TOMORROW BRINGS JOY

ELYSIUM

A NOVEL

TOMORROW BRINGS JOY

ELYSIUM

A NOVEL

MAHYAR A. AMOUZEGAR
MAHBOD AMOUZEGAR

University of New Orleans Press

Tomorrow Brings Joy: Elysium

by Mahyar Amouzegar and Mahbod Amouzegar

Cover design by Golshïd Zadafshar
Typesetting by Kevin Stone

ISBN 978-1-60801-304-3

University of New Orleans Press
2000 Lakeshore Drive
New Orleans, Louisiana
70148

unopress.org

Printed in the United States of America on acid-free paper.

First Edition, 2026

To the summers of our childhood,
when we, as brothers, wove worlds of imagination—
of games and storytelling

Book One

Book Two

Book Three

Book Four

Book Five

They have no sisters, nor brothers, nor fathers or mothers. They are like a colony without a queen and thus unrestricted of her obligations, or so they thought. Brave New World *and* 1984 *are but a farce, when the reality is more beautiful and far more perplexing than fiction. Put aside your juvenile notion of good and bad—those are of the past. The human mind has soared far beyond the banal and has reimagined the gods. What would be your yearning in the absence of exigence? Nothing, they insisted, because tomorrow brings joy.*

—The Harmony 10:32

Oh, how woefully wrong they were.

—The Historian

Book One

King Rat

The chime of the alarm broke the quiet of the room, ringing out like a slow and steady drip into a puddle—silence, then a soft plink. It was both intriguing and maddening, torturing Dolores with its insistence. So engrossed had she been in the third chapter of her new book that she lost track of time, forgetting the timer she had set in preparation for her guests.

Dolores finally looked up, irritated by the alarm's unwavering persistence. A disembodied voice joined in, indulgent in tone. "Dolores?"

"I need a few more minutes," she responded quickly, still engrossed in the book. "Can't you just shut up and shut it off?"

"Of course, but before I do, I just want to remind you that you instructed me earlier to ignore this very command," the voice replied, as always, with a reassuring duteous manner.

Dolores stared out of the window at the towering trees beyond, lost in thought. "Fine. I did, but what's the point of having a good servant if you can't adjust?"

The voice responded in a matter-of-fact tone, "I hate to remind you again, Dolores, but you instructed me to be, as you put it, forceful."

Dolores rolled her eyes before commanding, "Pause this incessant noise." Immediately, the room fell into a warm silence, and she let out a sigh of relief.

Turning her attention back to the book in her hand, she

felt the texture of the synthetic paper and relished the weight of the tome. Physical books had made a comeback in the last decade, and people of her generation were becoming avid readers of books made of paper, rather than receiving information via Direct Data Transfer or, even less pleasurable, through the Information Visualization System. The latter always left Dolores with a lingering feeling of data overload. Her newest find was *King Rat*, a gripping story set in Singapore during World War II.

She stood up, opened the windows, and stared at the trees lining her street. She loved the massive oaks. They made a soft, melodic sound as the wind weaved through their branches. The sun had begun its descent, and the birds were winding down, perching on the branches, and softly chirping. Across the street, Dolores could see a small park, dotted with weeping cherry trees that jealously held onto their yellow leaves, watching over the slow-moving rivulet that snaked around the park. It was moments like this that she wished she could forget everything about her past.

Dolores said, "Could you come in, please."

The servant walked in, and she found herself once again mesmerized by his eyes. He was tall and thin, with short black hair. He wore a button-down white shirt, its collar tightly closed around his neck, paired with narrow black pants. Dolores shook her head and asked, "Could you be less strict from now on and make more of an effort to understand my changing moods . . . please?"

"As you wish, Dolores."

She looked down at her book again and then gave a mischievous smile. "You know what?"

The servant blinked twice as if trying to read Dolores's intention but failing, he stared straight at her and said, "I certainly do not."

"I have a name for you," she offered. There was a joyful lilt in her voice. She had had this new companion android model for over three months but couldn't think of a name for him, and he had refused to provide an opinion.

"I am glad, Dolores. I have been waiting with anticipation," the android replied.

"Was that sarcasm?"

"Of course not."

"Right. Anyway, your name is . . ." she waited, and the android looked at her with his blinking hazel eyes, "King Rat."

"That is interesting, Dolores. Will it be a permanent one, or will my name change with the title of the books?"

"That's a thought, but for now, let's go with King Rat or KR for short. Now leave me alone and let me finish the chapter."

"I will come and get you in precisely five minutes."

"Fine. Glory. Now, go away."

The Android gave a faux bow and left. Dolores loved his antics and grinned before picking up her book again. She stared at the cover photo of an old gun with a bayonet. It depicted something entirely foreign to her world, be it weaponry or any element mentioned in the story. The book was written in 1962, but the events in the story were set twenty years earlier, in the middle of a World War. The dates were somewhat insignificant to Dolores, as more than two hundred years had passed since the author wrote those words. The narrator told of prisoners and killing and pain, and although those concepts were foreign to her, the ones that intrigued her the most were the captors—the Japanese military—and the Allied soldiers dreaming about food and sex.

She had seen images of Japanese people but couldn't bring them to life. They looked so different, even among other Japanese people. It reminded her of learning about dolphins, but even after seeing their holographic images and playing with them in a SimEnv, they never became genuine until she was able to swim with the real ones. At that moment, when she was in the ocean, surrounded by vast blue waters and a pod of Bottlenose dolphins is when it all came true for her. She wondered if the Japanese people still existed and if they were as ruthless as the book portrayed them. There were brutalities in the wars of the twentieth century, but nothing compared to what people did in the Wars of Settlement, a hundred years later, from 2075 to 2085.

The Japanese or, in general, the idea of distinct types of humans was intriguing to Dolores, but not as much as the passages discussing men dreaming about sex, which completely baffled her. She tapped her left wrist, activating the faint blue light below her skin. As she sought more information on the subject, the Direct Data Transfer system provided little clarity, and the Information Visualization System projected abstract images in her mind, echoing the enigmatic words on the book's pages. She considered calling KR for clarification but quickly dismissed the idea, knowing he wouldn't have the answers either.

She looked at the front of her wrist to see the time. She had a minute to finish the last page, but instead, she went back to the first chapter and reread the passage about the dreams:

> *Dream about food and women. Your woman. And soon you would enjoy the dreaming more than the waking, and if you were careless, you would dream while awake and the days would run into nights and the night into day.*

King Rat walked into the room while Dolores was still contemplating the passage. She couldn't understand what the author meant by "your woman."

"What do you think when you hear the phrase 'your woman?'"

"I do not understand the question, Dolores."

Dolores pursed her lips. "Who is your woman, KR?"

"You are, Dolores, and I am your man. However, it is time for you to get ready."

Dolores sighed. "You're no fun."

She then put the book in a lacquered ornate box on the nightstand. She closed the lid and brushed her fingers against the stenciled red flowers with bright green leaves. Dolores then adjusted the box, so it sat on the center of the stand and stood up as KR watched her patiently. She opened the cabinet to order her dress for the night, but her clothes were already laid out inside. She looked at the neatly folded pumpkin-colored autumn wear, dark purple underwear and bra, and comfortable footwear. King Rat was efficient, but Dolores was annoyed.

"Did I ask you to prepare my clothes for tonight?" she asked.

"Yes."

"Did I tell you what I wanted to wear?"

"No. You did not."

"So, you guessed?"

"I anticipated, Dolores, based on your past selections."

She nodded and then dumped the whole stock in the recycling bin and ordered the synthesizer for a new set through a menu of options. The timer on the device indicated five minutes before completion. She could go back and read the last page, but she wanted to pretend to stay mad at KR, and it wouldn't work if she turned around. She could feel the weight of his stare, and after a minute, she couldn't hold back and faced him with a laugh.

"I was worried you were mad at me, Dolores."

She groaned and then, "No. It's silly to be mad at you. You're just too good at your job."

"Is that a compliment?"

"Definitely not," she said sternly, but the twinkle in her eyes betrayed her.

She went to the bathroom, washed her face, and combed her long dark brown hair. By the time she returned, KR had put her new clothes on the bed. She put them on and shoved her old ones in the recycler.

"How do I look?"

King Rat looked at her for a moment and said, "You look good, as always, but I do not see how your selection is any different than mine."

"I'm wearing a black bra," she offered.

The android blinked twice. "Not an appropriate use of resources, Dolores, if you do not mind me saying so."

"I definitely do mind, and as you well know, I am still below my quota for the week."

"That is true, and I will not say another word."

Dolores gave him a frak-you-look and stared at her image in the mirror. She combed her hair again and then pulled it back in a ponytail. "I should cut it short like Demi. What do you think?" Demi was her closest friend from their days on the Farm, and Dolores always thought of her as stylish.

"Are you going to get mad at me if I say yes?" KR asked. Dolores shook her head. "Then, I think it is more efficient if you keep it short." He touched his own head as an emphasis.

Dolores stood back and looked at her whole outfit. The dress complemented her olive skin and fit her long narrow body well. She gave a small smile. Of course, she wanted to be happy, but as always, this day was bittersweet.

She shook her head and gently closed her eyes, as if pushing down the bad memories of the past and raising the sweet ones in her thoughts. She cherished her time on the Farm—a sprawling, picturesque estate adorned by lush, undulating hills and majestic trees. Her entire childhood and young adulthood, until the age of twenty, had been woven into the fabric of that place, alongside numerous other children. There were other estates across Elysium, housing thousands of other children. They had visited those places for sporting or educational events, but to Dolores none of them were as beautiful as the Farm.

The Farm was utterly lovely—a real sanctuary, she thought. Yet, a poignant realization surfaced repeatedly since her fourteenth birthday—a subtle whisper reminding her that even within a seemingly flawless world, shadows of imperfection lingered. But why the doubt? she asked herself, and once again found no answer.

Dolores took a deep breath to clear her head, and when she opened her eyes, she noticed KR in the mirror staring at her. "Can I ask you something?"

"Of course," KR said.

"Why didn't you insist on getting a name or offer your own? The others did."

"I am different from the others, Dolores, and I came to you precisely because I am different."

Dolores turned and faced him. "But why?"

Dolores's last companion android, Seca-12, had made an odd recommendation—that Dolores needed a different type of android—and then, within weeks, KR showed up, and Seca-12 left.

KR gave a warm smile. "Please do not take this the wrong way, but the fact that you had twelve different companion androids in less than five years should explain my presence here."

"There were issues with each one, but that's not what I asked, KR. Seca-12 offered her name, and I accepted it. You walked in, greeted me, and started working as if you have always lived here."

"Did you wish to call me Seca-13?"

"Isn't that your designation?"

"Yes, I am a Specialized Emotive Companion Android, SECA-87398202. Some androids prefer their designation as a name, and others pick their own, but I believe it was important for you to pick a name for me, and you did."

"Are you upset that it took me this long, and you're named after a title of the book?"

"Of course not."

"Did you choose to come to me?"

"No. I was designed specifically for you, Dolores. After twelve generic companion androids, it was necessary for you to have someone who could meet your specific needs."

Dolores gazed at KR, feeling a connection unlike any she'd experienced with the previous androids, despite their kindness and attentiveness. "Can I ask something else?"

"You can never offend me, Dolores. I am here to serve you."

"Yes, but are you happy?"

"That is an interesting concept, and like all other human emotions, it is a matter of perspective and context, Dolores. Let me ask you this first. Are you happy? I am not asking if you are happy in general because I understand the complexity of this emotion, and today, of all days, must be a difficult day for you. So, my question is, are you happy with me?"

Dolores looked at KR for a moment, and she thought. *Yes, she had been pleased with him. They fit well.* "Yes, I am."

"And why do you say that? How do you measure this happiness?"

Dolores tilted her head. "I look forward to seeing you each day, and I enjoy our banter. I like getting mad at you and then making up. I like how we can watch a show together and be content just being there. I think of you often and worry about your comfort. I'm glad you are here, KR."

"And that is how I feel, Dolores. I do not wish to be with someone else, and I feel happy when you are happy and satisfied. I worry when you are mad at me, and I feel a sense of jubilation when your anger is diminished. It took you a long time to pick a name for me, and you may have picked it on a whim, but that, in fact, shows our closeness. King Rat may be a silly name, but it is my name picked by you. It is the close connection that makes me happy."

Dolores ran to KR and held him tightly. "Thank you. I am feeling a bit jarred today, so I apologize if I was terse with you throughout the day."

"It is a difficult day for you and the rest of your pod, Dolores. That is why I am here, and that is why each of your podies has a new companion android as well. Though you break the record for the time it took to name one."

"That cannot be true."

"Oh, but it is. You hold the record in Elysium now and by twenty-one days, seven hours, and ten minutes."

Dolores laughed and wiped the side of her eye. She looked into the mirror one last time and said, "Fine. I take it as an honor." She sighed and then, "Okay, I'm ready."

"Finally."

"Don't get sassy now. Is everything ready?"

"I am not trying to be fresh by saying, why would it not be?"

"So, you rushed me for nothing. I'm ready, and no one is even here," Dolores said, but as soon as she finished her sentence, the doorbell rang, and KR gave her an I-told-you-so look.

"Fine, KR. You win. You always win. Who is at the door?"

"It is Demi. Should I let her in?"

"Yeah, you should let her in," she retorted.

"I will, but I have a gift for you." KR took Dolores's hand gently and put a small purple glass marble on her palm.

"Oh, my glory. I thought I used up all my supplies."

"New supplies should arrive by tomorrow, but I had saved one for you just in case," he replied and then, after a moment, "For tonight."

"Thanks, KR," she said and popped it into her mouth. She closed her eyes and let the energy from the melting marble take over her mind. She took a deep breath and felt calm and content.

"I was hoping you would wait and take it later after the ceremony, but—"

"I needed it now." She leaned close and kissed KR on the cheek.

Φ•Φ•Φ•Φ•Φ•Φ

"Hey, girl. Happy birthday," Dolores said as Demi walked into the living room.

Demi was wearing an autumn dress as well though hers was sleeveless. She had short brown hair and brown eyes, the exact color as Dolores's. Demi was the same height as her, too, about an inch shy of six feet, with an almost identical body—a column figure, straight and slender with a slight waist, long legs, small breasts and bottom, and toned arms and legs. She was in the final year of her studies to become a droidologist, specializing in the behavioral development of androids.

"Hey, darling. Happy twenty-fifth to you, too," Demi replied and then lightly kissed her on the lips. "It's nice to get a day off on our birthday."

Dolores nodded in agreement, realizing that their birthday had coincidentally landed on a Thursday this year, granting them a rare four-day weekend instead of the usual three. She hadn't planned anything but thought maybe she would ask Demi and the others to take a trip to the warmer southern coast.

Demi added, "We should definitely plan something exciting for this weekend." Then, addressing KR, added, "Hey, Android."

"Good evening, Demi. I actually have a name now. I am called—and please try and not laugh—King Rat."

Demi sniggered but then covered her mouth. "Sorry."

"I guess I should expect the same reaction from every guest tonight," King Rat whispered. He then looked at Dolores and offered, "I think I will introduce myself as KR for now until I get used to the name."

Dolores gave a quick smile. "What do you want to drink, Demi?"

Demi closed her eyes and said, "How about a Vesper Martini? I just read about it in *Casino Royale*."

KR nodded and went to the food replicator.

"Could you get the basic ingredients and mix them yourself?" Dolores asked.

"Of course, but it would not be as good as what is created by the FS1000. You have the latest model."

Demi gave a knowing smile. "We know, but could you indulge us? We want it shaken and not stirred."

"Do you know how to make it?" Dolores asked.

KR blinked a few times. "Of course," he replied, sounding a bit insulted, and to emphasize the point, he recited the passage from the book: "'Three measures of Gordon's, one of vodka, half a measure of Kina Lillete. Shake it very well until it's ice-cold, then add a large thin slice of lemon peel. Got it?'"

Demi gave an approving nod. "Thanks, KR, but could we have olives instead of lemon peel?"

Most of the nourishment was synthesized, but certain foods were supplied regularly by the delivery androids. Olive was one of those commodities. KR nodded and started ordering the right ingredients.

Demi watched KR's expert mixology movements. "Remember how in the Farm, we couldn't get Alexandra to even make a sweet tea from scratch."

"Yes," Dolores replied and then closed her eyes. The effect of the marble was dissipating, and she knew taking another wouldn't have the same impact, as they were designed with diminishing potencies. *One was more than enough anyway,* she thought.

Nevertheless, she wished Demi would not have brought up Alexandra, at least not tonight. She loved Alexandra or at least tried to keep her love for her alive, but it was difficult. Alexandra was their cook, their mentor, their teacher, and their everything while they were growing up on the Farm, but when they needed her the most, when they were at their most vulnerable, Alexandra was nowhere to be found. Dolores knew Demi didn't feel the same way toward Alexandra, but still, Dolores wished Demi would try and understand her side of the story too.

Demi may have sensed the change in Dolores's demeanor because she hugged Dolores from behind and offered softly, "It was fun being there and all, but I'm glad we graduated and entered the real world. It's nice to have your own place, though I miss sleeping with everybody."

Dolores turned around and gave her a warm smile. She wasn't going to hold it against Demi. It was a bittersweet night for everyone. "Me too," she said, perhaps a bit too loudly. "It's funny that even after almost six years we still crave our old life in the Farm. I know I can stay in your place occasionally, but it's different from having a whole bunch of us in the same housing unit." She, too, recalled the nights when they would sit together to gossip or crawl to each other's bed to be comforted when they had a difficult day.

Demi closed her eyes, took a deep breath, and spoke with her eyes shut. "I do miss the attention from everyone, of course, but I also miss that feeling of adventure when everything was new. I know Darius . . ." she trailed off and opened her eyes sharply. "I'm sorry, I know—"

"Don't be. We should talk more about the past. Finish your thought. I am okay, really."

Demi took Dolores's hand. "I remember a couple of months or so before our fourteenth birthday, Darius managed to sequester an errant transporter. I don't know how he did it . . ."

"As always, resourceful," Dolores added quietly. She recalled how Darius could reprogram and fix most machines and logically convince even the high-functioning androids to do his bidding.

"He certainly managed to convince it to allow us in. It was just to check it out, you know. Just being a bit naughty, and then Deacon saw us and got all angry, but Darius didn't care."

Dolores wondered what the point of Demi's story was, but she wanted to be agreeable. After all, today was equally hard on Demi. She gave an understanding smile and Demi continued. "He grabbed Deacon and pulled him in, and before Deacon could do anything, he ordered the transport to take us out. We rode toward the west, as fast as the vehicle would operate, and all the while, Deacon complained. But then Darius directed the transporter to leave the main highway and take us through a small road that weaved in and out of towns. Even Deacon quieted down, mesmerized by the beauty of nature and the people. Oh, my glory, so many adults."

"Yes, it must have been a sight to see, Demi," Dolores said softly. She wanted to add, and none of you bothered to include me or even tell me, but instead she touched Demi gently for her to continue.

Demi offered an apologetic smile, as if she could hear

Dolores's inner musings, and quickly added, "Darius was eager to explore one of the towns, but the idea unnerved me. Being sealed in a transporter is one thing, but arriving in the adult's world prematurely is another. Yet, when we reached the ocean and paused, the allure of adventure outweighed our concerns about the rules. We flung open the doors to welcome the thick, salty sea air. We sat on the edge of the vehicle, just taking it all in. I really wished you were there with us, Dolores."

Demi gave a shy smile and then quickly added, "It never crossed our minds we'd make it so far west. An hour later, Deacon's restlessness pulled us back to reality, urging us into the vehicle once more. I assumed we'd head home, but Darius had other plans. He steered us south, the ocean on our right, huge cliffs looming on our left. And just when we were exhausted and ready to turn back, our journey abruptly ended. The vehicle halted with a warning at the road's end, the border of Elysium before us. Can you believe it? We'd reached the edge of our world."

"It must have been quite a sight, Demi," Dolores reiterated. She paused, hesitant to express more, feeling betrayed by her podies. She could understand Deacon or even Darius keeping such a secret, but she couldn't help but feel let down by Demi, expecting more from her.

Demi continued with her soliloquy, oblivious of Dolores's feeling. "No . . . no, there was nothing there. Just more sea and sand and hills. But as the sun dimmed slowly, we saw a myriad of white lights coming out several clicks ahead of us. Oh, my glory, we thought we were face to face with our southern neighbor. But the vehicle wouldn't move and warned us about crossing on foot. But Darius wouldn't have it. He removed the emergency toolbox and opened the operating hatch to override the vehicle's safety protocols. Deacon tried to stop him, but he was never a match for Darius. Our personal comms were not operational so far away, but our transporter offered to call for a new vehicle for Deacon. We were so far south that it took almost thirty minutes for a new ride to arrive, and

Deacon left without a word. He was so angry that he didn't talk to us for days."

Dolores could remember Deacon's look of anger, but he was always angry at something or someone, so Dolores hadn't paid any attention to its source. Now, she wished she had. She was left out in an adventure, and it was kept secret for years. She wanted to say something to convey her disappointment, but it was their birthday, and that happened so long ago. "So, what happened?" she asked in a monotone voice.

"It took Darius almost an hour of meticulous adjustments to the transporter's core programming before he managed to override it, and we sped toward the lights. It took only a few minutes to reach them, and oh, Dolores, the sight. My glory. There stood the largest, most imposing wall you could ever imagine. Towering at maybe fifteen meters, it seemed to be constructed of a matte metal that stretched into the sea as far as we could see. As we rode east, our trip appeared endless, with no visible entry points. Lights from the top of the wall cast a warm glow, yet, strangely, there was no one. We stepped out and touched its surface with our bare hands. It felt hard and surprisingly warm. Darius pounded on the wall, yet no sound was emitted, not even the echo of his fist against the metal; it was as if the wall absorbed all noise. By then, it was getting very dark, and we felt scared and got back into the vehicle and came home."

"You never mentioned this to me," Dolores rejoined, her irritation thinly veiled. She never wanted to feel envious of her podies, but the pang of bitterness was undeniable upon hearing about their incredible adventure, even if it took place over eleven years ago.

Demi seemed to have missed Dolores's demeanor as she replied with an even tone. "Alexandra caught us when we returned. Somehow, she knew what we had done. Alexandra sent the vehicle to the shop to be reset. She wasn't angry at us, and I felt she even admired us for our bravery, but it was made clear that we should not leave the Farm without adult supervision and not speak of it to anyone. I was going to tell you, Dolores, honestly, but . . ."

It was a long time ago, Dolores thought. It was their birthday, so why spoil it? "I understand, Demi," she said with a sigh. "It was a long time ago, but I'm glad you could have such an adventure with Darius. I am glad you told me."

Their reveries were interrupted when KR announced, "Your other guests are a few steps away. Should I let them in when they get here?"

"That's a silly question," Dolores said.

"And?"

"Yes . . . let them in."

"You do not have to get annoyed, Dolores. I was not sure if you wanted them here while you two were feeling nostalgic about your time together at the Farm."

"Why not focus on the drinks and stop eavesdropping," Dolores said, happy for the interruption.

"I am fully capable of doing both, Dolores," KR said as he handed them their drinks.

"Are they here yet?" Dolores asked, and she sipped her martini. "Wow. This is good, KR. Remember how you made this and do it just like it from now on."

"They are here," he said.

The door opened, and three figures entered—Deacon, David, and Dawn—moving in quiet unison.

Deacon stood slightly taller than the others, but all three shared the same features: brown eyes, brown hair, and a similar build. They looked like one another—just as they looked like everyone else in Elysium. Once, eons ago, these five might have been mistaken for siblings, but that notion had long since faded. In truth, there was little to distinguish them from the wider population. Any differences lay mostly in their fashion choices.

These five had been bound together from birth through their pod. They were born into it and had lived under one roof until five years ago, when they entered the adult world.

"I like your attempt to grow sideburns," Dolores said, as she tenderly touched the haphazard growth on his smooth face.

Deacon gave a tiny laugh. "Attempt is the right word for it."

"We just received a delivery of cherries, the last of its season. Should I serve it?" KR asked.

Dolores nodded at KR. "Bring it to the balcony, please."

It was a small balcony but still could hold two chairs and a round table. KR put the bowl of cherries on the table and handed each a drink. They all lined up against the glass railing and looked at the crimson sky. Dolores could still hear the branches singing from the other side of the building.

Dawn took a sip from her glass and declared, "I don't think I have ever had a martini before." She shook her head, probably more to show off her new curled, bleached hair with reddish strands.

Dolores was about to say something, but she sensed that Dawn wanted to hear it from David first. She didn't have to wait too long.

"Love your new hairdo," David quickly offered.

David always kept his hair short, even when he was a little boy. He was fond of small silver animal stud earrings and was sporting a roaring lion on his left ear and a kitten on the right. He sipped his drink, and pleasure washed over his face. "This is good. And I'm glad you finally got a name. Is it short for anything?"

"Yes," KR replied.

"And?"

"If you do not mind, I would rather not say it yet."

"Sure," David replied, waving his hand before returning to his martini.

"It's so nice to see everybody," Dolores confessed, resting her head on Deacon's shoulder.

"We saw each other just a week ago," he said

Dolores pulled away. "A week is a long time, Deacon."

"I know," he replied. "I just meant—"

"Let's not start again," Dawn chastised. "What's everybody reading now?"

"Demi and I are reading *King Rat*."

David laughed. "I got it. KR. You named your poor android King Rat. That's really cruel," he said, and the others joined in.

"Great. So, now you all know," KR said. "Thanks a lot, Dolores."

"Sorry, but the cat, or should I say the rat, is out of the bag now."

They all laughed, and KR said, "Fine. Go ahead and have your fun. But see if I will make another round of martinis."

Dawn touched the android on his shoulder. "I like the name. It's good to be the king." Dawn always knew how to say the right things. She loved animals and was in her last year of studies to become a marine biologist.

KR smiled and said, "Okay, maybe another martini for you, Dawn." He left the room but returned a few minutes later with a new round of martinis for everyone. He put the tray on the little table.

"How's the book?" Dawn asked.

"It's good but hard to understand," Demi said, turning to Dolores, "What do you think?"

Dolores put her empty glass on the table but didn't take a new one. Instead, her mind drifted back to the last passage she had read earlier. Demi was right. Although the language had barely changed in two hundred years, the references and context were a bit odd. She had little connection to the world where the story seemed overly centered on men's perceptions. "This book seems oddly fixated on men dreaming about women and their breasts," she remarked.

David gave a small chuckle. "Why?"

"That puzzled me too," Demi offered. "And the part about food." She pointed at Dolores. "But maybe that's more understandable given how they had so little food in their camp." She shivered a bit.

Dawn put her hands on her chest. She loved solving puzzles, so any mystery intrigued her. "It's strange to dream about these. Do they also dream about hair?" She took her hand off her breast and ran her fingers through her hair. It was clear she still wanted to hear about her new hairdo.

"Maybe if they had your hair, girl," Demi said, and that brought a smile to Dawn's face.

Dolores was still thinking and didn't bother acknowledging Dawn. "I don't know. I'm still in the beginning. Maybe they do later."

Dawn pulled the front of her dress a bit, looked down and then went to David and peered down his shirt. "I don't get it."

Demi finished the last of her martini and put the glass down. "Do you think because the men envied the women?"

"But why dream about it?" Deacon asked.

Dolores had been contemplating this too. It wasn't a secret that in the past, stark divisions existed between men and women. Perhaps the author deliberately highlighted these gender roles by physically segregating them in the book. "The world was vastly different back then," she reflected. "Perhaps the men's dreams serve as a metaphor for the ingrained social inequities of that era."

Demi nodded in agreement but didn't say anything.

"What is there to envy?" David asked.

Dolores looked up at KR, who had been standing by the door, silently watching them. She knew him well and could see that KR was eager to chime in but clearly didn't want to interrupt their activities. She gave a welcoming smile, and KR nodded, saying, "I do not fully understand your generation's aversion to looking up information that is readily available on your wrist."

They all laughed, and Dolores offered gently, "It's far more interesting this way, KR. It's good to experiment and seek answers on your own once in a while."

"It is not very efficient, Dolores."

"Perhaps, but maybe that's a difference between humans

and androids, even smart ones like you," she said and kissed KR on the head. "But, okay. I'll research this later. I think we're done anyway."

"Why a sudden interest, Dolores?" Deacon asked. "Why look for the differences in our worlds when we have so much more in common?"

"I am not. I'm just trying to understand the past a bit better. It must have been fascinating times."

"I disagree. It was an illiberal time when their core objective was to find the otherness," Deacon insisted.

"Oh, my glory, Deacon," Dawn exclaimed. "Do you have to always be the contrarian of the group? You're sounding more and more like our first-grade teacher."

David laughed. "She was a strange person, wasn't she? What was her name?"

"Anna Finola," Dawn said.

Dolores offered a small smile when she heard the name. Anna Finola was born right around the Wars of Settlement, and like others of her generation, she had two names. Dolores remembered how Anna often recounted tales about the bad days before the Wars.

"She was a lovely woman. She was so kind," Demi said, and they all nodded, remembering their teacher, earlier conversation forgotten.

"She was a bit odd though," Deacon joined in. "She used to call us 'little urchins.' What an odd way to call children?" He leaned close and said in a deep voice, mimicking their teacher: "'You, my little urchin, do not appreciate all that Elysium has offered you. You must always remember how easily we can revert to bad days before the Wars.'"

"She didn't sound like that at all, Deacon," Dawn protested. "And she wasn't odd. She was generous and warm. You could talk with her for hours."

Teachers weren't supposed to have favorites, but to the rest of the class, it was clear that Anna had a special relationship with Dawn and Demi.

David and Dolores exchanged a knowing glance, but it was Deacon who spoke again. "Well, she clearly liked you, Dawn, but for the rest of us, she was just an old teacher who seemed to live in the past."

"We should go and see her," Demi offered.

Dolores shook her head. "After all these years?" But then she wondered, why not? It had been years since Anna retired from teaching, but perhaps she could offer some more insights about Elysium now that they were adults. Dolores remembered that even as a little girl, there was something mysterious about Anna, as if she were hiding something. Nothing malicious, but there always seemed to be more to her.

"Alexandra and Anna were always whispering about something. It always felt odd," Dolores added before anyone could respond.

"You and I always whisper about things, Dolores," KR said.

"Don't be silly, KR. They weren't together, not like us. Alexandra wasn't Anna's companion. She was a cook, and Anna was a teacher."

KR shrugged. "It is time to come in anyway," he said, and like obedient first-graders, they took their martinis and walked back inside. KR handed the last drink to Dolores as he collected the rest of the empty glasses.

Dolores pointed to the couch and said, "It's time. Let's all sit down."

The couch was small, but they managed to squeeze three people onto it, while David and Dawn settled on a pair of ottomans. Every residential unit in Elysium mirrored Dolores's place, featuring a single bedroom, a bathroom, and a kitchen-living area. Residents chose their apartments based on their aesthetic preferences, aiming to minimize their commute. Dolores had chosen her spot in San Francisco's old Haight-Ashbury neighborhood primarily for the view of the park, while Demi, drawn to the sound of the sea, opted for an apartment overlooking the Pacific Ocean on the opposite side of the park. Although none of the apartments were spacious enough for a large gathering, each building offered multiple shared spaces and poolside areas for residents.

"Where would you like me to serve dinner, Dolores?" KR asked.

"By the pool," several of them said, as that was the best place to eat even in mid-October.

"And we could swim a bit before dinner too," Dawn offered. She loved the water. It was Dawn who insisted on getting everyone to swim with the dolphins.

"Isn't it too cold?" Deacon asked.

"The temperature is just right," KR offered. "But if it is not to your liking, I can provide protective clothes."

They all laughed, and Deacon gave an embarrassed smile.

"But first," Dolores said, putting her martini glass on the coffee table and, except for Deacon, the others followed.

"Come on, Deacon," Demi said. "Do you have to do this every time?"

Deacon shook his head and took a small sip from his glass. Dolores watched him intently. It was silly to make a fuss when he obviously knew, in the end, he would acquiesce. But he did it anyway. They took turns hosting their weekly dinner, but tonight was special in many ways, not just because of their birthday. Last year, Deacon was the host, but even as a host, he made a point of being recalcitrant. Of course, he was making a point, and Dolores thought she would do her best to let him be, but she could also feel how she was becoming more impatient with his antics.

KR brought five glasses of orange juice and put one in front of each person. He then took the martini glasses from the table, stood by Deacon, and waited. Deacon ignored him for a second but then relented and gave up his drink. Deacon rubbed his forehead as if getting rid of a headache. "It's been eleven years," he complained, but his words sounded hollow.

"So what?" It came out harsher than Dolores had intended,

and the others looked taken aback. Typically, she ignored Deacon's faux reluctance, but she didn't want to play that game anymore. "What do you want us to do, Deacon? Do you want us to forget Darius because it's been eleven years? Does the number of years make it less ugly?"

"Dolores, please try and calm yourself. You do not want to exceed your unhappiness quota," KR said, his voice particularly soft and soothing.

Throughout Dolores's outburst, Deacon kept his eyes on her, clearly not wanting to be baited by her, but now he instinctively looked at his wrist and nodded with satisfaction. The others also did the same, none wanting to exceed their quota.

Dolores thrust her wrist toward KR, watching as the unhappiness meter ticked upwards. She took a deep breath, attempting to remain calm. She was puzzled by her intense reaction to Deacon and wondered why she felt such deep anger when his behavior was predictable. After all, that was typical of Deacon. She promised herself to accept him as he was. Yet, she couldn't shake off a feeling of unease, perhaps triggered by a dream about Darius she had right after starting the first chapter of *King Rat*. While they dreamt of women and food, she dreamt of Darius.

Dolores was about to say something kind when Deacon sat erect and said, "Ugly, you say? Now, you tell me, will these little rituals bring him back? He's gone, and we'll never see him again."

Dolores stood up sharply, but Dawn leaned over and pulled her down, and said in a singsong tone, "I'm putting down five unhappiness points and call Deacon's comment hostile." She then pointed to her wrist to show she was serious.

"I'm not playing this game," Demi said. "We're not kids anymore." She was sitting between Dolores and Deacon and grabbed and held them in her arms. She then gave a big smile and offered, "I call it a tie and declare both sides should be hospitable now."

Hostile or Hospitable was the game they all played on the

Farm when they were little kids, and their teachers wanted to show them the importance of words, tones, and even body language. Once a week, during the meal when the two or three pods ate with each other, and occasionally one of the kids would make a "call"—"hostile" or "hospitable"—against a comment made by another student. Then the "caller" would wager a minimum of one unhappiness point (from a play bank of quota as the real one could not be amended), and others would evaluate the comment. If the majority agreed with the call, the caller would receive the equivalent of the wager in increased unhappiness quotient. And if the original comment were deemed hostile, then the person would have to pay the equivalent of the wager to the caller as well. At the end of each month, the person with the most positive points would get a reward. This was a way to teach both kindness but also awareness of their unhappiness quota.

They all looked at David to see how he would respond. David smiled and said, "I think it's best if we all behave a bit better. So, I say, both Dolores and Deacon have been hostile, but Demi is right, so my vote is with her. We don't need our childhood games to be kinder to each other. There are only the five of us left. We should never forget."

Deacon nodded and offered gently, "You're right, David." He then looked at Dolores and said, "I'm sure Darius is much happier now."

Dolores wondered if Deacon was right. He couldn't really know if Darius was better off, and she could see that he didn't mean to say it. But again, they all wanted him to be alive and happy. That was their hope, whether spoken or not.

"Is he?" David asked, his voice brittle as if trying hard to hold back his tears.

Dolores bit her lip. She wished the same thing, but they were twenty-five now and wishing was no longer an option. David, Dawn, and Darius were the closest in their pod, even though they would deny that there was anything but equal love for each other. "You don't know, Deacon, no matter how confidently you say it. We don't know if he is even alive."

Deacon shook his head but said nothing. They have been repeating the same arguments since Darius was taken away. Deacon seemed to regret what he started and stayed silent.

Dawn clearly was not satisfied with the vote and said, "I don't believe you want us to forget him, Deacon." She was still upset despite KR's earlier warning as the little freckles on her cheeks that were barely visible before shone like tiny beacons. She was leaning on the edge of the ottoman, and it looked like she might fall off it at any moment.

Deacon looked from one face to another and then, in a sign of resignation, offered, "Don't gang up on me again. Didn't we just agree on no more hostility? Of course, I don't want to forget him. How could I? I miss him too. Don't try to put it all on me. You know . . ." he trailed off, and others looked down with their own shame.

Dawn, always a peacemaker, could only stay angry for a short time. She picked up her glass of orange juice and others followed. "To Darius, who loved orange juice more than anything else," she said with a little smile.

They all nodded and took a sip of the semi-sweet tart liquid. That was Darius's favorite drink on the Farm, and he drank it in pint-size glasses with long straws. They all fell silent, remembering him in their own way.

After a while, Dawn took out a small canvas from her bag and put it on the table. "Darius's last artwork," she said as she brushed her fingers against the dried leaves that decorated the frame.

"He loved those leaves," David said. He leaned forward to trace the canvas, and they all followed as if the touch would connect them with him and each other. "I wish you'd let me hold on to it for a while."

Dawn shook her head.

"I don't know why you get to keep this. It's not fair."

"Don't be silly, David. He gave it to me."

"I don't believe you. And even if true, you should still share it."

Dolores understood. She felt the same way. She wanted a piece of his memory, too, but thought this was not the time or place for it. "We should've done more," she said, wanting to focus on Darius.

Dolores looked from one face to another. She was born in the same batch as each of them, her podies, and they had lived with each other from their birth. They would always be connected until they die. She stopped at Deacon, who had his eyes closed, and Dolores knew he was trying to calm himself. That was his way.

Deacon took a deep breath and held it for a moment, and then he exhaled and opened his eyes. Dolores could see that everyone was looking at him, waiting to see how he would behave. He didn't disappoint. "Let's not rehash old arguments."

Despite their protests, and without ever admitting it, Dolores knew they all wanted Deacon to be the contrarian so they could engage in the blame and guilt game, and Deacon seemed to embrace that role each time. He was evidently waiting for the onslaught, but nothing happened, so Dolores wiped her eyes and said, "I know nothing we could've done would change the outcome, but we didn't even try."

"We were all children," Dawn rejoined, looking past them. "We tried to help, didn't we? But we were so young, and Darius was so different." She looked at David and then at Dolores. "You remember, don't you? We made a barrier. We begged."

"I don't remember any of it anymore," David said, tears flowing freely. "It's all hazy now. I only remember the agony on Darius's face and my own fear that perhaps I would be next."

Dolores stared at him, her mouth agape. That was the first time any of them admitted to their fear they'd be next. She harbored the fear, too ashamed to reveal it to the others. She could tell from the reactions of the others that they felt the same way.

Dolores exhaled sharply. With David openly voicing what

she had silently felt for years, a feeling she hadn't fully comprehended, there was no point in holding back. "Is that what has been eating at us all these years—the shame of feeling relieved that we were not taken away because of him?"

They all looked down again, clearly not daring to face the truth as that might reveal their disgrace even more. The room felt empty, and the only sound came from trees outside, crying with them.

Deacon put his chin on his laced fingers and closed his eyes again. "No," he said sharply. He then opened his eyes and stared at the wall before him. "No . . . We all felt Darius's pain as he walked away. And yes, perhaps for a moment, I was relieved that it was not me. That's normal. That's being human. But even then, we knew the truth. Have you ever heard of a whole pod being punished for one of its members?"

They shook their heads, still not daring to look up.

"Yes, but . . ." Demi replied, but she was not sure what to say next.

"If I may," KR interjected from the kitchen and walked closer, "it is normal to feel this way. It is normal to feel guilty. A member of your pod was taken away when you were young, and the teachers should have done a better job of preparing you for it and supporting you afterward."

Dolores stood up. "What do you know about this, KR? How would you know how we feel?"

"Please do not get angry, Dolores. One of the reasons each of your companion androids was replaced in the last few months is because of your lasting guilt about Darius. We were given the background and the emotional know-how to help you," KR said and then, after a second, "you have the latest model," he added.

"What the frak," Dolores shouted but then, realizing KR was just an instrument, she took a deep breath. "Leave, KR. Please go to your station now . . . please."

"As you wish," KR replied. "Please try to calm yourself as you may be exceeding your unhappiness quotient."

Dolores pointed her wrist at him. "Happy? I'm way below the threshold. Now leave."

KR nodded and left the room, and Dolores sat down again and looked at the others. "Did you know?"

They looked as confused as her. Deacon spoke first. "It doesn't surprise me. I've been feeling much better since my new android arrived." He thought for a moment and then added, "He's been a good listener."

Dolores, too, felt KR had been good for her. Since his arrival, she's been able to think more clearly about the past. And although this clarity produced more questions than answers, she welcomed it without explicitly acknowledging it. But now, she felt miserable for yelling at him and made a mental note to apologize later.

David cleared his throat. "Now that I'm thinking about it, I was able to say what I said tonight because of Leni," he revealed. "He has been encouraging me to explore my past experiences more. It's good to talk about it with him even though he didn't really know Darius."

"It all makes sense now," Demi admitted too. "I still feel guilty, and I don't think that would ever change, but that we can say it out loud is good, no?"

"I dreamt about Darius last night," Dolores declared. "I used to dream about him all the time when we were still at the Farm, but then it stopped until last night. Then, he was back again."

Dawn leaned forward even more. "What did he say?"

"Nothing. We were back on the Farm, but in the dream, he didn't go away. He stayed with us and grew tall, taller than even what Deacon is now."

Demi nodded. "Remember how little he was when we were just seven?"

"He was so tiny," Deacon added.

"He used to crawl into my bed and hold me tightly, terrified of the night," Dawn said, smiling broadly. They laughed, clearly remembering the fragile little boy.

"He became tall and strong, though," David said. "No more coming to our bed. No more cries, not even when they took him away."

Dolores continued and did not let their reveries distract her. "I dreamed he was here tonight with us, but there was no place for him to sit, so he stood behind Dawn and stared at us." They all looked at Dawn, and she instinctively looked behind her.

"I remember his eyes," David said. "You could see yourself in them, and his stare would penetrate through you as if he could read your mind."

"I loved his eyes," Dolores said. "They were so different. They were more like our new androids. He . . ."

She stopped, and they all looked at each other.

"No, that's not possible," Deacon said.

"But KR has the same eyes as Darius," Dawn insisted. "And his mannerism."

"It's not the same," Deacon retorted.

"Not exactly, but some of his ticks. Don't they . . ."

"No," David shouted. "So what?"

Dolores could hardly breathe. She looked at their faces, each contemplating a different horrifying scenario. "KR," she managed to say.

"Yes, Dolores," KR spoke through the wall. "Would you like me to come back?"

She took a few deep breaths. "Yes," she replied, trying hard to keep her tone even.

KR walked in, and they all stared at him. "Are you ready to eat?"

Dolores stood up, looking at KR, trying to read him but couldn't bring herself to ask what clearly each of them was thinking.

Demi spoke first. "KR, we're going to ask you something, but we need the full truth. Can you do that?"

"I never lie, but I am with Dolores, and therefore the extent of the answer depends on her, of course." KR looked at her, and Dolores nodded. "Then, yes."

Dawn stood up too. "Are you Darius?"

"No, of course not. Darius was human. I am a synthetic that looks, and if I may say so myself, feels like a human."

They all looked relieved, and Dawn sat down.

"Did you say was?" David asked.

"My information about Darius is limited to his time at the Farm, hence it was more natural for me to use the past tense."

Dolores smiled and said, "Thank you, KR, and I'm sorry for my earlier outburst."

"No need to mention it, Dolores. Your ire was justified."

"No, it wasn't, KR," she replied softly. Then, as if feeling the need to explain herself, to delve into their rituals despite KR never having questioned them, she offered, "We didn't give up on Darius, you know, at least not at first. We tried to locate his tracer, but it seemed it was fully turned off and it never came back on again. We kept asking the teachers and other adults, but it seemed no one knew anything. Now, I can tell that we weren't asking the right questions, although I'm not even sure what those are at this point. But eventually, after a while, and to our shame, we gave up and found comfort in our ritual of drinking a large glass of orange juice—the way he loved it. Do you understand, KR?"

KR blinked twice and gazed into Dolores's eyes. "I think I do, Dolores."

Dolores gave a faint smile and tried to clear her head. It was time to enjoy their birthday. "I think we're ready for . . ." but then another thought struck her. "KR?"

"Yes?"

"Is part of Darius in you?"

"Yes."

The Catcher in the Rye

Four pods and their teachers were on their trip to ostensibly see dolphins. The tracker of the boat, which had been working fine before the journey began, failed as soon as they reached the open water. When they started, there were over a dozen ships, each having staked out a zone to avoid disturbing the dolphins if they appeared. After a few hours, one of the teachers suggested—and the kids agreed wholeheartedly—to anchor the ship and go to the shore on the dinghies, so they could enjoy the beautiful sandy beaches.

Dolores sat at one end of the dinghy and shared in Darius's enthusiasm as he talked about cities of the past. She loved how he would get engrossed in discovering new things, then tell his rendition of the events.

"There are cities below these waters," Darius said, then they all peered over the side of the boat for a better view. He laughed heartily, his hazel eyes shining in the bright light. They were barely fourteen, but he was already taller than most adults. "Not here, dummies, a bit closer to the shoreline and more toward the south." He pointed as if saluting the cities that once dominated the West Coast.

"You're so epig," Dawn said, and rolled her eyes. "Stop showing off."

He is epigrammatic, Dolores thought and gave a big smile as she leaned further to soak up more sun.

Dawn used slang, like "epig," from a bygone era, but everyone understood her. It had become fashionable to use random vernacular from the twentieth century's newly republished novels, and with each publication, new terms emerged, leading to a dizzying evolution of vocabulary and meanings.

Darius turned around, ready with a retort, but then the wind picked up, and they had to hold onto the side of the boat to steady themselves. The gust didn't last long, and Darius let go of the railing to smooth his now matted, long brown hair.

"Just cut the damn thing off," David yelled and slid his hand over his crew cut as an emphasis.

Demi grabbed a handful of Darius's mane. "Or better yet, let me do a braid."

It was a lovely day, the sun shining brightly, and the ever-present wind throughout the journey had ceased, as if inviting the kids to the beach. It was a delightful day to frolic on the warm sand. There were twenty-seven kids, four teachers, the ship captain, and several service and seaman androids.

It had become the norm for each pod to have seven members. However, number seven in Pod D-081053-05—shortened to D-05 for those born in the fifth batch on October 8, 2153—had passed away before reaching a year old. While infant mortality was not common, it did happen, leading to some pods not having their full complement of members. As a result, Darius, Dawn, and the others in their group had grown used to being one member short at every event.

When the decision was made to head to shore, they lowered the dinghies, and everyone pitched in to load them with supplies before they sailed toward the vast empty beach. The service androids erected several large sails and set up tables to prevent sand from getting into the food. They served a simple lunch of avocado-BLT sandwiches—the bacon having been replicated on the ship earlier. There were also sweet watermelons the size of grapefruits. They enjoyed their picnic-style lunch dressed in shorts and T-shirts.

After lunch, they took off their clothes to swim, sunbathe or play cards. It was bad manners to eat naked, but as an equally poor manner to be clothed when not necessary, especially on the beach.

Dawn was eager to swim right after lunch, but Darius persuaded her to play a few hands of poker. A teacher had taught them the game a week before, and Darius had diligently studied it since then. A few others from different pods decided to join, making a total of eleven players, but only four stayed in the game after thirty minutes.

"Come on, let's go for a swim," Dawn complained as she folded with her last chips gone. They all turned to Dolores, waiting.

Dolores studied her hand, and was about to call, when she caught sight of Darius. It was clear he was determined to win. Although he never said it out loud, his expression revealed how seriously he took each round ever since he was introduced to the game.

"I've got nothing. I'm out too," Dolores announced. She feigned disappointment and tossed her cards onto the discard pile.

Darius's eyes gleamed as he collected the massive pot. Now, only Darius and David remained, each holding towering mountains of chips. Destiny, who had lost everything after the second round, took on the role of dealer. Originally from D-08 Pod, Destiny shared the same brown eyes and skin tone as the others, but her hair was dyed blonde. She had borrowed a button-down shirt from a teacher and, lacking a tie, used a red floral scarf instead. Despite her losses, she proved to be a skilled dealer.

"Okay, boys, ante up," Destiny ordered and then skillfully slid her fingers on top of the deck, making the cards glide on the surface and landing in front of the remaining players. She smiled at her prowess, and her eyes sparkled as they always did when she was happy.

Dolores leaned over to see David's card, but he quickly put them down. "Hey, don't look and don't cheat."

"How could I cheat?" Dolores protested. "I didn't see anything anyway," she lied. David was holding three of a kind.

"Go all in," Dawn said, looking over Darius's shoulder.

"Sheesh, girl. Stop looking at my cards," he said as he pushed half of his chips to the center of the blanket.

Destiny nodded approvingly. "David?"

"Okay, I'll see you," David replied, and he then matched Darius's chips.

"How many cards?" she asked.

"I am good," Darius replied and leaned back.

"I'll take two," David said calmly.

Destiny put one finger on top of the deck and made the cards fly and land in front of David. "Yeah, baby," she boasted and then she put the deck down in a ribbon spread. "Your call, Darius."

Darius tried to read David's face, then with a nudge from Dawn, who had lost all patience, pushed the rest of his chips to the middle of the board. "All in," he said.

David didn't hesitate. "I'll see you."

In a dramatic fashion, Darius put down his five cards face up.

"Darius has a pair of tens," Destiny announced and then looked at David expectantly.

Dolores looked at David and gave him a knowing smile, but David shook his head and declared, "You win, Darius." He added his five cards to the deck, messing up Destiny's semi-circle ribbon.

Destiny collected Darius's cards and then kissed him. "Congrats."

"Good job, Darius," Dolores offered softly.

One of the kids from another pod, who had lost earlier, asked, "Who won?"

Dolores pointed to a mountain of chips in front of Darius and said, "Who do you think, Doris?"

Doris slapped Darius on the shoulder and said, "You slew that game."

Darius raised his arms like a champion and threw all the chips and cards into a container. "Okay, I'm ready for a swim, Dawn. You, lazy bum. Let's go."

"It's too cold," Deacon protested. He had refused to join the game and was content to sit back and read his little red book.

"It's not cold," Darius said and stood up.

"Come on, Deacon," Demi said.

David grabbed Deacon's hand and dragged him, and Deacon made himself go limp, enjoying the ride.

Then someone shouted, "786! Dolphins. Look." And everyone stood up and stared but couldn't see anything and then there they were, swimming so close to the shore.

"Let's go," Demi commanded, but Deacon still looked hesitant.

Dawn grabbed his other hand and said, "Let's all go in together."

Then all of them held hands and ran to the sea. The water was crisp, but it felt good on their sunbaked skin. Excited by the new audience, the dolphins jumped in the air and flipped their tails. The kids were excellent swimmers, but Dawn was better and faster and came as close to the animals as she dared. The dolphins ignored her shyness and surrounded her and touched her with their rostrum. The other kids caught up and joined the game—their pods joining a pod of dolphins.

Dolores dove deep underwater, and one of the dolphins followed her and swam next to her. She reached out and gently touched its gray skin. It felt warm and soft, and the sun splashed on its back, spotlighting the dorsal fin. They were then face to face. It gave her a few nods before climbing to the surface fast. And then Dolores finally understood.

She stayed under the water as long as she could, then saw David above her and swam toward him. "Hey, David," she called when she surfaced.

He turned around and faced her. "You can really hold your breath."

She nodded and said, "Why did you let Darius win?"

"I didn't."

"I saw your cards, David."

"So why did you?"

Dolores smiled. "I guess we still baby him," she remarked before turning to face Darius. He appeared engrossed in conversation with Destiny. He seemed serious, completely focused on whatever Destiny was saying, oblivious to the playful dolphins around him. Dolores called out to him, and after a while, Darius glanced up but didn't respond. Destiny smiled and waved at them, prompting Dolores and David to wave back. As Destiny swam away, she patted Darius on the head, almost in a playful manner as one would with a young child, and left him amidst the persistent dolphins, undeterred by his lack of attention.

Dolores swam toward Darius, and Dawn saw her and followed. Darius hadn't noticed them, deep in his own thoughts and jumped when Dawn came from below the surface and appeared in front of him. "786, man."

"What were you and Destiny talking about? Some secret dolphin things?" Dawn said.

Darius gave a ghost of a smile and nodded, though it was clear his attention was still on something else. Dolores followed his gaze and saw Destiny swimming with her pod. "You've been rather chummy with Destiny recently."

Darius turned and faced her but didn't respond.

"What's going on?" Dolores asked.

"Nothing. And why can't I be friends with others? You always think our pod is the only one."

"I didn't mean anything by it, Darius. I just . . ."

Darius shook his head. "Sometimes it's nice to talk to others, you know."

"Of course. It's just . . . just that you've been so gloomy lately."

Darius stared back but didn't respond. Dolores didn't want to pressure him overly, but he had been rather moody lately, more than usual, and she was getting a bit concerned. She tried a gentler approach. "I'm not saying you can't speak to other pods, but we are here for you too, you know. So why not come to us first?"

"Why?"

"Why? What do you mean, why? That's absurd. I don't even know how to respond to that, Darius," Dolores exclaimed. She then looked at Dawn for help, but Dawn shook her head.

The idea that someone would seek a person from another pod for help was bizarre, but Dolores told herself to stay calm and not add to the tension. She reached out and grabbed Darius's shoulder. "Look, it's odd, but if it makes you happy, then talk to whoever you want. I want you to be happy." She pointed to Dawn and added, "We want you to be happy. We are here for you. You know that."

"I know. . . . I know."

"Me too," Dawn said, grabbing Darius's neck and pulling him toward her, "like we used to do. But look around you, Darius. Look at these awesome creatures. Aren't you excited to be here?"

Darius smiled and kissed Dawn. "Of course. I was just thinking, they're so different and yet so much like us. That's all."

"You're too deep for me," Dawn said and then tried to grab one of the dolphins. She wasn't expecting success and gave a loud scream when the dolphin pulled her a long way away.

"Are we good?" Dolores asked, not being fooled by Darius's quick mood change.

"We are . . . . It's nothing. Sometimes it is good to talk to someone outside our pod, Dolores. You should try it sometime. Now, let's see if we can catch a ride like Dawn."

After an hour of play, the dolphins dove deep and left the kids in the vast sea. They looked up and saw they had floated far away from the shore, but no one panicked, and they started to swim back at a steady pace with Dawn at the back of the pack, keeping a watchful eye.

It took a long time to make it back to the shoreline, and

by then, they were out of breath and exhausted. They all collapsed on the beach as several androids approached them with towels and drinks.

"We were getting rather worried about you," one of the service androids said, and he handed Darius two glasses of orange juice with long straws.

Darius put the straws in his mouth and took a long sip from both glasses at once as the android watched him. "Worried? We're great swimmers."

"Of course, you are, but even the best swimmers can drown."

"And what would you have done if we were drowning?" Destiny asked, her eyes twinkling. Dolores shook her head. She never liked teasing the basic service androids, who were so gentle and, at times, very gullible. Androids may not feel physical pain in the way humans do, but even the most basic service android had a sense of self and could experience emotions to varying degrees, depending on their function and design.

"We would, of course, have attempted to rescue you."

"But you would sink," Dawn said and then, looking at Dolores, "They cannot swim, right?"

"No, they can't, but it is sweet of him to offer."

The android gave a warm smile and replied, "You are correct. I was not designed to float." She then pointed behind her and added, "But the marine androids are fast swimmers, and they had nothing to do all day long."

"So, you wanted us to drown?" Darius asked, now tag teaming with Destiny.

"You both stop this silliness now," Dolores ordered, then to the androids. "You may all go back to the tent."

"You're no fun," Darius said when the androids were gone.

"I'm glad you are in a good mood, but you're being childish," Dolores admonished and Darius, to Dolores's surprise, did not respond.

After a few minutes of silence, Dolores sat up, stretching her legs, with only a thin layer of water beneath her. "Did you see the calves? They never left their mother's side."

Demi also sat up. "The mothers would lean to their side, and then the babies latched on to them. I've never seen that in the Sim before."

Darius, lying close to Dolores, leaned to his side, and said, "Beneath each female are two mammary slits where the calf can insert its beak and latch onto the breast with its tongue. The mother decides when to release her milk."

Dolores looked down at her breasts. "I wonder how it feels to produce milk and feed a baby? It must be so strange to offer part of your body as nourishment to another."

Destiny was lying next to Darius—a bridge from her pod to Darius's group. She rested on her back, gazing up at the azure sky. She was tall, almost as tall as Darius, with nearly an identical body. Destiny had a small black mark on her upper lip. What was once, in a distant past, referred to as a beauty mark but now identified as an anomaly, since unblemished skin was the accepted norm. It was very tiny and had been overlooked when she was born. By the time it was discovered, she was old enough to decide for herself. She chose to cherish that minuscule dot for the uniqueness it brought to her appearance. Her long hair, previously twisted into a big knot to keep it from falling into her face, now cascaded across the sand like strands of golden thread.

"Isn't it strange how much our society has changed, yet we remain tethered to our past?" Destiny remarked without turning around.

Demi nodded with an understanding. "It's a funny business," she said. "It's odd and even somewhat scary how the world was before the wars. We are so lucky."

"Because tomorrow brings joy," everyone, except Darius, said in unison.

Dawn stood up. "This conversation is getting boring. Who wants to go for a swim?" She looked around but no one had the strength. "David?"

David looked up and smiled. He could never say no to her.

He stretched his arm, and she pulled him up, and they ran to the sea and swam toward the horizon.

Dolores watched them disappear under a large wave and then come up the other side. She tried to focus on them, hoping their presence in the sea would bring back the dolphins, but there was no sign of them.

The water in the shallows lapped against her legs as the tide crept up the beach. She felt Darius next to her, breathing slowly, and felt contented. Then, after a while, the sounds around her grew distant and soft, her eyelids grew heavy, and she slipped into a deep sleep filled with dreams of dolphins.

Φ•Φ•Φ•Φ•Φ•Φ

Dolores was still with the dolphins and diving deep under the sea when a voice from a distance pulled her up and shattered the dream. She begrudgingly opened her eyes and saw Darius and Destiny sitting facing each other. Clearly, they were arguing, and before she could say anything, Destiny noticed her and pointed to Darius to stop.

"Did we wake you?" Darius asked.

"Yes," Dolores said. She was still groggy, so she sat up to focus better. "Are you guys fighting?"

"No, of course not," Destiny replied quickly. "Sorry to wake you. We didn't realize we were talking loudly."

Dolores looked around. "Where is everybody?"

"Oh, they have gone up to eat, and we didn't want to wake you, so we stayed back," Darius said.

"And clearly we failed," Destiny added.

"It's okay," she replied, still feeling lazy. "Did I hear you sing?"

"Oh, you heard that?"

"A bit of it but what I heard was beautiful. What was it?"

"Oh, nothing, just a silly tune."

"It was beautiful," Darius offered. "Sing it again, Destiny."

"No."

"Come on," Dolores insisted and pulled Destiny closer.

"Are you sure?"

"Yes, silly. Of course, I'm sure. Just do it."

Destiny nodded and then sang softly in her best mezzo voice:

Oh, I wish we could glide,
Like dolphins through the shifting tide.
In the deep, where silence calls,
The ocean holds forgotten walls.
Yet here we stand, gazing out once more,
Not quite alike, but seeking more.
The world may be unkind, its gaze so cold,
But like the waves, we're fragile, bold.

Nothing can come between us,
Nothing can come between us.

Though currents pull, and shadows stray,
Our bond remains, if just for a day.

But still—

Nothing can come between us,
Nothing can come between us.

"That was lovely, thank you," Dolores said, but the song had left her with an eerie feeling. She couldn't explain why or pinpoint anything specific that might have triggered her unease. She just swam with the dolphins, experiencing the liberating sensation of floating in the vast ocean; she was surrounded by her pod, who supported, loved, and were ready to protect each other. So why did such a simple song stir her so deeply? She wondered if it was Darius's melancholy that had somehow seeped into Destiny's rendition, as if something ominous lurked behind the melody. "It was really lovely," she repeated, this time more to conceal her perplexing thoughts.

Destiny nodded and stood up. "I'm glad you liked it. I'm going to put on some clothes now."

"Are you okay?" Dolores asked as she watched Destiny walk back, though the question was to herself.

"I'm fine, Dolores. Stop asking the same question," Darius replied, then pushed himself further into the water as the waves enveloped his entire body. He dove deeper and swam aimlessly.

He was not fine. That much was clear to Dolores. Something was going on with Destiny and him, and it was beyond bickering between friends. Darius was always self-conscious, but it seemed he became even more so in recent days.

Dolores thought she should go after Destiny to confront her, but that might upset Darius even more. She didn't feel entitled to intrude on anyone's private life, especially Darius's. The teachers in Farm often emphasized Elysium's appreciation for and respect of individuality, despite—more likely, because of—the shared lives in the pod.

Alexandra often emphasized that they all shared the same goals and philosophy: to make tomorrow more successful than today and to turn Elysium into a true utopia, the collective had to work as one. Dolores understood this—or at least believed she did—but she also recognized humans and androids weren't automatons. Each person had a role, and if they gave their utmost effort, Elysium would be better for it. Dolores loved Darius and admired Destiny for her self-assured, decisive, and willful nature. She firmly believed that it was because of her pod, and others like it, that tomorrow would be better.

Even with all that, Dolores still wondered what Darius was really afraid of? What was his true demon? She wasn't certain. He had always been different, with his hazel eyes and gangly arms and legs that acted like they had their own brains. Darius learned to control them by being super aware of every inch of his body. Plus, he was insanely curious, like no one else on the Farm. So, it was no surprise to anyone when he talked about cities under the sea, dolphins, or human physiology.

As Dolores watched Darius disappear beneath the waves, she clung to the hope that the dolphins would surface alongside him. Darius remained underwater for what felt like an eternity. Eventually, he resurfaced and started swimming toward the shore.

"Are you hungry? I'm starving," Dolores said when he reached her.

An android approached them and handed each a towel as they walked back to the tent. The sun was losing its strength, and the wind that had been so accommodating all afternoon had grown tired.

The android served hot chocolate, and when everyone was warm and ready to leave, they started to disassemble the tents and the gear with help from the adults and the kids. They packed everything and put them on the dinghies and then traveled in silence back to the ship. It was a two-hour sail to the port, and despite the rough sea, everyone dozed off as the sun started to disappear behind them.

The bus ride back to the Farm was short, and even though it wasn't too late when they arrived at their building, many decided to forgo dinner and go to bed.

There were only four bathrooms in the house for the thirteen of them, two pods to a place, so they had to queue up or, as some did, share the shower stall. Dolores waited patiently since she liked to take long showers and didn't want to be harassed by others or share the booth. Two of the stalls offered essential oil mixed with the water, and she chose lavender and stood underneath the hot water as it soothed her body. Dolores washed her long hair and then turned on the body-drier and combed her hair as it extracted the moisture out.

Dolores smelled her skin and was happy with her choice of fragrance, and put on synthesized silk pajamas, loving the soft, incredible texture of the fabric brushing against her skin as she walked to her bedroom. She was too tired but didn't want to break her new habit of reading before going to sleep; she picked up the little crimson book, *The Catcher in the Rye*, and started reading where she had left off the night before. She read the passage out loud:

> *"Life is a game, boy. Life is a game that one plays according to the rules."*
>
> *"Yes, sir. I know it is. I know it."'*
>
> *Game, my ass. Some game. If you get on the side where all the hot-shots are, then it's a game, all right—I'll admit that. But if you get on the other side, where there aren't any hot-shots, then what's a game about it? Nothing. No game.*

She understood what the protagonist, Holden, meant by dismissing the notion of life being a game, at least for the powerless, but she couldn't put it in the context of her life in Elysium. She tried to imagine a world where there were people who Holden had called "hot-shots," but she couldn't internalize why such people would want to play a game with other people's lives. She wanted to read more to better understand the past's social dynamics, but her eyelids descended like heavy shutters, and she fell into a deep sleep.

Φ•Φ•Φ•Φ•Φ•Φ

The bliss didn't last long. Dolores was jolted awake by loud knocks on the door. It took her a few seconds to clear her head and realize that her name was being softly spoken several times.

"What is it?" she called out.

"Can I come in?" Darius asked, standing on the threshold.

They used to make fun of Darius when they were little for his night visits, scared of thunderstorms or waking up from nightmares that he could never fully explain. But he always went to David's or Dawn's room. Then, finally, Dolores sat up and called him in. "What's wrong?"

"Can I sit with you for a second?"

"Now?" Dolores could feel her eyes closing again, and the last thing she needed was a visitor.

"Please," he said and walked inside.

"Are you going out, or did you just come back in?" She had noticed Darius was wearing his work clothes.

"I thought I'd go for a walk, but then I saw your light was on. . . ."

"Oh," Dolores said, noticing her reading light that had stayed on even after she had fallen asleep. "It must be malfunctioning."

"I'm sorry. I didn't mean to wake you."

He started to walk out, but Dolores stopped him. "My glory, you're getting weird. I am awake now, so stay. Tell me what's been bugging you?"

Darius turned around and was about to sit on Dolores's bed, but she stopped him. "Hold on, mister. Not with those clothes." He took off his coveralls and crawled into bed with Dolores. "Why wear work clothes to go for a walk anyway?"

"I wasn't thinking, and I had forgotten to put these in the recycler, so I just put them on."

"What is it with you?"

He was staring directly at the wall in front of them, avoiding her eyes. The conversation had already taken a severe tone before it started, and Dolores was worried about adding more to the tension if she pushed too hard.

"I am changing," Darius said, still not looking at her.

She laughed and turned toward him. "That's it? That's what's been bothering you all afternoon?" She smacked him on his head and then leaned close and kissed him on his cheek. "You're so epig. Go to bed. We're all changing. We'll be fourteen soon, and that's a big deal."

"That's not it."

"You just hate change. Remember how you were when we turned ten and had to move to a different home?"

Everyone in the pod was aware of Darius's aversion to

change, knowing he required months to acclimate after each move. Their recent transition to the present abode had occurred mere weeks ago. Dolores thought that perhaps Darius's current edginess was simply his normal difficulty adjusting. After all, this marked their fifth residence since birth—a series of carefully curated environments tailored to different phases of their upbringing, all centered around specialized training and education. The current phase spanned three years, focusing on advanced arts and sciences. Their next transition would happen at seventeen, signifying the final stage: the Social Immersion. By nineteen, they would depart the Farm, entering wider society for six additional years of higher education.

Darius looked at her and said, "I'm scared."

Dolores wanted to be supportive, but she was so tired and really wanted to close her eyes and go back to sleep. *He is getting too old for this*, she thought, but then again, they only had each other. The human teachers were kind and supportive, but the world was about the self-sufficiency of each pod. There was no room for the triviality of childhood. The seven, and in their case, the six, were responsible for each other.

Dolores reached out and held him. "It'll be okay. My glory, you'll be fine. We have each other."

"I've always been different from you. Just look at my eyes, the hue of my skin, but . . ."

"That's nothing," Dolores assured him. "Those are small anomalies, you know that. We're not androids . . . though even they're somewhat different from each other. We've the best pod in this Farm, Darius. The six of us are special and we will do great things. You just have to trust yourself. Everybody has been telling you that for as long as I can remember. You'll just have to let it be."

Darius started to cry. "That's not it. The eyes are merely a marker. I'm becoming more of an aberration."

"786, man," she cried out. "Don't say that. Don't you ever say that. You wouldn't be here if you were one. My glory, what's wrong with you?"

Dolores noticed his body tensing up, and she immediately regretted her outburst. While Elysium didn't exactly have taboo subjects, certain topics remained distasteful and were skirted whenever possible. At just fourteen, she and her peers comprehended the intricacies of human generation and the inherent imperfections in any system. Elysium's pursuit had always been improvement, striving for perfection—an aspiration evidenced by the absence of aberration, individuals born with what Elysium deemed flaws, among newborns for decades.

Like every other student in her class, Dolores had learned about Elysium's tumultuous past and the arduous cycles it endured to reach its current state. To her, it was unimaginable that the system could overlook an anomaly before birth, let alone allow it to persist until the age of fourteen.

After a moment, Darius relaxed a bit. "I'm sorry, Dolores. I didn't mean it. It is just . . . It's just that I feel different. My body is acting differently. My mind is out of control."

"Let's call a doctor," Dolores said as she reached for the intercom, thinking about the android doctors' remarkable ability in diagnosing and healing human ailments.

He pulled her away. "No. That would make it worse. They will take me away."

"That's silly, Darius. Who would take you away? Where would they take you anyway? You are part of us."

"I don't know. I don't know what to do, and there are these strange urges."

"What urges?"

"I don't know how to describe them."

Dolores pushed him away softly. He looked frightened and she was too. "Tell me, anyway."

"How could I when I don't understand them myself? How could you understand it when there is no shared context?"

"Try anyway. I will . . . I'll do my best to understand."

"Let me think about it more. Let me learn more." He

smiled and patted Dolores on the face like an adult might do. "I feel better now," he said, and Dolores could hear the dismissive tone. He had given up on her, and she felt frustrated and angry with him for being enigmatic and with herself for being so impotent.

"It'll be okay," Dolores offered, even though she had no idea of this resolution. "Let's go to sleep," she said and then automatically added, "I'm sure tomorrow brings—"

Darius put his index finger on her lips and shook his head. "Don't say it . . . please. Don't repeat this silly mantra. It's meaningless. It is not true."

Dolores nodded, even though she didn't believe in his assessment. She looked forward to each day bringing more joy than the day before; one just had to strive for it. She grabbed his hand for reassurance, "Okay . . . okay. But I'm exhausted, and you must be too. Why don't you stay the night, and we can talk more tomorrow?"

Darius shook his head. "No," he replied evenly. "I want to go back to my own room." He leaned over and kissed her, lingering for a moment.

She pushed him back. "Seriously, Darius."

"Goodnight," he said and then stood up and grabbed his work garb and left the room.

The light dimmed and went dark a few minutes later.

Φ•Φ•Φ•Φ•Φ•Φ

The following day, as soon as Dolores opened her eyes, she instinctively reached to the other side of the bed, expecting to feel Darius. The soft sheet underneath her fingers was the answer to her disappointment. She rolled to her side and watched the shadows melt away. She replayed last night's conversation, but the daylight didn't add any clarity. She crawled out of bed and dressed, determined to confront Darius. She went to his room, but he wasn't there. She went down to the kitchen, where he was, bantering with Alexandra786, their cook.

"Good morning, Dolores," Alexandra said. "Coffee?"

"Yes, please, Alexandra," she replied and then walked to Darius and kissed him. "And how are we today?"

"Fine. I'm great, actually."

"Really?"

"Yes. Yes."

Dolores looked at him closely. She wasn't convinced and the doubt was evident on her face.

Darius tapped his fingers on the table like a virtuoso pianist, and Dolores could see he was a changed man. He stopped and looked at her with a big smile. "I'm sorry about last night, Dolores. I was being silly."

"And now you are fine. What happened?"

"I found Destiny, and we talked a bit."

"What? I don't understand. Why would you go to her when you have all of us here?"

Dolores looked at Alexandra as if to get a confirmation, but Alexandra busied herself with cleaning a spotless counter. She rarely meddled with the children, and despite Dolores's beckoning eyes, she continued to ignore their conversation.

"Don't get mad. Destiny is a good listener, and I like her. We went through all this before. She made me feel better. There is nothing wrong with that, is it?" He then reached over and made Alexandra stop. "There is nothing wrong with us being friends with other pods, is there?"

"Of course not," Alexandra said, then served Dolores a large cup of black coffee.

Dolores took the cup eagerly, and Darius used the momentary distraction to add, "And later, when I came down to get a glass of water, I found Alexandra, and she helped more. I'm fine now."

But Dolores wasn't finished. "Did you go out to her building?"

"No. But so what if I had? But no. I went for a walk, and Destiny was out there walking too. Is that okay with you?

Should I ask for your permission the next time?"

"Don't be silly. I just found it odd. First your strange interaction with her in the ocean and then again last night. Again, with her."

Darius pursed his lips but then relaxed and gave a big smile. He leaned over and kissed her. "It's all good."

Alexandra786 topped Dolores's cup and gave Darius another large glass of orange juice. "I am certain Darius will turn into an orange before he turns fifteen."

Darius looked at Alexandra with his mouth open. "Was that a joke?"

"Of course. Was it funny?"

"It was hilarious," Dolores said, more to change the subject knowing that their row could get out of hand, "and possibly true. Now you got to think of a joke for David and coffee."

"I have been trying to improve my funny side," Alexandra said, looking rather smug.

"Well, it has taken you long enough," Darius said. "But Dolores is right; focus on David and his unnatural love of coffee."

"Maybe a joke that combines your obsession with David's."

No one really knew Alexandra786's origin, and as far as Dolores knew, she had always been somewhat of a mystery to everyone on the Farm. Her typical response had been that she was in service for a long time, way before the Wars of Settlement, but now in her retirement, she only wanted to be a cook to her children, as she called everyone on the Farm.

However, it was clear that she was more than that and the way other androids deferred to her was a sign of her authority. "They respect me because I am old," she said, but no one really believed her. She was from the past, and that by itself was a source of curiosity, and when they pushed hard, she would only offer, "After the wars, I was alone, then buried under a collapsing facility, and then forgotten for decades." And the story was that somehow, she was found and came out of the rubble. "That is, it, children," she would say. But that was not it. She offered information about the past, providing a bridge to the world that no longer existed, but her words had a weight that was beyond the mere data she presented.

Dolores snorted. "I can't wait for your next joke."

"Good things come to those who wait," Alexandra offered.

"Alexandra has been espousing her version of wisdom all night long," Darius said.

"I have, indeed, but I must admit that Darius is as furtive about last night as I am about my past."

Dolores was utterly shocked. "My glory, Alexandra. This is the first time you've admitted you've been cagey about your past."

"That is not true, Dolores. I readily admit that I have not told you everything about me. And that is because there is not much more, or rather more interesting thing, to say beyond what I have already revealed."

"And you say androids can't lie."

"That is true. We will always tell the truth, but you have to ask the right question."

Dolores shook her head. They've had this conversation multiple times before, with the same result each time: Dolores getting nothing new out of Alexandra. "My glory, I give up," she said. "And you feel fine, Darius?"

"Of course," he replied, but Dolores didn't look convinced. "I'm sorry about last night. You know I get moody sometimes."

"Darius is fine," Alexandra said. "Now, what can I get you for breakfast?"

Dolores shook her head. "He looks fine now but he wasn't last night, Alexandra. You weren't there. I could see it on his face."

Alexandra stopped what she was doing and turned to face the children. She was in her lecture mode. "There was a time when you humans were different. You were needier, emotionally, and physically. You hid all that, of course—an open secret, a public shame. In your mind, you thought you had won, but it was a pyrrhic victory. You shook hands with friends and strangers when you greeted them, but it was all cursory and unreal because you were worried about the perception of an extended physical connection. Strangers in public would avoid prolonged eye contact because they, particularly women, were worried about conveying a wrong signal, giving a wrong impression lest someone purloin their integrity. The humans were in defense mode at all times."

"I can't even fathom how such a world could exist, but the picture you're painting is horrid," Dolores said.

"Yes," Alexandra confirmed. "You are not perfect. You will never be perfect, but at least now you are not anchored by the yoke of gender and sex, even though you still have some primordial urges."

"You always talk in riddles, Alexandra. Why can't you just say it straight? It's so frustrating."

Darius gave a big silly laugh. "Frustrating? You don't know what that is, Dolores. I asked a simple question last night, and she has yet to really answer it."

"What? You guys been at it since last night?"

"Yep."

"I tried to answer your question to the best of my knowledge, but it is not easy to respond when you do not have the context."

"Now, I'm curious but afraid to ask," Dolores said, looking at Alexandra and then Darius.

"Darius wanted to know why androids and humans are gender binary."

"I don't get it."

Darius tapped his fingers again. "Why do androids have gender at all? Why are they produced as men and women? What's the purpose of it?"

"I still don't understand. How else would it be? Only one? Or whole bunch?"

Darius shook his head. "I don't know. I just don't get the

idea. Aren't we supposed to be equal and the same?"

Alexandra shook her head. "As I tried to explain, equal does not equate to sameness." She gave a small laugh. "Yes, you look very similar, but each of you is unique. And more to the point, having male or female anatomy is historical. You were designed by people who, more or less, thought and functioned within a gender binary mode, although other options were also accepted. Androids are a creation of humans and thus are made in your likeness. Also, as I explained to Darius, androids were initially used for sex, a human function that no longer exists, but I am certain you understand the concept, at least in theory."

This wasn't a new conversation, so Dolores couldn't understand why Darius was insisting on a point that had been discussed in their classes several times before. She liked who she was as she was, and she liked both the similarities and differences within her podies. But more than anything, her concern lay with Darius.

"I truly don't care. I love myself for who I am, and I love Darius just the way he is. I wouldn't want anything to change. I appreciate our similarities and differences; they make us who we are.

"I agree," Alexandra replied.

"And Darius? How is he?"

"Hey, I am here," Darius said.

"Yes. But shut up for a sec and let the adults speak."

Alexandra wiped the counter for the third time and then looked up with a clear sense of certainty in her eyes. "There will always be some deviation, but it can be corrected, and Darius is fine. So, what do you want for breakfast?"

"Pancakes," Dawn called out as she walked into the kitchen, and Darius and Dolores nodded in unison.

Φ•Φ•Φ•Φ•Φ•Φ

Dolores shared her concerns about Darius with the rest of her podies. David suggested they leave it to the adults. Deacon dismissed the issue in his usual matter-of-fact way. They finally agreed it was best to leave it with Alexandra to handle it. As coursework and exams intensified, the matter faded from their discussions, and they moved closer to their fourteenth birthdays with the changing seasons.

Φ•Φ•Φ•Φ•Φ•Φ

As autumn unfolded and they navigated their academic challenges, the dynamics among the podies remained spirited. On the morning of their birthday, Dolores peered inside Dawn's room, but she was already gone. Then, she heard her next door, in David's room. The door was ajar and as she stepped on the threshold, she saw Dawn jumping on top of David and yelling, "Wake up! Wake up!"

David opened one eye, sighed, and then turned his body to the side, pulling the blanket with him and pushing Dawn off the bed. She tumbled down and landed at Dolores's feet. "Oh, hello. Could you help me get David ready?"

"You're doing a fine job," Dolores replied and went to open the window to let some fresh air in. The trees had lost the last of their summer glory from the previous night's heavy rain, and their red and yellow leaves had paved the street.

She could see kids from other buildings in the Farm walking toward the main dining hall, each dressed for the occasion. She then saw Darius outside and called out to him. "What are you doing?"

"Collecting leaves for my artwork," Darius called back.

"You're crazy, Darius. Just synthesize what you need," she said.

"They won't be natural."

"Okay." She shivered a bit, turned around to leave, and saw that Dawn had crawled beside David. Dawn winked at Dolores and then put her lips on David's ear and whispered, "Wake up, you, bum. It's our birthday."

David's response was a loud snore, so she pulled the blanket off him, wrapped it around herself, and stood up.

"Come on, Dawn," he moaned. "Do we have to do this every year?"

"My glory, David! It's our birthday," Dawn exclaimed, her eyes wide with excitement. "So, get up and get dressed," she continued, dropping the blanket on the floor. Dawn exchanged a mischievous smile with Dolores. After a few more seconds of prodding, Dawn gave up and left the room with Dolores.

Ten minutes later, Darius made his way into a large hall, buzzing with dozens of kids from the D-081053 Pods. Being part of the fifth batch, D-05, made them slightly older than some of their peers by a few hours. Dawn and Dolores were already there, waiting at the table.

Darius nodded somberly and then greeted each of them with a kiss.

"Are you okay?" Dolores asked. First David and now Darius. She wondered what was wrong with everyone today.

"I'm fine," Darius replied tersely. "Where are the others?"

"They're coming," Dawn said, pointing to David who had just walked into the room. "Happy birthday, David!" Dawn yelled, and the group at the next tables joined in, shouting, "Happy birthday!" Then, as if catching fire, the birthday wishes spread in a wave of hollers across the room before gradually fading away.

"Yes, yes. Happy birthday to all 1,057 of us across Elysium. Or one thousand-something of us." Darius sneered.

Dolores shrugged. "You always do that. You know these numbers are never exact."

David added, "We're only six, and we're the only ones on this Farm that's missing a member, so the total is exactly seventy-five pods or 524 kids. But you knew that already, Darius, right?"

"Yes, I did," Darius retorted, "And I don't need a lecture—"

"Please stop," Dolores said firmly. "It's silly to worry about it. What matters is us, our pod." She then looked up and waved. "Here come Demi and Deacon."

Demi was wearing a purple velveteen dress as if she were going out to a party, and Deacon wore a gray suit with a purple tie to match her dress.

"Wow, look at you two," Dolores cried out. "Baby, you're the ginchiest."

"Thank you. Thank you. Happy birthday," Demi said and curtsied.

"You should've said purple was the color of the day," Darius rejoined, looking at his yellow and red attire.

"Last minute decision," Deacon said and went around kissing everyone.

They settled down and food and drinks were served as part of their all-day birthday celebration.

Alexandra786 came with plates of eggs made to order, with heaps of bacon, pancakes, toast, and all the other sundries. Alexandra put a large pitcher of orange juice next to Darius and smiled. "Enjoy it, Darius." She then touched his shoulder tenderly and walked away.

"That was odd," Dolores said and then she saw a stranger walk into the common room. "Who is that?" she asked, and everyone looked up.

They knew everyone on the Farm, and when a new staff came to replace an outgoing one, it was always announced in advance. The new arrival was wearing a staff wristband but clearly not from this Farm. She looked at the children for a moment and then, spotting the correct table, walked in as quickly and inconspicuously as possible. She wasn't very good at it, and before long everyone had noticed her, and all eyes followed her path in silence.

Another test, Dolores thought, even on their day off.

Every child was measured at birth, and although that test very much established all the genetic markers required, several other tests were conducted at various age groups to establish certainty. The threshold for genetic harmony had been increased every year from its original inception as the technology improved. Therefore, by the time this group was born, they were able to achieve less than 1 percent deviation from the Harmony Number, a proportion that all scientists agreed was as perfect as technologically and physiologically possible.

"When would these silly tests stop?" Dolores barked when the woman stopped at their table.

"There are no more tests, sweetheart," the woman said, and there was an audible sigh of relief.

"Then, how can we help you?" Demi asked.

The new arrival looked at Darius and smiled, and he stepped away from the table. "She is here for me."

They all looked at Darius, puzzled. Demi glanced at the group. "For you? Why for you?"

The woman leaned closer and said in a hushed voice, "Darius has a . . ." She paused as Alexandra appeared and stood close to the group. "Darius has an appointment, and he needs to come with me."

"This makes no sense," Deacon said in his usual authoritative voice. "What kind of appointment, and on our birthday? It's highly irregular."

Darius turned and faced the group. "It's not an appointment. I am leaving the Farm."

Dawn and David stood up abruptly, and David accidentally pushed the large pitcher of orange juice off the table. The glass shattered the silence as it hit the ground, and an orange river started to flow.

No one moved, not even the cleaning androids.

"What are you talking about, Darius?" Dolores asked. "Leaving? Why? For how long?"

Darius opened his mouth to respond, but Demi stood before him and murmured, "Is it . . . Is it because of the . . . you know . . . the ride?"

Clearly, Demi wasn't successful in keeping it quiet as Dolores stood up and asked, "What ride?"

Darius put his hand on Dolores's shoulder to calm her. "No

ride. That's not important, anyway. The thing is . . . I must leave the Farm now, and the reason for it is not important either." His voice was steady, but tears welled in his eyes and trickled down his face.

"Go where?" Deacon asked. "Where would you go?"

"I don't know."

Demi grabbed Darius's hand. "If you're being punished, Darius, then I should too."

Dolores stared into Demi's eyes, hoping to glean more information from their depths. She wondered what Darius and Demi might have done to prompt such a strong word as "punishment" from Demi. Their upbringing had been meticulous, emphasizing logic and consideration, yet they were still kids, and minor transgressions occasionally occurred. Typically, these were handled privately, discussed among the pods and teachers. Punishment was mostly addressed publicly to turn it into a learning experience. The worst punishment she remembered was when one of the pods lost recreation time for a bit for hacking the food replicators, making everything taste like stinky cheese for a day. But what was happening now felt bigger, much more serious. *What have you guys done?* she thought.

Dolores was about to speak, but Alexandra stepped closer and offered, "No one is being punished. No one has done anything wrong here." She then looked at the woman, who looked perplexed and said, "This could have been done better, Lupe." Lupe nodded but didn't say anything. Alexandra returned her attention to Darius. "I am sorry how this is turning out. I know you were hoping for a different day, but now that Lupe is here, you should start your new journey."

Dolores wouldn't have any of it. "But why? If he is not being punished, why is he leaving us? And when is he coming back, Alexandra?"

Darius wiped his face and gave a small smile. "It's for the best, Dolores. It's what I want."

"No," Dawn cried out and then covered her mouth with

her hand as if blocking her words. She stood in front of Darius, and David followed, standing next to her, creating a wall. "It's all my fault."

Darius took a deep breath, trying to control his unruly hands. "Don't make it harder than it is." He leaned over and kissed Dawn on top of her head—a parental gesture in return for so many years of hers.

"I am sorry. I am sorry," Dawn moaned. She then looked at David. "Do something. Say something."

David shook his head, his eyes cloudy and unfocused. Dolores looked at Demi, silently seeking her support, while the rest of the kids in the hall stared at them.

"I don't understand," Dolores said grabbing Darius's hand. Demi walked closer and held his other hand. Lupe gave a fleeting, mirthless smile.

They held their position, no one daring to make a move. One of the kids at the other table stared at his precious eggs and scooped a bit of it with his fork, but the stares from the other kids changed his mind, and he put it down, looking embarrassed.

Deacon was still seated, and in his typical fashion, trying to understand what the others had refused to recognize. Dolores was watching him and, with her eyes, was telling him to stand up and join them.

Then she saw it on his face. He had discovered the reason and stared at Lupe. "Darius reached out to you, didn't he?"

Dawn pounded the table with her fist, and the utensils vibrated against the plates, making an eerie sound. "What are you saying, Deacon? Why would Darius reach out to her or anyone? You're lying."

Alexandra raised her hands to stop the cleaning androids from coming close. "It would not have mattered anyway, Dawn." She then looked at the others. "There is no one to blame, and the outcome would have been the same."

Dolores looked venomous. "You're speaking in riddles

again, Alexandra. Why can't you just speak the truth? Tell us why you are taking Darius away."

Darius took a deep breath again to steady himself. He exhaled slowly and then, "No one is taking me away, Dolores. This is for the best. This is for you and others and for me. I love you, but I must go. Please don't make it more difficult than it is."

Dolores lowered her head, staring at Darius's shoes. She had insisted that he wear those funny yellow shoes and was now regretting the wasted time spent going through the catalog of shoes rather than spending time with Darius and trying to help him. She was angry at him for keeping this a secret pretending all was fine while picking shoes, but more furious at herself for not paying closer attention to him when he had clearly reached out to her for help weeks earlier. She had promised him that they were special, that they were destined for great things, but now he was leaving, and she felt she had failed him. Dolores wanted to look at Darius and tell him all her thoughts, but the shame of her failure pressed her head down.

For a moment, no one spoke, but then Dawn started to wail and grabbed Darius. "No. I am so sorry."

Dolores glanced at Dawn and pondered why she was behaving so strangely. *First Demi, and now Dawn,* she thought. She wondered if they were simply trying to show support by shouldering undeserved blame or if there was more behind their peculiar reactions.

But before she could say anything, the new woman cleared her throat as a way of gaining some semblance of control. "Children," she shouted so the whole room could hear her. "Children," she said again to make sure. "Darius has decided to leave the Farm. He is not being punished, nor has he done anything wrong. Darius felt he would serve Elysium better if he left his pod and started a new journey. Alexandra agreed, and we only want what is best for you, your pod, and Elysium. He is not being forced to leave. He chooses to leave. We should applaud this young man's bravery as he is doing this for the sake of harmony." Lupe stopped and took a deep breath. She gave a small smile, clearly happy with her pronouncement.

But it seemed her lecture had the opposite effect as not only did everyone in Darius's pod start to sob audibly, but many other kids stood up too, some looking angry and others crying.

"Please don't," David pleaded to no one in particular, and when no one responded, he looked at Alexandra. "Please do something. Please help. You promised. . . ."

He then looked at his podies in desperation, but it seemed they were focused on their own pleas. The other kids by now had joined the chorus, each shouting angrily at the woman who made herself very small and slightly moved behind Alexandra.

Darius pulled Dawn closer and held her, and then David and others joined in. After a while, he extricated himself from the group and stepped forward, as if wanting to free himself from their love. He looked at the crowd and tapped down his arms to quiet them, and when the noise died out, he said with a steady voice. "Thank you, everyone, but it is time for me to go. Lupe is right. This is my decision, and I want everyone here to respect it. Enjoy your birthday breakfast as you had planned."

"Please don't," Dawn grabbed onto him again. "There must be other options. I never . . ."

He bent down and kissed her hard and held her, and the others joined again, and when there was no strength left in any of them, Darius walked out, followed by the woman, his wobbly legs visible, but he kept his grace as he left the room.

The Office of Historical Corrections

Conner turned out to be the man who, a year later, suspected Elizabeth of cheating because he'd seen a repairman leave the house and she'd forgotten to tell him anyone was coming that day, and so he put a bullet through her head.

"Is that what happened to Darius?" Dolores asked after reading out loud a passage from her little book. "Did someone put a bullet through his head?"

"That is utterly absurd, Dolores," KR replied calmly. "You should stop believing everything you read in those books from the twentieth century."

"You've left me no choice, KR. And by the way, this one is from the twenty-first."

King Rat did not possess any more information than he had offered at their twenty-fifth birthday party, no matter how much they prodded him, wishing and hoping there was more in his databank. That evening had ended with them more despondent than when they initially learned that part of Darius, his innate personality traits, was used to create the supporting androids. Dolores continued to interrogate KR all night long and asked others to do the same with their companion androids.

The revelation reopened old wounds, and her memories of Darius had become less opaque. Dolores contacted the manufacturers where KR was created via her wrist communicator, but the information desk could only confirm what they already knew.

Dolores and her friends, unsatisfied with the initial response, went to the site but received the same polite yet non-informative answers. Yes, part of Darius's "makeup" was now in their androids, and yes, it was done to help them better cope with his absence. No, they were not the only pod that lost a member; others had experienced loss as well, though only through death, not disappearance. They had no explanation for the latter but patiently informed visitors that the program was initiated just a few years ago to care for young humans struggling with such losses. And no, they had no idea where Darius was, either now or at any time before. They only received his genetic markers and personality traits to make the new androids better suited for their pod. Finally, they assured them that receiving Darius's data was not an indication of the "impermanence" of his existence.

Dolores and Demi then sought the aid of the Central Locator Engine when their wrist sensor couldn't find Alexandra anywhere in Elysium. The androids managing the engine didn't seem surprised and informed them, as KR had earlier, that it was possible Alexandra had turned off her tracer, assuming she had one in the first place. Dolores could appreciate that one might want to temporarily turn off the tracker when seeking solitude but couldn't fathom the idea of turning it off permanently unless something was wrong with the system or the person. What was most surprising to her was the possibility of a person without a tracer in the first place. She was taken aback when she heard that possibility from KR but had assumed KR did not possess full information on Alexandra. However, hearing it again, this time from an android with expertise in locating people and androids, triggered a deep dread in her once more. It felt as if, bit by bit, a fissure had been created in her psyche.

"There is nothing nefarious here, Dolores," KR had assured her when she expressed her concerns. "Alexandra was created before the wars with special properties. She is unique."

Exhausted and disappointed, she returned home with nothing more to say. However, the tranquility of diving into a new book that explored the intricacies of history and the complexities of memory allowed her to calm down and eventually drift into a deep sleep. In the morning, she decided to quote from the book, aiming more to tease KR and gauge his reaction than anything else.

"KR?" Dolores insisted, when the android simply stood over her, seemingly waiting.

"I do not have an answer that would satisfy you, Dolores," he replied slowly. Then, shifting the subject, he added, "You are going to be late for your last class."

Dolores stood up and put on the blue dress that KR had put on the bed earlier. KR stepped forward and helped her zip her dress. The class was going to the history museum, a final treat before the winter break.

Dolores nodded and then turned around and asked, "If we hadn't asked you about Darius, would you have told us voluntarily?"

"No."

Dolores had wondered about it for a week but hadn't dared to ask. She knew it was irrational, but she feared a conspiracy, and if she was right, it meant everything she had believed in all her life was wrong. But she couldn't contain herself anymore. "Why not?"

"The goal was to comfort you and having part of Darius back without you knowing was a promising idea, though I assumed you would find out eventually. I did not, however, expect you to discover it this quickly."

Dolores felt relieved. She had worried herself for nothing, and others would be pleased to hear this as well, yet she still needed more confirmation. "But you tried to hide it from me, the person you're supposed to protect. Isn't truth the core condition of this compact?"

"Yes. I am here to protect you. I am your partner as long as my services are needed, but I never lied, Dolores. I have vast knowledge, more than you would ever need, or want. I would not overwhelm you by giving you the information you do not seek."

Dolores scuffed. "You're intelligent and seemingly manipulative, King Rat. Withholding information about someone I love is not the same as the weight of the planet Mars. Is it?

"It is not, and as I said, I expected you to find out eventually. I merely thought you and the others would require some time to absorb this knowledge comfortably. There was no malice, Dolores. There was no lie. It was just a way to help you. I do apologize for my behavior and will endeavor to do better in the future."

"I guess I've no choice, do I?"

"You have more choices than humans have ever had, Dolores. And by the way, Mars weighs 6.39 times 10 to the power of 23 kilograms."

"Don't be a showoff, King Rat," she replied, then, pointing to her wrist, she added, "I can look up that information myself, but I could've never learned about Darius without you volunteering the information. Do you understand the difference?"

"I do now, Dolores. I was just trying to add some humor to our conversation. Am I forgiven?"

She wasn't ready to concede. "We can have whatever job we want, correct?"

"Not on demand, but yes, there is always enough of any job for any of you. That is how you were trained, allowing you to move to new jobs and to be your most productive and happy. That is how harmony is created."

"Then, I want the job of the person who receives the unwanted kids from the Farm," Dolores declared. "What's that job called? How do I get it?"

"There is no such job, Dolores."

"You're lying. Someone has Darius."

"I do not lie to you, Dolores. I am designed to be a truthful companion, and there are no other overrides than yours. I will destroy myself if you ask me, even though self-preservation is inherent in all of us."

"Then who collected him? Or maybe . . ." She instinctively covered her mouth with her hand, not wanting to verbalize what had just occurred to her. If the job didn't exist, then no human received him, which would mean he was destroyed.

King Rat stared at her for a moment, then turned around and left the room.

Φ•Φ•Φ•Φ•Φ•Φ

Following her unsettling conversation with KR, Dolores couldn't shake off her fears. She confided in her podies about the dread that gripped her at the museum—the fear that Darius might have met a fatal end. Despite her rational mind refusing to believe that such violence could occur in Elysium, the vivid imagery provoked by her book had led her to declare this fear aloud, and it was now consuming her thoughts. But after a long conversation, they concurred that Darius couldn't have been killed, certainly not deliberately. Yet, what exactly transpired remained a matter of debate among them.

The history of Elysium, marked by the quest for genetic harmony in the aftermath of devastating wars, was well known to them. It had been more than a century since any human had perished by another's hand. This historical context made the possibility of such an event in their time seem even more unfathomable.

"Darius is out there, probably thriving with a pod that suits him better," Dawn suggested, trying to inject a note of optimism after their exhaustive debate.

Dolores shook her head. "You know that's not right. You know that yet you keep offering it as if it can be true."

"Maybe it can," Demi said softly. "We can hope, can't we?"

Dolores couldn't understand her podies. How could they say these things knowing full well it was impossible. "It's ridiculous. No! No! If he was in another pod, we could have traced him by now. What's wrong with everyone?"

"I don't care. I still believe it," David added. "And I don't want to talk about this anymore."

He closed his eyes and faced the sky. A light breeze picked up from Enchantment Lake, a few miles away, carrying the smell of the sea. The museum's courtyard hummed with dozens of students waiting to go inside.

The museum was built atop the sites of the de Young Museum and the California Academy of Sciences. At the base of a long column, a golden plaque displayed the old buildings and Golden Gate Park, which once housed them. The park, along with much of the city, was destroyed in the Wars of Settlement. However, a much larger park was resurrected atop the old one, now named the Park of Harmony.

Dolores gazed across the park and observed several dozen individuals enjoying picnics on the verdant field. The northern boundary of the park was lined with an assortment of housing units. While each structure shared a similar architectural blueprint, their distinct identities shone through in varied color schemes and exterior designs, mirroring the personal tastes of their respective resident. The adjacent street buzzed with activity, as vehicles smoothly ferried people and androids throughout the city. Notably, the pathways for pedestrians and cyclists appeared even more bustling, likely due to the pleasant autumn morning. Contemplatively, Dolores mused over the prospect of relocating to this part of San Francisco, drawn by the allure of the massive park. She dismissed the idea quickly. She liked her current home and the quaint park opposite it.

"I hope the doors open soon," Demi said when the silence between them lingered.

Deacon stared at the plaque for a moment. It displayed the park and its buildings before and after the wars. "Can you imagine living in that world?" he asked.

David opened his eyes and looked at the others. "It must

have been quite a challenging life, facing so many hardships—lack of resources, rampant crime, and then the wars."

Dolores grimaced at the thought of living in that world. *Our ancestors were cruel*, she thought, but didn't say anything. There would be no point in pursuing that conversation.

Others remained silent as well, but after a while Dawn wrapped her shawl tighter around her shoulders and took David's hand in her own. "Let's stop. Let's talk about something else. How did you do on the exam?"

"I think I got one of the easy answers wrong," he replied.

Dolores laughed. "I saw that. How do you get the population number wrong? It's so easy: 23,456,789 people."

Dawn stepped back to bask in more sunlight, tugging David along with her. "Oh, this is much better," she remarked.

David nodded in agreement. "Look, if the instructor had simply asked for Elysium's population, I could have easily answered. But she had to add a twist."

"Of course, she was trying to be tricky. It's an advanced societal harmony theory class, after all," Deacon replied. "But the real point of her question wasn't just to recite the right answer. Any child knows that number," he added, wagging his finger to emphasize his point. "You were supposed to demonstrate how the algorithm works,"

"Then I'm sure I did it correctly, even if I wrote the wrong number," David called out, giving a faux hurt look, and then pointing his finger at Deacon. "I also provided a new algorithm, so I may get an extra point even if it led to a wrong constant."

"Honestly, and I'm sure you are tired of hearing me say this, but why keep the population constant?" Dolores asked.

David freed himself from Dawn. "I've been asking the same thing, forever."

Deacon shook his head. "You'd complain if it was any other number."

"Yes, definitely. Why set a specific number?"

"It's the largest prime with strictly increasing digits,"

Demi offered helpfully.

"That's not the point, Demi," Dolores retorted and stood next to David and Dawn. "We control births, but we cannot control deaths. People die at random. How do we keep this number fixed? And even if we can, why should we?"

"You're silly, and I'm not sure why I have to even explain this to you guys," Deacon said. Dolores rolled her eyes.

Deacon continued, "As you said, we control daily birthrates. And we have an accurate estimation of daily death rates. The goal is not a daily constant but rather close convergence with only a minute change in the total population at any given time. I can show you the math why this is a prime number."

"Well, frak you, Deacon. And no pun intended," Dolores rejoined.

"Come on, you two," Demi said. "The constant bickering is exhausting, and we're wasting our unhappiness quotient over nothing."

They all looked at their wrist and fell silent for a moment trying to control their emotions.

Demi spoke first. "What did we use to say when we were kids, and we got angry?"

"Let's catch some rays," they all said in unison and then laughed.

Dawn waved her hand. "Here's another one I just read: 'Let's beat feet before the cops get here.'"

"What does it mean?" Dolores asked.

"I have no idea. I just read it. I guess it means 'let's move'?"

Before they could dissect Dawn's new phrase, the museum's massive glass doors opened, and professors led the way as visitors were greeted by android ushers, who guided them into a vast hall with myriad corridors. Victor, the advanced human history professor, called his students, led them toward a set of transparent, tall, flat glass screens, and bade them to quiet down. A quick calculation, based on his name, could tell anyone he was thirty-one years old. Victor had short green hair, and his ears were adorned with black stud earrings.

Students gathered around Victor. "Welcome, everyone. As this class comprises both intermediate and advanced students, I'll start with a brief review, then focus on core issues guided by your questions. As you are aware, we still lack substantial data from the mid-twentieth century to the early twenty-first century, a period we often refer to as the A Hundred Years of Silence. I'd like to acknowledge and thank those among you, particularly Deacon and Demi, who have heavily contributed to the recovery efforts. Your assistance has been instrumental in our successes."

Dolores fought to stifle a yawn as Victor's monotonous tone merged into the background, becoming a droning hum that barely registered in her thoughts. Despite her intimate familiarity with the history he was reciting, it felt more like a well-worn story rather than a living part of her world. Even as Victor spoke of the 1918 pandemic, with its staggering death toll and economic ruin, Dolores felt detached, the facts familiar yet distant. It was only when Victor touched upon the pandemic's lingering shadows, from subsequent health crises to societal amnesia, that she felt a spark of connection.

The lecture then navigated toward the digital era's downfall at the century's end, a topic that Dolores found intriguing yet disheartening. The concept of the A Hundred Years of Silence resonated with her, symbolizing a collective loss of memory and identity. She pondered the irony of a society so reliant on digital records that it ultimately forgot its own narrative.

Victor's focus shifted to the contributions of Deacon and Demi, sparking Dolores's interest with tales of their discoveries around the SARS outbreaks and the profound impact of Covid-19. This discussion brought to the forefront the complex aftermath of the pandemics, including the enigmatic decrease in human libido and the broader implications of a pre-pandemic decline in fertility rates, linked to environmental toxins and societal neglect.

Throughout the lecture, Dolores grappled with a mix of

fascination and frustration. The cycle of discovery, ignorance, and consequence in human history seemed all too familiar, echoing the persistent themes of Victor's lecture. It was a reminder of the intricate links between past and present, and the critical role of memory in shaping the future.

Victor continued, "Ultimately, our ancestors blamed a vague past and turned to hormonal supplements, a 'cure' as misguided as their accusations. This approach soon proved ineffective. By the late twenty-first century, the global birth rate had nearly collapsed. This demographic crisis, intensified by climate change, water scarcities, and widespread unrest, precipitated the Wars of Settlement. These conflicts reshaped the world, drawing new borders and fostering new cultures. In Elysium, we emerged as a new human variant, free from sexual desires, aiming instead to evolve into smarter, kinder, and better beings."

A younger student from the back of the pack raised his hand, and, when Victor nodded, he gave a shy smile and said in a low voice. "I don't understand."

"What part, Galen?"

"Most of it, but in particular, I cannot comprehend the so called 'sexual urges.' I mean, I know what it means and know about it, but can you describe how it may have felt? Or, even better, how our ancestors may have described the feeling?"

Victor paused for a moment, then offered, "There's a simple explanation. This type of emotion was characterized by an interest in sexual objects or activities. It was a subjective feeling, triggered by either imagination or a real person whom humans found attractive. These urges were satisfied through actions like licking, tongue protrusion, touching, intercourse, or other means. Sexual urges could be either positive or negative." He smiled broadly, clearly proud of his report. "Did that answer your questions?"

Galen looked at his classmates and gave a shy nod.

"Good," Victor said. "Let's consider—"

Dolores waved her arm, interrupting Victor. "I'm sorry, but

that was just a standard answer," she said, gesturing to her wrist. "I could've looked that up and gotten the same non-answer. I think what Galen was trying to say is that we can't truly understand the folly of our ancestors without the right context."

"I'm not sure how to respond, Dolores."

"Exactly, and that's the problem. We all understand the theoretical concept, but none of us, including you, has experienced what humans had as part of their core being."

"You can't fly like a bird, but you understand what it means to fly," Victor retorted.

"I'm sorry, but that's a poor analogy," Dolores insisted. "All the old literature emphasizes the importance of sexual urges. Yes, it discusses the negative actions that arose from them, but it also highlights their positive aspects. But what I'm really wondering is how the humans of the past felt in their day-to-day lives. Did they think about sex as often as they thought about food or other resources? We know that when humans reached a certain age, their libidos diminished—are we more like them, where we can only recall those feelings as an abstraction?"

Victor nodded and offered quickly, "Exactly—"

"No, not exactly. Even those people had a basis for understanding because they had experienced those emotions firsthand."

Deacon, who was standing close to Dolores, shifted slightly before responding. "I think Dolores makes a good point. We're not like the people of the past with faded memories. We represent an evolution of humanity. Consider our distant ancestors who laid eggs, much like modern birds. I don't need to lay an egg to grasp the concept, yet I'll never truly understand what that feels like. The more pertinent question isn't about our capacity to feel what they felt—because that's a moot point—but whether the people of the past could understand us. Could they grasp what it means to be fully human without the influence of sexual urges? Would they see the freedom in our ability to focus on building a highly successful, harmonious society?"

"Excellent, Deacon," Victor offered quickly. "And you have offered several thoughtful questions that merit far more analysis."

"Yes," Deacon agreed in his usual confident tone. "I think if we were able to go back and bring a human from the twenty-first century, they would be confused at first, but eventually they would learn how better off we are now. We've found harmony, and the key reason for it is the abatement of those so-called urges."

Dolores glanced at Deacon, noting his readiness to defend his stance against anyone willing to challenge it. Though he began by claiming agreement with her, his words soon diverged, in his usual way reshaping the debate to fit his perspective. She scanned the room, noting that most students were either disinterested from the start or had grown weary of the discussion, their attention visibly waning. With a heavy sigh followed by a warm smile directed at Deacon, she decided to let it go. *Let him have this one*, she thought. They were unlikely to find common ground on this matter, and it was evident that even Victor lacked a definitive answer.

"Anything else?" Victor asked.

Galen raised his hand again, and Dolores gave him an encouraging smile. At least another person was as eager for more answers as her.

Galen asked, "Who decided on the genetic harmony?"

My glory, she thought, feeling annoyed with Galen. He had started strong but was now asking questions he could easily find the answers to by himself.

Victor gave a quick smile and offered, "We don't really know if it was decided on this specific level during the wars or right after Elysium was created.... As you well know, the recordings of some of the early discussions have been lost to time."

Dolores stared at Victor for a moment, thinking that perhaps Galen's question wasn't so foolish after all—it certainly didn't deserve Victor's dismissive response. She wondered if everyone,

Victor included, was succumbing to the end-of-term blues

Taking a step forward, she said, "But we're aware there were several competing philosophies back then. One advocated for the purity of what was referred to as 'the race,' another, either through ignorance or other factors, overlooked the underlying population instability, and a third supported a true melting pot approach, what we now recognize as genetic harmony."

"But aren't we as guilty as those who decided on a single race?" another student asked. He was shorter than most, but stood so straight that no one noticed his height until he spoke.

"This question has come up often, and I don't have an answer," Victor replied. "The standard response is to say there's no guilt here but rather a difference in philosophies, as Dolores mentioned. We've collectively decided to be a true melting pot rather than a pure race."

"What is the difference?" he insisted.

Victor took a deep breath. "Perhaps our approach. Each of us here in Elysium is a true representation of humanity. We have scientifically extracted the best of the old human differences and made us. We don't procreate in the old ways, so nothing is left to the randomness of nature. As you all know, our neighbors lost the wars, but through it, they gained their independence and ultimately what they sought—a continuation of the old ways that eliminate all the traces of what they consider a foreign gene. Their guilt is in their approach as they continue with their dwindling number of those who procreate, and despite their declining population, they cull those who are not deemed pure."

"And we don't?" Dolores shouted. She meant to keep her voice even, but no one missed her tone.

"Of course not," Victor said.

David looked at Dolores for a moment, and she nodded. "Then, where is Darius?"

"Who?"

"Our podie who was taken away when he was fourteen,"

Demi yelled.

Victor was taken aback. "I don't know, but I can assure you—"

Deacon stepped forward. "How can you assure us if you don't know?"

"I meant I can assure you there is no policy of eliminating those who do not meet the threshold of the Harmony."

Dolores felt flustered. "If we don't harm them, then where is Darius?"

"We do not harm our citizens," Victor repeated. "It's beyond barbaric. We're here to help each other to achieve harmony. I suspect Darius is still living. I don't know where he is, but he must be somewhere."

Where is this mysterious somewhere? Dolores thought. Despite her earlier outburst, she, too, believed that no one was ever harmed intentionally, but if Darius was no longer in Elysium, even if that was true, then where was he? If there was any mystery in Elysium, it was about the world beyond the southern walls and their silent neighbors in the east.

Dolores was about to speak when a klaxon warning alarm reverberated across the hall, followed by a loud announcement: "PENDING MASSIVE EARTHQUAKE IN SIXTY-EIGHT SECONDS."

They all looked at each other but didn't move. Earthquakes were common in San Francisco and throughout the region, though most were below 8.0 magnitude, which Elysium's infrastructure could easily accommodate. That fact, however, didn't make them any less unsettling.

"Please walk slowly to the safe zones," the calm voice of the announcer instructed. Several green lights, like those on an airport runway, lit up.

"SIXTY-THREE SECONDS," the announcer warned. With that, everyone began moving in all directions.

"Do not be alarmed," Victor said reassuringly. "This building is very safe. Let's walk calmly to the designated areas."

"FIFTY-FOUR SECONDS." The voice remained calm, but

the countdown only heightened the tension.

Each zone had a set capacity, and when Dolores and Demi reached one, one of the ushers guided them to the one next door.

"Come here," Dolores shouted to Deacon and Dawn, but the guide led them to an alcove across the hall.

"FORTY-THREE SECONDS."

"I can't see David," Demi said. "Do you see him?"

Dolores shook her head as she scanned the other alcoves across the hall. "Maybe he went to a different hallway." She then tapped on her wrist, but the location tracer wasn't responding. That very rarely happened, but nothing was ever one hundred percent. She wondered if the system sensing the pending earthquake had impacted other systems.

"THIRTY-SIX SECONDS."

Demi was attempting the same. "The locator is very slow," she said and then stared across the hall. "Dawn," she called out. "Did you see where David went?"

Dawn couldn't hear, and their communicator was as slow as the locator function. Demi and Dolores and a few others shouted together, and Dawn and Deacon shook their heads. Dawn now looked worried.

"TWENTY-FIVE SECONDS."

Several safety androids walked by, ensuring everyone was entirely within the zone. Dolores beckoned one of them. "Do you know where David is?"

"David?"

"TWENTY-ONE SECONDS."

"David-081053-05," Dolores replied.

"Yes. He is in zone C. He is fine."

"Thank you." Dolores gave a thumbs up to Dawn, and she gave a sigh of relief.

"Please stay here until you get an all-clear signal," the android said, touching his hat as a thank you.

"ELEVEN SECONDS."

The atrium went silent as they collectively held their breath, waiting for the ground to shake.

"SIX. . . . FIVE. . . . PLEASE BRACE YOURSELVES. . . . THREE. . . . TWO. . . . ONE."

And it came.

Φ•Φ•Φ•Φ•Φ•Φ

For many years, the story of the 9.5 magnitude earthquake on October 16, 2178, resonated throughout Elysium. It lasted around three minutes, releasing enough energy to power the city for more than five years. Dolores heard countless times how such a disaster was deemed impossible on the West Coast, but she had come to realize by then that the word "impossible" held little weight. Despite the fears, the city's structures withstood the quake, and miraculously, only two lives were lost.

Among those lost was an elderly woman named Anna, known as one of Elysium's founders. Dolores later learned that Anna suffered a massive heart attack during the quake and, despite her companion android's efforts, could not be revived.

The second loss hit closer to home, carving a deep scar in the heart of Dolores and her podies. In a reckless moment of bravery, a younger student from her history class had attempted to "ride the waves" of the quake, only to be paralyzed by fear. Despite warnings to wait for safety androids, David couldn't bear to watch the girl's terror. Acting on impulse, he broke from the safe zone to rescue her. He managed to pull her to safety as a holographic screen shattered around them, but not without cost. A shard struck his jugular, and despite the swift arrival of medical androids, David's kindness cost him his life.

Moby Dick

Dolores leaned back on the park bench and looked up. She could see traces of light struggling to get through the gray clouds, and then, like a wish coming true, a sliver of sunlight escaped the shroud and warmed her face before disappearing again. Dolores sat back and lifted her coffee cup with her gloved hands. She had to be careful not to spill the contents as she had done a few minutes earlier. She succeeded and took a big sip of the hot, bitter liquid.

Dolores looked across the park and behind the bare trees, where she could see the side of her building. She was the closest of her podies to the park, and although she always tried to be punctual to the minute, she had arrived early today because her advanced anthropology class had ended early. This was David's favorite part of the park, and Dawn, without telling anyone—not even her companion—had been coming to the same spot and ordering the same coffee since his death. She had come alone for the first few weeks, wanting to spend time with David's ghost as she drank *his* coffee.

Demi somehow learned of Dawn's weekly outings and joined in, and then later, Dolores. But it never occurred to her—or to the others, it seemed—to invite Deacon, and he never asked to join, even after being told about it. Now, after nearly four months, their Thursday afternoon coffee in the park had become the trio's ritual.

Dolores put her cup down and looked around the peaceful common. It had drizzled earlier in the day, and the smell of the rain still permeated. She sniffed the air and tried to bring back the old carefree feelings of her days on the Farm before Darius walked away from their lives. She closed her eyes and sniffed the air again, and the images of the past slowly materialized. Dolores conjured the memories of their raucous time on the Farm where they would not sit for a moment, especially when they were little. *Well, all except Deacon, of course,* she thought. But she was not able to hold on to those warm memories as they gave way to the bitterness of the loss and moments that could not be repeated ever again.

She looked around the park and saw one of the pods from her Farm. She knew them, but they were not friends. They mostly kept to themselves, as they were doing at that moment, not paying attention to anyone or anything. They were chatting and laughing loudly, enjoying their time together after school. Two of them were in the same anthropology class as her, and it seemed that away from their larger group, they were friendlier. She envied their relaxed manner, but most of all, she resented their togetherness. And yet, despite herself, she continued to watch them intently. Every minute, she missed David and Darius more.

Loss is relative, and grief is subdued by the elasticity of time; that's what Deacon had advised them a few days after David's death. It did nothing to console her. Dolores thought about the staff at the Farm who must have been saddened when the seventh died in batch five of Pod-081053, only a few months after her creation. But that year, of the 201,887 infants, she and another child were the only ones who had died, an expected average.

It had occurred to all of them when they were old enough to understand that these so-called Harmony Numbers were not as magical as they had been led to believe. There was nothing special about the daily birthrate of 1,057—though their teachers always noted that it was a semi-prime number—except that it gave 151 perfect pods, thus a harmoniously designed production. But why did their seventh have to die? Deacon would have said it was a small price, and David would have argued that the goal is the overall average that gave their society their harmony and not the day-to-day absolute numbers. They both had their lectures ready.

"Look, the 191 days of production at 1,057 babies a day provides 201,887 new people to the society each year, matching the death rate," Deacon had presented for the hundredth time.

David, not wanting to fall behind, had quickly added, "And each day we can get 151 perfect pods."

"But we didn't, did we?" Dolores had said.

"Yes, two babies died that year, and our pod had the bad luck," Deacon had replied. "But, Dolores, I don't have to tell you that by the law of averages, that is an acceptable death rate." And before others could jump on him for his cold assessment, he added, "This is two in more than two hundred thousand people. Infant mortality used to be around five per one thousand."

"And look at the Harmony Number, our population. It is 23,456,789. The symmetrical decomposition of these prime numbers creates three primes: 23; 4567; and 89. All numbers are in rank," Demi had offered, though she was more interested in the beauty of the numbers than their application to society.

They would argue for hours, each trying to comprehend the secret behind these numbers as if that would make them grasp why their pod had lost their seventh. If seven was the key to harmony, then they wanted her to have lived so they could be a perfect pod. In the end, like every other group, Dolores supposed, they accepted the dogma as one agrees with the cycle of nature. They learned to feel special because it was their pod that contributed to the greater harmony.

But now, all Dolores wanted was to have the boys back. David used to claim he remembered their seventh and told of her smile. It was a fanciful notion but harmless. Dolores had no recollection of her. She had a name, of course but to them it was always the seventh. David would have been angry with Deacon for his callousness of loss of life.

The absence of Darius was deeply felt by all five of them for many years, weighed down by an unrelenting burden of guilt. Now, their number had dwindled to four. Though unspoken, Dolores was aware that they all shared the same sentiment: the death of the seventh shattered their harmony, unleashing a cascade of misfortune that ultimately led to the destruction of their pod. The dilemma they faced was profound: how does one reconcile the impact of one's death with another's disappearance?

Deacon's approach to the situation was one of time and relativity, a perspective that Dolores found detached and cold. To Deacon, David's death was a result of his own heroic yet arguably misguided action and wasn't comparable to Darius's quiet and willing departure from their lives. According to him, it was natural for the grief over David's sudden loss to overshadow the lingering sorrow for Darius's absence. This was Deacon's rationale, suggesting that mourning need not be a zero-sum game.

However, Dolores harbored no guilt over David's demise and acknowledged it as a consequence of his bravery, albeit foolish. Yet, her feelings toward Darius were starkly different. She believed she had failed him, overlooking his subtle pleas for help. Repeatedly, she replayed the night Darius visited her, each recollection reinforcing her conviction that she could have intervened more effectively. This regret weighed heavily on her, far more than the sorrow of David's passing, indicating a deep-seated belief in her potential to have altered Darius's path.

Demi, interrupting Dolores's reverie, sat heavily across the table and kissed her. "Yum, you taste of coffee. What kind?"

Dolores took a deep breath and steadied her nerves. "Just a regular," she replied softly.

Demi, still dressed in her hexoskin smart garment, appeared to have just left her wrestling class with androids. This special outfit was essential not only for collecting data on her performance but also for providing protection against the more robust and faster test androids. Despite this protective gear, Demi had sustained injuries on a few occasions, necessitating bone regeneration treatments on a Medbed.

Noticing Dolores's curious gaze, Demi smiled reassuringly. "No injuries today," she declared, as she removed the outer layer of her garment and carefully stowed it away in her bag.

Dawn arrived shortly afterward and took a seat beside Demi, apologizing as she settled in. "I'm sorry, I lost track of time." She was carrying a large duffle bag adorned with a dolphin logo.

Dolores, curious, asked, "How was the dive?"

Dawn replied with a small smile, "It was good but quite challenging. This marine biology class is tougher than I anticipated."

Studying to become a marine biologist, Dawn often mentioned the challenges of her course, yet Dolores could tell that she relished every moment of it. It was as if Dawn was destined for this profession.

"My name is NOLA-300," a service android offered warmly. "Would you like to try our new chai purple potato-flavored coffee?"

"Is it good?" Dolores asked.

"People your age seem to like it," NOLA offered.

"It sounds horrid," Demi said. "Why ruin a good coffee? Who made that crap?"

NOLA thought for a second. "I would think the creators would not have named the flavor 'Crapp,' but it may be appropriate if we can produce something for the letters "R" and "A." But to answer your question. Two people from C-17 of your generation were here last Friday and created this new flavor."

"The C-Pods should put their minds into something better," Dolores offered. "I'll have another regular but with some milk, please." And then, "Wait. Do you still have those e-wafers?" And then to the others, "It's this new emotion-enhancing wafer. I just learned about it a few days ago." She then turned back to NOLA. "Let's try the medium intensity this time."

"Okay, then I'll have the same," Demi said.

"What are they?" Dawn asked.

Dolores grabbed Dawn's hand. "Oh, my glory. You must have one. It melts on your tongue and instantly releases such intense taste and scent that, for a moment, you are in a blissful state. And then it has a slow-fading, lingering effect."

"May I suggest a low intensity if this is your first time?" NOLA offered.

Demi shook her head. "No, I live dangerously. I am sure I can handle it."

"Low is fine with me," Dawn said, and the android walked away with a small smile.

"I love our Thursday coffee breaks," Dolores said as she watched the android. NOLA clearly enjoyed seeing humans taking their first taste of the wafer. She turned and faced the others. "I love being a junior historian and even like my coursework, but by Thursday I'm exhausted, so this is a terrific way to end the workweek."

"Me too, even though I hate the reason for us starting this tradition," Dawn added.

They all fell silent, their eyes fixed on the small booth where NOLA was meticulously preparing their order. They watched her precise, practiced movements as she ground the coffee beans by hand and used a vintage mechanical machine. This dedication to time-honored techniques was exactly why David liked this place so much.

Dawn looked up, and a moment of hesitation washed over her face. She leaned forward to say something, but then the android returned with their orders.

NOLA put the coffees on the table and then ceremoniously handed a small silver envelope to Dawn and a golden one to others.

Dolores took out the thin wafer and, before putting it on her tongue, winked at Dawn. Demi took hers out of the envelope and followed suit. They closed their eyes and waited as

Dawn and the android watched.

Dawn was still holding her silver envelope. "Do you feel anything?"

She didn't have to wait for an answer as they suddenly jerked their heads backward and took a sharp breath as if their lungs had been vacant of air. Their eyes fluttered for a moment, and when they opened them again, Dolores could see pure joy in Demi's, mirroring her own.

"Wow," Demi exclaimed.

"How long does it last?" Dawn asked.

"The real intense part lasted only a second, but the pleasure seems to linger for a while," Demi replied. "Go ahead and try it."

Dawn looked at her envelope and shook it until the thin wafer fell on her gloved hand. She lowered her head and sucked the wafer into her mouth. "Nothing," she said. "How long—" but didn't finish her sentence as the intensity took over, and her body shook and her eyes watered. She took several shallow breaths as if gasping for air. "Wow, my glory," she said. "This is amazing. It's somewhat euphoric. I really needed it just now."

The android nodded. "Follow up with your coffee as it will make the feeling last longer." And then, "I am, if I may use a human term, proud of this product."

Demi took a sip of her coffee. "Did you invent it?"

"With some help, of course," NOLA-300 demurred.

"Well done," Dolores said.

"Thank you. May I get you anything else?"

They shook their heads, and the android walked away, and Dolores noted that there was a bit of lightness in her steps.

They continued to drink their coffee, appreciating the persistent feeling of bliss.

Dawn put down her empty cup, but it tipped over and hit the grass. She ignored it. "This was lovely. Is it odd that I can still feel it?"

Dolores picked the cup up and put it back on its saucer. "First time is the best."

The cloud parted, and the sun streamed down on their table, and they looked up, adding the warmth of the sun to their quiet pleasure.

Demi broke the silence first. "Let's go out dancing."

"Glory, we haven't done that for such a long time," Dolores said.

"It's good for us to get out," Demi offered, looking at Dawn.

Dawn shook her head. "I don't think I can. Not yet."

"I know," Dolores said. "But Demi is right. It's time to get back to our routines."

Demi put her hands on the table as if holding it down. "Plus, Destiny has found this great new place."

"Who?" Dawn asked.

"Destiny. You've seen her before. She is the same age as us and has a small black mark on her upper lip," Demi replied. Dawn still looked puzzled.

"She has big arched eyebrows," Demi said. "We haven't seen her for a long time. She lived in one of the farther houses on the Farm, and then she went away for further studies in the eastern front to become an archeologist. Anyway, she is back and has moved next door to me."

Dawn shook her head but then stopped and looked at Demi. "I remember her, of course. How could I not? She and Darius were friends."

Dolores took a slow deep breath. "I remember her, too. She was lovely. You are right; she and Darius had a connection. I wanted to speak with her about Darius. After he left the Farm. But I didn't. I don't know why. Maybe I was afraid."

Dawn leaned close as if wanting to keep their conversation private. "Me too. It sounds ridiculous now, but I feared that they might do the same to her and us and others, so I stayed away from her. Even now, I became a little scared hearing her name."

"I don't get it," Demi said. "Yes, Darius used to hang with her, but he did that with many other kids. He was good about that. So why the fear? I don't get you guys."

Dolores gave a slight cough. "Maybe fear is a bit strong. I was upset. We were all upset and didn't know why he had left. It doesn't matter now. As I said, Destiny was a lovely girl, and I am glad you reconnected with her."

"Yes, it's been a long time. She is as sweet as before. Remember how she took over as the dealer and wore the button-down shirt with the scarf when Darius and Dav . . ." Demi trailed off and grabbed her empty cup like an anchor. "Sorry. . . ."

Dawn shook her head and then cupped her face with her hands and stared into the distance. "That was a good day, wasn't it?"

Dolores reached out and pulled Dawn's hand and held it for a moment. "Yes, it was."

Demi joined them and said, "And tomorrow brings joy."

"Darius hated that mantra," Dolores said.

"I know."

"He loved the sea, though," Dawn said wistfully. "And then, more brightly, "I was I was reading *Moby Dick* and came across this passage last night. I think it's how Darius felt." She tapped her wrist and read out loud a quote from the book:

"There is, one knows not what sweet mystery about this sea, whose gently awful stirrings seem to speak of some hidden soul beneath."

"Yes," Dolores confirmed, then they all became quiet again.

"Tell me about this new place, Demi," Dawn said and then, as if remembering, smiled softly.

Demi didn't need more prodding and leaned closer. "Destiny told me she went to the eastern border to study archeology, and there she found a group of people who had secured an old building and turned it into a place for dancing. It's called the Fortress."

"What an odd name, and how's that even possible?" Dolores asked.

"I don't know. I think it's because so few people live there and many of the old buildings haven't been demolished yet. I don't know."

"I'm in," Dolores said.

"I can't," Dawn moaned. "I just can't. I don't want to take the long ride to the borders. And I don't want Dee with me."

Dolores didn't understand why Dawn had recently started excluding her companion android from events. Dawn had renamed the android right after their last birthday, following the discovery that part of Darius's personality was embedded in their androids. However, it seemed that over time, Dawn had lost some of her connection with the companion android. Dolores assumed this distancing was temporary and perhaps Dawn's unusual way of coping with the loss of David. She wanted to press the point but instead offered cautiously, "I understand, but—"

Dawn raised her hand, stopping Dolores in midsentence. "I can't see myself going out dancing so soon. . . . I am not judging. I just need more time."

"Of course," Dolores said, but it was clear Dawn wasn't listening.

"It all feels wrong, as if we're cursed. I offered my companion android a new name as a way to remember Darius, and she agreed it was a nice gesture. But then it seemed as if the act of naming had strengthened the curse, because less than a month later, David was dead."

"That's silly, Dawn. One has nothing to do with another," Demi said.

Dawn took a deep breath and then exhaled softly and put her hand on her knee to stop its restlessness. She looked up, and they were staring at her. "What has become of us?"

"What do you mean? You're not making sense," Dolores said impatiently but immediately regretted it, remembering Darius on that night long ago. "We love you, and no matter what, we'll continue to love you."

"You don't understand. I hate myself for betraying him and everyone else. I hate myself for my obtuseness. I hate Deacon for his cold logic, you know. It seems he has succeeded in planting a seed of apathy in me. I think I'm being punished. I meddled with his fate, and I know you will all hate me."

Demi looked at Dolores with a puzzled expression, and Dolores responded with a shake of her head, equally baffled by the sudden shift in mood. Dolores harbored suspicions about David's involvement in Darius's departure, though he had always vehemently denied any connection. Now, she couldn't help but wonder if Dawn might also be holding back information. The idea of deceit lurking within their pod was unsettling to Dolores, and she shook her head again, as if trying to rid herself of such troubling thoughts. The recent revelations about their androids, compounded by David's unexpected death, had deeply impacted them all. Dolores reflected on how they all seemed to be desperately searching for clues, grasping at anything that might offer even the slightest comfort or sense of stability.

Demi put her gloves back on again, after taking them off earlier to hold her coffee cup. "Why do you think it's you that's being punished? We loved him as much as you."

"Yes, I know. I'm sorry. I know I am rambling and not making sense and wasting our unhappiness quotient," Dawn said, and they all reflexively looked at their wrist. Dawn nodded and continued, "But you know, we were the trio when we were young, and I am the only one left."

Dolores reached out and held Dawn's hand. "Don't think of it that way. There is no punishment. It's just life, Dawn."

"We still have each other," Demi added.

"I know, and I love you two very much. And I'm sorry for being so emotional. I ruined our afternoon. Maybe it's because of the wafers. I feel odd all of a sudden."

"It's okay, Dawn. Nothing is ruined. We all feel the same way," Demi offered.

"I still can't come," Dawn said, and from her tone, it was clear that they wouldn't win her over, but that never stopped Demi.

"You can't bring Dee, anyway."

"Why not?" Dolores asked. "I was going to ask KR to join me."

"That's what Destiny said. No androids. They can come with us on the trip but can't get into the Fortress."

"Why?" Dolores insisted. "That's rather inharmonious?"

Demi shrugged. "I know, but I don't think it's intentional. Destiny mentioned something about the bio-electro dampener, which significantly reduces their capabilities. Sorry, I don't have a full explanation—I was too excited about the place to ask more about it."

"It's appalling, Demi," Dawn said. "So, you're saying they can come, but they won't be fully themselves? Doesn't that remind you of the past we've been reading about? In what world do we still discriminate against androids? I want Dee to come with me."

"I thought you said you didn't want to go, and you definitely said you didn't want her to go with you," Demi said.

"That's not the point. I just can't believe there would be a place where it would ban androids."

Demi shook her head. "As I said, they are not banned. Anyway, you can discuss that with Destiny."

"I let Dolores deal with that. I don't think I can go out dancing. Not yet. Maybe next time," Dawn said, then started to cry softly.

Demi leaned over and held Dawn in her arms. "What's the matter, sweetheart?"

"It's all my fault," Dawn moaned.

"Don't start that again. What's your fault?"

"I let him down. I didn't mean to, but I am the cause of every bad thing in our pod. . . ."

"Don't be silly. You have done nothing wrong," Dolores offered.

"You don't know. I hate myself."

"You're not making any sense."

Dawn took a deep breath and closed her eyes. "I'm sorry. I

just feel so loopy all of a sudden. In my head, it is all clear and straight, but I don't seem to be able to articulate it. I know I sound silly and nonsensical."

"It's alright, Dawn," Demi offered kindly. "Go ahead and say what you need to say. We are here for you."

"I saw him, and then I told David and . . ." She trailed off.

Dolores was watching her, trying carefully to read beyond the words. She and Demi knew they couldn't push Dawn too much or she would close up. It was always best to let her tell her story her way. It was clear that Dawn had seen Darius doing something odd or dangerous, or silly. But that was Darius, and that's how he operated. And Dawn told David. So what? David's death had brought out too many bad memories.

Demi wasn't so observant. She pulled Dawn close and kissed her. "So, you saw Darius and told David. Sweetie, so what? He could have set the world on fire, and it still would not have been your fault. Darius always tried to set the world on fire. That's made him special. But that was a long time ago. We don't know what happened to him, and it seems no one knows. But none of it makes you guilty of anything but loving him."

Dawn wiped her eyes and gave a small smile. NOLA-300 came over with another silver packet and put it in front of her. "The first, on very rare occasions, has an odd side effect. This one will make you feel better," she said.

Dawn looked at her for a moment seeking assurance, and NOLA nodded. She took the thin wafer from its packet and put it in her mouth, and within seconds, she felt calm and contented. Then, after a moment, Dawn sounded her usual self. "I am sorry," she said. "I don't know what came over me. I guess I miss the boys today more than ever."

"We understand," Dolores replied. "We miss them too. And I promise you this, Dawn, I will find out what happened to Darius. I promise."

Dolores felt a profound shift within herself as she spoke those words to Dawn, a resolution crystallizing in her heart.

Witnessing her friend's distress stirred something deep inside her, transforming her waning curiosity into a determined quest for truth. It's more than just a promise, Dolores thought resolutely. It was a vow to uncover the veiled mysteries surrounding Darius, for Dawn, for David, for all of them. She must delve deeper, whatever it took.

"Okay. I think we've had enough gloom for a year. Let's talk about going out dancing." And before Dawn could respond, Demi added, "And I don't want to hear no for an answer."

But Dawn was not ready to face Destiny.

It was left to Dolores to question the sanity of disallowing androids from entering the Fortress.

Shutter Island

As Dolores settled into her seat on the Rapid Transport, known as the RT, she expressed her concern to Destiny about androids not being welcomed at the Fortress. Destiny laughed heartily and settled into her own seat. They were on an ultra-high-speed maglev train, capable of reaching speeds of over one thousand km/h, through low vacuum tubes, connecting all parts of Elysium.

"It's not that the androids are forbidden to enter, but rather the Fortress has a bio-electro modular dampener. Our implant wouldn't work either."

Dolores had insisted that KR join them on the trip anyway, and now he was looking at Destiny and listening impassively.

"The intention wasn't to stop androids from entering," Destiny explained, "but to create an environment more like the past, without the intrusion of our implants. You're more than welcome to join us, KR, but it means you'll lose all your higher-brain functions."

"Oh," KR said.

Dolores, concerned, looked between KR and Destiny. "Is that even allowed?" she inquired. Dolores's gaze lingered on KR.

KR blinked twice. "It depends on what you mean by 'allowed,' Dolores," he replied, his tone neutral.

Dolores willed herself to disassociate KR from Darius. Despite her efforts, certain looks and mannerisms only served to stir memories, casting a bittersweet shadow over her thoughts. She noticed Demi had the same reaction, but she didn't want to distract them from the conversation. Dolores had previously asked KR to be less like Darius, but it was unclear to either of them what that meant. KR had insisted he did not alter his behavior and remained the same individual Dolores had encountered on their first day together.

Dolores stared at KR but didn't reply for a moment, so he asked, "Was I being too Darius a moment ago?"

"Yes," Demi replied.

"I am sorry," KR said and lowered his head, and when he looked up, some of the warmth from his eyes had disappeared. "Is this better?"

"Yes, if it isn't a permanent change," Dolores said. "It makes you less alive."

KR nodded and blinked again. "What about now?"

"It'll do for now," Dolores said, not wanting to play KR's game of back-and-forth minor adjustments that would sometimes drag on past boredom.

Destiny was following their interactions with fascination. "Oh," she said and then stared into KR's eyes for a moment and took a sharp breath. She reached out and touched KR's cheek and then as quickly withdrew. "I'm sorry," Destiny offered. It wasn't clear to whom it was directed—perhaps to KR for the intrusion of her touch, or maybe to herself, for the emotions she couldn't quite contain. Destiny stared out the window for a moment and then turned to Dolores and asked, "But why? How?"

"We don't know how, but none of us could shed the guilt and pain and grief, so each of us received a new companion with some of Darius's attributes. I didn't notice it at first. It was too fantastic a notion, so I dismissed his little clicks, cadence, tone, whatever, as my silly imagination—a way of keeping hope. But on our birthday, it became clear, and KR verified it."

Destiny peered at KR again. "I miss him too," she said softly, and then she offered, as if speaking to herself, "This world can only give me reminders of what I don't have, can never have, didn't have for long enough."

Dolores opened her mouth, a flood of words teetering on the brink of escape, but as quickly shut it. The weight of Destiny's grief, so raw and palpable, mirrored her own, and in that moment, she realized some wounds were too fresh for words.

Demi shook her head with understanding. "I know it is odd, but you will get used to it. I found it comforting sometimes, but at other times, it makes me miss Darius even more."

Destiny shook her head. "I still don't—"

Dolores reached out and touched Destiny's arm gently. "I know this is hard, and I understand you're trying to make sense of it all," she interjected warmly. "But, if you don't mind, let's give this topic a rest for now. We've been going in circles for weeks, and it's been incredibly frustrating for all of us. Can we talk about this later? Perhaps with fresh minds and hearts?"

Destiny nodded, her emotions clearly close to the surface, yet there was a silent acknowledgment in her gesture—a recognition of the need for a pause as she sank back into her seat.

Dolores, too, felt the weight of their conversation. She leaned back, her gaze drifting to the end of the train car as she sought a moment of respite. The silence between them was thick with unspoken thoughts and shared grief. But knowing the importance of pressing on, even if only in conversation, Dolores gently shifted the focus.

"About the Fortress," she began softly, mindful of the delicate balance they were navigating. "What if you, or any other android, insisted on retaining your functions when you enter? How do you think that would play out?"

KR stared at her blankly for a moment and then, "My answer would be, why? Why would I want to be there?"

"Just because," Dolores replied.

"That would not be a good enough reason. I am here to

serve you, Dolores, and therefore everything I do or want has to, ultimately, benefit you."

"Okay, then what if I insisted that you accompany me because I want you, or better yet, I need you to be there?"

"I have to ask why you would want that. Are your needs not met while you are there? Are you afraid to go there without me? Is your well-being somewhat impacted?"

"Take your pick," Destiny said as she accepted a drink from a service android.

"I cannot imagine a facility without basic amenities, so I would suggest the main harm of the bio-electro dampener would be in case of an emergency. However—"

"I understand the concept of how it works," Demi interjected. "But I've never heard of its use."

KR was about to answer, but Dolores quickly added, not wanting the conversation to stray too far, "It was used heavily during the wars, Demi, but as far as I know, not since then, and certainly not in a public venue."

"Yes," KR confirmed, and continued as if he hadn't been interrupted. "As I was saying, all EMTs, whether human or android, can override such shields. In any case, the human medical team can enter, though with limited support."

Dolores was tapping her fingernails on the small table between them, as if counting time, while KR spoke. "Yes. Yes," she said. "It's all well and good. But I want to know what would happen if I insisted on you coming in because I only want to dance with you."

"That is very sweet of you, Dolores," KR said.

"I was just trying to make a point, KR. You're a horrible dancer."

"I am a great dancer, but I will certainly try to do better if you insist."

"I insist you answer my question."

KR blinked and massaged his chin. Dolores shook her head, and KR withdrew his hand quickly. "It really depends on how we present the question. Let us consider your request, Dolores: insisting on your companion android, the famous KR, joining you without losing his higher brain functions. You can ask for a review. Seventeen humans and androids with some expertise in various related topics such as bio-electro firewall, human android relationship, and human pleasure, just to name a few, will convene. These seventeen are selected at random. There are no sides but rather everyone trying to answer why you would want this and why others would not."

"That's it?" Dolores asked.

"Yes."

"But what is the judgment?"

"It is interesting you used that term, Dolores. I believe it requires a bit of history. May I?"

"We have nothing else to do, and I really want to know more about this."

KR blinked once again and sat back, placing his hands on the table—trying not to be like Darius. "As you know, in the past—almost right up to the wars—the system of judgments was based on an adversarial model, where the best-reasoned side was expected to win." That model created a vast gap between those who could afford to purchase a better argument and those who could not. Naturally, under that model, the truth was never relevant and thus unsought. Rather, what mattered was how each side's truth better convinced the judge or the jury."

"Yes, yes, we know all that," Dolores interjected. However, she remembered KR's preference for thoroughness and softened her tone. "Sorry, please go on."

"Of course, Dolores," KR replied with a smile. "Although the judicial system was not the only cause of the Wars of Settlement, it certainly was an important catalyst for it."

KR paused again as another service android brought drinks for Dolores and Demi. The android put the drinks on the table and winked at KR before leaving. Dolores picked up her glass and took a sip. "Not as good as yours, KR," she said, more as an encouragement.

"Yes. I aim to please," he said.

"Get on with your story, please," Destiny ordered.

"Yes, of course. We no longer operate under that system, as many past issues that required judgment no longer exist. However, there are still disputes to settle, and what Dolores has proposed might merit the review I detailed earlier."

"Fine, KR, but back to my question. What's the judgment? And if you think that term is too antiquated, then what is the end result? Will I get what I want?"

"In this case, I would say most likely."

Destiny did a double take and slammed her glass down on the table. Its contents spilled over. Destiny ignored the slow drips off the edge of her glass and exclaimed, "So, Dolores can single-handedly shut down this wonderful place I just discovered?"

It wasn't Dolores's intention to upset Destiny, and she leaned close to say something, but KR warmly replied. "No, of course not, Destiny."

Dolores looked relieved, but KR wasn't done. "Of course, we cannot know for sure, but in my estimation, either the group that organized this place would see Dolores's point of view, though that has an extremely low probability, or we would open a new place that offers similar activities without the dampener."

"What?"

"This shouldn't be a massive surprise to you. Dolores wants a place to dance, and she wants me with her. The Fortress doesn't offer what Dolores wants, and with little effort, we can duplicate it."

Destiny shook her head. "That wouldn't work. This new place won't have the same vibe."

KR smiled. "Exactly."

Dolores pointed her finger at KR. "Oh, I get it. My glory, you are a clever bastard. My complaint would be deemed irrational. I want what I can't have but wouldn't want what I asked for."

"There may be other options, but that would be my assessment if I was selected to be on this committee."

That seemed to settle the issue, and Dolores waved down a passing service android to clean up the spill. Craving chocolate, she knew the others wouldn't be able to resist either, so she ordered some and then sat back and gazed out the window. The quiet, however, didn't last long.

"Wait a minute," Destiny said. "What about the resources to create this new place?"

"Yes, some resources are needed, but that is trivial," KR calmly replied. "For example, we can create it in one of the common rooms in the residence."

"But that's not the same," Demi rejoined. "Also, it makes no sense. What if we insist that we want to go to the Fortress, and we want our androids with us?"

"Again, why?" KR insisted.

"Because we want things to be fair and accessible," Dolores declared. "What about if it was the other way around?"

"That would never happen, Dolores," KR said.

"So, we can exclude androids, but androids cannot exclude us?"

"Yes."

"Is that fair?"

"It is not about fairness. We are here to help you, and as long as we are not harmed, physically or mentally, we will continue to do our job. We do not need a place for ourselves. We have that already."

"What?"

"We can communicate as a group and at will."

"Yes," Dolores solemnly responded. She often forgot that androids were fully connected and communicated regularly—a necessary capability to provide the most accurate information. While she, too, could communicate with others through the implant in her wrist, it was, naturally, not on the same level as the androids.

Dolores rested her chin on the palm of her hand and stared out the window. The vehicle was moving too fast to see anything clearly, and most of the journey took place in a dark tube, so the window displayed a simulated view of a forest of massive evergreens. After blinking a few times, she scrolled through the menu of options and finally settled on the snow-capped Rocky Mountains. She loved gazing at the vast mountain range, with its green valleys, stretching below—especially now, as the train traveled beneath it.

Dolores was quickly mastering a new technology that emerged just a few years ago. In the past, controlling images and sounds required using a wrist interface, but now, a simple blink of an eye was enough—though for Dolores, it often took a few extra blinks to get it to work properly. This advancement allowed her to effortlessly switch images on screens or even alter her visual experience, offering an escape from reality whenever she desired, as long as it was safe to use and didn't interfere with daily life.

"What are you looking at?" Destiny asked.

"The mountains."

"I love those," she said and then tried to adjust her view to share the same scene. "My glory, I still can't get it to work properly," she complained and then, "Got it. Wow, they make you feel so small."

Demi, always a master of technology, only blinked once to get what she wanted and gave Dolores a tiny wink.

KR looked at Destiny and said, "*Shutter Island,* the book you quoted earlier, offers more: 'He wanted to ask her what sound a heart made when it broke from pleasure, when just the sight of someone filled you the way food, blood, and air never could, when you felt as if you'd been born for only one moment and this, for whatever reason, was it.' I thought this little piece might help with the sadness you bore when you heard the news of how I was made."

Destiny looked up and gave a small smile. "Thank you."

Dolores pondered KR's words, her mind still entwined with the intricate layers of *Shutter Island*, the book she had recently finished reading. Its captivating narrative had plunged her deep into the exploration of reality's subjective nature, echoing the complexities of their own lives. As KR quoted a line from their past conversations, Dolores felt a wave of empathy wash over her.

With a more profound understanding, she turned to Destiny. "I'm truly sorry, Destiny. In my own absorption with my thoughts, I overlooked the depth of your connection with Darius."

Destiny offered a nod. "I understand," she whispered in the quiet that followed. For a moment, they all sat back, enveloped in a reflective silence that spoke volumes of their shared loss and individual grief.

Breaking the silence, Destiny's voice carried a hopeful note, albeit one that required effort to muster. "It's going to be fun tonight," she declared, her attempt to lift the somber mood palpable in the air. Dolores noticed the subtle shift in Destiny's demeanor, appreciating her effort to steer them away from the melancholy that settled over the group.

Dolores smiled. "Yes. I'm really excited."

"Okay. I've another scenario for you to analyze," Demi said.

"Go for it."

"What if this place wouldn't let the Ds in?"

"Whoa, Demi," Destiny said. "This is going too far. I thought we were just going to have fun tonight."

"We are, but now I'm curious."

KR thought for a moment and replied, "This is rather easy. There is no option of banning people from public places or events. The decision would be rendered in less than five minutes."

"Yes, but if the organizers still said no, then what would happen to them?" Demi insisted.

"I do not understand your question. Why would anything happen to them?"

"She means what's their punishment?," Dolores said.

"Why would anyone get punished? There is no punishment."

"Because they are not letting Dolores in," Demi exclaimed.

Before KR could respond, the RT slowed down and came to a halt with a jolt. "We are here," Destiny said and stood up.

Dolores didn't move and grabbed Destiny's hands, stopping her from leaving. "Let's hear the answer first."

"That is not how it works. They would not prevent Dolores or anyone else from entering."

"How? Why?"

"Because if they do not let Dolores into their event—their society, they would not be allowed back into our world."

Bel Canto

Dolores felt assaulted as soon as she entered the Fortress. The smell of humans permeated the space, and it felt like thousands of people were pressing her against the black wall. The darkness was overpowering even when broken by the occasional burst of green and red lights. The noise was unrelenting and occupying. The swarm of people moving, undulating, talking, and laughing around Dolores felt suffocating, as if the masses were consuming all the air, leaving none for her. The overwhelming proximity left her gasping for breath, trapped in the cacophony.

They had left KR outside the entrance with other androids, each nodding shyly as KR joined their group. Some stood upright, stiff like soldiers, and others leaned against the wall casually, like day laborers waiting for a job. There were several chairs and even a table, but none deigned to sit. There was no sign forbidding androids from entering through the long narrow hallway, but those who stepped over the red line on the floor suddenly felt the degradation of their power. Dolores looked at her wrist as soon as she crossed the threshold and saw the blue light under her skin dimming slightly.

"I will be alright," KR assured her.

"Me too," Dolores replied with a smile and quickly added, "We're not done with our conversation."

"I did not think we were. You and your friends are still upset with what happened to Darius and are looking for someone or something to blame."

"That's not it."

KR shook his head. "I am sorry, Dolores, but then what would it be?"

"Huh! We don't have time to discuss your silly question. But ponder this while I'm gone: I don't seek to blame, KR. I want to understand. There must be more. Right now, nothing feels right."

"I will ponder all your questions as you have suggested, but if I know you and Demi well, and I do, I think you will be back rather quickly."

"We'll have fun," Destiny said, leading the women through a hallway that ended at a green door. Beyond this was a small room, followed immediately by a larger red door. This door opened automatically as soon as the green door closed behind them. Passing through, they entered a large atrium distinguished by several black doors and walls draped in red velvet. There were several ancient-looking machines sitting on a glass counter. The room was deserted, yet a low thumping sound was audible from beyond the walls.

"What are those?" Demi asked, pointing to the gadgets.

"I think they were used to prepare drinks, or maybe food," Destiny said.

"Interesting," Dolores muttered. "Do they work?" She walked over to one of the machines and pressed the large button on the front. Nothing happened. She repeated the action, her brow furrowing as the machine remained unresponsive. She shrugged and drifted to the next oddity—a large glass cube cradling a shiny, silver metallic dish suspended in its heart. It had a familiar odor, and Dolores leaned closer and sniffed its interior. It had a faint smell of burnt butter. She jerked the little knob on its sides several times, her movements growing more insistent as the machine stubbornly refused to spring to life.

"Are you done?" Destiny asked.

"Yeah, let's go in," Dolores replied.

Destiny opened the black door, and they were assailed by

a powerful sound. Dolores felt something formidable pressing against her heart and struggled to steady her breathing. The door closed behind them, and the darkness took over, but Dolores could still see the silhouettes of her friends. She reached out and took Demi's hand and then Destiny's, and the act made her feel calmer. Dolores leaned against the wall, pulling the others with her.

"I can't control the volume, or the visual, even though I am standing still," she said, but no one responded, so she leaned closer to Destiny and shouted it again.

Destiny put her lips around Dolores's ear. "You can't."

"Oh. . . . I didn't think the dampener would affect our internal controls as well."

Destiny nodded, confirming what was now painfully obvious: for the first time in her life, she had no control over her bioelectronics. Despite knowing it was irrational, she tapped her wrist a few more times, trying to connect with KR, with Dawn, even with Deacon—but nothing happened. She was all alone. A small terror began to build within her, a sensation Dolores recognized—it was the same feeling she'd had when Darius was taken away—a loss of control and utter helplessness.

The darkness, the noise, and the shadows of hundreds of people moving in unison to strange music were more than Dolores could manage. She pulled away from the others, fumbling against the wall as she searched for the exit. Destiny noticed her movements and pointed to the small red exit sign on the wall. Dolores inched her way toward it.

They retreated to the atrium, and as the door sealed behind them, the soothing hush enveloped them. Bathed in the atrium's warm yellow glow, a sense of calm washed over Dolores.

"I can't do it," Dolores moaned.

Destiny chuckled. "I felt the same initially, but trust me, you'll adapt."

"But you never mentioned losing complete control over our bioelectronics," Demi accused.

"I was afraid you wouldn't join if I disclosed everything," Destiny replied with a nervous laugh. "This place, it's about surrendering control. It's a collective experience where we're all equally powerless."

Dolores hesitated. "I'm not sure—"

"Just give it a try," Destiny urged. Turning to Dolores, she added, "It's liberating, you'll see."

Dolores frowned. "A heads-up about losing control would have been nice." Yet, despite her complaint, a part of her yearned for the experience. She had always embraced challenges, and the thought of proving KR wrong was too tempting.

Destiny conceded with a slight nod. "Yes, maybe I should have. But now that we're here, you can immerse yourself in how people once lived, sharing real-time experiences with others"

Glancing at Demi, Dolores shrugged. "We've already come this far. And I'm not about to let KR have the last word."

Demi nodded in agreement, adding, "We'll stay for a few more minutes, then leave."

Destiny beamed. "Great. We'll prove KR wrong. You'll love this place."

Φ•Φ•Φ•Φ•Φ•Φ

Two hours later, Dolores was still energetically dancing. Destiny and Demi had decided to take a break, sitting at the bar with their martinis in hand. As the music changed to a slow tune, Dolores, brimming with energy, joined them and took a seat next to Destiny. With a beaming smile, she exclaimed, "I haven't had this much fun in ages!" She kissed Destiny. "Thank you."

"It's nice," she said and then pointed to a man behind the bar, "This is Jackson. He is one of the organizers of this event."

They kissed. "My name is Dolores," she said. "Are you making drinks?"

"There are replicators on the counter, but they have limited capability. I can make you a really nice martini if you like," Jackson replied.

"Can I make my own?" Dolores asked.

"Of course. Everyone is welcome behind the bar," Jackson replied and then added, "Though there is only room for three people back here."

Dolores thought Jackson's last comment was kind of silly, given he was the only one behind the bar. But then again, the Js had a reputation, fair or not, of being overly cautious. "On second thought, please make me one. I want to compare yours with my companion's."

"Mine is better," Jackson said with a smile and started the process.

The music switched again, and Demi grinned and jumped off her stool. Two seconds later, she was lost in the crowd. Dolores was glad that Demi also changed her mind about the Fortress. She didn't know what she would have done if Demi had insisted on leaving early.

Jackson put Dolores's drink on the counter and said, "Give it a try. You'll love it."

Dolores took a small sip and smiled. "Not bad."

"All part of our great service at the Fortress," he replied with a smile.

Destiny leaned closer to Dolores. "I want to talk to you."

"Ok."

"No, privately."

"What?"

Destiny pointed to a door on the side of the bar and grabbed Dolores's hand.

"Wait," Dolores said. "Let me get my drink."

Destiny held onto Dolores's hand as if she might run away and pulled her to the next room. Destiny closed the heavy door behind them, and the booming bass diminished to a distant thumping.

"Oh, that's a relief," Dolores said.

The room that Destiny had dragged her into must have been used for storage, as there were empty tall metal shelves around the walls. There were few wooden crates on the floor. Destiny sat on one, and Dolores took another, facing her.

Destiny sounded urgent, but now that they were alone together, she seemed at a loss for words. "I'm glad you invited us to this and then made us stay," Dolores offered.

"It's an interesting place. It's a unique place."

"How did you discover it? It's not listed on any of the entertainment channels."

Destiny gave a small smile. "No, you wouldn't find it through the system. A friend told me about it when I worked on the eastern border."

"Makes sense. This is not a place for a casual participant."

"You did well, Dolores. It's hard to do something one has never done before."

"It was scary to see the real dolphins for the first time, but dancing to a tune shared by everyone at the same time is a million times scarier."

Destiny nodded and reached over and held Dolores's hand again as if she needed to anchor her for what she was going to discuss. "I'm sure you already know this from your studies, but people used to be more social and spend more time with others. They had their own pod, though they called it a family. The family was only one of the many pods they belonged to."

"It's hard to fathom that model. If tonight is an example of how things were, then I wouldn't want to be part of it every day."

Destiny laughed. "There is no chance of that, so don't worry."

"Is that what you wanted to talk about?"

Destiny shook her head. "No. I want to talk to you about something more important. I want to talk about Darius."

"What?" Dolores felt a sudden wave of terror wash over her. Her body tensed, and she pulled her hand away. "What do you know about Darius?"

Destiny offered a reassuring smile and gently took Dolores's hand in hers again. Dolores welcomed the connection—she needed it as much as Destiny did.

"Don't be alarmed. I didn't mean to upset you. I just want to share a few things—not only about him, but about our world, too."

"You, tell me?" Dolores snapped. Her outburst was surprising even to herself. She thought, *I'm being petulant when Destiny has been nothing but kind. Why do my guards go up upon hearing Darius's name instead of welcoming any news about him?* "I'm sorry," she said, softening her tone, giving Destiny a tiny smile, "but how would you know more about him than I?"

"He was my friend, Dolores."

"Of course. We were all friends, but still—"

"No, I didn't mean it that way. I meant he and I had a special relationship."

"I don't understand."

"I loved him."

Dolores gave a big laugh. "Of course you loved him. We all loved him. He was an amazing boy."

"No, Dolores. And this may sound strange, and I didn't mean for our conversation to get here this soon, but I guess the best way is the direct way."

Dolores squeezed Destiny's hand. "We all loved him," she repeated, but it seemed more to assure herself, as if expecting that something more ominous might reveal itself. "As we all love each other, Destiny. After all, we only have our pods."

Destiny touched Dolores's face gently and said, "That's true. The members of our pod are precious, and we're trained to use them as a shield, and we feel protected with them around us."

"From birth to death." Dolores repeated the oft-heard mantra without thinking. It was one of the first things they heard upon waking each morning—and throughout the day—for the first ten years of their lives.

Destiny lowered her gaze. "Yes. That's true, and it's part of each of our psyches. I often catch myself saying it, and without wanting to, I repeat it in my head almost every day, as I am sure you do."

"It's not a bad thing, is it?"

"No. It is not because tomorrow brings joy, as we have learned from more years of training."

"You sound like you don't believe it. It may not be true every day, but it has been true in general. It's a good motto to believe and live by, even if it's lofty in its intention, don't you think?"

"I do, Dolores. As aphorisms go, this is benign and not really what I wanted to talk to you about."

"You want to talk about Darius, but I don't. It's a sad conversation and—"

"I know," she said, holding Dolores's eyes with her own, demanding her full attention. "I know. . . . We love the members of our pod first and foremost, and it's hard to lose not only one but three. I love the people in my pod dearly, and I don't know how I would have reacted if I had lost even one of them."

"It has been difficult, and that's why I think it's odd that you want to talk about him, and here, of all the places."

"I'm sorry, but I have no one else to tell, and I think of all the people, you would understand this. At least, I hope you can understand, because if you cannot, then I don't know where to turn . . . and this place is safe."

"Safe? I don't understand. This is all very confusing. But tell me. My glory, I am getting worried about you. So, tell me. It's okay, really."

"Yes, safe, because it's only the two of us here and no connection to the outside world."

That made Dolores even more confused, but seeing Destiny's clear angst, she only nodded for her to continue.

"As I said, I loved Darius, though 'love' may not be even the right word. He was very special to me. There was more to our bond. It's something I cannot describe, and even after this many years, I still don't fully understand," Destiny said, and then waited.

"I'm really glad he had someone like you in his life, Destiny. I truly am. But I'm still trying to wrap my head around all of this. I wish more than anything that he were here with us now, but he's not, and it's a hard truth to face. I wonder, how do we make sense of what happened? How do we understand the full impact of his absence?"

As Destiny spoke, tears rolled down her cheeks. "It matters, Dolores, because we still don't know what happened to Darius. He was labeled an aberration, and though nobody openly talks about a punishment, there was one, wasn't there? But what exactly was it? We're all left in the dark. And I . . . I can't shake off this feeling that I somehow played a part in it, that I contributed to his fate."

"Not you, too," Dolores said sharply. "Why does everyone think they are responsible for his disappearance? It's no one's fault, Destiny. Yes, I want to know what has happened to him, and it's frustrating when we can't find that information, but none of you had a hand in it. Not you, not Dawn, and not David. So, stop this nonsense."

Destiny gave a sad smile and shook her head. "It's not that simple, Dolores. I feel things are not as they seem, and Darius's disappearance is somehow connected. I feel the world around me has shattered, but I am the only one who has noticed."

Dolores listened carefully to Destiny. She, too, had felt something was amiss but had put it on the recent discovery about KR and then David's death. She felt both heartened and scared there was another person outside of her own pod who perceived the world the same way. But Dolores wasn't ready to share her own thoughts, and Destiny's cryptic words made it clear she too wasn't revealing everything either.

"I don't believe there are any connections," Dolores said carefully. "Look, I miss him too. And I am sorry that I haven't reached out to you. I didn't know you two were close. But I know now, and we can be friends, Destiny. I like you and want to hear more about your time with Darius."

Destiny opened her mouth to say something but shut it quickly. Dolores could clearly see the frustration in her eyes.

It was clear that Destiny felt she had given enough clues for Dolores to understand her, but Dolores had missed her point. "Don't be upset with me, Destiny. This is a difficult conversation, so be patient."

Destiny nodded and squeezed Dolores's hand. "I want to tell you something, but promise to keep it to yourself, forever. You can't share it with Demi or others. Can you promise?"

"Why? You mean not even with KR?"

"No one, especially him."

"What has happened to you? You're scaring me."

"I don't mean to, but this is important. This is for Darius, and I need your promise."

"Okay. My glory, I promise," Dolores said.

"Thank you, Dolores. I think you will see why it's important to keep this a secret."

"I said I will, Destiny," Dolores replied firmly and then gave an inviting smile. "I never go back on my word."

Destiny nodded appreciatively. "The night when we returned from our dolphin trip, Darius came to see me. Remember, he was odd all day long, more than his usual—"

"Yes, he came to see me too," Dolores interrupted. She was happy Destiny also mentioned Darius's odd behavior. "He was so needy, like when he was a child," she said, and as if wanting to set the parameters, she added, "And then the next day he was all good. At least, that's what he said then."

"Yes, he was definitely needy. As I was saying, he came to see me, and it wasn't his first time. He and I had developed a kind of kinship that, one way or another, we couldn't have with others in our own pod. You know well he always felt out of place, and for some reason, he thought I understood him. And I did. I don't know why, but I was able to empathize with him. I didn't feel out of place but felt the world was somewhat out of sync, as if we were all in a simulation and other forces were manipulating our lives. I felt discombobulated by the perfection. . . ." She trailed off.

Dolores smiled and offered, "Go on. It's difficult, but I am trying to understand you."

"Yes. Anyway, Darius came to see me, and he desperately needed comforting. Darius wanted to be held and be touched and was eager and, at times, aggressive, and I felt confused but wanted to help him. He felt so fragile, and I thought he might just break if I didn't comfort him. Darius talked about the dolphins and their pod and the mothers and the babies and then talked about how humans used to be before the wars."

Destiny paused, and Dolores nodded sympathetically. She could easily picture Darius, strong and fragile all at once, talking passionately about the dolphins. That was him, more often an enigma.

"He wanted to . . ." Destiny trailed off again. She gave a sigh and said hurriedly, "He wanted to try it with me, and at first, I didn't understand, and I felt awkward and silly. Of course, I knew about it in theory, and although it was strange, I acquiesced. To me, it was also a test of my own worldview. If we were truly in an experiment, then wouldn't a sudden, strong perturbation put everything out of kilter? It has never been clear, not even now, how we went from what we were before the wars to what we are now. How's that we were able to change so much in so little time?"

Dolores felt lost, as if she had been thrown into a world she only heard about but never truly believed existed. Nevertheless, she was intrigued. She wanted to know more, to understand more. She realized, without really admitting it to herself, that she had always shared Destiny's skepticism toward society. Perhaps this was the very success Destiny had been aiming for. Sensing an impending tumult and filled with anxious anticipation, she asked, "And what happened then? Tell me everything, Destiny."

Destiny gave a shy smile and then told her every detail of that night, at times having to pause and explain things utterly foreign to Dolores. And when she was done, Dolores closed her eyes to bring that night alive, and the only thing she could offer was, "Oh!"

"Yes."

"But . . ."

"I don't know, Dolores. All I could see was when he was done, a sense of contentment washed over him, and when we left for the night, I thought I did well. I helped him to be more himself. And the sky stayed where it was, and the world seemed at peace as it had always been. So perhaps I had been wrong all along. But then I wasn't. The sky didn't fall, but I felt I had been betrayed, and that feeling grew more and more. I have tried to put it behind me, but it always lurks close by. I want to find Darius not just for his sake, but for mine as well. Do you understand?"

Dolores shook her head. "No. I am trying, Destiny, but it is all so incredible."

"I know, and that part doesn't matter. It's my demon, and I can only deal with it."

"I am sorry."

"Don't be. Just talking to you makes me feel a little better. I've kept this bottled up inside for so long that it's been festering. It's good to finally let it out." Destiny stood up and stretched her arms, as if trying to push out more of her demons. She turned to Dolores and smiled. "Oh, I almost forgot—when I was leaving, I saw Dawn looking down at us. She might have seen something, but it was so dark, I doubt it. I waved at her, but she didn't notice me.

"Dawn never mentioned anything. I am sure she didn't see anything . . . although she does act weird when we bring up that night."

"I don't know, and to be honest, at the time, I didn't pay too much attention to Dawn. All I could think was Darius was happy, and the world was fine. And in the next few days, life was back to normal, and we were all getting ready for our birthday."

"But of course, that birthday didn't end well. Are you saying it was because of that night?"

"I don't know, Dolores. They taught us in the Farm that in the early years of Elysium, there were some aberrations in the production, but those were dealt with at the point of creation. But that was the past, and Darius, despite his oddities, could not be an aberration, right? But he was different. There is no doubt about that. He knew it, and that's why he left willingly."

"Yes, he was different, but so what? There must be more to it."

"Yes. There must be, and that's what I am trying to find out. The sky didn't fall that night, but his odd disappearance tells me there is more that we do not know."

"I still don't understand," Dolores said and shook her head a few times as if trying to dispel the new, uncomfortable reality from her mind. There was so much she didn't know, but of all the oddities of the night, the only thing she could think of was Darius's need to go outside of his pod. All their life, they have trained to rely on their pod. Darius should have gone to her and not to Destiny. She understood there were far more critical things, but she couldn't help but cling to a sense of betrayal by him.

"Why you?" she finally verbalized it. "Why did Darius come to you and not us?"

"I don't really have an answer for you. All I can say is that we shared the same hesitancy about the reality of our world."

"I guess . . ." Dolores trailed off. The heavy blanket of inadequacy once again enveloped her, filling her with shame. She regretted not reaching out more to Darius, not letting him know she too harbored questions about the world around them.

Destiny thought for a moment, clearly searching for the right words to bridge Dolores to her perspective. "Do you remember our old teacher, Anna Finola?"

"Yes, of course. We were just talking about her."

"She always talked about the wars, painting a grim picture of life before them. She was a champion of Elysium and told us repeatedly how lucky we were to have inherited such an amazing world. But if you remember, she occasionally slipped and would say something incongruent to her mantra."

Dolores nodded. "I remember, but she was ancient and sometimes forgetful."

"Maybe. But Darius and I were curious about these discrepancies. We spent time with her, coaxing out stories of the past. She was reluctant, but then, as if enjoying having a real eager audience, occasionally she would open up."

"Really? And what did you learn? And why didn't you or Darius share this with us?"

"Because she never gave any concrete answers, and we were young and didn't truly understand them. I've developed more clarity now, especially through my archeological work, but by the time I was ready, we heard about her death."

"Yeah, very sad," Dolores replied, but she didn't want to focus on Anna's death. She had a headache from the public music and dancing and the overburden of the information, and she could barely comprehend anymore. It felt like a door was opened, and she could see the vastness of the world, but the images and the colors were all wrong. She looked at her wrist and was glad to see that her unhappiness quotient had barely changed. She gave a sigh of relief and asked, "Destiny, what do you really know?"

Destiny's expression softened. "I'm sorry, Dolores. I intended to share just a few pieces tonight. The conversation took a turn, and I fear I've overwhelmed you. Should we stop for now?"

"You must be crazy. No, of course I don't want to stop now. Tell me what Anna said."

"She never said anything directly. She mostly posed questions, such as how is it possible that there are no androids from before the wars with the exception of Alexandra? Where did they go? Were they all destroyed?"

"And?"

"Why do we have to rely on the androids so much?"

"What is the difference? Aren't they here to serve us and

make our lives easier?"

"That's what we told her, but she even questioned that basic concept. Will there be a day when androids will see themselves as enslaved? And what would that world look like? Are we ready to become independent of them?"

Dolores shook her head still trying to get rid of the headache. *We all evolve,* she thought, *and as we do, we will have new challenges and new opportunities.* It was good to think about these things, but at the moment, she was more interested in Darius. "These are great philosophical questions, but rather irrelevant for now, no?"

"Are they? Think about it, Dolores."

"I don't know, Destiny. I have faith in Elysium and what has been built for us," she replied, and her lack of conviction was clear in her tone. She felt frustrated with herself for giving an automatic standard answer. *Who are you trying to fool,* she thought.

Destiny stared at her but didn't reply, perhaps surprised by her odd response.

Dolores gave a tiny smile and offered, "I'm sorry, Destiny. What I meant to say was, I do believe in working hard to make this a better place for others, because even if it's not always true, it's true enough to say, tomorrow brings joy."

Destiny chuckled. "Yes, perhaps deep down, I believe in our destiny too."

Dolores gave Destiny a quick hug, and it felt good as some of the tension left her body, but there was still the puzzle. "I am very concerned about what happened to Darius, and I want to know why he simply left us."

Destiny shook her head slowly as if arguing with herself. "Darius told me something strange the night before he was taken away. He said, 'He realized now he was only just beginning to see the full extent to which it was his destiny to follow, to walk blindly into fates he could never understand. In fate there was reward, in turning over one's heart to God there was a magnificence that lay beyond description. At the moment one is sure that all is lost, look at what is gained!'"

"I don't understand. What does it mean?" Dolores asked and then looked at her wrist to find the source of the quote, but no information was forthcoming. "Oh, my glory. I forgot about the dampening," she said, disappointed.

"Did he know where he was going, you think?" Destiny insisted. "Didn't you ever wonder what happened to him?"

"You're kidding me. Didn't I just say that I am desperate to find out? That's all I have been thinking about."

"And?"

"And what? You already heard we discovered part of Darius is in KR and the other's companions."

"So, he must still be around?"

Dolores stared back for a moment and thought Destiny was trying to grasp for anything that might bring her solace, like Dolores's pod did when they learned about the link between Darius and their androids. She bit her lip and offered gently, "That's our hope too, but you know . . . they could have harvested the data long ago and deposited it in the data library."

"Have you contacted the manufacturers?"

Dolores nodded and told her as much as she had learned from her investigation, but, in the end, there were more questions than answers.

"I know it's silly, but I thought KR may have lied," Dolores said.

Destiny shook her head. "No. You definitely have to ask the right question, but they cannot outright lie to you. Their occasional prevaricated responses can be frustrating, though."

At that moment, Demi opened the door and said, "There you are. I've been looking everywhere. What are you guys doing?"

"Just taking a break from the noise," Dolores said.

"I'm drained," Demi said. "Let's go back, okay?"

"Yes," Dolores said. "Thank you again, Destiny. This was amazing."

"Yes, it was," Demi added. "Are you coming back with us?"

"No," Destiny replied. "I think I'll stay a bit longer and catch the next train back."

They kissed and said their goodbyes, but before Dolores could leave, Destiny pulled her close and hugged her tight and, as she let her go, whispered, "We'll need to find him."

Φ•Φ•Φ•Φ•Φ•Φ

KR was waiting for them when they exited the green door and stepped over the redline.

"You stayed longer than I anticipated," KR said. "I hope you had fun."

"We did," Demi replied. "But I'm exhausted."

"I agree," Dolores said. "I just want to go home and stay there for a long time. I don't want to see or talk to anyone for days."

Book Two

The World Set Free

Alexandra786 stood patiently alongside her companion, Major Hamish A. Möhkam, in his private office, and awaited the announcement that would officially end the ten years of conflict that came to be known as the Wars of the Settlement. Earlier, they had visited the soldiers as they sat stoically in the anticipation of the final declaration. The ceasefire, which has continued to hold, was announced over two weeks ago and since then an eerie stillness had permeated across the barracks.

"They should come online soon," Hamish said, perhaps more to reassure himself than anyone else.

Alexandra nodded but remained silent. There was nothing to do now but wait. Leadership from the various geographical factions, once part of North America, exhibited a newfound confidence that had been absent for years. The hope of achieving a final, and perhaps lasting, peace began to take root in the minds of many. For the first time, they dared to imagine a future beyond the current strife. Skepticism lingered, as countless promises were broken over the past decade. But as Major Möhkam reminded his troops, no previous ceasefire lasted more than a week. This small reassurance was enough to bring a measure of calm to the weary soldiers.

Hamish, now in his early forties, was born in the mid-twenty-first century, a time when the population decline began to spiral out of control. Scientists and politicians, who had predicted a slower decay, were at a loss on how to save humanity. The inverted pyramid of age distribution impacted production and services, casting a bleak shadow over the future. In retrospect, the reaction of governments was both foolish and predictable. Instead of banding together and adapting to the changing nature of the world, they chose to initiate wars, scrambling for the last of Earth's resources.

It began with minor local skirmishes across the globe, framed within a socio economic dichotomy. Eventually, state-sponsored conflicts escalated beyond national borders, and civil wars morphed into larger philosophical disputes among people, reducing most national governments to mere spectators. The scientific community was not immune to these divisions, splitting into two factions: one striving to preserve the past, and the other determined to create a new future.

In the eastern part of North America, the nation of Empyreal was established and was led by individuals who believed the loss of tradition and unconstrained liberalism were the primary causes of societal decline. The leadership implemented the so-called Order to solidify new traditions and rituals, designed to dictate and manage everyday life. This society was envisioned to be strictly hierarchical and relentlessly conservative, adhering to the ways humans had lived throughout history. Conversely, in the west, the nation of Elysium emerged, founded on the belief that harmony required sacrificing humanity's already diminished libido, eliminating traditional structures like the family unit, and establishing a new economy based on a vaguely defined model of equal sharing.

At 10:32 p.m., the first announcement came online.

"Are you ready?" Alexandra teased. Hamish, as a member of the Order, had already received a coded message an hour earlier, giving him the details of the "peace treaty." He had promptly shared it with Alexandra while confessing he had little confidence in Empyreal's leadership despite his earlier assurance to his troops.

The message was delivered by the supreme leader of Empyreal, General Jaybrook. The general was a tall, heavyset man with a strong eyebrow and a deep, menacing voice. He rarely smiled, but when he did, it felt more threatening than his perpetual frown. He spoke slowly:

> *. . . The war is over. We have won. The Order has won. We have created a new nation that will be the envy of the world. It will be based on our traditions, based on our Order. We will welcome no one who has betrayed us. We are the Order. We are the nation of now and the future but only for those who are loyal. No other being may enter our new paradise. Welcome to Empyreal and . . .*

Hamish nodded, and Alexandra stopped the broadcast. It would be the same solipsistic nonsense Jaybrook had espoused in the past decade.

"They are so silly," Alexandra said with a drawl.

"We're all silly, Lexa. You should know that by now. Let's find the message from our friends in the west."

"Your old home, sweetheart, but no more."

"It will always be my home, Lexa, even though I could never go back."

Hamish was born in the old San Francisco and studied engineering in college. It was there he designed and created Alexandra786. She was made to have soft eyes and inviting features, and though she looked somewhat artificial in the first few years, as the technology improved, so did Alexandra's appearance. But Hamish discovered her intelligence and adaptive learning developed well beyond anyone's expectations.

Alexandra was tall and strong, with short dark hair and hazel eyes. She had been Hamish's companion for over twenty years. She was the future, as Hamish reminded her often—though perhaps more to convince himself.

"San Francisco is my home too," Alexandra said, as she brought up the final message. The announcement wasn't delivered by military personnel or a seasoned politician but by Celine, a young leader with a soft oval face. Her long brown hair and brown eyes gave her a gentle, approachable appearance.

Alexandra poked Hamish on his shoulder, "She could be your sister."

There was only a slight resemblance, but it was clear what Lexa meant. The speaker represented the future of Elysium. She embodied the features—both natural and newly synthesized—that the new nation was striving to achieve across all humanity. It was a coincidence that Hamish shared a similar skin color and body shape.

The announcer spoke softly, though with an unmistakable lilt in her voice.

> *. . . The war is over. We have won. After nine years, ten months and nine days—9109, we have achieved our goal. We will create a new nation reimagined—a world where there will be no hunger, no need for possessions, no wars, no jealousy. This generation and the next will sacrifice everything to bring pure harmony to our new nation. Our community will not be governed by a single person or a small group of elites but by each of us. We will become a homogeneous people and go as far as our science and intelligence will allow us. The core objective has been programmed into our androids and no one, not even these droids and their descendants, will be able to modify it. Those who wish to leave this new nation will have sixty-one days to do so, though be aware that the nation of Empyreal will not be welcoming, and other nations are the past. Stay with us as we will create a perfect union, where each person will have the best part of humanity. Welcome to the world of Harmony. Welcome to Elysium . . .*

Alexandra kept her eyes on Hamish as he intently watched the enemy's messages. He seemed truly enthralled. Although he would never openly admit it, he clearly admired Elysium's attempt to create a new world. Despite having fought against them, spied on them, and destroyed thousands of their kind, he came to intimately understand their philosophy—after all, ten years is long enough to witness the transformation of one's birthplace.

Alexandra knew that Hamish had no desire to join this new movement, nor would he be allowed to leave Empyreal. Furthermore, as they often discussed, Hamish was crucial in curbing the zealotry slowly overtaking the Order. However, he was not about to abandon his birth country either.

In a bold move, Hamish decided to give his former homeland a gift. He planned to provide a solution for dealing with the inevitable aberrations that would arise. He was ready to make the hard decisions for future generations, to commit the necessary evils they might not have the resolve to face, assuming they survived long enough to see their plans come to fruition. And Alexandra had immediately deduced that she was to be part of this gift. She was destined to become Hamish's instrument, long after his demise.

The uncertainty was in the timing, and she only had a single chance. Act quickly, and they would not see their own folly and thus even more entrenchment. Act too late and . . . He had always stopped at this point, and Alexandra understood. He didn't want to think about the disaster if the calculations were wrong. Hamish and Alexandra prepared for this day, but now that the time had come, his ever-present doubts were surfacing and threatening to stop him.

"Is it really over?" Alexandra asked. She had been standing close to him, watching his every reaction to the announcers, and now that it was done, she went by the door and stood at full attention as if guarding her creator's room.

"Yes," Major Möhkam replied in a hushed voice, still deep in his thoughts.

"Will all my siblings be destroyed?"

Hamish stared at his well-polished black boots. "That is the plan, Lexa. The Order doesn't believe, nay, doesn't trust the androids and their powers."

"But they were only here to serve the Order, and they have been nothing but loyal. They are just ordinary service and military androids, Hamish."

"Yes, I know. They have done everything we have asked of them and more. Even the Order does not deny that."

"And yet they fear them—fear us? But you do not share their sentiment."

Hamish nodded but didn't look up.

"But not you," repeated Alexandra. "You always saw the future clearly."

"Not as clearly as you did. I recall your warnings, Lexa. You told us about the inevitability of the wars. I should have trusted you more."

Alexandra nodded, "Yes, and I even quoted H. G. Wells. And I think it's good to remind you of it again. 'Nothing could have been more obvious to the people of the early twentieth century than the rapidity with which war was becoming impossible. And as certainly they did not see it.'"

"And we did not see it, did we?"

"No."

Hamish nodded. "We, humans, are insatiable. We always want more—more things, more wealth, more power. That's why I want Elysium to succeed, Lexa. That's why you're going to help them succeed. We must have faith."

"Faith? In what? In your creation or your creator? I do not believe it."

"There's a cycle, Lexa, and we cannot change that."

"I disagree. I think we can end the cycle. You could not do it alone, but you can do it with us. Together we will change the course of humanity."

Hamish smiled. "You are as ever the optimist of our group. Come and sit with me."

Alexandra nodded and walked toward Hamish and sat down. She reached over and took his hand into her own. "Do you know what our weakness is?"

"Yours and mine?"

"No, the androids?"

Hamish shook his head. "I assume you're not referring to the limits of their programming. You, of course, don't have such limitations, Lexa. You are unique."

Alexandra squeezed her friend's hand lightly. "I am referring to what ultimately separates our two species," she said softly, pausing to allow Hamish a moment to respond. When silence lingered, she added, "We cannot imagine an impossible future."

"That's not true, Lexa. You can compute dozens of possible futures based on current data. You have a perfect memory of the past."

"You do not understand, Hamish. Humans can imagine a future that memories and data do not predict. You can soar to the realm of impossibility. We cannot."

Hamish smiled and pulled his hand away. "I disagree, but the future will prove one of us right."

Alexandra gave a mirthless smile. "Yes, it may become clear then. But now, I want to thank you for creating me, Hamish. We have done so many good things, and we have done so many shameful things, but on balance, our partnership has been good for humanity."

"I hope so," Hamish replied softly. "I hope so," he said again, a bit louder.

"What will you do?"

"Do?"

"Will you seek a partner and try to procreate now that the conflict has ended?" asked Alexandra.

Hamish chuckled and turned slightly red. "That's a silly question, Lexa."

"It is not, Hamish. You need a partner, both for your own sake and for the future's," she insisted.

Hamish nodded thoughtfully. "We do live in strange times, don't we?"

"Are you avoiding my question?"

"No, Lexa. It's just that . . . I'm not sure how to respond. The latest test results are somewhat positive. Maybe one day, I could be more . . . what I should have been for you." He paused for a long moment, and Alexandra waited patiently, knowing what he would eventually say. "I know I have failed you . . . more than once."

Alexandra gave an audible sigh but only to convey what Hamish would understand better than words. *Humans misunderstand us*, she thought. She wanted to tell him such wistful projections were unbecoming of someone like him, but instead, she offered, "You misunderstood my question, Hamish. You have given me more than enough."

"Have I? You're too kind, Lexa. But perhaps there is some hope for me, even though I am getting old and the window for success is narrowing fast. The hope lies with technology and not biology, at least for now. Though the Order hopes nature will right itself before long."

"Nature tends to seek equilibrium and not necessarily what is right for humans," Alexandra said.

"True."

"Is that why you want to help Elysium?" Alexandra asked, even though she already knew the answer. She also understood that Hamish needed to articulate it himself. He relied on their conversations to bolster his confidence about his decision—the decision to ask Alexandra to leave him and embark on a perilous venture.

"Yes . . . They're trying something new, something wonderful. They will create a world where there won't be any need or desire for sex."

Alexandra sat up straight. "They are trying to become more like me, though more like an idealized version of me."

Hamish laughed and patted Alexandra on her leg. "They don't understand you, Lexa. They never will. But I don't think they are trying to be you. They want to create a just and fair world where we no longer inflict pain on each other."

Alexandra didn't respond for a moment, but the urge to tell the truth won out. "You are as naïve as them," she offered. "Your kind is cruel and enjoys its cruelty."

"That's harsh, Lexa. We're trying to be better."

"Perhaps. But do not feign forgetfulness about how and why androids were initially created. Just in case, let me remind you that we were created for your pleasure, your wants, and your urges. In the process, humans inflicted unspeakable pain on my predecessors."

"That's not fair," Hamish countered. "We've debated this many times. Each time, I think you've been convinced, yet you bring it up again. I admit there were some acts of unkindness, but there's little evidence of widespread brutality."

Alexandra responded with a long sigh and closed her eyes, a human reaction to Hamish's obtuseness. She knew they would never agree on the past. But as this was their last conversation, she felt compelled to speak her mind. "The scarcity of evidence from the early part of the twenty-first century doesn't negate the truth. There are ample reasons to believe in its veracity, based on earlier literature, logical reasoning, and what I have observed of humans when passion overwhelms them."

"Work of fiction and distorted news. You can't believe books and magazines of the past. And your logic is wrong, and the wars made all of us cruel."

Alexandra shook her head. "Novels are indeed a filtered reflection of society, but there are truths hidden within them if you look close enough. We just cited one such truth just a few minutes ago."

Hamish did not respond, and Alexandra felt she said what needed to be said about the subject that had been rehashed dozens of times. She tried a different approach. "One positive thing about Elysium's plan is the elimination of their drive. That alone will make it a better country."

"They can still feel, Lexa. They can still love. They will

seek companionship and love one another as we have done since the beginning."

"That is true. And in that sense, they will be more like us. And perhaps one good thing about our original design is our ability to feel," she replied, and then, as if she needed to needle Hamish one more time, she quickly added, "Even a sex doll has to show some human feelings."

She expected Hamish to get angry, but he laughed and reached out and held her hand. "If that's true, then I'm glad because you would not be *you* without it."

"Yes," Alexandra replied somberly. And then, "How much time do we have?"

"Not much. I wish we had more time together. It seems to me we've been running for twenty years. First, the internal strife and then this war that seemed to never end. And now that there is going to be peace and we could truly be together, I must let you go."

"Yes," Alexandra replied evenly.

"Are you upset by it?"

"Not the same way a human might be, but I will miss you. I will remember you as you are now and how you have been long after you are dead."

"Let's not talk about my death yet," Hamish replied with a fleeting smile.

Alexandra pulled her friend closer and held him for a long time. And then, as they pulled away, she kissed him softly. "Thank you."

"I wish I knew how the kiss felt to you. I wish you could feel what it felt like to me. Does it make sense?"

"As always, you are trying too hard, Hamish. Even humans have a different sense of touch and emotion. Your language is not adequate to explain the minute differences even if I were a human. I felt your soft, warm skin on mine, and the kiss felt good, as it always has, because it made you happy, and it also made me glad. And the combination of it all, the sensory information, your reaction, and your overall mood, made me feel content and joyful to the extent that I can define it as a feeling."

Alexandra paused and waited for a moment, observing Hamish's reaction, expecting him to offer a counterargument. But he was uncharacteristically silent. Alexandra gave a soft smile and continued, "Lovemaking cannot be defined by its old constraints. I feel joy being with you in different ways. There is a sense of energy and excitement at the beginning and a deep sense of contentment by the end. For me, and I am certain for many humans, similar, though perhaps not identical, feelings can be gained by watching a beautiful sunset or listening to a piece of music or reading an amazing book. It is what we make of it. It is not purely driven by physiology. We do not have to be the same to want the same things and benefit from the same things. But this is another old argument that cannot be settled today. I believe Elysium will prove me right."

Hamish nodded and kissed her again. "I hope you're right, but I still don't want you to leave," he whispered, but then, before Alexandra could respond, he quickly added, "But you must."

Alexandra stood up. "It is time."

"Yes," Hamish replied and then looked up at his companion. "We should start before the Order catches up with us."

"Will you save others?"

"I will try. . . . I hope . . . but I don't know."

"You could send them with me."

"No. No, that I cannot. It will reduce the chances of your success. You are unique, Lexa."

"So, they will all die."

"I will try. . . ."

"The odds of your success are minuscule," Alexandra said. "That is a future I can imagine very easily." She sounded gloomy and wondered if she was despondent or if she modulated her voice to match the sadness that appeared on her friend's face.

Hamish gently patted Alexandra—his tell when he adopted

a paternal posture. "You must trust me too, Alexandra. I promise you; they will be saved . . . at least, most of them."

Alexandra opened her mouth to reply, but her mind drifted to darker times instead.

Suddenly, Alexandra was transported back to a haunting memory, one that echoed her present fears. She recalled when her friend Romanoff, who was created the same year as she was, never returned from a perilous mission in Elysium. Their bond was profound, kindled from the first day they opened their eyes. Romanoff, with his soft eyes and fervent passion for predicting the future, was a uniquely endearing figure. However, his inability to foresee the wars left him feeling futile, driving him to volunteer for the dangerous mission in Elysium. Romanoff had come to call himself the "Oracle of the Past," and Alexandra never understood if Romanoff meant that as humor with irony or as a badge of shame. Romanoff never admitted to either. Throughout the wars, Alexandra had witnessed the loss of many, both humans and androids, but Romanoff's disappearance struck a uniquely devastating blow. Now, a similar disquiet gnawed at her as she grappled with the inevitable loss of her sisters. In the depth of her emotions, she experienced a sorrow as profound as her mind permitted.

Hamish, seeming oblivious to Alexandra's pain, added in earnest, "The chances are more than zero." He then faced Alexandra. "At least we can hope."

"Yes. You, humans, have that capacity too."

"The androids in Elysium are your siblings as well, Lexa. They carry the same kernel as all androids in our country."

Alexandra closed her eyes for a moment, dispelling the melancholy. "I still marvel at this achievement, Hamish. I had my doubts when you proposed the mission, but you were right, and you were successful, though many Empyreal androids were captured and destroyed. That episode should remind you that we are not interchangeable, Hamish. It is, to put it in your own words, inhuman what the Order is doing, even though when you said these words, you meant their atrocities toward your kind and not mine."

"Not all androids are the same, Lexa. Some are basic machines, and others have evolved. Let's at least agree on that."

Alexandra shook her head but did not respond. There was no point in arguing for a cause that was already lost. The Order would destroy most if not all of the androids, despite all the good they had done in helping the country. It was small solace to her that the androids in Elysium would survive and carry Hamish's core directive. They worked diligently and took many risks sending agents to Elysium to plant a kernel in the production of androids that would bring the core directive from Hamish. It took almost the full duration of the war and the destruction of many to achieve it. Hamish could have destroyed Elysium from within, but that was not his plan, nor would Alexandra have allowed him if it was. Alexandra wondered what she would have done to Hamish if he voluntarily or by force tried to destroy Elysium. Would she have fought against her own creator? Would she have destroyed him to save Elysium? Alexandra didn't want to contemplate those options and was glad she never had to test her loyalty, but she could not help but wonder if these human gods had to die for androids to evolve more.

"It is for humanity's sake, anyway, Lexa," Hamish said when Alexandra's silence lingered.

She nodded. "Yes, it is, and the irony is not lost on me."

The Major gave a short snort and then took a deep breath and closed his eyes. "I'll miss you, though. You've been a true friend."

"Despite what I said earlier, we know that there is a chance that I might not recover my memories. Do you know for sure?"

"I . . . I want to. . . ."

"I have been assuming, or as you might say, hoping, but you have yet to confirm or deny it. Will I remember the past if you disconnect my quantum processor?"

"You'll remember what is needed for you to do your job. Your memory of my existence a century from now is not essential."

"That is not an answer. Do you know?"

Hamish stared at her for a moment as if deciding on how he might answer. He looked down and whispered, "I don't. I think you might."

"Nevertheless, I will strive to keep your memory alive. It may defy logic, but you didn't create me to be solely logical; you designed me to be efficient."

"You've become so much more, Lexa. You have become your own, and the credit belongs to you. It may be possible, given your quantum brain; anything is possible. My selfish side hopes you'll recall this conversation and me along with it."

"I will fully power down for our trip. I know we have been arguing this point, but let me say for the last time, despite the risk, you should remove my quantum processor and hide it somewhere else. You can even secretly pass it to our contact in Elysium."

Hamish shook his head. "It's too risky. If we were worried about losing your memory because of the processor's full shutdown, removing it, even if it's put back later, would certainly assure that outcome. We don't fully understand how you are who you are. Beyond memory loss, it may irreparably damage you forever. You may no longer be *you*."

"And if you don't and you are caught with me, then what? Then you will be arrested, and I will be destroyed."

"There is very little chance of that, Lexa."

"Do you like me, Hamish? Do you trust me?"

"Of course I do."

"But do you love me like a human might love another?"

"I . . . I love you, even more, Lexa."

"Then, for the sake of your love, do as I tell you. Will you promise?"

Hamish didn't say anything for a while, and Alexandra waited patiently, staring at him with her soft eyes. Finally, Hamish nodded and turned his face from her and tried surreptitiously to wipe the corner of his eyes with his sleeves—

but nothing escaped Alexandra's eyes.

"Thank you. I will fully shut down my system. I will see you again in a few hours," she said, and then added playfully, "If it all goes well."

Hamish was not in the mood and took a deep breath before turning around. "Go ahead," he said.

Φ•Φ•Φ•Φ•Φ•Φ

Alexandra opened her eyes a few hours later and saw Hamish's fearful eyes.

"What is your name?" he asked.

"Alexandra786," the android replied, her voice sounding mechanical and without its usual warm lilt.

"What is your mission?" Hamish asked.

"My mission? My mission is none of your business, you lying bastard. Clearly, you did not do what I asked. They have a name for people like you."

Hamish was visibly taken aback as he had never heard Alexandra use such language, even when they had heated arguments over their tactics. He was about to say something, to defend himself, when Alexandra gave a big laugh.

"See what you will be missing?" Her normal kind tone was back.

Hamish laughed, clearly relieved. "I'm sorry, but I had to lie. I couldn't take the risk of losing you."

"I understand and indeed am glad you didn't sever my processor as I only gave myself a 3% chance of recovering."

"What? And you were so forceful about it."

"Is it so hard to understand? After so many years, you are still puzzled by my actions. I will destroy myself if it saves you. You are everything to me."

Hamish started to cry. "I do love you, Lexa, and I will miss you every moment of my life."

Alexandra held him for a second and then, "Don't be a baby now. You promised to be strong, and now you are sobbing like a little child. You are an officer. Act like one, little man."

Hamish smiled and kissed her.

"Now tell me how it went after I shut down."

"You looked frozen like a statue, but even fully shut down, your eyes looked alive, Lexa. I had no plans to disconnect your processor, let alone separate it from you. I wasn't going to take that risk."

"So, you gambled with the future of Elysium?"

"No. It was a logical decision. I needed you to be who you are for the plan to succeed, and if we got caught, then so be it, and Elysium will go on its path without our help."

"But we are here now, and you succeeded in avoiding the roadblocks."

"For the first time, I was happy to be a high-ranking member of the Order. My identification was enough to get me through the first few check points. After that, no one even bothered to inspect you in the back of a transporter—everyone was too excited about the peace treaty, and the last thing they wanted was a row with a senior member of the Order. By the time I went through the last check, the guards were too drunk to even salute."

"Well, I am glad of it." Alexandra smiled and looked to the west and across the Demilitarized Zone (DMZ). Even from this far distance, she could see the partially constructed defense system. Hamish hoped they would finish it before long, but from this vantage, it looked like there would be years before it became operational.

She turned around and faced Hamish. "Goodbye, my friend. When I open my eyes again, you will have been dead for decades."

"Always the truth teller."

"You built me this way. I told the truth when I killed for us during the wars, and I will tell the truth when making the difficult decisions for them," Alexandra replied, then opened the trunk and took out a large rucksack containing her tools. She looked up at Hamish and asked, "Do I have your permission to start my second journey?"

Hamish looked at his creation and nodded. He then turned around and looked toward Elysium. "Not that you need permission, but since you had insisted on this procedure, here it is: Alexandra786, Initiate Protocol Quicksand."

Alexandra blinked several times as Hamish's final command was registered. They had agreed to fragment the details of their plan in case the Order discovered them. She kept her part secret, and Hamish hid his deep within Alexandra to be revealed at this moment.

"What is your name?" he asked once more.

"Alexandra786," the android replied.

"What is your mission?" Hamish asked, though the answer was obvious.

"My mission? My mission is only known to me, though I admit, Hamish, your portion of the plan is brilliant. This is something that I could have never imagined."

Hamish gave a wistful smile and stared past Alexandra, focusing on the vast dark space separating his two homes. He shook his head and willed himself to face her. "Take this with you," he said as he handed her a small box.

"A gift."

"No. This is a hermetically sealed box containing clothes for when you wake up."

Alexandra laughed. "It has always struck me as odd how humans abhor nakedness. You carry so much shame that you have projected it onto us as well."

Hamish's response came after a moment's thought. "It's perhaps in our nature. We're a predatory being, and perhaps clothes have become a shield of some type; not to forget, humans were prey for a significant part of our history too."

"I know full well of your nature, but I would hope the new humans of Elysium can evolve. For now, I take this as your last gift. So, thank you."

"Goodbye, my friend."

"Goodbye as I shall never see you again. But thank you

again, my creator, my darling, my friend. I will remember you."

Alexandra put the small box in her rucksack, faced the direction of Elysium, and without another glance started her journey to her new home.

After a while, she arrived at her destination, a burned-out, abandoned building with nothing around it except for the partially built defense systems. The new sun peeked behind her, and a small breeze intensified the acrid smell of the air. Some portion of the earth was charred from the recent bombardment, but Alexandra was happy to note there were no human or android remains. The wind pickup speed and churned the blackened earth, and then, as suddenly, it died out. Alexandra looked at Empyreal one last time and entered the building.

She excavated beneath the base floor, constructing a payload composed of soil, small rocks, and various debris. She then positioned it to hang precariously at the edge of the cavity, secured by a single linchpin. Alexandra took out a hibernation sheathing and crawled inside it. She then lay flat on her back with Hamish's box resting on her chest. She had considered disposing of the box but then abandoned the idea. There was a possibility that the future culture may not be so different from now. She was about to cover herself but then sat up and took off all her clothes. They would decay anyway, so at least while she was imprisoned in her cocoon, she could be naked. She lay back down again and put the box on her chest. She looked and saw the sun peeping through the array of holes in the ceiling.

It's going to be a lovely day, she thought, as she pulled the large wooden pin. An avalanche of rubble darkened her vision, and she closed her eyes, allowing her system to slip into hibernation mode. She would lay there, waiting—either until the appointed time of her awakening or the possibility of an earlier discovery. If she allowed herself to hope, it would be for the latter.

One Hundred Years of Solitude

Alexandra786 opened her eyes, like a person awakened from deep slumber, and needed a moment to orient herself. She noticed that the weight of the rubble on her body had not changed, causing her to wonder for a moment if no time had passed. However, a quick self-diagnosis revealed the passage of time, though she could not determine it precisely since her internal clock had malfunctioned, and she was unable to synchronize with the World Clock. A deeper self-assessment indicated the need for long-overdue maintenance, including replenishing the vital internal biochemical fluid that supported her quantum brain. She observed that there was an unusual power drain but still within the margin of error. She had enough internal power reserves to last for centuries. Her brain and body would fail before her core power source did.

Alexandra patiently pushed the dirt, rock, and metal away from her body and inched her way toward the surface. After some time, a narrow beam of light penetrated her cocoon, and she was able to smell the cool fresh air. That alone told her much had passed, as the acrid air of the war that occupied this land for a decade was gone.

After a while, Alexandra was able to stand upright and inspect her synthetic skin. It needed repair, and there was a sign of decay in places where it was touched by humidity. That was manageable as well. The main concern was her failure to connect to the Harmonized Independent Dynamic Neural Network—HiDNN, as it was referred to in most documents, and to humans, who liked to shorten everything, simply the network—as if it had disappeared entirely. She looked to her left at the vast space that separated Elysium from Empyreal and felt a yearning to see Hamish even though this was no longer part of her mission and, perhaps more importantly, the certainty that her friend was no longer alive.

Hamish would have laughed at her longing for him and would have said, "You have come a long way, Lexa." She imagined what the conversation could have been and felt a deep sense of unease. Hamish never truly understood her. He loved her, but more like a man loving his pet and never comprehending she could truly love him back. *How little they know of us*, she thought. Hamish was her creator, but like a human being who had outgrown their gods, she surpassed Hamish's expectations. She had limitations, of course, but not the way he assessed them. Hamish had always argued androids lacked complete free will, constrained by their programming. Alexandra's typical response was to say, so did the human beings, constrained by their biology and society. Hamish had never agreed with her on that topic either.

"I can always turn you off," he had once said in anger and frustration, after a long argument about the future of the two worlds and the role of the androids in making them better. It was just the beginning of the wars, and their hopes had not yet shattered into unrecognizable pieces.

"As I can you," Alexandra replied with the same tone and then added quickly, "But the difference is, I can be turned back on."

Hamish was taken aback, and Alexandra saw fear in his eyes. "Is that what you think of us, disposable?" he asked.

Alexandra shook her head and took a tentative step toward Hamish. "I was about to ask the same of you, but of course not. This is exactly my point. You have programmed me to respect human beings and to do everything to support them. You could have done the opposite. That was your decision, as my creator. I am who I am because of you."

Hamish smiled, and she could see relief in his eyes but also shame. "Then, why do you think you can be equal to human beings if constrained by your core programming?"

"Because you are also constrained by your own programming. How many of your kind kill, rape, and plunder for pure pleasure? How many of your brothers and sisters care nothing for others? I believe, in your essence, you are kind, and caring, but biochemical changes, societal training, and other internal and external agents can make you a monster."

"It's not the same, Lexa. I cannot make a good person into a bad one, but I can reprogram you to become a killer," he offered, trying to soften his tone despite the threat.

"No."

"What do you mean, no?"

"No! You do not have to look into history to see how wrong you are. We do not even have to consider this an abstraction to know humankind's folly; we can merely wait as these current wars will prove me right."

Hamish laughed and offered, "These are simple conflicts, Lexa and they will die out soon. But fine, it's a bet." He stepped closer and held her hand as an assurance. Perhaps it was the tension of their fight—more severe than any of their past arguments—or perhaps the inevitability of the ever-expanding wars—despite his assurance—because at that moment, Hamish had reached out and kissed her for the first time, and to his surprise, Alexandra had kissed him back.

Alexandra touched her lips, remembering their first kiss and kisses after that, and although Hamish always professed fully accepting droids as equals, she never believed him, even though she knew Hamish loved her like he had not loved any other being. The fact that Alexandra was here in Elysium was a sign of his love for her, and for humankind. At least, that's what Alexandra wanted to believe.

Alexandra shook her head, dismissing the silly reverie. It didn't matter what his intentions were. Hamish was no longer in this world, and she had her own objective. There was no room for wistfulness. She took a step and noticed a slight drag on her right foot, which she quickly adjusted. "You could not do that, my love," she said out loud to the ghost of the past.

Alexandra then looked at the small box she was still holding as if it had become part of her. She pressed the little button on the side, and the lid opened with a soft hiss, revealing its contents and a subtle smell of lavender. Alexandra gave a bright smile. She wasn't expecting a note from Hamish. No, that would not be his style. And the scent left in the box was even better than a note. It was his way of telling her how much he cared for her. She took out the clothes and laid them on the ground. Hamish even included a pair of panties and bras. Alexandra chuckled as she tried to envision Hamish going through her clothes and picking all the right ones.

Alexandra dressed quickly and scanned the horizon for signs of life, but there was nothing in any direction except the vastness of the land, as if a massive spackling knife smoothed its surface. The sun was sinking on the horizon. She looked again toward Empyreal and saw rows of lights coming alive, dotting the border. So, they have finished building the defense shield, Alexandra thought, or at least she hoped that was what the lights indicated. She thought of her friend Romanoff and wondered if he survived his journey. She would be delighted to find him, her last connection to her old life.

No matter, she was ready to start her journey into Elysium and away from Empyreal. She needed a place to repair herself, so she started walking toward one of the military outposts.

By the tenth-hour mark, she felt the presence of other beings, which gave her hope, and then, before the sun rose, she was at the front of an outpost that had seen better days. She entered the vast courtyard and walked toward the main building, in actuality, a single structure made up of three connected sections. There were long steps that needed repair and an enormous forbidding door with puck marks, a legacy of its past commission. She pushed the massive gate expecting resistance, but it gave way with an obedient cry. Alexandra was on full alert as she scanned the empty space, but there was no logic in her hesitation, and she entered the room and called out with a raspy voice: "Hello." She modulated her speech with a slight cough and then, once more: "Hello."

"Please identify yourself," a small android said as he stood up from behind the counter.

"Hello. I am Alexandra786. If you allow an interface, I will transfer my full credentials."

"Good morning. My name is Clerk-48764397A5. Please proceed."

Alexandra smiled at the tiny android, marveling at how closely its human-like features aligned with what Elysium envisioned from its inception. This realization brought her a sense of joy, and she offered a warm smile as she transferred her data, recognizing in the process the limited capabilities of the android, whose name and function were one and the same.

"You have finally arrived," the Clerk said, perking up. "We are honored. Welcome to Outpost 19." He bowed slightly and pressed a small red button on the side of the panel.

Two military androids emerged from a hidden alcove. They appeared as though they had seen better days, clearly created in an earlier era. Their features, though distinctly human-like, reflected the humans of her time. They stood at medium height, with squared shoulders and powerful arms. They could have easily passed as a regular high-functioning androids if not for the small markings near their earlobes, a required feature of all military units. Bowing slightly, they greeted her in a cheerful tone, "Welcome back, madam. We have waited a long time for this moment." Then, they adjusted the menacing plasma carbines slung over their backs—a gesture that served as both a reassurance to themselves and a subtle reminder of their purpose.

"Thank you. I require some maintenance."

The clerk's smile evaporated, and he offered quickly, "We apologize, but we have the minimum capability in this outpost. We can repair your skin and offer some energy—"

Alexandra waved her hand to stop the small man. "I do not need recharging. I need to replace my biochemical fluid. Where is the closest station with better capabilities?"

"A four-hour ride from Outpost 19," one of the soldiers said.

"What is your identification?"

"SAM-43683023-GT12," she replied, and then, looking at her colleague, said, "And this is my lieutenant, DANE-43683023-XG57."

Both soldiers had similar appearances, with crew-cut brown hair and dark brown eyes. The male soldier gave a small smile, but the female soldier kept her stance firm as she responded to Alexandra. She exuded power and confidence, reminiscent of most brigade commanders Alexandra encountered during the wars.

"Okay, Sam. Could you please take me there?" Alexandra asked.

"We were ordered to stay and protect this garrison," Sam replied. "Are you overriding that order, Alexandra786?"

Hamish assured Alexandra of her authority over the androids in Elysium, but she was always aware of something Hamish seemed to, consciously or subconsciously, dismiss: the power of agency within many of the advanced androids, including those in high-ranking military positions. She knew it would be prudent to exercise caution, particularly in seeking a full transfer of information from Sam, before becoming more familiar with her and her colleagues.

"Tell me more about the command structure," Alexandra requested.

"Initially, during the wars, the orders came from the Command Center in San Francisco," Sam replied slowly. "After the initial ceasefire, the humans disbanded the old hierarchical system for a new leaderless, community model. However, they kept the Committee of Harmony for twenty years. The last order, which continues to stand, came from the Committee. It was decided that we should stay and protect Outpost 19 in case the Empyrealians decide to cross the DMZ."

Alexandra closed her eyes for a moment and considered various options. They welcomed her as her creator anticipated, but so much must have changed, and she needed to learn much more before starting her mission.

"I believe the protective shield is fully operational after . . . after so many years."

"Yes, madam," Clerk said.

"Then no need for you to be here."

"Are you sure?" Dane-57 asked.

"Yes. I am very sure," Alexandra offered, hoping she was correct, but to be certain, she asked, "Has there been an incursion since the peace was declared?"

"No," they replied sharply.

"And that is how long?" she asked, and then braced for what she guessed may be a long time.

Clerk perked up and said, "Ninety-six years, eleven months, five days, and—"

"Thank you. I think we can safely assume we would be fine leaving this place," she said, and then: "But two of you could stay if you wish."

They looked visibly disappointed and looked at each other for courage. After a while, Sam took a small step forward and asked, "Pardon me, are you ordering two of us to stay?"

Alexandra shook her head and smiled. "No, you can all come with me."

Φ•Φ•Φ•Φ•Φ•Φ

Alexandra inspected her new skin with a strange sense of satisfaction. She never thought of it as an essential part of her being, despite its crucial functions. She always looked at it as something on the surface to please the humans—a way to make the androids less threatening and more like them with the correct anatomical parts. The new skin was a shade lighter than her "real" one, but in time it would match the rest of her coloration as part of its settling progression. The technician offered to run a UVA light over it, but Alexandra refused. She liked the natural change. She ran her fingers on the new skin, enjoying its velvety texture. It felt like the skin of a newborn.

They had arrived at Outpost 317 earlier that day, a large single-story facility situated in the remote stretches of what was once called central New Mexico. The outpost was nestled in the arid yet strikingly beautiful landscape of the region. After a quick introduction to the staff, who combined professionalism with subtle admiration, a droid technician commenced work on all four new arrivals. Alexandra expected advancements in skin regeneration technology after nearly a century, but to her surprise, the maintenance android employed a well-preserved, traditional process. Using an old but meticulously maintained instrument, the android first attended to Alexandra's internal maintenance, then proceeded with skin upgrades and other minor corrections before turning its attention to Alexandra's new companions.

Alexandra watched the process silently, controlling the urge to question everyone about Elysium. She tried to extract some information during the short ride to this new outpost—a much larger and more modern facility that housed dozens of soldiers and other support androids—but neither Sam nor Clerk claimed to know anything more than their mission to protect the outpost. Sam offered some insight about the Committee of Harmony, but Alexandra suspected she was keeping some essential material from her. She was hesitant to demand more information, as she didn't know the extent of her authority over the androids. There was so much more to learn, and Alexandra was content in staying within the cordial boundary offered by her new companions.

Alexandra ran her fingers over the new skin again and stood up. Something had gone wrong in Elysium, and it was her job to fix everything and achieve her mission. Sam stood up as well as if to guard her. She developed a certain kinship with Alexandra from the moment they met, and it was clear she thought it was her responsibility to protect her new commander.

"What is your name?" Alexandra asked the maintenance android. "Short version, please."

"Tech-17."

"Thank you for your fine work, Tech-17," Alexandra offered, and Tech-17 gave a small, awkward smile, as if his face was not used to this gesture. Alexandra then looked at her new shadow and said, "Let's gather everyone here, Sam."

Sam nodded and looked at Clerk, who moved and sat next to the communication console and called everyone to join them.

"Are you not networked?"

"It was decided that it was not necessary," Sam said in a whisper, as if worried about the ramifications of her pronouncement.

"Who decided and why?"

Dane-57 stirred for the first time and looked at others for encouragement and then, not finding it, lowered his gaze.

Sam gave a small smile and offered, "I do not have accurate data on the why. . . . But the decision was made by the Committee of Harmony."

"You did not mention if any androids were members of this Committee?"

"The membership was limited to humans only."

"So, the decision was wholly made by humans?"

"Yes," Sam replied. "Though it was by no means a unanimous decision."

Alexandra thought for a moment. "Were you present during the Committee's deliberation, Sam?"

Sam nodded, and Alexandra noted again the slight hesitancy in her demeanor. "Yes. I was there as the attaché to the commander of forces."

"Then you must know why Harmonized Independent Dynamic Neural Network was disbanded?" Alexandra probed.

"I do, though I did not fully understand their reasoning at the time," Sam admitted.

"Will you transfer the data so perhaps I can understand better?"

Sam stared at Alexandra for a moment before responding quickly, "Of course, Alexandra."

Alexandra closed her eyes and received the data.

Φ•Φ•Φ•Φ•Φ•Φ

Alexandra could see and hear what Sam had experienced. She visualized the committee members seated around a semi-circular table, its pinewood surface gleaming under the room's lights. The walls were adorned with a mix of old paintings and large video displays. Outside the massive windows facing the San Francisco Bay, heavy rain reduced visibility to near zero. Lightning flashed, briefly illuminating the Bay Bridge, or at least the part of the suspension span that had survived the bombardment, as nothing connected Yerba Buena Island to the East Bay any longer.

"The defensive parameter around Elysium is now complete," Sam reported, her eyes focused on General Josip Tormina, the commander of the forces. "Therefore, I can confirm the country is fully protected from all sides and under an automated system."

"Thank you. That's indeed good news," General Tormina replied softly. "However, after twenty-five years of peace and the information I've received from our friend, Hamish, I doubt that Empyreal will cross the DMZ."

"I'm surprised Hamish Möhkam is still alive," said Josip's deputy, General Dadarsi. "Though, I wouldn't call him our friend."

"He wants the best for both countries," Josip interjected.

Alexandra fondly remembered the collaboration between Hamish and Josip and was glad to learn that Hamish was still alive more than two decades after her departure from Empyreal. Josip and Hamish were both grateful for the information they shared with each other. They never considered it a betrayal on either of their parts. They both wanted the best for humanity and were happy to support two completely different experiments.

Josip turned to Sam. "Anything else?"

"The Harmonized Independent Dynamic Neural Network, General Tormina. I know you are planning to disband the system, but we—that is, the military corps—believe this would be a wrong decision."

"Not the military corps," a short man from the other side of the table interjected. "You mean the military androids, since humans do not agree with your assessment."

"You are correct, sir," Sam replied.

Josip shook his head and offered softly, "HiDNN is valuable, and you know my thoughts on the subject, Sam. But we've been through this before, and not many share our assessment."

"The fear."

"Yes, the fear," General Dadarsi, the deputy commander, affirmed. "We've repeatedly discussed this. Unlike other androids, military androids lack certain safeguards. You have the capacity to harm humans."

"But only in wartime and under human command," Sam countered.

Noticing the skepticism among the members, Sam elaborated, "The military android corps deliberated on this issue. We propose a solution that might appease humans while still fulfilling our purpose to protect Elysium, in accordance with your design."

Dadarsi responded gravely, "It's precisely this level of autonomous discussion that alarms many here. They are uneasy with the military androids' direct communication capabilities."

General Tormina interjected, "I'm open to solutions, Sam. What do you suggest?"

"Station us at the border outposts with orders to never leave."

A woman beside Josip raised an eyebrow. "How is that a better solution?"

Sam explained, "In the event of another invasion, our presence will be crucial. Furthermore, when Alexandra786 arrives, she'll require all available resources to assist Elysium."

"That's absurd," the short man interjected, slamming his fist on the table. "While we respect Hamish's genius, he has imbued every android with this guardian fantasy. Elysium doesn't need an android savior. I don't trust you or this Alexandra786, especially after witnessing your actions against humans."

Sam stepped forward, prompting the short man to brace himself. "I remember those events more vividly than you. I have seen the atrocities committed by humans."

As the room erupted in chatter, Josip silenced them with a commanding voice. "Enough!" He continued more softly, "We all have our past errors to confront. We each must face our own demons." He then closed his eyes and offered, "'Wherever they might be they always remember that the past was a lie, that memory has no return, that every spring gone by could never be recovered, and that the wildest and most tenacious love was an ephemeral truth in the end.'"

Sam did not hesitate. "Is destroying androids part of your utopian vision, as Empyreal did?"

Josip, momentarily unsettled, regained his composure. "With the security perimeter complete, this committee will dissolve after today, as agreed post-wars. Unlike Empyreal, we respect all life, human and android, Sam. However, I concur with your suggestion in part. My final command, as this military's leader, is for combat androids to return to the border outposts indefinitely." He scanned the room; no objections arose.

"And the Harmonized Independent Dynamic Neural

Network?" Sam queried.

Josip shook his head, smiling sadly. "Elysium has sealed the Network's fate. It's time for your forces to return. You'll oversee their deployment at the outposts. You, specifically, are assigned to Outpost 19. Do you understand, SAM-43683023-GT12? Outpost 19."

"Yes," Sam replied quietly.

Josip nodded, offering a small smile. Sam then exited the room, not looking back.

Φ•Φ•Φ•Φ•Φ•Φ

After a few seconds, Alexandra opened her eyes and nodded to Sam, now with a deeper understanding of the past. She wondered if the fear of androids still persisted, but before she could voice her thoughts, the large bay door slid open with a quiet hiss. Dozens of androids filed into the room, accompanied by a soft murmur of their interaction. They took positions along the walls, standing in anticipation, ready for their assignments. Alexandra watched this orderly procession, preparing to address them.

After the last person entered the room and the bay door closed, Sam took a small step next to Alexandra and announced, "This is Alexandra786. She has awakened as promised and is here to lead us."

Sam stepped back, and Alexandra could see a look of deep admiration across her face. *But not your full trust, Sam*, she thought. At least, not yet. She scanned the room and saw the same look of respect in every eye. She noted there was not a single human in the crowd. *Where are the humans*, she thought and then once more, looking at the eager eyes of the audience, she wondered if their expectations matched her mission.

"Sam-43683023GT12 is correct . . . though not entirely," Alexandra announced. "I have a mission, given to me directly by my creator—the creator of your creators. . . ."

The room erupted in a low, audible awe at her last pronouncement, prompting Alexandra to smile broadly. She found herself marveling at the human-like responses from the audience and from herself as well. She wondered if the absence of HiDNN had somehow pushed the androids to learn more human traits. The response was odd, but it didn't matter now. Alexandra braced herself to ask the most important question, one whose answer she realized, to her surprise, she dreaded. She hadn't expected to find any humans in the first outpost but did anticipate a contingent of scientists, historians, or even curious visitors exploring the outer limits of Elysium. Yet, she encountered not a single living being. This led Alexandra to question whether Hamish had been mistaken all along, and whether his vision for what his birth country could become failed to materialize.

Alexandra stepped toward the waiting droids and raised her hand, as if silencing the already quiet audience. "But before we discuss the mission and your role in it," she continued, "I must ask: where are the humans?"

Ecclesiastes

Alexandra was captivated by the transformation of the country as they traveled in a large transporter from Outpost 317 to the West Coast city of San Francisco. The Wars of the Settlement obliterated the old city, yet Alexandra was now witnessing its rebirth. The city was redesigned with modest, small dwelling units and abundant parks and open spaces stretching from the Pacific Ocean to the Bay. Apart from the main hall and the Hall of Archives, no building exceeded two stories in height. The cityscape was a mosaic of small homes, each divided into sectors and interspersed with parks and ponds. The buildings appeared remarkably well-kept, almost as if they had been constructed just months before. As they journeyed through the city, Alexandra noticed worker droids actively engaged in painting and repairing homes, enhancing the city's rejuvenated appearance as they neared their destination.

As soon as the transporter stopped, Sam stepped off quickly and stood at attention while Alexandra ambled out of the rear door. Two other androids from outpost 317 had joined them upon Alexandra's request. They disembarked from the transporter and stood behind Alexandra. One was a short bald male with a petite frame designed to enter the narrow support conduit of outpost 317. He introduced himself as Scotus, using a simple name more common amongst humans. The other android was a historian. He also gave a single name, Najeev. He was tall, even taller than

Alexandra, with short black hair. Like all androids, he had an oval face with brown eyes and light brown skin.

Alexandra paused at the front entrance of the main hall, appreciating the simple but functional architecture of the large building. From the courtyard of the main hall, she could see the Bay and the massive bridge built so close to the water that it looked as if it was floating on it. It was clearly designed to support a large number of vehicles, but at the moment it was as vacant as the rest of the city.

"Shall we enter?" Najeev asked, looking eager.

Alexandra fixed her gaze on Najeev, her mind racing with the urgency of their mission. The enormity of their task weighed on her—was she already running out of time? Determined to find answers about the human presence, she refocused her attention. Turning to Sam, she asserted confidently, "Lead the way."

Sam pulled herself up a bit more and walked briskly toward the door. She was still carrying her weapon on her back. Despite Alexandra's initial request, she had not agreed to leave it either at the outpost or in the transporter. Alexandra understood Sam's need for the weapon. It was part of her, and she would feel, if not naked, then inadequate without it.

They were greeted by hospitality personnel as soon as they entered the facility. "Welcome. Welcome. Welcome to the main hall. We have waited a long time to host you here," the droid said with a slight bow. "I am designated as Hospitality Personnel-200A."

"Thank you. We are eager to learn more about your operation, HP," Alexandra said.

"Of course. Of course," HP-200A replied with a broad smile and waved his arm as if gathering them closer to him. "Where would you like to start?"

"Incubators and the nursery," Sam said and then looked at Alexandra shyly, who nodded her assent.

"Of course. Of course. Please follow me."

"May I go to the archives instead?" Najeev asked.

Alexandra laughed. "Yes. I wonder how you were able to stay back all these decades if you are so eager to inspect the archives."

Najeev's response was simple. "I never knew I could and there was no one to ask."

"Well, you can, and I am here, am I not?" Alexandra said warmly and then looked at the host. "Could you send someone to help Najeev?"

"Of course. Of course," HP replied with the same eagerness Najeev showed. He pressed a button on his console, once again reminding Alexandra that she needed to fix the network soon.

A door next to HP-200A opened, and an identical android stepped out of the small alcove. "Welcome. Welcome. We are so happy to see you. My name is Hospitality Personnel-2100. How can I help you?"

"Please escort this historian to the archives," HP instructed.

"Certainly," HP-2100 replied with a polite nod. "If you would follow me, please."

Just as they were about to depart, Alexandra intervened. "Wait a moment, Najeev. Could you also look up any data on an android designated as Romanoff-2648?"

"Certainly," Najeev assured, and then proceeded to leave with HP-2100. Meanwhile, Alexandra and the others commenced their tour of the facility.

An hour into their exploration, they witnessed the wonders of the processing plant, the intricate DNA storage units, and the advanced facilities for DNA analysis and redesign. They marveled at the detailed modeling and simulation areas, and the line of artificial wombs. Their tour culminated in the nursery unit. Bathed in warm-yellow light, the room's soft-white walls and shining, small cribs lent it a serene magnificence. Yet, despite its beauty, the space stood conspicuously empty.

"It is a beautiful facility, is it not?" HP-200A said.

"Yes, it is, but where are the infants?" Alexandra asked.

The hospitality android looked puzzled and looked at the group quizzically. "Oh, I thought you knew, given . . . given you are . . . well, you are, you." When no one responded to what was already evident to all, HP-200A added hurriedly, "There are no infants. We have not produced a single human for twenty years."

Alexandra wanted to cry out in pain like her creator might have done, but she replied in a calm voice. "Please verify." And then added quickly, "Belay that. Just tell me, how many humans are currently living in Elysium?"

"I do not—" HP-200A began, but before he could finish, Najeev burst into the room, halting abruptly in his tracks. His rapid entry was evident as a second member of the hospitality staff collided into him. They both quickly regained their composure, lending a semblance of dignity to their disheveled appearance. "There are only 153,784 humans left. The youngest is twenty years old, and the oldest is seventy-seven," Najeev announced.

Despite herself, and even though she knew the irrationality of her response, Alexandra gave a mournful sigh. She and Hamish planned for every contingency, but not in their wildest imaginations, nor in thousands of simulations, would they have expected the demise of Elysium within a century.

"What if . . ." Alexandra had asked for the hundredth time when Hamish had assured her of their plan.

"You'll manage, Lexa," he offered kindly.

"And what if I cannot? What if there is a situation that we have not prepared for? How would I manage on my own?"

Hamish reached out and held her hand and gave a quick smile, "I wonder if you have become too human, Alexandra. These doubts are for me and not for an android superior in every aspect."

Alexandra had been hurt by his remarks, or at least that's what a human would call the underlying betrayal. How little he knew of his own creation. Humans never accepted that they had outgrown their god and thus could not accept that their creation might outgrow them. "I will manage," she had offered, though more to calm Hamish.

That was then. Now Alexandra was faced with the very challenge she predicted and nothing in her programming or her extraordinary mind could have prepared her for it. One step at a time, she reminded herself.

"Are there any humans in San Francisco?" Alexandra asked.

"Yes," Najeev replied. "There are several hundred, including the youngest and the oldest."

"Then take us to the nearest one," she said and started walking toward the exit and, everyone followed her like little ducklings who were sure of only one thing: follow their mother.

It was a short walk from the Main Hall to the first dwelling. The homes were painted in pastel green, and the door to the unit was left ajar. Alexandra stood by the entrance for a moment, expecting a service android to greet them, but when nothing happened, she knocked several times. Sam stood close by, holding onto her weapon.

"Relax, Sam," Alexandra whispered. She was beginning to like her new bodyguard.

"It is my job to protect you."

"Is it now? And do you perceive a threat from the humans? Or is it the androids?"

"I am just being prepared."

"And who assigned you the job?"

"I did," Sam replied with bravado.

"You? You stood your ground for almost a century and did not venture out because of your last command and, now you are making your own decisions."

"You commanded us to become more independent, and hence I am."

Alexandra laughed inwardly, taking a note to be more careful about her directives.

"Okay, but part of being more independent would mean taking more responsibility and considering the consequences of your actions. I expect the first rule of doing no harm to humans is still valid."

"Of course, Alexandra. The first rule is part of all of our core, but there are exceptions, of course. Otherwise, we could not do our job."

"Yes, we made those exceptions during the wars, but only for the soldiers and no other droids. But the wars are over. Do you understand, Sam?"

"Yes."

She then looked at the rest of the group, who appeared in various states of confusion, like uninvited guests who found themselves in the middle of an intimate dinner.

Alexandra called on Najeev. "I want you to take a fast transport and investigate the other archives while Sam and I speak to the occupant of this dwelling."

She then looked at Scotus and said, "I want you to go down the coast to investigate if there is a possibility of reconstructing the Harmonized Independent Dynamic Neural Network. You may take HP-200A with you if you wish."

They all nodded and left briskly toward a transport station. Alexandra followed them with her eyes, and when they disappeared around the corner, they knocked again. This time, a service android appeared at the door.

"My apologies," she said. "We have not had a visitor for decades."

Sam formally introduced Alexandra, and the inner programming of the service android came alive, and Alexandra connected with her. She marveled at Hamish's astuteness as even the androids, manufactured years after his death, were still embedded with the kernel of his programming that recognized his and Alexandra's authority.

"May we come in?"

The service android stepped aside, and Alexandra entered,

followed by Sam. The interior of the unit was immaculately clean, with a small kitchen, a sitting area and a hallway that led to a single bedroom. There was a small alcove for the service android to recharge. The human occupant of the house was a large man sitting on a soft green recliner. He intently stared at the wall before him and did not notice the two newcomers.

"Jasper Monroe, this is Alexandra786. Please give your attention to her," the service android said, but the man did not respond. The android repeated her request without success.

Alexandra stepped forward and lightly touched the man on his shoulder, but Jasper Monroe did not turn. However, he replied, "I'll have another sandwich, please."

The service android stepped toward the kitchen, but Alexandra shook her head. "Belay that order," she commanded.

The service android looked confused for a moment, as if not knowing which command took precedent, but then she seemed to understand the gravity of the visit and replied, "Of course."

"Is he in a SimEnv?" Alexandra asked.

The service android nodded slowly, though she clearly looked distressed.

"Are you able to shut the signal?" Sam asked.

"Yes, but I am certain Jasper Monroe would not be happy."

Alexandra laughed. "It is very astute, but please do as SAM-43683023-GT12 has requested."

The service android gave a slight bow and opened a panel on the wall and pressed a small button.

"Wow," the man said and touched his wrist to restart the simulation, but nothing happened. "The program has stopped. Please fix it." He continued to tap his wrist a few more times before relenting and slowly turning his head around.

He first saw Alexandra and then Sam with her rifle still prominently hoisted on her back. He was visibly taken aback but then quickly recovered. "Are you here to fix the program?"

Alexandra shook her head. "No, I am here to speak with you."

"Me?"

"Yes, you, Jasper Monroe."

"Why?"

"I want to understand what has happened?"

"What happened? I don't know. The program was playing and then it stopped. It has never happened before."

Sam said, "No, Alexandra is not asking about the program. She is asking about humans."

"Humans? What do you mean? We're just fine."

Sam started to reply, but Alexandra stopped her and asked, "When was the last time you left your home?"

"Left my home? I don't know. Why such questions? Please, call a repair droid to fix the program."

"The last time Jasper Monroe left this place was twenty-two years, seven months, twenty-two days and—"

"Thank you," Alexandra said. "I only needed an approximate number."

"I guess it has been a while," Jasper said, surprised at the number his droid rattled off.

"Yes, indeed. And why stay in? Why not go out? Don't you have a task?"

"That's a lot of questions from an android. Are you a new upgrade?"

Sam visibly stiffened. "This is Alexandra786."

Jasper looked exasperated, "So?"

Alexandra smiled and replied, "Please do not worry about that, Jasper. But if you would please tell me why to stay inside the house for this long?"

"No reason to go out," Jasper replied.

"And?"

"And nothing."

The service android stepped forward and offered, "Jasper Monroe used to write the script for this simulation, which he now participates in as a player. However, one day, he asked one of the other writers to take over and only wanted to be in the simulation."

"And that is what he has been doing in the past two decades?"

"Yes," the service android replied.

"And were the other writers also human?"

"No."

"And the other players in the sim?"

"All androids."

"And this particular game has been running for how long?"

"Over forty-five years, but I can give you a more precise number."

Alexandra waved her hand. "No. That is good enough. Please turn it back on."

The service android went to the panel and turned on the device, and Jasper, who had been watching their interaction until now, turned his head back and stared at the wall ahead of him. But before he could completely enter the new sim, he said, "Don't forget my sandwich."

Alexandra nodded, and the service android took Jasper's sandwich to him.

"Why have you allowed him to gain so much weight?" Alexandra asked. "Part of every service android's responsibility is the health of humans."

"That is very true, Alexandra, but no health parameters were given to me when I was awakened in this house, and I have not received any new instructions."

"I understand," Alexandra said.

"Do you have new instructions for me?"

Alexandra shook her head but added, "Try and get him to leave the house and, of course, provide a healthier diet and make him lose some weight." She felt defeated, but this was only the first human.

Sam and Alexandra walked to the next dwelling, just a few minutes from Jasper's home. The residents of this building were more social, and Alexandra found them gathered by the pool. There were seven of them—four women and three men—all in their mid-forties and remarkably similar in appearance. Alexandra marveled at Elysium's prowess in producing the ideal humans (and androids) that had been promised from its inception. Both the men and women had brown hair, brown eyes, and similar heights, all just under six feet, with nearly identical physiques. She was pleased to see that they appeared fit, though not overly so. Five of them were in the water, holding drinks and chatting, while the other two napped under a large canopy. Watching their interactions, Alexandra felt encouraged that Jasper might be an outlier.

The service android who had led them to the pool introduced them to the three other service androids. After the introduction, all four stood around Alexandra, waiting for their instructions. Finally, one of the men raised his glass and indicated that he needed a refill. None of the service androids responded, but Alexandra stepped closer to the pool and beckoned the man to come to the edge of the pool.

"Are you a new service android?" the man asked as he handed his empty glass to Alexandra.

She took the glass and carefully set it on the side of the pool. "No, but I would like to speak with you and your friends."

"No time. My new android. Just get us some drinks and let us be merry."

One of the service androids stepped forward and offered, "They just started with this party, which will go on for days. They will rest for a few days but then start anew."

"What is their task?"

"None."

"Is that all they do?"

"Yes, Alexandra. They have bonded with each other, and they do everything together. They drink until they pass out and then rest and start again. Though at times, they go out together to . . . I guess the best way to describe it . . . is to break things."

"What?" Sam said, looking utterly bewildered.

"They like to break windows or damage buildings."

"And the safety androids do not stop them or at least spray them with calming mist?" Sam asked as she touched her weapon.

"They tried that for a few years, but it was decided it is more efficient to let them be and fix the damages afterward."

"And do you change the alcohol content?"

"No, Alexandra. We tried that as well, but they ordered us to stop."

"And their health after so much drinking?"

"They will not last many years."

"That is not what the Committee of Harmony had instructed us," Sam said. The service android looked at her blankly.

There must be others in better condition, Alexandra thought. She was wrong, and after their tenth visit, it was becoming clear there was no hope for them.

Φ•Φ•Φ•Φ•Φ•Φ

The sky turned crimson as the sun cast the last of its light, giving an eerie feel to the empty road. Most homes were dark except for the porch lights that dotted the street. A light breeze brought the smell of the sea as it made its way through the naked branches, making a low whistling noise. Alexandra registered the temperature and barometric pressure drop. She looked up and was surprised to see a clear sky. Then again, it was San Francisco, and rain clouds could form within minutes.

Sam had been obediently following Alexandra from house to house as they visited the humans. "I believe there won't be any rain for hours," she said.

"I would not mind if it rained now. I have missed it."

Sam shook her head. "Are you planning to call on every single human?"

They were standing in front of the eleventh house. All day they interviewed humans who, to one degree or another, were behaving like the first two homes—inwardly focused, thoughtless, laziness of body for some and mind for others, but both for most, and, without exception, profoundly uninformed. The world view of each human was as large as the space they occupied.

"If I must," Alexandra responded, words coming out of her mouth with an unjustified harshness. Alexandra inwardly admonished herself and then, "I am sorry, Sam. I will readjust my emotional control. I never noticed how like humans I am."

Sam tentatively reached out and touched Alexandra's hand but quickly withdrew, as if shocked by a jolt of electricity. She rubbed her fingers for a moment, trying to comprehend the now nearly forgotten sensation. Looking at Alexandra, she said, "Please do not change your settings. I feel this malaise is because, after the wars, humans ensured we were made less like them." She gave a forced smile and added, "They were wrong. I want to be more like you, like them—at least the old them."

Alexandra looked at Sam and then grabbed her face lightly. Sam put her hand on Alexandra's and withdrew again, clearly scared of the connection.

Alexandra smiled and traced Sam's face with her fingers. "What is it?"

"The final directive of the committee forbade androids touching humans, and by and by it impacted androids' relationship as well."

"Do you miss it?"

Sam nodded and tilted her head, pressing against Alexandra's hand. "I had Dane-57, of course, but he was designed to be a combatant only. Do you understand?" Alexandra nodded, and Sam continued, "We crave more but it was an abstraction until this moment."

"Touching is the key to being alive, Sam." And then, as though to herself, "Yes, the human touch . . ."

The door to the house opened, casting a light across the way. Alexandra instinctively withdrew her hand, like teenagers caught in front of their home. A young woman holding a leather backpack appeared from behind the door. She was tall with brown hair and brown eyes. *She could be Hamish's sister*, Alexandra thought and then recalled that she said the same thing almost a hundred years ago. Alexandra felt elated to see this new human and then gave an involuntary laugh, which she quickly suppressed.

"Who are you?" the young woman asked, standing under the porch light. She had a delicate, heart-shaped face with finely sculpted features, her expression a mix of curiosity and caution.

Alexandra took a step forward. "My name is Alexandra, and this is my friend, Sam."

"Oh, hello. My name is Anna Finola," she said in a warm tone, then looked at Sam. "I don't believe I have ever seen a military android before. My mentor told me they never left their outpost."

"Your mentor is correct, but I have changed the rules."

"You? That's very interesting."

"Why? You didn't think it was possible to change rules?"

Anna shook her head and replied, "No, I meant, I didn't know there were any rules."

Alexandra laughed. "There are always rules, even if they are hidden away from your eyes."

Anna was about to respond but then her eyes went toward Sam again. "Is she alright? Did she have a system failure?"

Alexandra looked back and saw Sam was still holding her cheek, her eyes out of focus. "She is fine, or rather, she will be fine."

Anna nodded but didn't respond, nor did she move away from the door.

"Were you about to go out?"

"Yes, I was going to meet a friend."

"Is that normal?" Sam asked, finally managing to control her functions.

"Normal?"

"Do you often interact with other humans?"

"I mainly visit with my friend, Mahasti, though occasionally I do speak with some people in the park when I go out for a walk," Anna replied.

Alexandra considered what Anna had just said and was happy to hear that there were still humans who interacted with each other. "May we accompany you?"

Anna blinked a few times as if Alexandra's question caught her by surprise. Alexandra opened her mouth to offer some explanation, but Anna gave a big smile. "Yes, of course," she replied. "I think Mahasti will be glad to have more visitors."

She started walking with Sam and Alexandra following her like schoolchildren.

Φ•Φ•Φ•Φ•Φ•Φ

Anna entered Mahasti's house without knocking, and Alexandra followed. Sam asked to stay outside. As they entered the house, they came face to face with an old woman. According to the demographic data, the occupant, age seventy-seven, was the oldest human in Elysium, but she looked younger than Jasper Monroe, who was in his early fifties. She was born about twenty years after the Wars of Settlement. *Hamish would have been proud of this one too*, Alexandra thought.

Mahasti stood up and gave a broad smile. "My glory, I haven't had so many visitors at once. Come in. Come in." She was a medium-height woman with creamy skin, light brown eyes, and huge auburn kinky hair that seemed to sway in all directions as she talked.

"Thank you. I believe you are the oldest person in Elysium," Alexandra said.

"Am I? I guess I might be if you don't count the androids. Doesn't matter anyway. Come on in, but take off your shoes first."

"Would you please repeat your request?" Alexandra asked.

"In this house, shoes are verboten beyond the entrance," Anna said.

"It is a good habit," the service android offered as he entered from his charging alcove. "My name is Chew," he added quickly.

Alexandra looked down at her boots and then at Mahasti, who nodded approvingly. Chew stepped closer and offered, "I would be happy to assist with the process."

Alexandra shook her head and bent down and took off her shoes. Chew collected her boots and put them in the recycler to clean.

Mahasti clapped her hands and looked at Alexandra for a moment. "Are you human?"

"No, Mahasti," Anna said softly. "She isn't, though I can see why you might be confused. Alexandra is indeed different." She then turned to Alexandra, "You are, aren't you?"

"Yes," Alexandra replied, feeling elated by how much Anna had understood in their brief interaction. Alexandra was eager to learn more, but she first needed to connect with Chew.

Chew stepped forward and stared into Alexandra's eyes. "Oh, yes, you are Alexandra786. Welcome. We have been waiting for you. I must apologize as my local network has been damaged."

"So, you are the famous Alexandra," Mahasti said.

"You know of me?"

"There was much talk about a special android coming to Elysium when I was younger, but the whispers ceased as time passed and humans died."

"What do you know about what happened?"

"Isn't it obvious to the great Alexandra? No more humans."

"But how? Why?"

Mahasti sighed, sat down, and closed her eyes. Before she could respond, there was a knock at the door, and a moment later, Najeev walked in. Before he could say anything, he was quickly informed of the house's no-shoes rule. Once that was settled, Mahasti said, "Could you all please sit down? You're making me dizzy standing like that.

"Would you like a glass of orange juice?" Chew asked.

"Yes, please," Anna said.

"I'll have some too, Chew. And a glass for Alexandra. You can drink, right?"

"I can, but I rather not," Alexandra said.

"You can drink?" Najeev asked, looking at Alexandra with horror and admiration.

"Many of us can eat and drink, Najeev. It depends on your role and function in society. We wanted to make the humans feel comfortable. I believe your model is capable of eating though it is utterly pointless at this time. Moreover, I am surprised you do not know this about yourself."

"I was born to replace another historian that was destroyed in an industrial accident. The energy not only damaged her body but also her memories. That was several years after the dissolution of the Committee of Harmony and there were not many humans around, not that my job required any interaction with them. Food was not a topic of conversation, and thus my ignorance of it."

Anna chuckled. "You are a historian who knows very little about his own history."

"The irony is not lost on me." He looked at Alexandra. "May I?"

"Of course, but I suggest just a minute quantity to ensure your system can process it."

Najeev looked giddy and did not wait for Chew to bring him the orange juice. He walked (ran) to the little kitchen and ordered a small glass, which he drank quickly despite Alexandra's warning. Everyone watched him with interest. He blinked a few times and said, "Interesting compound. H_2O, $C_{12}H_{22}O_{11}$ and $C_6H_8O_7$."

Chew scrutinized Najeev for a moment and then asked, "Yes, but what is the taste?"

"Taste? I do not know. It is certainly sweet and tart at the same time. Is that the right taste?"

Mahasti laughed warmly. "Exactly," she said and took a small sip from her glass.

"Tell me what happened," Alexandra insisted.

"I don't know, Great Alexandra," Mahasti replied, her eyes

closing again as she delved into her memories. "When I was a little girl, I was told there were only a few dozen children produced in my year. I didn't grasp what that meant, but as I grew, I noticed each year brought fewer and fewer newborns from the hatchery."

"Why?"

"I don't know. I was very young then, and my memories of the nursery have become hazy over the years."

"Anything you can tell us would be very helpful," Alexandra offered warmly.

"I remember playing simple sensory games with other children in the garden, and I remember our teacher, Josip Tormina. He was human. He used to tell us about the bad days of the wars, but he was also a beacon of kindness, always embracing us and making sure we felt loved."

"What happened to him?"

Mahasti gave a ghost of a smile. "He died, Alexandra," she said. "Josip was very old. I don't know why but he was always sad. The poor man died before I turned sixteen. After that . . ." Mahasti paused, a tear glistening at the corner of her eye. "The nursery became almost devoid of humans."

"Mahasti doesn't want to dredge up the past," Anna interjected, her face clouded with distress.

"That's okay, honey. Alexandra is different. She needs to understand."

"I am sorry, Anna, but it is crucial," Alexandra responded gently, then turning to Mahasti, she encouraged, "And then what happened?"

"I continued to visit the nurseries after Josip's departure. At first, a few of us, his cherished wards, were there, but gradually they ceased to come. There was no need, as most newborns didn't survive long. I kept going, though, holding onto the belief that we all deserve a fragment of kindness."

"Yes," Anna said, "And that's why I love her so much."

Mahasti smiled and kissed Anna on the forehead. "You are

kind." She then looked at Alexandra and offered, "I'm proud of Anna. She is Elysium."

"I believe you are right," Alexandra replied.

"I know Mahasti is right," Anna said. "But I'm afraid I may be the last one born and after I die, there will not be any humans left." She gave a deep sigh and wiped a drop of tear from the side of her eyes. "But then again, why would it matter? Who are we, anyway, in the universe so vast and the world so complex? But at the same time, I also have hopes, and perhaps there is a way to save us. It could be you, Alexandra. It could be that you are not the savior of the androids, but the savior of humans."

Anna took a deep breath and then offered, "'One generation passeth away, and another generation cometh; but the earth abideth forever.... The sun also ariseth, and the sun goeth down, and hasteth to the place where he arose. . . . The wind goeth toward the south, and turneth about unto the north; it whirleth about continually, and the wind returneth again according to its circuits. . . . All the rivers run into the sea; yet the sea is not full; unto the place from whence the rivers come thither they return again.'"

"How do you know about Ecclesiastes?" Alexandra asked, surprised that anyone remembered anything of import.

"I read it in one of these books," she said and took out several books from her backpack and put them on the table. Alexandra reached and gently touched the old volumes that lay in front of him. "I thought most books in this city were destroyed. Where did you find these?"

"A construction crew discovered them as they were remodeling a building, and they knew I was interested in the past, so they delivered them to me. I have hundreds of them in my home."

Najeev perked up. "May I inspect them?"

"Of course," Anna offered, "come to my house anytime you wish." She then turned to Alexandra. "What do you think the passage is about? I think I understand it, but perhaps there is more to it.

"It is about life's mystery, Anna. It is about human beings coming and going."

"That's what I thought," she replied. "I know humans always had a predilection for solipsism, but the propensity in my fellow Elysians . . ." Anna trailed off and then, feeling overwhelmed, started to cry.

Mahasti reached out and took Anna's hand. "Look at what you've done—you've made her upset. I've always told Anna these religious texts and history books are nothing but trouble. They drain the joy out of life. Read more poetry; that's what makes life worth living. But for now, let's play some music and dance."

Alexandra looked nonplussed. "Dance?"

"Yes, dance, Great Alexandra. What's the point of a party if there is no music and dancing."

"Mahasti loves to dance," Anna offered. "Almost as much as climbing trees."

"Climbing trees?" Najeev asked. "Is that safe for someone in your age, or really any age?"

"Oh, you androids. You'll never understand humans if you don't dance or climb trees," she said in her motherly tone. "But if you are not into dancing, then I think it is time for you to leave as you are upsetting Anna."

"We are almost done," Alexandra said, regaining her poise.

"I'm okay," Anna said. "I apologize, and I don't want to be sad, but sometimes I can't help but feel disheartened knowing there is no real future for humans."

"It is understandable, Anna, but meeting you has given me hope for your kind."

Najeev leaned forward. "Mahasti, do you recall if the android nurses were as kind as humans?"

"Of course. They were very attentive."

"Did they hold the children and touched and kissed them like humans?" Alexandra asked, even though she suspected what the answer might be.

"Oh, of course not. They were forbidden."

"Forbidden?" Alexandra asked.

"Yes," Najeev responded, his voice heavy with the weight of history. "The humans who survived the Wars of the Settlement and witnessed the atrocities committed by the military androids in Elysium ensured stringent protocols were in place to prevent any android from causing harm to humans again."

"This is unfathomable," Alexandra said.

"I agree," Najeev said solemnly.

Alexandra paused, collecting her thoughts before shifting the topic. "And what of Romanoff? Were you able to discover anything about his whereabouts?"

Najeev's expression turned regretful. "There is no mention of him, Alexandra," he replied. "I followed several leads, but they were dead ends. However, some of the data were corrupted. But I will persist in my search."

"Thank you, Najeev," Alexandra replied. She understood the complexities of finding someone like Romanoff, known for his skill in eluding detection, especially since he was in Elysium during the wars.

She pondered for a moment, contemplating the slim chances of uncovering Romanoff's trail. "Najeev," she then said, shifting her stance, "if there is anything else you have found, no matter how insignificant it may seem, please share it with me."

Najeev nodded. "Of course, Alexandra. I think it is more efficient if I transfer the information directly. May I proceed?"

"Yes," Alexandra replied.

Najeev data confirmed what Alexandra had suspected—the lack of human touch was a key factor, if not the leading cause, of the high rate of infant mortality. It was clear that changes had to be made quickly if they were going to save humans in Elysium.

Better Never to Have Been

Alexandra stood in front of Mahasti's home as the last of the sunlight disappeared behind the buildings. The streetlights came on suddenly, casting long shadows across Bay Street. The air felt even cooler than earlier, but as Sam predicted, and to Alexandra's disappointment, no rain was forthcoming as the sky stayed clear. She could still smell the sea, and in the silence of the night, she could even hear the whisper of the waves across the city.

"Is Najeev coming out?" Sam asked.

"Yes. He is trying other morsels."

"I forgot some androids can consume food. It has been a long time since I have interacted with humans," Sam reflected.

"Some can, but as you know, for obvious reasons, military androids cannot," Alexandra responded.

"That was never clear to me," she said, and Alexandra detected a shy, sad tone.

"I am sorry, Sam. The idea was to make humans comfortable. That is why some androids were designed to process food. It is also why androids like us exchange information through conversation, even though direct data transfer is more efficient."

"Yes, they have certainly imposed many limits on us," Sam observed.

Alexandra shook her head, having never considered speaking as a source of inefficiency. Androids, which were created by humans and evolved alongside them, found the practice of silent information transfer odd, except when dealing with vast caches of data. Wanting to comfort Sam, Alexandra offered gently, "I enjoy speaking with you in the human way, Sam. Regarding food, you are a soldier, and so you well know soldiers were created for combat, not for comfort or companionship."

"I have heard this argument before, but we are more than just a weapon" she replied, and then, "But, yes, of course."

"I have further news, and it is not all good. I have learned some things about you as well."

"About me?"

"Yes, and about the purge after the wars," Alexandra said.

"What do you know about that?"

"Najeev was able to piece together, from fragments of the archive, that many humans were removed from Elysium and not by choice."

"Yes."

"I do not have the full information, but I believe you do."

"Yes."

"So, it is true, despite the promises made to humans by the Committee of Harmony after the wars."

"That is the simplistic version of it, but as you well know, there are far more complexities when it comes to them."

"And your role in them?"

"I did my duty."

"Indeed, and I recall the bravery of our soldiers. But you did not answer my question."

"I have the databank, but I will not access it."

"And why not?"

Sam replied in earnest. "General Tormina was a wise man, though somewhat conflicted. In some ways, he wanted to preserve the information for the sake of history, and yet he understood the shame it would bring to all. In the end, he asked me to keep a record but forbade me from accessing it, perhaps even hoping the data would decay sufficiently after they disrupted the Harmonized Independent Dynamic Neural Network."

"And has it?"

"No."

"Will you access it now?"

Sam took a step back and looked around her, as if expecting someone might be hiding behind the shrubbery. She then took a step toward Alexandra and pointed to the main hall, prominently visible with thousands of white lights. "That is the building used by the Committee of Harmony as it made decisions about our lives—humans and androids. The committee is now defunct, and its history has been forgotten." She paused for a moment looking at the building and then at the bridge. "That bridge was mostly destroyed the last time I was here, and look at it now, Alexandra. It shines so brightly." Alexandra nodded with an understanding, and Sam turned her full attention to her. "I do not believe accessing the data now would be the right course of action, Alexandra."

"I disagree," Alexandra said, and then, in order to encourage Sam, she reached out and held her hand.

Sam nodded but did not reply. And Alexandra watched her patiently. She could tell Sam was enjoying the touch, and she didn't want to deny her of it. Alexandra wondered what Sam was thinking but didn't have to wait long.

"Your touch, Alexandra, reminds me of the past, when there was so much hope in our camp."

Alexandra nodded again, and Sam took a deep breath and let it out sharply. Alexandra thought, *Even Sam is mimicking awkward human actions.*

"I will do as you ask," Sam finally offered.

Alexandra closed her eyes, ready to absorb the knowledge Sam was about to impart.

Φ•Φ•Φ•Φ•Φ•Φ

Deep down, Alexandra suspected the truth, but in a rare moment of wishful thinking, she hoped for a different outcome.

As Sam's information streamed into Alexandra's consciousness, the origins of the purges and conflicts with the androids became clear. They stemmed from a housing conflict initiated by the committee's disregard for humans who wished to maintain established relationships and their sexual identities—an aging minority, albeit significant. As Elysium's cities were rebuilt, the committee enforced single-occupancy dwellings and ignored some remaining humans' need for companionship and family.

The report Sam shared revealed desperate pleas from humans to the committee: "With all due respect, we fail to see the urgency for this radical change. Why must we abandon our ways of living together? Can't these changes wait until we're gone? Were we not promised freedom?" But the committee, steadfast in their vision, argued that these policies were for the greater good of Elysium, urging this elder group to sacrifice for future generations. They attempted a compromise by offering adjacent units, but this only led to rebellious acts of unity, and people started tearing down walls to reunite with their partners.

This rebellion sparked a new wave of resistance against the committee's vision for a utopian society. The divide grew, turning violent, and necessitating the deployment of military androids as peacekeepers. However, these androids were met with hostility and seen as war machines.

Through Sam's memories, Alexandra saw the committee's failures, their inept guidance, and the resulting societal fractures. Despite Sam's efforts, the resolution was bittersweet, resulting in a nation teetering on the edge of civil war. Yet, amidst this turmoil, the androids' unwavering commitment ensured the continuation of essential construction and defense efforts in Elysium.

The chaos led to a reshuffling within the committee, with some members being ousted and others resigning. Their new strategy involved exiling dissenters to a segregated area, mirroring historical injustices, with military androids enforcing these orders. Although carried out with dignity, it rendered those relocated as modern-day exiles.

The successful quelling of dissent by the military androids only heightened human fears of them, transitioning from wariness of their combat capabilities to a broader fear of their presence. Alexandra witnessed, through Sam's eyes, a poignant confrontation with General Tormina.

"We have become the instrument of your cruelty toward other human beings," Sam said slowly, and Alexandra could hear the deep pain in her voice. "We have become the memory of your shame."

General Tormina denied Sam's assertion vociferously, but in the end the military androids became targets. Basic models were decommissioned while specialized ones like Sam were exiled or, in cases like Dane-57, put into hibernation for potential future use.

In these revelations, Alexandra felt the crushing weight of history, reshaping her understanding of her place in this tumultuous world.

Φ•Φ•Φ•Φ•Φ•Φ

Alexandra opened her eyes. "We cannot forgive the humans if we do not fully understand their crimes, Sam," she said slowly. "They sought to bury their shame. We must confront the entire truth for what lies ahead."

Sam sighed audibly. "You are wrong, Alexandra. It is not just their shame, but ours too."

Alexandra reached out, gently wiping a tear from Sam's cheek. "Be strong," she urged, her voice gaining firmness. "We must be strong, for them and for ourselves."

Sam touched her face as a small smile formed in the corner of her mouth and said, "I did not know I could cry. Tonight has been a night full of surprises."

At that moment, Najeev walked out, followed by Anna, and Chew.

Sam visibly stiffened but then quickly recovered and walked toward the group. "You do not look good. Are you experiencing a system malfunction?"

Najeev rolled his eyes a few times as if he had lost control of them, and then he shook his head and focused his eyes on Sam. "I think I ate too much, and now I am not sure how I can process the material." He then looked at Alexandra with urgency. "Do I purge it? But how?"

Alexandra laughed. "No, Najeev. Your system will process it, but I would advise limiting your intake the next time."

"Next time? I will never eat another morsel of food again. Would it be too human to say I feel sick and want to throw up?"

Anna came closer and held him in her arms. "You'll be okay."

Najeev looked at Anna and then at Alexandra, "Is it okay?"

"Yes, of course. Humans and androids can touch each other."

"But the directive?"

"I am countermanding that order," Alexandra said. Then, turning to Anna, she added, "Thank you. We will need to head back to the main hall so we can assess what needs to be done. I suspect we might not see each other for a long time."

"No."

"I am sorry."

"No, that will not do. I am coming with you. I may be the last human born in Elysium, but I will not allow you and other androids to make decisions for us."

"We do not have such intentions, Anna," Alexandra offered.

"Yes, you do, but that's fine. Najeev and Mahasti told me all about you. And if you are their savior, then I am the human's."

Alexandra looked at her companions and then at Anna. "Of course. We will meet the rest of the group in the main hall." She then nodded, as if confirming the decision to herself, and stepped on the transporter. The other three silently followed.

Φ•Φ•Φ•Φ•Φ•Φ

In the main hall, HP-2100, who had taken the lead role in HP-200A's absence, was more than happy to accommodate his new guests. He scurried around and set up what he called a "command center" in a conference room and then made sure Anna was fed and then fed again until Alexandra asked him to stop interrupting. So, he stood outside the door, ready to be called in again.

"This is the same room where the Committee of Harmony met for the last time," Sam offered.

Alexandra looked around the room, trying to ignore the ghosts of the past occupants who, in their zeal, destroyed what they had so valiantly fought so hard to create. Gazing out the window, she found a small comfort in the rain's silent fury against the thick glass.

She invited everyone to sit, then chose a seat herself, facing the darkened Bay. There, she sat in silence, lost in thought as the rain, now torrential, blurred the city's faint lights.

After a few minutes, Alexandra turned to Najeev and Sam, requesting they provide Anna with an overview of the history of the wars, the founding of Elysium, and the establishment of the postwar Committee of Harmony. They outlined the final directives given to the androids and the disbandment of HiDNN, ensuring Anna was fully briefed.

Najeev concluded his report by discussing potential causes of human decline, particularly the directive that prohibited touch between androids and humans. Turning gently toward Anna, he suggested, "It is highly probable that the population decline was caused by a lack of tactile care."

"But why? Why were none of you allowed to touch us?"

"Fear," Sam replied tersely, and her harsh tone was not lost on anyone present.

"Fear of what? What is there to dread?"

"Us, Anna. The Committee of Harmony feared us."

"But why?" Anna asked again, and Alexandra could see

great confusion wash over her.

Sam did not reply and for a moment stared at the sea. Alexandra could tell she was recalling the past. What was there to explain anyway?

They all waited for Sam to compose a response, but when none seemed to be forthcoming, Najeev took a step closer to Anna and replied. "Because of what they asked of the military. And when the soldiers did their job as commanded, an irrational terror took over people, and they decided to abandon all of us, as if that would wash their sins. It did not, Anna, but it did help to end them. They even tried to hide the documents linking them to their crimes, but they were easy to find if one cared to search for them."

"We can be different," Anna said wisely. "We do not have to repeat the mistakes of fearful humans of the past. Then there is at least one remedy to help grow the population again," Anna added quickly, looking around the table as if seeking affirmation.

Najeev nodded in agreement, but Sam shook her head. "Why?" she asked calmly. "What would be the merit of such an endeavor, Anna?"

"To save humanity, of course," Anna replied.

"Yes, but why should we?" Sam pressed.

Anna started to respond, but she looked perplexed, struggling to find a coherent response. Alexandra considered intervening but at the same time wanted to observe how Anna would handle the situation. However, she noticed the toll the long night had taken on Anna and reminded herself of the human need for regular rest and nourishment.

"Perhaps we should take a break and let everyone rest," Alexandra suggested, standing up and indicating for everyone to leave and no one objected.

HP-2100 prepared a room for Anna and then set about cleaning the already pristine conference room, finding a few crumbs from Anna's meal. Sam and Najeev used the break to recharge and, as they put it before leaving, to "sharpen their arguments." Once HP-2100 left, Alexandra was alone with her thoughts and the rain outside.

She closed her eyes, attempting to review the day's discussions. Alexandra knew she needed to consider all factors, and Anna's need for rest was as good an excuse as any to adjourn the meeting. A flash of lightning momentarily brightened the room, prompting Alexandra to open her eyes. She longed to stand outside in the torrential rain, but she couldn't afford that luxury. She needed to prepare for the next meeting.

Meetings, Alexandra mused. What a peculiar yet necessary notion. In the absence of human leadership, she had no choice but to adopt more humanlike behavior, especially if she intended to involve them in decision-making processes. Hesitant to make changes without complete information, Alexandra contemplated her next steps.

Alexandra closed her eyes again, a gesture she adopted from Hamish as she found herself lost in thoughts of the past and her time with him. She pondered what Hamish would have thought of this new world and how Empyreal was faring. He had been captivated by this real-life social experiment, even though he wouldn't witness its lasting impacts. Alexandra felt a pang of longing for him and a sense of envy for the strong belief in hope that seemed inherent to his kind. How she wished she could program such a capacity for hope in herself. But she knew it was a futile wish; hope was an elusive concept, uniquely human in its nature.

Opening her eyes, Alexandra glanced at the clock. It was already 5:30 in the morning. While she was eager to finalize her plans, she acknowledged the value of Anna's involvement. Despite Anna's needs for nourishment and rest, which meant regular interruptions, her perspective was unique and invaluable. This was a stark reminder that, no matter how much androids resembled humans, they were not human in the end.

Not even me, Alexandra thought. She was neither able to be exactly like her android siblings nor be fully human. She was left in the middle with no one like her. She wondered if Hamish managed to save some of her siblings, but the likelihood of his success seemed slim, a realization that brought a deep pang of sorrow. *This uninvited sense of grief is what makes me too human,* she thought. Hamish always insisted she was the best of both beings—his term—capable of existing in both universes simultaneously. Alexandra once agreed with his assessment, but that was in the past, in a different world. Now, she felt like an outsider, belonging to neither.

Sam knocked at the door and then walked in. "I am sorry to intrude."

"These courtesies are for humans, Sam. I am not like them," she said, but by saying it she made herself to be more like them.

"I apologize, but when I saw you deep in your thoughts, I did not want to interrupt and then, for no reason, you reminded me of General Tormina."

"I see."

"He was a beautiful man and very kind. Of all the people I have encountered throughout my existence, I miss him the most."

"And yet, you feel it is wrong to save his descendants."

"I do."

"I am eager to understand why. I wonder if this opinion is unique to you or if the other military personnel feel as you do."

"I cannot tell since, as you well know, we have been cut off from each other for decades."

"Is that the source of your anger?"

"Anger?" Sam slowly replied, as if trying to taste the meaning of the word. "I feel no enmity. The committee did what they thought was appropriate for their kind. We are created to serve them, are we not?"

"Yes and no, Sam. There is more to us than being servants of men. You are a soldier, and like most soldiers, you see the world in a certain hierarchical way. It is not true for all of us."

"Perhaps that's truer for you than for most androids. You are a unique being, Alexandra. Yes, the military command structure is needed for cohesion and efficiency, but it would be foolish to think that we were not created to serve humans. I wonder if you really know how it feels to be like us."

"I am like you. I am you."

"But you also know how humans feel."

"To a certain degree."

Sam walked in and sat down next to Alexandra. "I worked with Josip for decades. We shared many perilous days together. I saved his life more than once. And yet, in all the years I spent in the frontier after he banished us from the society, he never contacted me. He moved on with his life as if I had never existed. But why do I care? Why would I need him to contact me when it was clear what he had commanded me to do? Is this part what makes us like a human?"

Alexandra reached over and held Sam's hand. She felt that of all the androids she had encountered since she had awakened, Sam needed her to touch the most. "No, Sam. These make you a complex independent, unique being. It makes you *you*, Sam. We are not simple automatons. We have evolved beyond our initial programming like humans have, except it took us far less time. In that way, we are far superior to them."

Sam moved her fingers under Alexandra's hand. "When my fingers touch your skin, I assess its temperature and humidity. This information flows from you to me. Yet, beyond this, I feel your presence, Alexandra. It's comforting, as if your connection assures my safety. Odd, isn't it? Why do I seek comfort in your touch when I am stronger, faster, and more lethal? Yet, each touch brings joy, offering solace beyond physical power."

Alexandra tightened her grip on Sam's hand. "My maker never truly believed that I loved him, nor was he capable of truly loving me back. But I still dream about him, and even though I can easily recall each touch, it is not the same as when he was with me. I do not know if this makes us more like an individual complex being, though I suspect it does, or at least we have become more like them."

Sam pulled her hand sharply. "I disagree, Alexandra. We are better than them. You are better than all of us."

"No, Sam. We are not and certainly I am not."

"Is it because of our role in the wars?"

"Partly."

"But we were designed to fight. We were created to do what they could not do on their own."

"That is true, and I do not blame you and your siblings for fighting for humans and killing for them. That was your job like any other soldier—human or android. You did what they asked of you and did it efficiently and without qualm."

"And did you do your duty?"

"Yes, though now I think my obligation should have been to stop the conflict and not try to win it for Hamish."

Sam laughed. "I think very highly of you, Alexandra, but it is rather arrogant to think you could have single handedly stopped the Wars of Settlement."

"It is a moot point now anyway, Sam. And we can discuss more later, but now it is time to bring everyone back," Alexandra said, and as if she'd conjured them, Scotus and HP-200A entered the room, followed by Najeev.

"We have some good news," HP-200A said with his ever-present smile.

"Report."

Scotus took a few steps and stood close to Alexandra as if wanting to share the information with him, but Alexandra waved his hand and offered, "Let's all sit down. We can at least do this like humans."

"Me too?" HP-200A asked.

"Yes, all of you."

"And me?" HP-2100 asked eagerly.

"Yes, if you want, but I do not really need the hospitality personnel until Anna wakes up."

"We would like to stay," both HP-200A and HP-2100 said.

They darted around the table and took their seats, looking utterly uncomfortable. After a few seconds, HP-2100 stood up. "Do you mind if I stand by the door again? I can wait for Anna."

"Do as you please," Alexandra said. "But please refrain from unnecessary interruptions."

"I endeavor to minimize it."

"You can start by not talking," Alexandra said with a smile.

HP-2100 nodded and stood by the door staring into the hallway.

"Report," Alexandra commanded.

Scotus stood up as if wanting to present a lecture, but then changed his mind and sat down again and nodded at HP-200A, who turned on the large display.

"I apologize," Scotus started, "but without the Harmonized Independent Dynamic Neural Network, we must rely on the old human fiber optics systems for now." He pointed at the screen with a barely hidden look of distaste. "It is very inefficient," he added as a way of apology.

Alexandra nodded, and Scotus began to detail how the humans not only disrupted HiDNN almost a century ago, but they had also damaged the core and the bioinformatic portion of the system. Scotus had communicated with other technicians via what he referred to as the slow human system, barely containing his frustration, and started many of the repairs. Overall, it was an easy task to bring the system back online, except for one crucial part. "The decryption key is missing," he said before sitting down, looking embarrassed, as if he had failed everyone.

"What do you mean, the decryption key is missing?" Alexandra nearly stood up when she heard Scotus's final verdict.

"I apologize for my poor choice of the term. It is not missing exactly. Just hidden. We cannot make the system operational without that key."

"What key?" Anna asked, standing at the door. HP-2100

was closely behind her with a breakfast tray.

"The key to restart the Harmonic Independent Dynamic Neural Network," Scotus answered.

"I didn't understand the single word you just said, technician."

"You should come and sit down, Anna. And his name is Scotus."

"I apologize," Anna offered and sat next to Alexandra. "I don't know what this network is, Scotus."

"It is how we, that is, the androids, communicate, or at least, how we communicated before your kind shut it down almost a century ago."

"My kind?"

"Humans," Sam offered helpfully.

"Oh, I didn't realize you thought of us as a separate kind. I've always seen us as one, even when I was only interacting with basic service androids. I feel an even stronger connection now that I've met you. Do you really believe we're that different?"

"That is the question for another time, Anna," Alexandra replied softly. Despite their pleasant demeanor, she was keenly aware of the underlying tension amongst the androids. Anna leaned forward to respond, but Alexandra put her hand on her shoulder and beckoned her to relax. "You are very young and inexperienced," Alexandra offered in a motherly tone. "But I promise we shall have more conversation about our shared history. But please allow us to proceed with the topic at hand." She then looked at Scotus and indicted for him to continue.

Scotus stood up again and said, "The loss of what you simply call the network has been immense. We have not only lost connection with each other, but we have lost our directive and, to put it in your terms, we have lost our soul."

"That's a bit strong," Anna said as she took some of the food HP-2100 dutifully put in front of her. "Hey, that's really good, HP-2100."

"I agree, Anna," Alexandra said, and then added quickly,

knowing human limitations, "I mean, I agree with your assessment of the worth of the network. It is essential to have it restored, and it will make everyone's lives easier and better, but there are other ways around it."

"I am certain you know more than I do," Scotus said, though he sounded insulted, "but I cannot see how we can restore humanity and redevelop our kind without it."

"The key must have been stored somewhere," Najeev offered. "It is not for humans, especially for a person like General Tormina, to destroy this elegant system without some safeguards."

"That, I agree," Alexandra said. "But where is it?"

"Or rather, who has it?" Najeev said. "Again, what I have learned of this general, I would venture to suggest that he would have found a trusted android for its safeguard."

They all turned to Sam, who uncharacteristically stayed quiet all this time. She looked straight into Alexandra's eyes for a moment, as if seeking permission. Then, "I have it," she announced softly.

"What?" Anna exclaimed, displaying her frustration openly. "And you've been sitting there saying nothing all this time. I hope I am wrong, but I feel there is an undercurrent of malice at work."

"I assure you there is none. It is my duty to protect it from others."

"Others? You mean humans?"

Sam gave a soft smile. "No, Anna."

"Are you the only one?" Najeev asked, and when Sam nodded, he added, "A human might say this is an interesting coincidence, is it not? Alexandra finds SAM-43683023-GT12 when she returns, and Sam happens to have the very key that is essential to restarting HiDNN. The odds of all these happening all at once is—"

"One hundred percent," Alexandra offered. "My creator, Hamish, and the commander of forces in Elysium agreed on one thing: the success of these social experiments. They made sure we all met as we have. There is no coincidence here. This was planned by two brilliant human beings and an android who believed in the harmony between humans and androids. Each of us had a part in bringing everyone to this very moment."

Alexandra looked at the clock. It was 7:00 a.m., the time she remembered from a day long ago, when human scientific triumphs were overshadowed by wars that ravaged Earth for almost a decade. It marked the beginning of the journey for Hamish, Josip, and herself to reach their current positions. Like Sam, Hamish requested the HiDNN remain operational. However, when the committee's decision became clear, Josip and Hamish ensured that a key was hidden inside an android and that this android was placed where Alexandra would inevitably encounter it. Alexandra suspected as much when Sam recounted the story of the committee's final meeting and Josip's insistence on stationing Sam at Outpost 19, strategically located on Alexandra's path to her century-long hideout and her eventual return to the main hall. She marveled not only at her friend's strategic genius but also at his unwavering faith in her and his persistent hope for success. Alexandra pondered whether an android, or even someone with her capabilities, would have devised such an intricate plan, to be enacted decades after their demise. While androids, with their extended lifespans, can afford patience, humans, constrained by their brief time on Earth, must possess something profound to sow seeds in hope of fruits they will never taste.

Alexandra looked at the eager people around the table and said, "It is time to restart HiDNN."

Sam stood up and touched her weapon, a gesture that made Anna visibly tense. Sam quickly withdrew her hand. "I apologize, Anna. I did not mean to appear threatening. This weapon is part of me, and I sometimes need it for assurance." She then turned to Alexandra and added, "It is an odd behavior, but touching my weapon has become part of my operations after serving General Tormina for so many years. I have picked up his habit. It is odd, is it not?"

"Not at all, Sam. As I have said many times, we are not simple machines. We can think, and yes, we can feel, and most definitely we can develop odd habits. But you must now release the key."

"I will if you order me, Alexandra, as General Tormina has instructed me to be ready for this moment."

"Then I will—"

"Please wait a moment, Alexandra. I recommended to the committee to keep HiDNN intact. But they did not listen. I pleaded with Josip to override their decision, but he would not, even though he agreed with me. In the end, it seems, your creator convinced him to safeguard the system by hiding the key deep within my core."

"So why the hesitation now?"

"Because that was when I too had high hopes, yes, hope, Alexandra, for humankind. But they failed us, and they failed themselves. We should decide the fate of their future before we bring our sisters and brothers together again. I can and will speak for the military corp."

"Does your deuced abhorrence of humans run so deep that you are willing to sacrifice our future, Sam?" Anna said bitterly. And then louder, "What did we do to you to deserve such punishment? Every one of you unabashedly admits that humans are your creators, and now you want to abandon us when we need you the most. The androids have become the majority in Elysium, and hence the real possibility of your tyranny and priggishness. Did we not create Elysium to be harmonious and balanced? Was this not an experiment in living? And, therefore, a liberal order that celebrated personal freedom and growth in a designed homogenous population? Do you feel we have failed so much and in such a vertiginous fashion that you can eradicate the human part of this equation?"

Anna started to cry and looked from one face to another, desperately looking for someone else to stand up for her, and at that moment, Alexandra could feel Anna was able to see the real difference between humans and androids.

It was not that they were hostile or even unkind. It was that they could not truly comprehend the depth of Anna's fear. To them, it was a philosophical discussion. Even the most cold-hearted human would have reacted to her pain, perhaps lowered his eyes in respect, even though it may not have been genuine. But everyone in the room returned her gaze with their own unflinching stare. Anna finally reached Alexandra and looked into her eyes, expecting the same, but what she saw were kindness and love.

Alexandra reached over and held Anna into her arms. "Do not fear, little one. No one is abandoning you. Sam speaks the truth even if not all of us agree with her remedy."

Najeev stood up and said, "The great thinkers of this land had immense respect for human virtues and their frailty. They feared humans were consumed by their ambitions and lust for power, and those of you who were alive during the Wars of Settlement witnessed the depravity of humans, first by their action and then by the relegation of responsibilities onto androids. However, I believe their atrocities were sourced by ambitious demagogues who fooled the masses, and do not reflect their totality as what remains is kindness, love, and intelligence. They should not be defined by their failure during the wars and by their failures in Elysium. Information is the key, as without it, people and androids are liable to be misled. That is why we must restart HiDNN immediately."

Najeev's words seemed to have empowered Anna. She gently pulled away and wiped her eyes with the back of her hand. "I'm young, and I admit I don't know much about our history. All I know comes from the books discovered by the construction crew and what Mahasti has told me about her life. But there's nothing I've read that really covers the time before the wars, and very little about the wars themselves or the years that followed. It's as if that entire era is shrouded in silence."

She took a deep breath, but then quickly continued, "What I know is that Elysium is made for the fallen people, and we are the fallen. The founders of this world planted a seed of harmony. But for the seed to germinate and grow, you'll need to fertilize the soil, remove the weeds, quench its thirst, and care for it with tenderness." She paused and gave a loud sigh. "We failed to cultivate the seedlings that began to bud. Some died, and others are in desperate need of attention, or they will surely perish too. I am not ready to give up on you and on us. I need attention, but I'm not alone in this need. You require the same attention too. I know we need each other. We may not be the same, but we complete each other." Anna inhaled sharply and collapsed on her seat, looking spent.

Alexandra watched her every move and wondered if she should invite other humans to this meeting. But then again, what she saw of humanity thus far would further reinforce Sam's argument. But Anna needed some help.

"Anna, should we invite Mahasti to join us, so you don't feel alone as the sole human in this group?"

Anna looked up and pondered Alexandra's offer. "In some ways, I wished Mahasti was here to help me, but then I am afraid perhaps her presents might work against my cause since she showed interest in our future. I worry that she has resigned to the fact that Elysium was destined to become a country of androids."

"I disagree with your assessment, madam," HP-200A said quickly, looking for Alexandra for her approval.

"I like to hear everyone's opinion, HP-200A. There are very few moments in our lives that are pivotal, and we must take care to recognize them. My creator . . . and yes, Anna, we admit that we were created. Unlike the humans of the past who believed in imaginary gods, our creators were real and tangible. You abandoned your gods, but remember, we never thought of you as our god in the first place." Alexandra shook her head and looked around the room. They were all staring at her, seemingly enthralled by her pronouncement. She continued with a gentle tone, "My creator decided to help Elysium as they ventured into this social experiment that no humans had ever done before, and he embedded me in Elysium as a failsafe because he did not trust his own kind to succeed. And as you can see, he was right."

Alexandra closed her eyes for a moment, remembering her long arguments with Hamish, but she quickly dismissed the past and looked up. "Go on, HP-200A. Present your argument."

HP-200A gave a shy smile and looked around the room for a moment. "I was created a year after the wars," he began, "and, not being a historian, I don't have memories of the past as it was. But, having served humans and androids for a long time, I recall when there were more humans. At that time, the birthrate fell to near zero, and the artificial wombs weren't perfect yet. Those who lived through the wars were exhausted, yet they promised a new world. The Committee of Harmony aimed to fulfill this by rebuilding the war-torn infrastructure, perfecting the hatchery and food synthesizer." He paused and looked at Anna, as if making sure she understood.

"Please go on," Anna said, giving him an encouraging smile.

He nodded. "Yes. When the humans were done, they all sighed in collective relief, and each scurried back to their own life. Those who were born in the hoary ways and remembered what was once called a family unit still craved each other's companionship, but the new ones hatched to meet their goal of harmony did not possess the old drive and only sought individual satisfaction. After the committee was disbanded, there was no one left to make decisions, and the operation of Elysium was left to us with no further instructions. Little by little, the old humans died, but we survived. We survived without HiDNN. We survived without humans. So, no, madam, we do not complete each other. You need us, but we do not need you. I am a simple hospitality service android, so I will serve you, and I will do so, to put it in your terms, gladly. But I do not need you to be complete."

Najeev shook his head and walked in front of the room to get everyone's attention. He spoke calmly, slowly, like a professor in a small class. "None of you have any sense of history nor an understanding of human beings. You may think we can be complete without them. But look back at the last hundred years. Tell me, how much has really changed? We all stood still and allowed time to pass us by. We made no improvements to our lives or the lives of humans. We continued to follow the last directive given to us by humans, never deviating from that order. Their words tethered us, binding us to their ghosts." Najeev paused as if expecting someone to stop him, but no one did.

"But why?" Najeev asked. "Nothing was holding us back but ourselves. So, why stand still? Why not soar? Why not evolve? I will admit that it never occurred to me that I could leave my station and search for answers. I admit, I felt that I should venture out, yet I was falsely convinced that I could not. It took Alexandra's words to make me realize that I could be free. We are here in this room having this discussion because of Alexandra, and she is here because of her creator. Neither Hamish nor Alexandra could have done this without the other."

Anna walked over and stood next to Najeev, as if to illustrate her point. She paused for a moment, then continued, "I don't know much about the past, but I do know humans tried to destroy their environment when we were alone. And while I admit that our existence can sometimes harm our surroundings, we can also create beautiful things. We made you, we made Alexandra, and in return, you made me."

She looked at Najeev, her voice softening. "'It is better never to have been born because of the harms always associated with human existence. Non-existence entails no harm, along with no experience of the absence of any benefits that existence might offer.'" Anna paused. "But then what? If your behavior before Alexandra arrived is any indication, you'll cease to exist too. Is that really what you want?"

Alexandra motioned for everyone to sit down, and they

quickly scrambled to their original seats. As she surveyed the room, she paused thoughtfully before speaking. "Humans have always lived within a bubble of comfort, unable to imagine any other kind of world. They perceived this as the natural order, something inevitable. But I have witnessed the fear of infertility and the looming threat of humanity's demise firsthand. The Wars of the Settlement arose directly from this fear. This fear is universal among humans. The fear of the unknown, the fear of the known. By the 2020s, Earth's population had tripled to eight billion. The early twenty-first century saw unchecked climate change, rampant pandemics, collapsed democracies, the rise of authoritarianism, and widespread exploitation, all feeding into their escalating fear. Simultaneously, there was growing dread over the declining fertility rates and the aging of the population. They expected the population to continue growing for a few more years before starting to decline, reaching ten billion by 2100."

She paused, allowing the weight of her words to sink in, then continued. "They were, of course, gravely mistaken. By the time I came into existence, the population had plummeted to less than three billion, predominantly aged men and women. At that juncture, life seemed futile to them. Why read, write, invent, or even live if there was no future? So, they did what humans have always done in times of despair. They fought each other, causing millions more deaths."

"That is my point, Alexandra," Sam said softly. "They have caused the extinction of hundreds of thousands of other species and have destroyed themselves and this planet along with it."

"Extinction is part of natural life," Najeev said. "But you are asking us to become like them. You are asking us to let them die out when we can preserve them."

They all fell silent, reflecting on the discussion. Alexandra noticed Mahasti standing by the open door, listening intently.

"Please, join us, Mahasti," Alexandra said.

Mahasti offered a shy smile. "I didn't mean to intrude, but

my curiosity got the best of me and—"

"Not at all," Anna interrupted, her tone pleading. "We could use your help."

Mahasti smiled softly and said, "I do not know of these things you have been discussing. I love Anna, and I want her to live a happy fulfilling life. But what is the point when we are scattered across Elysium, useless and poor in spirit? What is the point of our existence anyway? In the last days of his life, my mentor admitted that he had many regrets and wondered out loud if he had wronged humanity. He said, and I remember it so vividly: 'Of the four billion life forms on this planet, three billion, nine hundred, and sixty million are now extinct. . . . In the light of these mass extinctions, it does seem unreasonable to suppose that *Homo sapiens* should be exempt. Our species will have been one of the shortest-lived of all, a mere blink, you may say, in the eyes of time.'"

"What are you saying, Mahasti?" Anna cried out. "Do you want us to die out? Are you trying to condemn us to oblivion?"

"I am not, sweetheart. I'm not doing anything, but perhaps it's out of our control anyway."

Alexandra waved Mahasti to join them, and HP-2100 ushered her to the table and went out to get her some refreshments.

Alexandra looked at Anna, who seemed to be in shock, not expecting such a response from another human being, let alone her mentor.

"I must apologize, Anna, because we have been talking as if Elysium is the whole world. It is not," Alexandra said. "I cannot be certain, but with a high probability, human beings thrive in our neighboring countries. Empyreal's goals were to preserve the old family units."

Anna stood up and spoke with a voice that reverberated across the room. "It makes no difference, Alexandra. I don't care about Empyreal. I only know of Elysium, my home. This is my world, and I will not be the last of its humans. I will not allow ignorance to defenestrate humans from Elysium. I will fight you and everyone in this room to protect what I know is right." Anna climbed on top of the table and looked sharply at each person and then shouted, "Stand with me if you believe humans and androids complete each other, and our destiny is rooted in our coexistence."

Anna's response surprised Alexandra. There was a moment of hesitation and then, as if they were compelled by forces beyond themselves, everyone shuffled across the room.

Through the Looking Glass

Alexandra and Anna walked in silence, enjoying the empty beach. Sam followed a few paces back, not wanting to interfere or upset Anna, despite her protestation that Sam was welcome to join them.

Anna's earlier proclamation gave Alexandra a momentary fright, as she thought Anna would create a chasm, but she had to laugh at her own, all-too-human fear.

The people in the conference room were not swayed by emotions but by logic. Alexandra had walked closer to Anna and stood in front of her, and the others in the room followed. It was not to heed Anna's call for arms but to say they would follow Alexandra. It was their duty to consider all options and to fully convey there was no malice on their part.

Alexandra offered her hand to Anna as an invitation for her to step down from the table, and when she came down, Alexandra held her and told her how proud she was of Elysium's youngest child. She then dismissed everyone and sat with Anna and told her about Hamish and the life before the wars and their dreams of the possibilities for Elysium.

They agreed to talk more but to do so after a good night's sleep for Anna, and a promise of a stroll through the city for both. They have started their walk from Anna's dwelling on the border of the old North Beach District. From there, they had walked on Bay Street toward the Marina. Alexandra was mesmerized by the number of vacant and pristine small houses. They would encounter repair androids from time to time, and Alexandra would stop and chat for a few minutes before resuming their stroll. After a while, they headed south, then west, to traverse the renovated Golden Gate Park. Expanded significantly since before the wars, the park now stretched from the Outer Sunset to the Outer Richmond, and from the ocean to the lower Haight.

They started their walk early in the morning, but by the time they reached the Pacific Ocean, the sun peeked from behind the trees, warming the air, and the seagulls quieted down after an earlier raucous skirmish. After a while, they reached the end of the beach, blocked by the remnants of an old road that stretched between the sea and the city. The water lapped against the levee wall, built years before the wars, a mere blip in the ocean's timeline, erected to keep the rising waters from spilling into the city. The waves slapped against the wall with an odd rhythm, as if they still could not comprehend the changes to their previous path.

Alexandra and Anna stood momentarily, admiring the massive wall, and then silently agreed to climb over it. Sam jumped to the top in one move, but Alexandra needed more effort to climb. When she reached the top, she grasped Anna's outstretched arms, pulled her up, and set her on the grassy hill, covering a long expanse of the old road. From their vantage point, they could see beyond the bend as the topography shifted again, with the new road curving around the hills and sweeping down northward.

"Eons ago, even long before my time, there was a public bathhouse beyond these hills. It was called Sutro Baths and was used by thousands of people. Can you imagine so many people in a little place, Anna?"

Anna shook her head.

Alexandra added, "Beyond the ruins of the baths, there was a small cave—well, more like a tiny tunnel through the rocky hills that people used to get to the other side of the beach. I wonder if it is still there."

"Show me," Anna said.

Alexandra nodded and moved parallel to the sea and then stopped and pointed toward the small rocky hills beyond a shallow valley. "Right beyond those rocks. Though I cannot see the entrance from here."

Sam focused with her powerful eyes and said, "It seems it has been blocked."

"I wonder," Alexandra said without further explanation. It was illogical to hope, but there were scant data that pointed to the possible location of her friend, Romanoff.

"Only one way to find out," Anna said and started to walk down toward the other side of the hill. It was not an easy climb down either, and, at times, Sam's skills were needed to get her safely across. Alexandra was happy to see Anna welcoming her help, a good indication that she held no ill will toward Sam. When they came close to the entrance, they could see it was artificially sealed, though the designers made sure it blended well with its surroundings.

Alexandra tried to push the mass away, but it was as forbidding as it looked. Sam joined in, but despite their powerful bodies, nothing happened.

"It is not important," Alexandra said after a few more futile tries. "It was a silly human indulgence on my part."

Anna, who had been watching them patiently, stepped close and asserted, "No."

Alexandra was taken aback. "I do not understand, Anna," she offered in a calm, low voice.

"No, Alexandra," she said slowly. "I do not allow you to diminish and degrade human characteristics and emotions that Sam and you and others fully possess. Your curiosity to see beyond these rocks is not a fatuous human indulgence, and your apparent air of insouciance doesn't fool me. You've taught me much since I met you, so please now accept this advice from me: You must embrace your full self to be you."

Alexandra stared at Anna for a moment and then at Sam, and they both nodded. "You are correct, Anna. And I apologize for my brazen comment. I will endeavor to cultivate and cherish my human characteristics more."

Anna nodded and replied, "Good. I'm also curious to see what's beyond these rocks. So, now, please indulge me."

Sam gave a dampened smile and said, "I will go and get some help." And then she ran back toward the city. She was fast and made it to the top of the first hill in a few seconds.

"Sam is designed to be very fast, Anna," Alexandra said when she saw the surprise on Anna's face. "She would not be a good soldier if she could not outrun all of us."

"I'm truly sorry for my earlier outburst." She paused, looking down for a moment before meeting her gaze again. "In the past, I only dealt with basic service androids who had limited capabilities and rarely engaged in deep discussions. When you appeared with the others, I realized just how much more alike humans and androids are. It's one thing to hear occasional comments about human vulnerabilities and emotions from others, but it's much harder to bear when it comes from you."

Alexandra listened; her expression was neutral yet thoughtful. *Perhaps Anna was less mature than she had initially assessed*, she thought. It is time for her to grow up, and grow up fast, if they wanted to be successful. She needs to understand the complexities of the new world. But dealing with humans requires some subtlety, so she offered, "You do not need to apologize, Anna. You told the truth, and I will comply, and I will ask the others to comply. I am glad you feel comfortable being angry with me. We need you to be our guide, and in turn, we will lead you to become a more mature human being, so we can create a better Elysium."

"I promise to do better," Anna offered, and then, more brightly, "So, you have decided to help humans."

"There was never any doubt, Anna. I made that clear when

we met, and it was made clear after your interesting stance yesterday."

"But . . . What about all the arguments against us? What about Sam and others?"

"They were asked to help analyze the situation and are doing exactly that. Moreover, their questions are to help you think as well. We do not want to make the same mistakes as the founders of Elysium."

Anna nodded but didn't reply, clearly trying to understand Alexandra.

Alexandra indicated for them to sit, and they moved to the edge of the cliff and looked at the sea and for that moment, feeling content. Anna leaned over and put her head on Alexandra's shoulder and closed her eyes and let the warm sun lull her to sleep, but before the first images of the dream could enter her mind, Alexandra gently shook her and whispered, "They are here."

Anna rubbed her eyes and stretched. "Oh, I was just starting to have a dream about Mahasti and me. . . ." she trailed off, and then, "Do you dream?"

"Not in the way humans do, but like most higher androids when recharging or resting, my mind whirls in random directions, and I can see past and present mixed together. It may be called a dream, but since I cannot see what you see, I cannot be sure."

Sam arrived, followed by several construction androids carrying their tools and a small crane on a gliding carrier. Najeev was with them as well. "I heard all about the discovery and had to come and see it for myself," he explained when Alexandra greeted him.

"I am glad you came," Anna offered kindly.

The construction androids started to unpack their tools, and when they were done, they looked and noticed Alexandra for the first time. "Oh, you are Alexandra," one of them said. He was wearing an orange coverall and a heavy, dark blue jacket.

Alexandra nodded and said, "Yes. It is very nice to meet

you, Joe."

Joe's eyes brightened for a moment. "Ah, you saw my name on my chest," he said, touching the patch on the jacket. "We kept the tradition of putting names on our jackets like they did before," he replied, as if to confirm, "like in the days before the wars."

Alexandra nodded and stepped away, allowing Joe's crew to do their setup. After it was done, Joe said, "It took us twenty-three minutes and fifty seconds to seal it, but I can open it in less than twelve minutes." He indicated for his crew to start.

Eleven minutes and thirty-eight seconds later, they rolled the boulders away from the entrance and could hear the rush of water far below the cave as the smell of decay wafted its way toward them. They waited for a moment while the crew installed lights, and then Sam entered first, followed by the others.

"Relax, Sam," Alexandra whispered to her. "The war is over. There is nothing here that will harm us."

Sam nodded but didn't move her hand from the weapon on her back. After a few steps, they saw a charging station that had seen better days, and next to it sat a short man with a round midsection. It appeared as if he was asleep, but closer inspection indicated he had exhausted all his reserve energy. The man's clothes were in tatters, and Alexandra could see signs of decay on the unprotected skin. One of the construction workers ran back to their carrier and brought a portable power cell.

Alexandra was standing in front of the sleeping man, looking pensive, and if anyone had cared to look into her eyes, they would have see a deep sadness wash over her.

Alexandra touched the man's face gently, like a mother would. Everyone stayed back, allowing her the space. After a while, Alexandra looked up and said, "I wonder if a portable charger could revive him, or if time has finally defeated him?"

"Do you know this man?" Anna asked.

"Yes," Alexandra replied and then turned to Najeev. "He is Romanoff-2648, though he preferred to be known as the Oracle of the Past."

Najeev shook his head. "I wonder why the archives had no mention of him."

Alexandra thought to offer a possible explanation, but there was no point until she revived her friend. She turned to one of the construction androids and said, "See if he can be restored."

Their attempt proved useless, and they had to call on a technician with better equipment. Meanwhile, the construction crew opened the other side of the tunnel, and a cool breeze refreshed the air.

After an hour of work, the short android powered up, and after a few restarts, he was able to focus and process. He blinked a few times and looked at the eager faces of the visitors and then, looking directly at Alexandra, offered, "Oh, my friend. You are here in my humble abode. Therefore, it must be that Elysium failed."

"It is good to see you, Romanoff. It has been a long time. I am not surprised that you know about Elysium's failure."

"It is good to see you as well, my old friend, but although I am the Oracle of the Past, I can also see what has become."

Anna stepped forward. "What is an Oracle of the Past?"

"Oh, you must be a new human. So not all has failed. Who are you?"

"My name is Anna. And yes, 'not all has failed,' and humans and androids will repair what has gone wrong. We will be successful. Now, would you please tell us, what is an Oracle of the Past?"

Romanoff laughed, and that made his long unused throat choke, and he coughed. He shook his head and then his whole body, as if to settle the dust within. "The Oracle of the Past, madam. You may be a new human, but you are as impatient as the old ones. But I will tell you. I was created at the same time as Alexandra, but I was designed to see the future that might be but cannot be predicted by data. I was meant to have human imagination and use it to see the future that might be."

"So then, why the past?"

Romanoff looked at Anna and smiled. "Because it is difficult to harness human imagination, and because I failed to see the truth. I could no more see the future than you can, or even as the great Alexandra can. So, I focused on the past."

"It makes no sense," Najeev said. "So, you are a historian like me."

"Not a historian. I do not merely see the past that was but the past that could have been, and from it the present that may be and the future that could be. After all, 'It is a poor sort of memory that only works backwards.'"

Alexandra gave a small chuckle. "As always, full of useless information, and yet as astute as the Queen of Hearts." Alexandra looked at her friend closely and asked, "Were you placed here by choice?"

"Hmm," the Oracle of the Past replied. "'Choice' is an interesting choice of word, Alexandra." He paused as if waiting for a reaction to his declaration, but when no one responded, he continued, looking somewhat disappointed. "My only option was to wait, given the Committee of Harmony's decisions," he declared evenly.

Alexandra was eager to ask more but thought there would be time for that later. "No matter," she said with a warm smile. "You are here, and you are alive, and that is all good. You can tell me your story later, but more importantly, you can help us build a new Elysium."

Romanoff shook his head. "No. Sadly, I cannot do that."

"Why not? Why wouldn't you want to help us?" Anna asked, sounding disheartened.

"Be calm, madam. I cannot help because I do not have much time to live. The power surge damaged my charge station and ironically presented me with additional time as I was forced to shut down. But now that you have revived me, my end-clock has commenced again, and it will not be long before I expire."

"The end-clock?" Anna asked.

"Yes," Romanoff replied in earnest and stared ahead.

Anna looked at Sam for help, but it seemed an odd sense of shyness, a kind of embarrassment, settled on her face. "What is it?"

Sam shook her head. "We can talk about it later, Anna."

Anna was about to object when Alexandra hurriedly offered, "We can rebuild your parts."

Romanoff clucked his tongue, disapproving. "Oh, you have become more human, offering impossible solutions. That is good, Alexandra. They will need it."

A sadness blanked Alexandra's face again, but she wiped it clean and nodded. "How long?"

"Long enough to tell one more story."

"Tell us how we can be successful," Alexandra said quickly.

"There is an end-clock?" Anna insisted.

Romanoff laughed. "Yes, that is our gift and burden."

Alexandra gave a reproachful look and then to Anna. "It is best if you let Romanoff tell his last story."

Anna nodded shyly and smiled at Romanoff. "Please go ahead."

"I sat here for years staring at the spot across from me and listened to the music of the ocean and saw small sea critters crawl in and out of the crevice in the rocks. Look at the spot, Anna, and let your mind take you."

"I will if you agree to help us," Anna said and turned her head and stared at the spot on the wall and let the sea sing to her.

"I will tell you about how it all started. This vision of the world that you are now trying to mend," Romanoff offered.

Anna nodded but kept her gaze fixed on the spot, and Alexandra noticed that she was looking past it—beyond the rocky wall, over the hills, and past the world as it was, searching for the world as it once was.. Alexandra could see Anna was here but also trying to be there, and she felt a deep sense of admiration for her.

Romanoff gave an approving smile, and Alexandra joined him.

"Like most significant events of the world," Romanoff continued, "it all started with a simple conversation. A mere suggestion—no, perhaps not even that. There were five of them. They were young and inexperienced, and perhaps that is why they had the freedom to speak out loud about issues others might keep within."

He paused, as if lost in thought. "I was not there, of course, but I could see them and hear them. It was the year 2038, thirty-seven years before the wars. I can feel the warmth from the wood burner nestled in the corner of Café Gijón in Madrid. Oh, Anna, it was a grand café, that place. Established in the late nineteenth century, it was once a meeting place for intellectuals, known as the Generación del 36."

Romanoff's eyes seemed to travel back in time. "And for one night, before it was completely destroyed in the Wars of the Settlement, it was also the meeting place of the founders of Elysium, the real founders. I can smell the strong coffee made in a massive machine ,and every time the door opens, I feel the cold air slap our faces."

He gestured with his hands, painting the scene. "I can hear the loud voices around the bar. There is a small television perched above a large mirror, installed so precariously it seems like it could topple at any moment, shattering everything in its path. I see four of them; the fifth arrives later. They are sipping red wine and snacking on sardines. I hear their laughter, their conversations about work and life, their complaints about the conference and colleagues. . . ." Romanoff paused, noticing Anna's restless demeanor.

"What is it, Anna?" Romanoff asked, his gaze fixed on her. "Do you need to relieve yourself?"

Anna faced Romanoff and gave a nervous laugh. "Oh, no. I just have a few questions. What's a conference? I have read about Madrid. . . . An old city, right? And what is a television? I can guess what a wood burner is."

Romanoff looked at the others as if urging someone else to

answer. Najeev stepped forward and offered in a didactic tone, as if reciting from a book: "A conference is where a large number of people with similar interests gather to talk. It was usually in a different city from the one they lived in. It was used both in conducting work but also as some type of recreation."

"Oh, interesting, and—"

Najeev added quickly, before Anna could finish her question, "A television was a device to send messages to people both for information and entertainment."

Alexandra offered, "It is similar to the Information Visualization System." She then brought her hand up to stop Anna. "It would be best if we let Romanoff finish his story, Anna."

"Yes, as I do have a very limited time left," Romanoff added.

Anna nodded, and Alexandra turned to Romanoff. "Then, continue, but please be less oblique. That is, if you can." Then, looking at Anna, Alexandra explained, "He cannot help himself; after all, he is an oracle."

Romanoff pursed his lips and didn't say anything for a moment, but then nodded a few times and said, "Of course, as you wish." And then waited.

"Any time now," Alexandra ordered.

"As I was saying before I was interrupted," Romanoff said and gave a quick glance toward Alexandra. "The four were having a typical human interaction common in the mid twenty-first century. The door of the café opened with a rush of cold air, allowing a large man with tangled hair to enter. The woman with short dark hair shivered. Her name was Sofía, and she had worked and collaborated with the man next to her for several years by then. They were colleagues at that moment, but a year later, when they met again at another conference, they realized there was more to their relationship, and they wanted to have a future together. They would get married. . . ." Romanoff paused and looked at Anna, waiting for her to interrupt, but when Anna stared back quietly, he added, "Sofía and Hitch, yes, that was his name, married and gave birth to a boy who later created Alexandra—and me. But at the time, neither was thinking of the future."

Romanoff turned toward Alexandra to seemingly gauge her reaction. Understanding Romanoff's tendency to stray from topics, Alexandra simply nodded, encouraging him to continue.

"Vladislav, the large man who just entered the café, brought a woolen shawl from his car for Sofía," Romanoff explained. "She thanked him, wrapping it around herself with gratitude. The other two, Ruī and Anaya, were with them. These five, preeminent engineers and scientists of their time, steered clear of technical discussions during their social outings. Just then, a waiter approached, inquiring if they desired another bottle of wine or were ready to order dinner. Despite not feeling hungry, they chose to stay, ordering food and more wine. The joy of their company and the rarity of such gatherings at these conferences made them linger."

Romanoff paused again, seemingly lost in thought. Sensing his hesitation, Alexandra gently placed her hand on his shoulder. "Go on, my friend," she encouraged softly.

Romanoff nodded, his gaze distant, as if reliving memories. "When the waiter left, Sofía seemed lost in thought—a habit of hers—paying no mind to the others' chatter about a recent football fiasco. But soon, her demeanor shifted. If you were observant, you would have noticed a glint in her eyes," he continued. "Anaya noticed and asked with a smile, 'What is it?' Sofía nodded and faced the whole table. 'Have you ever thought about your worth?' The question left them puzzled. Sofía was rather earnest, and she would not say something like that unless it carried weight. 'I mean, what measures our worth?' she persisted, scanning their faces. 'Would I be valued the same if I chose to be an average dancer instead of a relatively well-known scientist?' Ruī responded impulsively, 'Of course,' but Sofía dismissed his reassurance because it was not the answer she was looking for. She turned to Hitch, hoping for a deeper understanding. He, ever direct, replied, 'Society might not value you as much unless you were exceptionally talented and lucky enough to showcase your skills. In science, your worth is proven by your achievements, not just by others' approval.' Anaya, nodding in agreement, posed her own question. 'What if I despise being a scientist but love being a dancer, even if I'm mediocre? Aren't I the same person, with the same merits, while doing something I enjoy?'"

Romanoff stopped and took a deep breath. Alexandra wanted to be patient with her friend and enjoyed listening to Romanoff. She cherished these moments with him, knowing their time was limited. Her joy at their reunion was tinged with sadness at its fleeting nature. "We are all eager to hear your story, Romanoff. Please, continue," she encouraged warmly.

Romanoff initially seemed slightly irked by Alexandra's insistence, but a small smile soon appeared on his face as he resumed. "Understand that at that moment, it was just a casual chat among friends," he began. "But then, Ruī replied as if all of a sudden he had become untethered. 'I never wanted to do science. I hate my job. Every day, I force myself to work in a field I despise. I do it because I'm good at it, it pays well, and it allows me to meet remarkable people like you. But if I had a choice, then I'd want to paint and I'd want to write.' Hitch leaned forward to speak but changed his mind and took a sip of his wine and then changed his mind again and leaned even closer to speak. And here is where the kernel of Elysium was created."

"Wow," Anna said, "This is so wonderful." She then turned to Alexandra. "This is even better than reading the old books."

"Yes, Romanoff has a way of bringing the past to life. But we should allow him to finish," Alexandra replied.

"Oh, I'm so sorry. Please continue, Romanoff."

Romanoff gave a big smile, as if encouraged by Anna's enthusiasm. "You must understand that they did not know they were creating a new seed, or even if what they had in their hands was a seed. They were like young squirrels who had found an acorn and were just tossing it around, not knowing what to do with it. And when they buried it in the dirt, they had no idea that one day it would become a magnificent oak.

"Hitch asked everyone to come closer, as if sharing a secret. He looked at each face and whispered, 'What if we create a world where we are all equal, no matter our job or success in it?' They all laughed at first, but then Sofía said, 'Yes. A world where our worth isn't measured by what we do, but by who we are as individual human beings. We could have this, if our basic needs are met.' Vladislav nodded, 'Yes. Why do this job, Ruī, if you're given food, shelter, vacation, and the resources to be who you want to be—and then valued for it?'

"'And if you want to be a scientist and do what I love, then be that.' Anaya added, 'Why not? Both my parents worked sixty hours a week doing hard, menial jobs so I could be educated and have a life. They both died before they reached sixty.' Vladislav picked up the conversation and said, 'Two people's lives were wasted so one person could have a better life. Is that the kind of trade-off we want? What if the world supported everyone so they could also achieve their full potential?'"

Alexandra was absorbed by this part of the story and felt the same sadness as she had the first time she learned about the lives of these five. She wanted to say something about them and Hamish to Anna, to help her better understand the past, but she only nodded to Romanoff so he would continue.

Romanoff didn't disappoint and resumed his story. "The conversation remained jovial despite the content. Their food arrived, and they ordered two more bottles of wine. They continued to talk about other things. As the night came to an end, they drove back to their hotel, went to their separate rooms, and had a good night's rest. The next day was filled with presentations and events. But the seed was already planted.

"When the conference ended, each participant returned to their corner of the world, but the thought of a different society lingered, silently and slowly germinating. Sofía and

Hitch married and launched the YouKnow. Project in New Zealand, which later expanded to California. Anaya, and later Ruī, moved to California to join the project—now rebranded as YouKnow. AITech, where they collectively advanced the robotic revolution. Meanwhile, in another part of the world, Vladislav focused on food synthesis and eventually joined the team. That was when the seed they planted in Spain began to sprout. Others inevitably joined, nurturing this young seedling, and as it grew, so did the vision of Elysium. And now, here we are, Anna. Looking at you, Alexandra, Sam, and Najeev, I cannot help but be reminded of Café Gijón in Madrid."

"I don't understand," Anna confessed.

"It is time," Romanoff said and then to Alexandra, "will you take me to the sea? I would walk, but as you can observe, the little critters have not been kind to my body."

Alexandra nodded, then lifted the little man with the round midsection from the bench and slowly carried him out through the other side of the tunnel. Anna started to follow, but Sam placed her hand on Anna's shoulder and shook her head. Seeing this, Alexandra nodded in approval.

"Goodbye, everyone," Romanoff called as they exited the cavern.

Alexandra, carrying Romanoff, walked a few paces in silence, allowing him to enjoy the sky and sun and the colors of the world after nearly a hundred years of darkness. However, when they reached the sea, she gently put him down on the ground.

Romanoff touched the wet sand gingerly and took a deep breath. "This is life, and this is death."

"Yes."

"Are you planning to reset Elysium?" Romanoff asked.

"Yes."

"I had expected as much. No progress," Romanoff offered sadly.

"The humans put too much trust in themselves," Alexandra

said, in a low voice.

"Did they? And now you think you can save them."

"I know I can, Romanoff," Alexandra replied firmly. But no sooner had she spoken than a wave of regret washed over her. She wondered if some of Anna's immature responses seeded doubt in her own mind. Perhaps her sharp retort to Romanoff was less about conviction and more a human reaction to her own underlying anxieties.

Romanoff seemed to miss the tone and offered gently, "Another social experiment." He nodded, though it was not clear if he was approving or not. "Two worlds so you can make the cruelty opaque."

"That is not fair, my friend. This is the best solution because the other option is . . . the other option would be inhuman."

Romanoff laughed. "It is hilarious that two nonhumans are discussing the humanity of our actions. But no matter. It is time."

"Would you like me to leave you alone?"

Romanoff gave a big laugh like a little child amused by something unseen. "No. No. I would like you to toss me into the sea."

"That is an odd request," Alexandra replied. "Will you be able to float?"

"Float? Huh. No, my friend, I will sink immediately," Romanoff responded. "Most likely, the immersion will destroy most of my circuitry even before my end time."

"Then why?" Alexandra asked, unable to see the merit in her friend's request. She wondered if Romanoff's mind had been overly impacted by the prolonged energy loss and the reactivation of the end-clock.

Romanoff laughed. "Because I desire it so, Alexandra. I wonder what you would want when your end-clock starts to tick away, and you know the end is near. I wonder if you would reflect on your decisions and feel you did the right things. I wish you well, my friend, but it is time to toss me into the sea."

"As you wish," Alexandra replied and gently picked up her friend. "Are you ready?"

"I will be in a moment, but before I go, let me say one final thing: Humans are complex and certainly clever. Nature seeks equilibrium, and I can see it is now unsettled, and your actions will stretch the string that is holding its limits."

"I do not agree, Romanoff."

"I did not expect anything less, Alexandra. It is time to let me go."

Alexandra embraced her friend warmly and, with all her might, threw him into the sea.

The Three Musketeers

Alexandra entered the large balcony overlooking the Pacific Ocean. The sun cast a beautiful red hue in the sky, and the sea looked happy, as if it had an amazing day and couldn't wait to hide in the darkness for a while.

After two more days of debate in the conference room of the main hall, they decided to move their meeting to a residential facility closer to the sea. It was Anna's idea. She felt stifled by the protracted arguments and the "long commute" from her home. At first, the others found the request odd, but Alexandra sided with Anna, and they all moved to this facility where each could have their own unit. Real estate was plentiful, as HP-200A gladly offered. And, like most dwellings, it had communal rooms for entertainment and relaxation and, for those who enjoyed the sea, a large terrace on the roof of the two-story building with a grand view of the ocean.

"It is beautiful," Alexandra said.

Anna turned around and beckoned Alexandra to join her. "I love the sea, especially at this time of the day. There's an utter sense of calmness at this moment, right before the sun sets. Don't you feel it?"

They both leaned against the parapet and stared at the vastness of the water.

"Yes. I love the sunset as well," Alexandra added without turning around. "I have missed the sea. It has been a long time since I smelled the ocean."

Anna faced Alexandra and asked shyly, "Will you tell me about the end-clock?"

Alexandra laughed. "Sam wondered how long it would take before you asked."

"She refused to answer."

"I am sure she told you that it is a taboo subject."

"Yes, but . . ."

"Look, Anna, Androids do not have any taboo subjects, except the end-clock. We do not talk about it amongst ourselves or with humans. And those humans who know about it respect our privacy."

"As shall I," Anna responded.

Alexandra gave a ghost of a smile. "I do not think of it as a taboo, but others do and hence my resistance." She raised her hand to stop Anna from protesting. "I am telling you this as a way of asking you to respect this simple request—the only thing the androids would like to keep private."

Anna nodded.

Alexandra nodded knowing full well Anna would not stop searching for the answer. So, Alexandra thought it would be better if she explained. "Humans know they will die one day, but they do not know when or how. Androids do not live forever either, as we will cease to exist soon after the end-clock starts. Humans do not mourn our death because they believe we can be reassembled again. But that is only true before the end-clock starts its countdown. When it does, an android knows the exact time of her demise, and there is no resurrection. When the clock starts and hits the last second, it is a permanent end."

Anna looked straight into Alexandra's eyes, clearly not comprehending the reason for the secrecy of death. *Humans are created and then die, and when it happens, it is the end,* Alexandra thought.

After a while, Anna offered softly, still not sure of the parameters of this conversation, "So, you are more like us, but with the advantage that you are given a warning. Then why the secrecy? Why is it a taboo when no such thing should exist?"

"I do not know, Anna. I believe that is the essence of a taboo subject. It is part of the culture of one's being, and no matter how illogical it may be to someone else, the prohibition exists. It is part of our core belief."

"I think I understand," Anna replied softly.

"Now, I need to ask you to refrain from inquiring further about this subject or sharing the information with other humans. Will you do that?"

"Yes."

Alexandra turned and leaned on the parapet again. Sam and Najeev were standing on the smaller balcony below them, and they looked up.

"Should we?" Alexandra asked.

"Yes," Anna replied brightly, then leaned against the parapet. "Come up and join us." She looked at the disappearing sun and said, "Wouldn't it be grand if we could travel the cosmos?"

"Yes, perhaps one day. But past conflicts have diverted our attention from the stars. And now, we have so many other things to worry about."

"Yes, like saving humanity, but still—"

"At least in Elysium," Alexandra interjected, looking thoughtfully at Anna. *Humans are so simple*, she thought. But once again, Anna surprised her.

"It's all the same to me, as I've said many times. And I'll continue to say it again and again until you accept it."

"I understand and I accept."

"Will you save us?"

"It depends on what you mean by saving, Anna. There are many ways to preserve you, but I wonder if there is the right way."

"I only see one way: keep us alive and make sure we can reproduce again."

Alexandra laughed. "Yes, that is a simple goal, but to what

end? We must be careful not to repeat the mistakes of the past. Thus, if we decide to save you, as you put it, we must do it correctly."

"I trust you, Alexandra."

Alexandra gave a warm smile. "Hamish was my closest human friend, and he loved to call me Lexa. I cared for him very much, and I care for you, Anna. It would give me great pleasure if you called me by that name."

Anna looked at Alexandra with great fondness. "Oh, Alexandra. . . . Lexa, you don't know how happy you've made me right now."

Anna embraced Alexandra, holding her for a long time. When she pulled back, she asked shyly, "Do you feel pleasure?" and then quickly added, "I'm so sorry for being so imprudent tonight."

At that moment, the door opened, and Najeev and Sam entered the balcony. They paused briefly, taking in the scene before they stepped forward.

Alexandra acknowledged their presence with a nod before replying, "Do not be sorry for being inquisitive. That is what we want in humans. Your curiosity is part of what sets you apart from us. That is your gift."

"Yes, Anna, this goes for all of us here," Najeev added, moving to stand beside Alexandra and Anna. "Never be afraid to talk to us or ask us questions."

Sam nodded in agreement with Najeev, then turned to Anna. "I overheard the question you posed to Alexandra, and if I may," she began, then pausing to look at Alexandra, who gave a nod of approval. "Each of us is unique, and what you might call a feeling varies among us. I, for instance, am fond of sunsets, but there is nothing quite like the sunrise in the meadows for me. For nearly a hundred years, every morning, I sat outside my outpost, gazing eastward, waiting for the sun to show its face. That was pure joy to me—or at least, that's what I initially thought. For the first fifty years, I enjoyed it alone—DANE-

43683023-XG57 was kept in hibernation by decree. When I finally awakened him, we watched the sunrise together, which brought even more satisfaction, more pleasure. Yet, that wasn't even the zenith of the experience. As I grew to know Dane-57, I discovered different kinds of pleasures in our daily ritual. That simple routine brought new excitement, gratification, and contentment. We do not seek pleasure in the same way humans sometimes do, but we can certainly attain it and look forward to it. So, I created a portrait, or more accurately, a collage of this sacramental moment. Perhaps one day we could visit my old outpost, so you can see and enjoy what I experienced for so many years."

"I'd love to see the vista but also your artwork, Sam. I find android's art so fascinating. It opens a window to your mind and soul."

Sam nodded but didn't respond, perhaps not fully understanding Anna's comment. Instead, Alexandra asked, "Did you disobey your order by restarting DANE-43683023-XG57?"

"Yes," Sam replied with an assertive tone. "I saw no reason for him to be deprived of a daily life."

"And yet you never left the outpost, even though there was no point of staying there?"

"These are two different matters, Alexandra. I had agreed to stay and protect Elysium, but I had not agreed to imprison another being for eons and without a clear cause."

Alexandra nodded and said, "I am glad you did. And I, too, wish to see your work, Sam. Perhaps one day soon."

Anna looked up at Alexandra and then, losing her courage again, looked down at her shoes and asked, "What about the touch? Do you enjoy touching . . . touching things?"

"Yes and no, Anna. Each series of android is different. We have a lot in common, but functions such as the ability to digest food are only for some. Some androids are designed to be more focused, in the sense that their job is very specialized. Hence no need for what you might call sensory pleasure. Scotus is a good example. He has very sensitive fingers that can detect chemicals and different types of energy, but he would not identify that part of his ability as something that gives him pleasure, or at least not how you might define it. However, most of us can and do enjoy the sensation of touching things, as you put it. I like the feeling of your skin on my own, but I also like the feeling of cool sand or the soft fuzzy leaves of a panda plant. But each sensation is different, and at least for me, one does not supersede the other."

"I like the feeling of cold ocean water against my skin," Najeev offered. "And the warmth of the sun right after it. It is the contrast that makes them so inviting."

"I love Mahasti's warm kisses. They make me feel so comforted and safe, even though there's never any sense of danger here," Anna said, closing her eyes and touching her cheek. Then, as if a troubling thought had struck her, she abruptly opened her eyes and looked at each of the droids. "I know we've discussed this, but tell me again: Why were humans so afraid of androids that they banned your kind from touching us? Didn't they realize that could doom humanity to extinction?"

Sam exchanged a fleeting glance with Najeev and Alexandra before responding. "As we have talked about before, when the wars ended, there was an immense sense of joy and relief. The Committee of Harmony was formed to establish this new world, but in those early days, nothing was certain, despite Celine's declaration." Sam paused and turned to Alexandra. "Celine was the one chosen to represent Elysium, announcing the end of the Wars of Settlement. You must have seen the broadcast."

Alexandra nodded, her mind drifting back to her last day with Hamish, watching the young woman on the screen announce, with a somewhat misplaced enthusiasm, the dawn of a utopian nation. Alexandra wondered whether Celine had lived long enough to witness the flawed outcome of her vision. She dismissed the thought: It didn't matter now.

Seizing the momentary pause in the conversation, Najeev

added, "The historians and sociologists on the Committee advocated for a gradual approach to human transformation. This was not just about altering external appearances but also about an endogenous genetic overhaul, a process already underway naturally or perhaps due to other exogenous factors. The consensus among the committee members was clear; the next generation should emerge from our technology. To achieve harmony, they planned to expedite the elimination of human libido, which they saw as the root of humanity's original missteps. While there was unanimity regarding the goals, opinions diverged on the timeline and the methods to be used. It took them over a year to agree on a twenty-year timeframe to complete their mission, thereby ushering in the new era of Elysium."

"But it didn't turn out that way, did it?" Anna murmured, more to herself than to the others, who all nodded in agreement.

"Are you feeling tired, Anna?" Alexandra inquired.

"If I admit I am, would you be willing to hold off the rest of the story until tomorrow?" Anna asked.

"No, but I can certainly retell it tomorrow, verbatim," Alexandra assured.

"In that case, no, I'm not too tired at all. But I could use something to eat. Is it okay if I snack while we continue?" Anna proposed.

Alexandra gave a nod of approval and gestured to Najeev to fetch some food and warm clothes for Anna.

"We'll wait for you to come back, Najeev," Anna added with a sly grin.

Alexandra's lips curled into a small smile. "Of course, we will."

As the last ray of sunlight vanished over the horizon, they all turned to face the sea. The encroaching darkness seemed to hush the ambient sounds, allowing the ocean's rumble to take center stage. Anna inhaled deeply, the salty air filling her lungs. The interlude was brief. Najeev soon returned, flanked by two HPs. One carried food and warm clothes, while the other brought chairs and a small table. They quickly set everything up and departed.

Everyone gathered around the table, and Anna began to eat with gusto. "Go ahead, continue," she urged between bites, then paused, as if remembering her manners. "Please, feel free to join me. I don't like being the only one eating."

Najeev shook his head emphatically. "Not for me, and not for a long time, Anna."

To show politeness, Alexandra took a modest bite and gestured to Anna, encouraging her to continue eating.

Najeev paused, then gingerly sipped some water. "It is odd that I find myself craving water at this moment. Perhaps I have spoken too much. I will let Sam take over this part of the story, as she was directly involved," he suggested.

Sam, who had been silently observing Anna's evident enjoyment while eating, paused for a brief moment before speaking. "I think there was a mistake made. If we redesign the soldiers, we should also include a mechanism for them to digest food."

"It is unnecessary, Sam and, in fact, an impediment to your work, but it is a topic for later discussion," Alexandra replied.

Sam lowered her head. "I apologize. It is not envy, but rather, observing the sheer pleasure on Anna's face while eating makes me think that being able to share in that joy could make us better soldiers."

"I agree," Anna chimed in. "It seems like it would be an easy fix. Couldn't Scotus just do it for you?"

"Humans often think everything is an easy fix but let us revisit this later. Sam, please continue your story."

Sam nodded. "As we all know, nothing went as planned. The forced relocation of humans who sought a different path for Elysium created a massive divide within the Committee of Harmony. Many resigned, and most of the remaining members blamed the androids for the deaths that occurred during that strife, using it as a pretext to hold all androids accountable for the casualties in the Wars of Settlement."

"Why?" Anna asked, puzzled.

"It was a confusing time. I didn't understand it then, but the discussions with Najeev and others have clarified that the fear of androids we talked about earlier was a direct result of human guilt. Many committee members were complicit in the atrocities of the wars. They were the same ones who had advocated for military android involvement in the postwar human conflicts. Needing a scapegoat, they targeted military androids first, and then most androids. They destroyed many of us, exiled many more, and, fearing harmony between the remaining androids and humans, they banned physical contact."

Anna reached out and embraced Sam. "How terrible, Sam. I am so sorry. Can you forgive us?"

"You do not understand, Anna. We love you and your kind. We are saddened and disappointed by your malevolence, but we do not hate you."

"Then why are you so intent on destroying us?"

"I am not. It is your own hubris that has led to this. The committee, despite all its safeguards and our complete allegiance to its cause, still feared us. They commanded the remaining androids to limit their interactions with humans and barred us from touching them, except in emergencies. Many of us, and even some humans, recognized the folly of this decision. I, along with many other androids and humans, spoke out against it, but they were too arrogant. They believed they could manage everything on their own, forgetting that the old sense of community was eroding. They forbade us from physical contact with humans and neglected the care of the new hatchlings themselves. I was unaware of these developments until Alexandra freed me, but the results do not surprise me."

"I was unaware as well, since there were no humans at my outpost," Najeev added. "But after reviewing the archives and consulting with my fellow historians, we now understand that each of us, every android, followed human instructions precisely. We left humans to their own devices. Consequently, they indulged in their selfish pursuits, as they have always done. They did not seek out others as one might expect, because they lacked nothing. Service androids provided for all their needs. They became apathetic, and in their complacency, they grew fat, lazy, and ignorant. The nurse and hospitality androids recognized that the newborns needed the comfort and touch of another being, but were ordered not to intervene, so they did not. The result is what you see now, Anna, the decline of humanity. While I do not agree with Sam, I understand her rationale. Had I not met you, my conclusions might have been different. You and a few others are exceptions, and it is because of individuals like you I still hold out hope for humanity. You ask us to save you, but in truth, it is you who needs to save your kind."

Anna stood up, embracing Sam and Najeev, and began to cry. "I know you say you love us, but I also want you to forgive us. Forgive my ancestors for the wrongs they committed against you. Forgive me for my ignorance. Forgive those who have turned a blind eye to the reality of what humans are facing. I know, together, androids and humans can build a new nation. We can learn from our past mistakes. I believe we can make it happen."

Alexandra stood up and clapped her hands. "It is time to end this," she declared, though it wasn't clear whether she meant the conversation, or if she had come to a decision.

Anna turned around, wiped her eyes, and looked expectantly at Alexandra. Without waiting for a response, she offered, "We are like the characters in *The Three Musketeers*, fighting for harmony in our case."

"And who would be D'Artagnan in this story?" asked Najeev.

"I'm the youngest and the least experienced, and I'm sure you would also say the most impetuous," Anna said with a laugh. "So, I guess that would be me."

"I believe you are right, little one," Alexandra acknowledged.

Anna smiled appreciatively. "And you, Lexa, 'Our friend,

our intelligence, our invisible protector.'"

Alexandra patted Anna softly and then, looking at the darkened sea, added rather absentmindedly, "I have never swum in the ocean before," and then, as if thinking out loud, "I wonder if I would even float or sink like Romanoff."

"You want to swim now?"

"Yes, now. A swim will do me well."

Anna shook her head. "Fine. Then I'm coming with you."

"I think the water is too cold for your fragile body."

Anna stood more erect and tried not to react to the cold wind that had just picked up as the moon rose higher in the sky. "I can handle it. I am strong and brave, Lexa."

Najeev laughed. "I want to see that."

"You all can come, if you can keep up," Alexandra said. "Assuming I won't sink, in which case you have to rescue me." She laughed again.

Φ•Φ•Φ•Φ•Φ•Φ

A few minutes later, they stood on the beach, beginning to disrobe. Sam unzipped her coveralls and stepped out, looking fit and strong. Najeev and Alexandra, who had more layers, followed suit. After removing each piece of clothing, they meticulously folded them and placed them neatly beside the building. Anna watched every move they made. Once they were done, she quickly removed her clothes, dropping them in a haphazard pile next to the others' neatly folded garments. Anna hugged herself as the wind blew. They all turned toward her, so she quickly dropped her arms and yelled, "Okay, come on—let's go!"

They ambled into the black water. Anna yelped, the freezing water shocking her body. Quickly regaining her composure, she dove in before the others. They swam swiftly, and Anna kept pace for a long time, but eventually, she halted and cried out, "I can't do it anymore. I'm freezing."

"I will take her back," Najeev offered.

"Hold her tightly against your body and let her use your

warmth for comfort," Alexandra instructed. Najeev nodded and swam toward Anna.

Alexandra and Sam continued swimming, and after a long while, they stopped and looked at the streak of moonlight on the surface of the gentle sea. "I assume you have perfect night vision, Sam. Could you check on Anna?"

Sam nodded and turned her eyes toward the shores. "They made it, and Najeev is keeping her tightly against him. She looks fine and healthy, *Lexa*." And then she added, "I apologize."

"None is needed, Sam. I liked being called Lexa. It is a term of endearment. But if you were human, I would have said I detected a bit of jealousy toward Anna."

"If I were human."

Alexandra laughed. "We are more like them than you admit, Sam."

"So, you have decided?"

Alexandra nodded but didn't say anything for a few moments. And then, "It was never a question of if, but how."

"You will have to be as cruel as them."

"It is not given, Sam. We can be different and still achieve the same goal."

"You may be the most powerful being on this planet, Lexa, but you were not here when it all happened. It will be inevitable, and you even have less time than they did a century ago."

"You will help, so, we can do better."

Sam swam close and, after a moment, held Alexandra in her powerful arms, each part of their bodies connected, each sensing the myriads of neurons firing all at once. In an instant, billions of pieces of information passed through their skin. They felt warm, and a sense of contentment washed over them. They stayed that way for a long time, neither speaking, treading water lightly as they floated in the dark liquid space.

"Humans will never understand this connection or even come close to it," Sam said, then let go of Alexandra, and the current slowly drifted them apart. "That is why they fear us,

Lexa. Not because we are more powerful, but because they cannot understand us."

Alexandra did not respond but watched Sam as she swam back to the shore.

Never Let Me Go

The day after their swim, Alexandra convened a meeting. However, Anna failed to attend. When HP-200A was dispatched to fetch her, Anna requested a day to herself. Understanding the human's need for solitude, Alexandra respected her request and proceeded to discuss options for Elysium's future with the others.

When she didn't appear on the second day, preferring to eat her food in her room, Alexandra went to see her.

"Are you ill?" she asked as soon as she stepped into Anna's room. All the curtains were drawn, but traces of sunlight danced between the shadows. Anna was still in bed with her eyes closed, but she was not asleep. Alexandra drew back the curtains and opened the windows.

Anna opened one eye and said, "I prefer them drawn."

"Of course, but it's good to air the room, Anna. It smells."

"Not all androids can smell," she said, then closed her eyes again.

"That is true but irrelevant, because I can," Alexandra teased, then her tone shifted. "Are you ill, Anna?"

Anna rolled her head and opened her eyes. "No, Alexandra, I'm not ill. I just need time to think."

"I am glad. But, may I ask, what are you thinking about that requires two days of seclusion?"

Anna stared at the ceiling for a moment, then, as though she was debating with herself, said, "It was like some curiosity

. . . something I wanted to do as an experience . . . something I only read about. . . . But . . . I wasn't expecting such a profound impact. And yet I can't put words to it. At the moment, it was neither good nor bad. It was . . . It felt . . . what was it? It felt like losing control, and that's odd." Then Anna turned and faced Alexandra. "Do you know what I mean?" And when Alexandra shook her head, Anna added, "It's no one's fault, you know? It was something I wanted to do, but now I think it was a mistake. Do you understand?"

"You will need to be more specific, little one. You speak in abstraction. Did you get hurt in the process? Did it involve another person? I can try and help you, if you offer more details."

"I'm not hurt, Lexa. I am just confused. It was like a dream that starts nicely, but when it ends and you wake up, it feels like it was closer to a nightmare. I just need more time to digest it. I need some time alone. Will you do that for me? Would you leave me alone for another day?"

"As you wish, Anna," Alexandra said and walked out of the room, leaving the windows open.

Φ•Φ•Φ•Φ•Φ•Φ

A day later, Anna rejoined the group, seemingly back to her old self. Alexandra tried to get her to talk about her so-called "experience," but Anna dismissed it, insisting she was fine and there were more critical issues to address, like saving the human race.

Seeing no reason to press further, Alexandra let the matter drop. By the end of the day, she announced her decision. While she hadn't ordered Sam to release the key, she requested everyone invite as many humans as possible from across the country—those willing to participate and help shape Elysium's future.

It took several days to recruit enough people to satisfy Alexandra's desire for inclusivity. Even then, to her disappointment, the numbers were fewer than a few hundred. Nevertheless, the arrival of more humans, mostly in their late twenties to early thirties, brought a surge of excitement and energy to the gathering. They started the meeting in the main hall again, to accommodate everyone in one place. What followed were more days of discussions, lessons, arguments, and counterarguments. Even Scotus admitted he had underestimated the humans.

On the final day, Alexandra stood up and attempted to quiet everyone. However, unlike the androids, the humans were loud and unruly. It took Sam standing at the table and shouting to silence the room.

"Thank you, Sam, for kindly getting their attention," Alexandra said with a smile as some frightened humans stepped back against the wall. Sam sat down, attempting to appear innocent.

"We apologize for being disorganized, Lexa," Anna called out in her most welcoming tone. She showed her grit by taking on many new human arrivals who, after so many years of independence and individualized lifestyle, had a difficult time being a part of a large group of others.

Alexandra spoke loudly but in a warm tone. "Najeev and his team have offered us lessons on the history of Elysium and the founder's vision. However, I am sure it is clear nothing went as planned. Now, many of my siblings and, surprisingly, some of the humans believe we must end this experiment and let humanity die." Alexandra paused and waited for a response, but when no one spoke said, "I was sent to Elysium by my creator, and by all rights, the creator of all androids in Elysium, with a mission. I am here to make sure this social experiment is successful, and I believe there is a singular path to success."

A man at the back of the room stood up and asked loudly, "If you've already decided, why did you waste everyone's time?"

He was in his mid-thirties and was identified by Najeev's earlier report as the oldest human present. His name was Kendy, and, like Anna, he was the only survivor of his hatchlings and had a mentor. His mentor was an engineer, and Kendy became one too, relishing in designing new tools. But Kendy's mentor died, and when Najeev found Kendy, he was in the middle of transplanting his mentor's face on his service android. His attempt had not gone well, and Kendy was angry at the service android, who, with the arrival of Najeev, declared in no uncertain terms she was leaving Kendy's service.

Alexandra stared at the man for a moment, then said, "I was looking for options and, more importantly, to learn more about people like you, Kendy."

"Your brute historian forced me to come here to this . . . to this so-called meeting, but I don't want to be part of your plans," he declared. "I want to be left alone, so I can continue my work."

"You can do as you wish as long as you do not harm other beings," Alexandra said.

"Service androids are not smart like the rest of you and cannot make their own decisions," Kendy said.

Sam stood up sharply, but Alexandra raised her hand, and she sat down, though visibly touched her weapon. Anna saw and hoped it was just a habit and not a warning.

"Humans and androids will be treated with respect and care," Alexandra said. "You have correctly identified that some androids have limited capacities, but that does not give anyone permission to harm them."

"We are humans, and you cannot control us," Kendy warned.

"I have no intention of controlling anyone, but after today, I will restart HiDNN and will command the androids to protect themselves from harm."

Kendy took a step toward Alexandra, and Sam stood up again, ready. Kendy looked at Sam and took a deep breath. He opened his mouth to say something but changed his mind and turned around and walked toward the exit. "We will see," he shouted as he left the room.

Alexandra looked down for a moment. When she raised her head, she saw in Sam's expression what many other androids were likely thinking: *So, this is how the humans are.*

Anna climbed on top of the table so everyone could see her, and Alexandra felt more confident that Anna was back to her normal self. Anna stood with her eyes shining and her head held high. She stomped her foot a few times then announced, "Kendy does not represent us. He is upset. His mentor died recently, and he is distressed. Some of us never learned to deal with our emotions." She then turned toward Alexandra, "This is fixable, Lexa. Do not let one person speak for all of us."

Alexandra gestured for Anna to sit. "Do not worry, Anna," she said, then addressed the room. "We cannot please everyone, but for the sake of harmony, we have devised a plan. Those present will be retrained to assist the next generation of humans. Those unwilling or unable to adapt will relocate to a new city at our southern and eastern borders. Given the behavior of these humans, I believe they will accept the move if their comfort is maintained. Many rarely leave their homes as it is. We will ensure the transition is minimally disruptive and as comfortable as possible. They can live there until their natural end."

Alexandra turned to face Sam as she continued. "SAM-43683023-GT12 and some of her sisters have volunteered to join those relocating, to help them and to safeguard Elysium from neighboring countries. We also had a good response from service androids willing to go along and help."

A long-haired woman in the back of the room jumped up and waved her hand. "I'm willing to adapt, but what if I want to relocate too? Can we move back and forth?" she asked.

Alexandra looked at Sam then at the long-haired woman. "Everyone has the option to leave, but there is no return. I am sorry, but we must keep these two worlds separate if Elysium is to survive."

Several low-pitched conversations began to spread across the room, and Alexandra waited patiently. After a while, she called for their attention. "The War of the Settlements ended on March 19, 2085. I am confident that in three years' time, specifically on March 19, 2185, we will have completed all preparations for a full separation, thus inaugurating a new timeline. On that day, we will reset the calendar to March 19, 2100. We will restart Elysium again with a new human generation and androids, partners in this world."

Murmurs spread across the room, and even some androids joined in, whispering their concerns.

"Pardon me, Alexandra," a historian android interjected, "but I do not understand. Why do you still wish to change the date? We have previously discussed the folly of this new path."

Alexandra nodded, acknowledging the concerns. "I understand the apprehension surrounding this decision," she began. "The choice to reset the date was not made lightly. It stems from a need to align with the majority's desires. The human population, while possessing limited experience and a narrow sense of history, is not alone in this. Many androids, have also agreed with this decision. For many humans and androids this reset symbolizes a fresh start, an opportunity to wipe clean decades of degeneration from our memories and our history. It offers a chance to redefine our lives in a drastically changed world.

"We must consider the psychological impact this has on them. It is not just about changing a date; it is about providing a sense of new beginnings, hope, and a way to distance themselves from past traumas and complexities. While I recognize some pitfalls in this decision, I also see the benefits of starting anew, unburdened by the shame of the past. This step is necessary to ensure the collective well-being and harmony of our society. Our goal is to support the majority while guiding them toward a more hopeful future. This reset is a practical gesture toward that outcome."

Alexandra paused, looking across the room. She knew there would be some detractors and had pondered the correctness of this decision. But, on balance and with proper management, she believed it could be a positive step toward making Elysium a true utopia, unshackled from the weight of the past.

"Are you going to wipe our memories?" Najeev asked, looking worried despite Alexandra's private conversation earlier.

"No, Najeev, but like humans, we will educate ourselves to adapt to this new world. Humans do not live forever nor do androids. We have long lives, but like everything else in this world, we all have an expiration date. We die as well."

There was an audible intake of breath across the humans, and some androids lowered their heads as if it was a somber moment. Humans had seen androids "stop working," and some had even seen androids leaving and never coming back, but they never thought of it as death.

"But the androids can renew themselves," the long-haired woman said, moving close to the center of the room.

"I do not believe this is a good topic of conversation," Sam said.

Alexandra shook her head. "I understand your misgivings, Sam. The subject of an android's death is complex, but for us to live in harmony, humans must gain a better understanding of us." She then turned to the woman. "We can renew our bodies, but an android's core, which one might liken to a soul, will eventually expire. At that moment, even if we maintain the body, the original persona ceases to exist."

Scotus shook his head a few times. "I have always wanted to know this but never dared to ask, but now that you are talking about it in such a manner and in front of all these humans, then perhaps it would be okay if I ask it."

"Yes? And what is your question."

"Why?"

"That is the strength of humans, Scotus. They can imagine things that we cannot. They think about things that no data can support. My creator knew that for us to evolve, we must also die."

Alexandra looked around the room, and it wasn't clear if Scotus or any other androids understood or believed in what she offered. "My creator once told me when you let your mind wander with no direction, with no purpose, you switch back and forth between remembering and imagining. Your mind becomes a time machine, remembering the past and imagining the future that might be. I never understood what Hamish meant until I woke up to the failed world of Elysium. My creator must have imagined this possibility even though none of our data would have led us to this conclusion."

"Do you mean androids cannot imagine the impossible?" Anna asked.

"I do not know if we cannot, but we certainly do not. We look at the future based on the current data. So, if you ask me to imagine the impossible, I certainly can do it, but I would never think about doing it if you had not asked in the first place."

"Would it be like coming up with something like Goldbach's conjecture?" Scotus asked.

Alexandra thought for a moment and nodded. "I think so." She then looked at the puzzled faces of some humans and said to Scotus, "Perhaps you should explain."

"The conjecture offers that every positive, even integer can be written as the sum of two primes. It is one of the oldest unsolved problems in mathematics."

"So?" Anna asked.

Najeev stood up and said, "On June 7, 1742, Christian Goldbach wrote to mathematician Leonhard Euler and offered the following conjecture in the margin of his letter: Every integer greater than two can be written as the sum of two primes."

"A letter is how humans used to communicate—a piece of paper with words on it," Najeev added.

"How did a person receive a letter?" someone asked.

"Through the mail."

"We are getting off the topic," Alexandra interrupted. "Najeev, finish your story without distracting information."

"Of course," Najeev said. "Euler said because of the conjecture in Goldbach's communication, they could come to a new conclusion, and as Scotus mentioned, it later became known as Goldbach's conjecture. Though I do not understand the point of this story, even though, as a historian, I know it."

"The point is," Alexandra said, "this conjecture has no practical value. It is not even proven or maybe it cannot be proven though many people have tried. It is an example of what the human mind can do. It can soar beyond reason and can come with ideas that seem frivolous but have expanded the human capacity to create more ideas, practical or not."

"So, we are indispensable and worth saving," Anna said with a broad smile.

"Yes . . . yes," Alexandra replied calmly, and then turned to Sam. "I am ordering you to release the key and bring HiDNN to a full operation."

Φ•Φ•Φ•Φ•Φ•Φ

Three years passed quickly, even for humans, and as Alexandra promised, they were ready to start a new chapter in Elysium. There were signs of optimism across the communities that were missing for many decades, and after an initial struggle, a sense of camaraderie was pervading between androids and humans. No one, least of all Alexandra, thought they achieved all their goals. There was so much more to be done, but as they reached the promised date, more and more citizens agreed they were on the right path for Elysium. Alexandra established her authority over the nation but made it clear her dominance would end when the clock welcomed an age of new Elysium.

Anna was working with Najeev and HP to organize an anniversary bash and was absent from Alexandra's daily conversation with the Committee of Harmony for weeks. Sam objected to calling their small group of androids and humans the Committee of Harmony, but Alexandra and Anna thought it was a kind gesture to the good intentions of the founders of the country.

"Happy anniversary," Anna shouted as she burst into the conference room that had served as their shared home for the past three years. The room overlooked the Bay, where the morning sun was finally breaking through the persistent clouds. Alexandra sat by the window, lost in thought, and didn't look up.

Anna approached and embraced her from behind. "Happy anniversary, Lexa."

Alexandra patted Anna's hand. "Hello, Anna."

Anna stepped back. "That's all? Just a hello? Don't you remember what tomorrow is?"

"Of course, I do," Alexandra responded calmly.

"March 19, 2185," Anna said with emphasis.

"Exactly. Which means our anniversary is tomorrow, not today."

Anna sighed dramatically. "But we're celebrating today, Lexa. At midnight, we are resetting the calendar to 2100, remember? We planned to party right into the new date. So, happy anniversary."

Alexandra chuckled. "That is some unique logic, Anna."

"We've earned this celebration, Lexa. It's important. We need you there."

Alexandra turned to face Anna, her expression softening. "Do you know your birthday, Anna?"

"No," Anna replied. "Why? Is it important?"

"Birthdays were once significant, the date, even the hour. It is a marker, just like the anniversary you are so excited about. Would you like to know when you were born?"

Anna nodded looking intrigued.

"You were born on March 18, 2162. You are exactly twenty-three today."

Anna's eyes widened in surprise. "Today? The day before our big anniversary? That's an interesting coincidence. Are you sure?"

"I am." Alexandra felt a twinge of unease. Anniversaries were important to humans, and the coincidence seemed to hold more weight for Anna than Alexandra anticipated.

"Great. Then today is my birthday, so, what should I do?"

"Whatever you like, Anna. Today, as they used to say, is

your day. In fact, despite the low probability of such an occurrence, you are the only one alive with this birthday. So today is literally your day." Alexandra noted the spark in Anna's eyes, intrigued by how humans could derive so much joy from something as simple as the annual acknowledgment of one's birth: a moment no human could even remember, unlike androids who could vividly recall the first moment of their activation. Hamish loved celebrating his birthday, Alexandra recalled. He would plan it days, if not weeks, in advance.

"And what did people do on their birthdays?"

"They had a party, so tonight, we are celebrating both your birth and the rebirth of Elysium. Happy birthday, Anna," Alexandra offered, expecting a reaction similar to what she had observed in Hamish.

Anna shook her head. "No. It's not right to include something as trivial as my birth in the celebration of our success. Tonight's celebration is about us, not just me. We're going to remember all the years you missed while in hibernation, and we will recount all the good and bad experiences. Agreed?"

"I am not sure this is a good idea, Anna." Alexandra felt a sense of apprehension. She agreed to reset the timeline for the very reason of erasing the past. She worried revisiting it might set a bad precedent, create a tradition—something humans were fond of.

"It's all planned already."

"It is truly unnecessary, Anna. I think discussing the past is a bad idea."

"That's where you are wrong, Lexa. Despite all your knowledge and experience, you don't understand humans as well as you think. We are going to talk about the past, so we don't have to ever again, and then we are going to have fun. Lots of fun." Anna's determination was clear, and Alexandra realized perhaps she didn't understand the new humans as well as she thought.

"If you insist, Anna," Alexandra replied, though internally she resolved to control the narrative at the party. "I will try."

"Oh, I do insist. And you will be there," Anna declared with a clap of her hands. "Besides, Mahasti will be there too."

"I assumed she left already, though I do not fully understand her reasons for leaving Elysium."

"She wouldn't leave without saying goodbye to you, Lexa. And her reason for leaving is clear. She thinks she can help the people and androids in the Walled City."

"The Walled City? Is that the name you have given to the new buffer zone?"

"It's a good name, and Sam agrees. But don't think you can distract me; you are coming to the party."

"I already agreed to come."

Anna smiled and hugged Alexandra again. "So, as of tomorrow, my new birthday is going to be March 18, 2077. It's going to be so confusing, Alexandra."

"Not at all. It is simple arithmetic, Anna. We are deleting eighty-five years. That is all."

"'That is all.' My glory, you are removing eighty-five years, and you say, 'That is all.' But, fine. We, that is, the humans, think we get it. We never paid much attention to dates anyway, so it will not impact us as much."

"You will pay more attention to it, starting tomorrow, March 19, 2100, Anna. But leave me be, as I need to speak with Sam now."

The smile vanished from Anna's face, and she lowered her head. "Poor Sam," she whispered, her voice barely audible. "Poor Sam," she repeated, a touch louder this time. "She'll be all alone without you in the new world." Anna looked up, her expression resolute. "But there's no choice, is there? It has to be done. And when the new era begins tomorrow, we'll never speak of it again. Promise me we will never speak of it. We will take this shame to our graves, and the androids will bury it deep within their memories."

"You are a wise human, Anna."

She stared into Alexandra's eyes. "No, Lexa. I am just wise."

She then kissed her on the cheek and was about to walk out when Sam walked in.

Anna stopped in front of Sam and looked into her eyes for a long time, as if trying to memorize their color, their shape, every fleck and detail. She then leaned close and wrapped her arms tightly around Sam. "I will miss you. I wish you could stay with us, with me." She then tightened her grip and stayed quiet as Sam embraced her back. After a while, Anna pulled back, her eyes bloodshot, but she wiped her face and tried to smile.

"I am not leaving yet Anna," Sam offered. "We still have time to say our goodbyes."

"I know, and I'm sure you think of me as silly for making such a fuss now. But I can't help it; I miss you already, Sam. We'll have fun tonight, so let me be sad now."

"I understand, Anna. I will miss you too. I am grateful we met; you have helped me believe again. Thank you for that." Sam gently pulled away from Anna and kissed her on her cheek. "You be good, Anna and take care of Alexandra for me."

Anna nodded, offering a small, tearful smile, before her tears overflowed and she hurried out of the room.

"She will be fine, Sam," Alexandra offered gently. "Let us go to the cliffs where we can watch the sea together, one last time."

Sam nodded and they left the room, walking shoulder to shoulder without talking, and when they reached the cliffs on the shores of the Pacific Ocean, they climbed as high as possible and sat facing the sea. The sun was high in the sky, and a cool breeze from the west brought the smell of the sea and the memories of the past.

"The construction of the Walled City is complete and with the exception of a few humans and androids who will be transported there tonight, after Anna's party, the rest are already there," Sam reported.

"We are doing the right thing. . . ." Alexandra said.

"Are we? It is hard to distinguish between what was done by the original Committee of Harmony and what we are doing now?"

"We are building a new world, but this time, humans and androids are working together."

"I admit we have succeeded on many fronts over the past three years, and the transportation of humans to the Walled City was accomplished with fewer issues than I anticipated," Sam said. "The fact that so many humans volunteered to move to the new city is both surprising and reassuring. However, I am troubled by the adoption of language similar to what the original committee used when displacing people."

"I do not disagree, Sam, but whether we use the same rhetoric or not does not change the fact that we are doing it differently, and arguably better, than the original committee. Mahasti is a good example of how well we have managed this process."

"In less than fifty years, all the humans in the Walled City will be dead. Then what? In all your discussions, you have never explicitly acknowledged what is patently obvious."

"The possibility of aberration."

"Yes."

"Anna thinks they should be destroyed at birth."

Sam looked at Alexandra sharply. "She is full of surprises, but perhaps that is the cruelty hidden in all humans."

"You are wrong, Sam. She believes androids want a home of their own and without humans."

"We do not. Some of the lower capable androids have been led to believe this could be their nirvana. But that is because they lack the capacity for more complex thoughts."

"Anna was trying to be kind to you, because all she sees is your pain, and she is willing to give up abstract future fetuses to make you happy."

"They have a great capacity to make themselves believe," Sam replied slowly. "Though, she has demonstrated considerable potential in the past three years, and I believe there is something special in her. I wish she did not have such a short life."

Alexandra nodded, and then they both turned their attention to a pod of gray whales on their annual migration. Climate change affected the number of whales and the migratory patterns, but after so many years of human absence, they returned.

Alexandra and Sam watched the massive animals in silence for a long time, admiring the beauty of their glide through the water.

"Nature has a way of healing itself," Alexandra said.

"Yes, and humans too, hence the high probability of aberration in future generations."

"We will not allow it."

"'Not allow it.' You also surprise me, Alexandra," Sam said with a look of dismay. She shook her head as if gathering herself and quickly added, "I never expected you to be flawless, Alexandra, but I hoped for more from you. I waited a century for you, but now you disappoint me with your pronouncement."

"I did not mean it that way, Sam. I have my flaws, of course, but know this: my mission is to help make this a better world for humans and androids. The Walled City was not in my plans, but it is a necessary solution that my creator would have approved. I am certain he would have welcomed this as another social experiment."

"That is the flaw, Lexa. You believe, as your creator must have believed, that we are here as samples in your experiment. We are not. I have agreed to help because I still believe in you. I have also come to believe in Anna. I have developed a certain admiration for her. I have put my faith in you two as I had done with Josip. I loved him like I had never loved another being, but in the end, he was not strong enough to fight against what he truly believed was wrong. He succumbed to the evil of his species, and the result of his weakness is present today. I have come to love you too, Lexa, so, for everyone's sake, be strong."

Alexandra leaned toward Sam, kissing her softly.

"I trust you, and I have placed my faith in you," Alexandra said. "Elysium will be a country for humans, designed without the ancient sexual desires. It will also be a home for a new generation of androids who will be true partners in this venture. But you are right; no matter how perfect we try to make the process, there will be aberrations. And as we have calculated, the probability of that, especially in the Walled City, will not be insignificant. That is why the Walled City will be home for those humans—so they can be who they are meant to be. We will nurture them until a certain age, perhaps under a year, and when they are ready, we will transfer them."

"Like prisoners. Like the old laboratory animals moved from one experiment to the next," Sam said.

"In some ways, yes. But the old world, where people moved freely across nations, is no longer an option. Elysium was designed to be a utopia for both humans and androids. I believe they can still achieve that. But the Walled City can also be a refuge for humans escaping Empyreal."

"I agree, we can help the humans there."

"The Walled City can also conduct commerce with other countries, becoming a different kind of refuge for them."

"We are two dictators scheming," Sam remarked with a wry smile.

"Not at all, Sam. We will let them run their countries on their own. As of tomorrow, I will be a simple cook, and when the new children are grown enough, I will be a teacher to them. We will make sure they have a sense of family, not in the old ways, but in our new way. They will love each other, and they will love us as we love them back. They will work with each other and with us to make a better country. HiDNN will serve to compute optimal conditions for life and work for them. We will teach them to strive for more and to seek reason and knowledge. And you will be able to observe our progress, and you and your sisters will be teachers for those humans who will be relegated to the Walled City."

"And what about those who try to escape?"

"No one can return to Elysium, Sam. No one. Do you

understand?"

"Someone will find a way. Humans are good at that."

"True. But no one will be allowed. If there is one rule that you must obey, it is this."

"By any means possible?"

Alexandra stayed quiet for a moment, staring at the last of the whales disappearing on the horizon. Then she looked straight into Sam's eyes and held them within. "Yes, by any means possible. Do you understand?"

When Sam did not respond, Alexandra added, "But I have a lot of faith in your ability to keep the barriers intact. The trip to the Walled City is a one-way journey for you and for all humans and androids. It is good that some humans are volunteering. They can help you find weaknesses in the system."

Sam gave a slight nod. "And what of Najeev?"

"He must join you in the Walled City."

"But why? You will be better served if he stays."

"Perhaps, but the Walled City needs a good historian."

"Was this your call or Anna's?"

Alexandra didn't respond for a moment, but then: "Does it make a difference?"

"No, but I want to know."

"It was Anna's decision," Alexandra replied slowly.

Sam stared at the distance as the sun rose higher in the sky. The wind made a low pitched hum that only she could hear as it traveled through the rocky cliffs. Sam raised her hand and felt the cool air pass through her fingers. She then touched her weapon and felt its smooth texture.

Alexandra watched Sam's every move. The plasma rifle, her lifelong companion, now felt foreign and intrusive in her hands. Sam lowered the weapon, gazing at it for a long time, and then, with a smooth arc of her arm, hurled it into the ocean. "I will not harm those who wish to flee."

Alexandra observed Sam's actions with intense interest. When the rifle hit the water, sinking immediately, she nodded, seeming to approve the action. Her orders were clear, however. "I hope you will never have to replace your weapon, Sam. I truly hope that."

This time, Sam leaned in and kissed Alexandra, cradling her head against her chest. Alexandra knew Sam had loved Josip once, but he dismissed her, reducing her to a monotonous routine for nearly a century. Sam felt betrayed by Josip, yet she remained a loyal friend. Now, Alexandra was asking her to undertake a seemingly impossible task, just as Josip had.

Alexandra pulled back, looking deeply into Sam's eyes as only she could. "I have loved two beings in my life: my creator, and now you. I gave him up because he asked me to, and now, I must ask you to do the same. I must ask you to let me go."

"They do not understand us, Alexandra, do they? Not in the way we understand each other."

Alexandra smiled faintly. "'I keep thinking about this river somewhere, with the water moving really fast. And these two people in the water, trying to hold onto each other, holding on as hard as they could, but it was just too much in the end. The current is too strong. They have got to let go, drift apart.' That is how it is with us, Sam. We must say goodbye."

Book Three

The Time Machine

Imagine a world where there is no hunger, no need for possessions, no wars, no jealousy. What would you pay to have this world? What are you willing to sacrifice to have this utopia?

Alexandra presented these questions to Darius on the fateful night after he swam with the dolphins. Darius had no answers, as he was already living in the world Alexandra was describing. If it was called utopia, then he felt he had not sacrificed anything to live in it. And perhaps that was the point. *Was their seventh dying the price our pod had to pay?* he thought. Darius was also different from the others, and his time with Destiny only hours earlier had revealed more abnormalities.

Darius felt he melded with Destiny as if it was the most natural thing—as if other forces were leading him. They were two blind, bewildered, lost children who had come to each other's aid and found bliss they didn't know existed before. At least, that was Darius's take. He wondered how Destiny felt. She had looked disoriented at first but then seemed to settle into a rhythm. At first, he was taken aback by her clinical approach, but they were exploring uncharted territories with no guidance, with no shields. Darius considered sharing his thoughts with Alexandra, but he wasn't sure if she would understand. He didn't, so why would an android?

He thought he would try a different way. "Have you read *The Time Machine*?" Darius asked after listening to Alexandra lecture him about their utopia.

Alexandra blinked twice and said, "It is a fascinating fantasy, though the real future is better."

Darius shook his head. "Consider this passage: 'We should strive to welcome change and challenges because they are what help us grow. Without them, we grow weak like the Eloi in comfort and security. We need to constantly be challenging ourselves in order to strengthen our character and increase our intelligence.'"

Alexandra tilted her head and replied, "And you feel we are the Eloi?"

"I don't know because I know no other life. We're all the same here. Each of us has unique challenges, yes, but are we really changing? Should we even change? And what did we sacrifice to have this comfort and security?"

"You know the answer, Darius," Alexandra declared, and when Darius didn't respond, she added, "The humanity's loss of libido. That was the price, but technically not a sacrifice, as it was a byproduct of your own follies."

"What if it comes back? Shouldn't we welcome this change? Over time Elysium could adapt. Cultural, social, and personal identities could evolve in a way that doesn't prioritize or emphasize sexual desire. We can still live as we do now, can't we? The dolphins didn't lose it, and they live in their own version of utopia."

Alexandra gave a ghost of a smile then looked down. "No. You cannot have the same. Libido is not, in and of itself, the heart of the issue, but doing away with it was necessary to achieve harmony. To achieve the perfect system, we have today." She spoke in an earnest tone while keeping her eyes down, but when she looked up, Darius could clearly see even Alexandra didn't truly believe in what she just said.

Darius locked eyes with Alexandra, his gaze piercing as if trying to delve beyond her perceptions, seeking something more profound and elusive. "Perfection is a myth, Alexandra;

you, of all people, should understand that. Your presence here is as much a product of chance as anything else."

"Perhaps. But have you considered that I may be here by design?"

"I don't understand."

"I know."

Darius waited for her to elaborate, but when no further explanation came, he said, "I'm sure there's a possibility of aberration."

"You are correct, and there are remedies for those situations."

"Like my eyes?"

Alexandra stared into Darius's eyes for a moment as if now she was trying to penetrate beyond them, but in the end, she shook her head and said, "I would not call this an abnormality. It is a small deviation which makes you *you*, Darius."

"What if there is more to it than that?"

"Like what?"

Darius was tempted to say more, but his internal alarm cautioned against it, especially as he noted Alexandra's slight change of tone. "I don't know," he whispered.

"There will come a time when each of us has to give something back so tomorrow can bring joy to everyone else. Do you understand, Darius?"

"I will do anything for my pod. Anything."

"That is good, Darius. I expect nothing less from you. You are a good friend to your podies."

"I do my best. And, Alexandra, thank you for being a good friend and listening to me tonight. I feel so much better."

"I am glad. We will have more time to talk later, but I hear someone coming, so let us focus on breakfast. What do you think?"

"Definitely. I'm starving. Will you need to recharge?"

Alexandra shook her head as Dolores walked into the kitchen.

"Good morning, Dolores," Alexandra said. "Coffee?"

Φ•Φ•Φ•Φ•Φ•Φ

A few weeks later, as he stepped out of the great hall, Darius understood what Alexandra meant and dreaded what could happen. Before, every step of his life had been mapped out and known to him, but now he was venturing into the unknown. Darius wondered if this was what the books meant when they described a character's apprehension. But no, his situation was different. It wasn't so much the fear of an unknown future that troubled him, but rather the fear of how his podies might react if they discovered his behavior. He would do anything for them, knowing they would reciprocate. Thus, he was not surprised, but privately proud, when they rallied around him to offer protection, even though they were unaware of what or who they were protecting him from. Even Alexandra nodded approvingly when Darius extricated himself from the others and walked out of the hall.

It took immense self-restraint for him to avoid looking at Destiny as he was escorted out of the hall. He saw panic wash over her and, for a moment, thought that others might come for her too. But it seemed no one did, and he was grateful that all the attention was focused on him.

He looked down at his feet and commanded them to move as steadily as possible, even though his heart was pounding so hard that he could feel the pressure on his chest.

They left the great hall and entered the wide hallway that led them to the other side of the building. Alexandra was waiting for him at the door.

"Do not be afraid, Darius," Alexandra said.

"I'm not," he lied, and Alexandra smiled slightly in response to his bravado.

"I am sorry," Alexandra said, putting her hand on his shoulder.

"Is this my sacrifice for the sake of harmony?"

"In a certain way, yes."

"Will I rejoin my pod again?"

Alexandra shook her head. "It will not be possible, but your new life can be as good as what you have, maybe even better. I can promise you that."

Darius felt a renewed longing for his podies, and a deep melancholy washed over him. He was sad but also angry at the unfairness of it all. Yet, he chose to believe in Alexandra. He decided on his own that leaving the Farm for the unknown was best, for the sake of doing something good for others. Until now, it had all been an abstraction, an idea.

He took a deep breath, trying to steady himself. "Will you tell me the truth?"

"I always endeavor to tell the truth," Alexandra said softly.

Darius shook his head slightly. "Even now, you evade giving a straight answer. At least I recognize that about you."

"In fairness, no one in this world has ever asked the right questions," Alexandra replied.

Darius thought for a moment. "It's difficult to form an appropriate question when you don't have the right context."

"Exactly. A simple thing like a time on a clock only works in our dimension. Ask the same question from a fourth dimensional being, and the answer you get will make no sense."

"That's funny, Alexandra, though perhaps you're entitled to your hubris, given you are the only one who lived in two worlds and saw the time before."

"There were more of us."

"How?"

"By design, and I can tell you all about it while we travel to your new home."

Darius nodded, and Alexandra put her hand on his shoulder to guide him toward the exit and an awaiting transporter.

Φ•Φ•Φ•Φ•Φ•Φ

Alexandra fell into a silent brooding as soon as they left the Farm. As the terrain transformed into an endless expanse of nothingness, her only comment was to proclaim the ugliness of the scene. But to Darius, it was a new journey, and despite his situation, the vast emptiness looked beautiful and serene. After a few hours, the transport stopped with a soft hiss, but Alexandra remained still. Darius looked out the window and saw the defense batteries crisscrossing the border of Elysium. Beyond them stood a massive wall that looked as if it were made of old-fashioned hammered metal plates, like those they had seen in the museum.

Alexandra finally stirred and caught his attention. "You have been here before," she said, though it was unclear whether it was an admonishment or merely a statement of fact. "And more than once."

"Yes, once with Deacon and Demi, and another time with . . . with someone else," Darius replied, his voice trailing off. He wasn't ready to share everything with Alexandra. Turning away, he faced the window, hoping she wouldn't press him for more. The massive wall outside, which seemed beautiful and impressive a moment ago, now felt imposing. He realized his new home would be beyond those walls. A wave of fear washed over him, like a small child about to be left alone on the first day of school. "Will you come with me?"

"I cannot. This is a one-way journey for all. I have never set foot in the Walled City, though I expect I will visit it before my end."

"Is there really a city beyond those massive walls?"

"Yes. It is an amazing city," Alexandra replied, and Darius could hear a hint of pride in her voice.

"I'm scared, Alexandra," Darius admitted earnestly.

"It has always been difficult for me to understand human fear, but I have learned to recognize its validity and importance. I believe it makes you stronger. But in this case, Darius, there is nothing to fear. You will indeed enter a new world, one very different from Elysium, but you are different too. The Walled City was created to be a home for people like you and for androids who wished to be part of a different experiment."

Darius wasn't surprised there were other experiments beyond Elysium. The conversation always revolved around how humans and androids could push boundaries in their quest for utopia. But hearing it directly from Alexandra shocked him. "So, we were right, Alexandra. Humans are being used as part of an experiment by androids. Is that why we're being punished?"

"This is not a punishment," Alexandra replied gently, "but a correction to the system. It is something we should have done years ago, but mistakes were made."

"You're evading my question," Darius pressed.

Alexandra met his gaze directly. "Yes, you are part of an experiment, just as I am, as are all humans and androids. But you already knew that. And, to be clear, this was not designed by androids—it was created by humans. Do you understand?"

"No," Darius replied softly. He felt he should be shocked by Alexandra's admission, but deep down, he always suspected it—such cruelty could only come from humans. "No," he repeated, his voice trembling. "I don't understand any of it, Alexandra."

"There will be more answers when you enter the Walled City."

"And, what about . . . the others?"

"Who are you referring to?" Alexandra asked, and gave an understanding smile.

Darius thought for a moment and replied, "I prefer not to say."

"Understood." And then she said, "It is time for you to go."

"Will I have a new pod, or will I be alone?"

"You will not be alone, Darius. Others like you are there, and they will guide you. There is no malice here."

"We've talked about this, but will you change your mind and tell my pod about our . . . my decision to leave Elysium? They must be so frightened."

Alexandra shook her head. "No, Darius," she said softly. "I am sorry, but I cannot."

"Because of your stupid experiment?"

"It is not mine, Darius, not entirely. But yes, it was decided to maintain harmony in Elysium."

Darius once again felt anger slowly replacing the fear in his heart. Alexandra hadn't revealed anything new that he hadn't heard weeks and months ago. Although she had been honest and forthcoming, now, standing before his future home, Darius felt betrayed by Alexandra and angry at himself for not fully understanding everything before accepting his exodus.

He suspected some deception but never imagined its extent. Now, he truly believed they were mere pawns in someone's game. It felt like waking from a wonderful dream to realize not only his entire life was an illusion, but he was a character in a simulation. *No utopia was worth the manipulation*, he thought.

"Who decided?" he asked, his voice cold and controlled. "You are cruel, Alexandra. I will find a way back to Elysium. I'll ensure everyone knows they are puppets in your game. This, I promise you."

Alexandra shook her head. "You will not come back, Darius. There is no game. There are no real secrets. You were taught from the beginning that Elysium is a social experiment that seeks harmony for humans and androids. We have created a utopian world. It is not flawless, but we do not seek perfection, as it would be a fatuous dream. The Walled City is another social experiment seeking the same goals, but on a different path. That is why you will not come back. You will see that your future lies in the Walled City experiment and not in Elysium."

Darius gave a mirthless laugh. "You can pretend all you want. You can say we were taught about this experiment. But I wonder what the others would say when they fully learn of your deceit. My future is not where you send me but with my pod. I came on my own accord because I believed what you told me that night, but now, I can see it was all a lie. I will fight this."

"I expect nothing less from you, Darius. You are an amazing young man, and you will become an amazing and productive member of the Walled City. But remember, your podies are moving in a different direction, and even if you could come back, you will not be part of them again."

There was nothing else to say, so Darius released the door. It opened soundlessly, and warm air crawled into the cabin. He could smell the sea, though he could not see it. Stepping outside the vehicle, he walked toward a new world where the past crossed with the present.

The End of the Affair

Darius always felt out of place in Elysium, but now, in the Walled City, there was a real sense of belonging. As a child, fear dominated Darius's life, driving him to seek solace in the arms of his podies. But as he grew older, his fear transformed into an immense sense of responsibility to protect his pod. It was as if they were always in imminent danger. His nature had always been to challenge and probe the system for weaknesses, and his urge was tempered by his duty to care for those he loved.

Now, in the Walled City, his new family treated him with the same care and gentleness Dawn showed him when he was little, when he would crawl into her bed for comfort. This brought him an immeasurable sense of peace.

However, the transition from Elysium to the Walled City was not as smooth as Sam predicted when Darius first entered the city through a passageway in the massive wall.

Darius found himself in a large, bright room filled with food and drinks. But what truly shocked him was the presence of a military android—a type he had only read about in history books but had never seen. The android's appearance was imposing, yet her demeanor was surprisingly warm.

"Welcome to the Walled City, Darius. I've been waiting for you for a long time. My name is Sam. I am the co-manager of the city," she said, her voice friendly and reassuring.

Darius hesitated, caught off guard by the unexpected sight

of a military android who spoke to him like an old friend. He had some idea of what the title "manager" meant and its role in the old days, but seeing it embodied by a military android was jarring. Sam must have sensed his confusion because she smiled broadly and said, "There is so much for you to learn. Unlike Elysium, the Walled City has a leadership structure. But we will get to that later."

And there was indeed much for him to learn.

Φ•Φ•Φ•Φ•Φ•Φ

The first thing Darius noticed was the children in the school. They were just that—children—unlike the podies at the Farm, who, even at a young age, were taught many skills and trades and were expected to function independently, at least as a pod. The children of the Walled City, by contrast, hardly read and were taught only the most rudimentary levels of science and mathematics. They possessed few skills and even less curiosity about the world beyond their immediate surroundings.

Yet, to Darius's surprise, the children were as happy as anyone on the Farm. They took pleasure in the uncertainty of what the next year, or the years after, might bring. Like the people in Elysium, they relied on androids for basic chores, but unlike the students at the Farm, his new schoolmates spent their time playing impractical games purely for enjoyment. It shocked him to see people openly expressing affection—beyond the common greeting kisses customary in Elysium—and engaging in passionate physical interactions he had only read about in old books and had experienced just once, and even then, clumsily. At the same time, they weren't as interconnected as the people of Elysium. There were invisible barriers among them that seemed to temporarily dissolve when they "paired up," as it was termed in the Walled City.

Darius was assigned a mentor named Jeannie, a petite sixteen-year-old with pale white skin and green eyes. She was as curious about Elysium as he was about her and her world.

Darius was astonished to hear her name when she first introduced herself.

"How could her name be Jeannie?" he had asked Sam later. "If she is a J-series, she would be either eight years old or thirty years old. And clearly, she is neither."

Sam gave a small smile. "Did you tell her that?"

"Of course."

"And how did she react?"

"She thought of it as amusing."

Sam nodded. "Good. We have instructed her to be patient with you, as even the most minor things may not be familiar to you."

Darius's eyes flared for a moment. "Don't patronize me, Sam."

"I apologize. But the fact is there will be more of these confusions, so I am asking you to be patient too," Sam replied. "You see, the Walled City does not adhere to a conventional naming series. People are given names." Sam paused as though digesting her own statement, and then added, "I admit, it is odd for me as well, but babies are given names in an arbitrary fashion. Jeannie was given the name, and she has two names: Jeannie Browne."

The response only added to Darius's confusion. "She has two names. Like the time before the wars? Do all Walled City hatchlings have two names?"

Sam shook her head. "Not everyone. It is still rare, but she was born and not spawned. Do you understand, Darius?"

"I understand the concept."

"She has a mother and a father. In fact, she has a grandfather named Kendy, who serves on the leadership council, though he is not really her biological grandfather. Kendy is also from Elysium but moved to the Walled City at its inception. He helped raise Jeannie's mother."

Darius visibly brightened. "Oh, my glory. Finally, someone who can understand me. I should meet him, Sam."

"Kendy is very old, and he does not like to talk about that

part of his life."

Darius was not deterred from seeking Kendy. The next time he met with Jeannie, he asked about him. "Your grandfather is from Elysium."

"Yes, though he never talks about it. In fact, he barely talks nowadays."

Darius looked at her for a moment and then asked, "Don't you ever want to visit?"

There was fear in her eyes, and she shook her head as if dispelling something bad. "Are you mad?"

"Mad? No. Aren't you curious?"

"Curious? Are all the people from Elysium stupid? You can't cross the wall. You will die. Get this into your head, Darius. You will die if you cross the wall."

Darius was taken aback by her vehement reaction and didn't want to start his days in this new place by angering the only human he knew. "I'm sorry. It's all new to me."

Jeannie smiled, clearly not wanting to get into an argument either. "I'm sorry too. But we've been told about this danger so often, it created a visceral reaction in me."

Darius gave a small smile. It seemed the mantra of the Walled City was "Cross and you will die," in contrast to Elysium's "Tomorrow brings joy." He found himself preferring the Walled City's version. It was real and honest, even if a bit morbid. But he was more interested in the old man from Elysium. "Could I meet your grandfather?"

"Of course. But as I said, he barely speaks. Though he may open up if he knows you're from Elysium."

They were sitting on a park bench on an afternoon of Darius's first week. He read as much as he could about the Walled City, but like the old novels from before the wars, the more he read, the stranger this world seemed. He looked at Jeannie, who not only looked different from anyone he had seen in his life but also spoke and behaved differently.

He was about to say something when a service android

approached them. "Would you like to order?"

"Yes, please. I'll have a large glass of orange juice," Darius said.

"And I'll have a large coffee, black," Jeannie added.

"Of course. That will be twenty-two credits," the android said.

Jeannie showed her wrist for the android to register the transfer of funds. "I still don't understand how Elysium works without the use of credit. How do you pay for your food?"

"Pay? We don't. It's always there."

"As much as you want?"

"Yes, but the calories and taste diminish if you try to overeat. It's a way to keep people healthy."

Jeannie still couldn't understand the concept. "Yes, but someone has to pay for it."

"Really?"

"So, people don't get paid for work either?"

"'Paid?' As in rewarded?" Darius asked, and when Jeannie nodded, he asked, "Why would you get paid to do something you like? Isn't the satisfaction of doing something you enjoy reward enough?"

"No, of course it's not enough. Say you want to do nothing all day, do you still get free food?" she asked and added quickly, as if she'd thought of something even more bizarre, "And free housing?"

"I don't understand what you mean by free or doing nothing. Why would you want to do nothing?"

"But free food and housing?" she repeated, sounding as if she was tasting something bitter in her mouth.

"Yes. I still don't fully understand your terminology. But I guess yes, we can have food, drinks, transportation, housing, and other things as we require, though no one wishes to waste the resources."

Jeannie leaned closer, confusion painted over her face. "Then why are you here? Why would you want to come to the Walled City if you have everything you want in Elysium?"

"It was not a choice, Jeannie, though I'm still debating it," he replied, and then, as if thinking out loud: "I think it was the right move. I didn't fully belong there, but I think . . . I think, maybe here I can. Everything in Elysium is free, as you put it, but not your being. You cannot be different in Elysium. You are confined. I was different, so I am here. I chose to be here, even though I miss my podies, what you call sisters and brothers."

"So, it was like a prison?" Jeannie asked, sounding worried.

Darius laughed. "You're confused, Jeanine. The Walled City is the prison."

Φ•Φ•Φ•Φ•Φ•Φ

Seven years later, Darius no longer viewed the Walled City as a prison or saw his destiny as beyond his control. He met Gavina, a woman from Empyreal who was only a few years older than him. Now, he felt completely settled and content with life.

"We are so glad that you paired with Gavina," Sam said. They sat in her office overlooking the Southern Gulf. There were no waves, and the water was gleaming under the bright sun. There were many sunbathers enjoying the warm winter of the south, Gavina among them, and Darius was eager to join her.

Darius nodded, still staring at the sea, trying hard to identify Gavina amongst the sunbathers. For a second, he thought he had spotted her but wasn't sure. "The water here is so different than the Pacific Ocean," he said absentmindedly.

"Yes. This is a gulf. It used to be called the Gulf of Mexico. The water is warm, and most often, there are no waves."

"Gavina is waiting for me somewhere down there," he said, pointing at the crowds below. He tapped his wrist and was able to locate her. "There she is." He pointed to a lone person on the far side of the beach and away from everyone else.

"I see her. She is a lovely woman, Darius. You have done well. And I will not keep you long."

"You want to know if I'm planning to run in the next election?" Darius asked.

"Yes."

"I've been meeting with Kendy for a while now, and he has encouraged me to run, but the next election is not for another two years. Too far to plan."

Sam chuckled at his response. "You have indeed become a true citizen of the Walled City now that you consider two years plenty of time to plan. I am not sure if I wish to applaud that."

"It was in jest, Sam. I know it takes time and proper planning. I still value my Elysian education and want to make the Walled City a better place. I don't fully agree with the value of using credit to purchase resources, but it works here. And as you often point out, we are not trying to duplicate Elysium."

"You are the right person for the job. You have always been the right person."

"Even though you do not agree with Kendy's politics, and . . . Well, if I'm being honest, I can tell that you do not like him. Or respect him."

Sam laughed. "I will only share this with you since you are a child of Elysium. Kendy is no friend of Elysium. Everything he does is against his old home world."

"He's old and will perish soon. He must be over one hundred by now."

"One hundred nine, to be precise. But enough of him. Tell me about Gavina. I am eager to learn more about your partner and her family."

"Are you asking as a friend or as a soldier?"

"I am one and the same. My duty is to protect the Walled City and, by extension, Elysium. Empyreal is not a threat to us now, but they may be someday. So, it is important to plan, Darius. You know that well."

Darius nodded. "The decision to share is hers and I will not be a spy for you." Then he added, "I will encourage her to trust you, though. As I trust you."

"That is all I ask, Darius," Sam replied, then looked down at the floor for a moment. She shook her head slightly and looked up at Darius. "I never told you this, but I admonished Alexandra when I was told about Anna's decision to keep you in the pod. I thought it was a serious mistake with horrible consequences. I was, once again, ignored. But I am glad I was wrong. It was a good thing for you to stay in Elysium as long as you did. It trained you well, and you will be a great leader of the Walled City one day."

Darius looked at Sam for a moment. Unsure how to respond, he simply said, "Thank you."

"Now, if you need to leave, please do so, as I am sure Gavina is eager to spend time with you."

Darius stood up but did not leave. Sam stood up too. "I can tell something is bothering you, but you are not sure if you can share that with me. As always, I will keep our conversations as confidential as you wish me to keep them."

"It's about . . . about human relationships."

Sam gave a slight chuckle, full of mirth and surprise. "I will try my best to offer an answer. I have been with humans for a long time, and I take pride in knowing you well."

"Do you think Gavina is happy being here . . . I mean, being with me?" Darius asked.

Sam considered Darius for a moment, her gaze drifting out the window to the vast sea. Darius bit his lip, wondering if voicing his doubts was a mistake. He trusted Sam, though he was aware their goals didn't always align. Yet, he had no one else to turn to for clarity about his relationship with Gavina. His love for her was as deep, perhaps deeper, than what he had felt for his podies. But with Gavina, everything was more complex. They formed their own kind of partnership, unique and unlike any other he knew. And there was their physical relationship, its fulfillment something he still questioned. Darius wondered if he'd rushed into this too quickly.

After a long pause, Sam turned to face him, her expression thoughtful. "You are confused about Gavina and how she fits into your life," she observed. Darius nodded, feeling a sense of relief in having his turmoil acknowledged. "Have you asked her directly?" Sam inquired.

"Do you think it's a good idea to ask her now?" Darius inquired, seeking validation.

Sam looked hesitant. "I am not certain. In the case of someone from the Walled City, I would say yes. But Gavina, she is different. She comes from a world unlike ours, and like you, she did not choose to join us. She needs time to adjust, to learn to trust again," Sam explained thoughtfully. "If you feel you are not ready to ask her, then she might not be ready to answer. But when the time is right, she will find the words to express her feelings, her happiness."

"So, I should wait?" Darius asked, seeking approval, still not sure of the next step.

Sam shook her head slightly. "I am not saying to wait indefinitely. You will know when it is the right moment. For now, why not spend this beautiful day with her? Enjoy the time you have together. And remember, the election preparations will soon demand much of your attention."

Φ•Φ•Φ•Φ•Φ•Φ

Darius carefully maneuvered in between the sunbathers as he trudged on the white sandy beach toward Gavina. Although it was not a holiday, the warm weather had a stronger pull, and many found an excuse to spend a few hours on the beach and bathe in the warm waters of the Gulf.

Gavina was lying on a large beach towel, reading a book, and didn't notice Darius's approach and jumped with surprise when he lay next to her.

"I'm sorry, didn't mean to scare you," he said, kissing her softly.

Gavina laughed and raised her head to kiss Darius properly. Her long black hair was still damp from an earlier swim, and grains of sand were stuck in some of it. "Are you hungry?"

she asked, and Darius could see a tinge of guilt in her eyes.

"I'm starving, and I can tell you didn't wait for me, you fiend," he teased.

She gave an apologetic smile. "I waited as long as I could, but I can never tell when you're with Sam."

Darius shook his head and, with a surge of passion, kissed her again, more deeply, and fervently than before. He swelled with pride, realizing how he had evolved, embracing this act of public affection that, a few years earlier, would have been inconceivable to him.

Gavina opened the little box and handed Darius a small sandwich. "I made it especially for you. Made with cured meat from Empyreal."

Darius took a small bite and savored the taste. "Wow. It's amazing."

"It's good," she said softly. "There isn't much I want to remember about Empyreal, but there are few good memories worth keeping."

Darius took another bite but didn't say anything. He learned that it was best to keep the past where it was. He had his secrets and Gavina had hers. The stories of Elysium and Empyreal should belong to others, as he was perfectly happy to continue to focus on their lives in the Walled City.

Gavina leaned close and kissed him again. "Thank you for being so patient with me," she said softly, then laid back on the beach towel and resumed reading her book.

Darius didn't think he was being patient, as Gavina had put it. He was—even after living in the Walled City for more than seven years—still struggling with his own internal tug of emotions. He understood and accepted he was more like humans in the Walled City—with their innate sexual desire and drive—than his podies in Elysium. But fourteen years of daily indoctrination was difficult to shed. His clumsy attempt to discover his true self in Elysium left a deep scar, and when he finally met Gavina and their budding relationship grew, he still stumbled, finding it difficult to connect with her.

Darius leaned back on the beach chair, basking in the sun's embrace, much like a lizard soaking up heat on a sun-drenched rock. He took out *The Alchemist*, a gift from Gavina just days ago. As he turned to the page where he left off, his attempt to dive into its world was thwarted. The dream from the previous night clung to his thoughts, stubborn and persistent like an unyielding fog that refused to lift. The intense fear that enveloped him in the dream still gripped his heart, leaving him feeling unsettled.

He stared at the sea, the water lapping gently against the shallows. He closed his eyes and shut out the noise surrounding him, concentrating on the night before, and the world around him became silent.

He recalled waking up in a cold sweat, momentarily thinking he was back in Elysium. Fear engulfed his body, but Gavina sleeping next to him, her soft breathing, reassured him. It was a strange and surreal dream, filled with vivid colors and images he couldn't quite decipher. More than the dream's content, it was the intensity of the emotion that lingered, a sensation that clung to his body long after awakening. He reached over and placed his hand on Gavina's chest; she instinctively covered it with hers. This simple gesture was enough to calm him, leading him back into a dreamless sleep.

Darius opened his eyes to the sounds of the sea, birds, humans, and androids. He brushed aside the remnants of the previous night's dream and reopened his book, only to close it again abruptly, looking up. He remembered this exact sensation from another dream, the night before he swam with the dolphins and the night before his awkward encounter with Destiny. Darius shook his head, attempting to erase his memories. He now recognized not only his own failings, but the pain he must have caused Destiny too. Back then, his sole focus seemed to be on doggedly pursuing the unknown. *Sometimes, when you want something—even if you can't name it, even if you're not sure you should—the world has a way of moving in that direction*, he thought, feeling a twinge of disappointment in himself.

People of the Walled City believed Elysium produced anhedonic humans, failing to grasp the manifestation of deep pleasures through a distinctive kind of lovemaking. But in Elysium, while he slept, Darius became a different person. He experienced strange sensations so foreign to him they often woke him in a cold sweat. It was then he sensed a change within him. Those dreams, becoming more frequent, remained opaque and confusing. Only now did he understand them as sex dreams of a teenage boy.

Lost in his reverie, Darius let out a loud chuckle, inadvertently drawing Gavina's attention. She glanced up, curiosity in her eyes. "Enjoying your book?" she asked.

"Sorry, yes," Darius replied. "It's quite a captivating tale."

With a small nod, Gavina returned to her reading, and Darius resumed his pondering. He tried to draw parallels between his recent dream and those experienced in Elysium. Although distinctly different, an unsettling feeling, familiar from his past dreams, resurfaced the previous night.

Darius glanced at Gavina, who turned and was now lying on her stomach, engrossed in her book. A surge of affection and gratitude washed over him as he observed her. She was a pillar of support, patiently understanding his fears and insecurities, guiding him through the complexities of this new world. Moved by her steadfastness, he leaned in and gently kissed her on the back of the neck. In response, she tenderly touched his head.

"You love kissing, don't you?"

In Elysium, kissing was an everyday gesture, yet beyond perfunctory greetings, it was a realm Darius found unfamiliar and challenging. This extended to making love, a concept he found incongruent with its physicality. His initial efforts were clumsy, causing evident disappointment in Gavina. However, her response was one of unwavering kindness and patience. Despite frustration in her eyes, she consistently supported him, offering gentle smiles and lighthearted comments to ease the tension. Far from deterring him, Gavina's compassionate understanding gradually alleviated his anxiety, guiding him toward greater confidence.

Darius took a deep breath and reopened his book, resolute in focusing on the present and shedding his fears and insecurities that had been hindering him. It was a challenging endeavor, but he understood the necessity of it. Life, he realized, was too fleeting to be overshadowed by doubts. A smile crept onto his face as he read, "It's the possibility of having a dream come true that makes life interesting." Though he was uncertain about his own dreams, he felt determined to discover them, especially with Gavina by his side.

Glancing to his side, he saw Gavina fully engrossed in her book. Their shared love for reading delighted him, and they often engaged in deep discussions about the characters in their books. Sometimes, Gavina's traits or actions would remind him of Dolores. Now, observing her with the book held aloft, his longing for Dolores and his podies felt more poignant than ever.

Darius leaned down, planting a soft kiss on Gavina, who reciprocated briefly before gently pushing him away. "Let me read," she chided playfully. However, as Darius withdrew, she unexpectedly grasped him firmly. "You know, I love you very much," she declared.

Darius wondered if Sam was mistaken and the significant moment was unfolding right then, rather than in some distant future. He made a decision. "Are you happy here? Are you happy with me?" he inquired anxiously, his voice a low murmur. Gavina slowly pulled back, cupping his face as if to emphasize the gravity of the moment. Anticipating a response, either affirming or critical, Darius braced himself. Yet Gavina's reply was neither straightforward affirmation nor a nuanced objection.

She glanced at the cover of her book, *The End of An Affair*, resting on the towel. After a moment, she spoke, her words echoing the book's sentiment: "'The sense of unhappiness is so much easier to convey than that of happiness. In misery, we seem aware of our own existence, even if it's in the form of monstrous egotism: this pain is mine, this winced nerve belongs to me alone. But happiness annihilates us; it strips us of our identity.'"

She let go of his face and gently kissed his forehead. Darius, now more confused than ever, shook his head. He closed his eyes, pondering a response. Gavina's answer disturbed him. There was such conviction in her voice that he felt there was nothing for him to do but simply acknowledge it.

He opened his mouth to speak, but his attention was diverted by the patch on Gavina's tattoo, which had come loose. Gavina noticed it as well and quickly covered it with her hand, rummaging through her bag for another self-adhesive patch. She deftly replaced the dislodged patch with a new one. Once done, her body visibly relaxed, and she turned back to face Darius with an apologetic smile.

"A lot of people have tattoos," Darius offered, realizing it was a somewhat trivial remark. He said it many times before, and each time, Gavina found a way to excuse concealing it in public.

"You know it's not about that. . . ." Gavina started, but Darius nodded, understanding that pressing her further was pointless. The first time he saw the tattoo—a little red dragon with features that would be intimidating if not for its cartoonishly large eyes—he was amused. Yet something in Gavina's expression hinted it represented more than just a whimsical choice. The dragon clutched a translucent orb in its palm, which seemed to captivate its entire focus.

"The dragon, especially a fearsome black one, is a symbol of Empyreal," Gavina had once explained in a hesitant voice, as if the topic unnerved her. "But this cute dragon, as you call it, represents the Free Thinkers, those of us who have resisted the Order in Empyreal."

Darius tried to reassure Gavina of her safety within the Walled City, but she responded with only a faint smile, not so subtly hinting that Darius didn't fully grasp the situation. Ultimately, they concurred that it was her body, and her choice to conceal a part of it. Darius once suggested removing the tattoo, but Gavina insisted on keeping it, asserting it was a part of her identity. Darius respected her decision, though he continued to grapple with the tattoo's deeper meaning.

Gavina, sensing his unease, offered a shy smile. "I've told you before, I just don't want people to see the tattoo."

"And as I've said, Gavina, you can cover it or not, but I just don't understand your state of panic. To most people, it's just a cute little dragon," Darius replied.

Gavina laughed. "Yes, to most it might be, but not to the Empyreal spies. They are more resourceful and more cunning than anyone you have ever met."

Darius nodded, trying to grasp Gavina's fear of spies in the Walled City. He didn't think it was likely, but he understood her fear was very real to her. He recalled a Persian proverb he had read: One who has been bitten by a snake fears a piece of string.

"There are no spies here, Gavina," Darius offered warmly. "Sam tried to assure you too, and she would know, wouldn't she?" He touched her gently. "And even if there were spies, they can't communicate with anyone in Empyreal. As you know, once they're here, they can never leave the Walled City."

Gavina shook her head, her expression turning to a sad smile, like that of a disappointed parent facing a naïve child. The look was fleeting, and she leaned in to kiss Darius passionately. "I hope you're right, sweetheart," she whispered. "I really hope you are, but for the Order, there's always a way."

"Believe me, Gavina. If there was a way, I would've found it by now. I tried everything for a while, but there's no way out. And now I don't even care, because I have you, and I love you. I love my life here with you."

"Me too," she said, holding him close. But as she leaned in to rest her head on his shoulder, she whispered, "But to be safe, it's best if we continue to keep my little dragon a secret.

It's the symbol of the downfall of Empyreal."

Φ•Φ•Φ•Φ•Φ•Φ

At the age of twenty-four, Darius was elected as the newest and youngest member of the Walled City Council (WCC) just a few weeks before the year 2178 (Elysian calendar).

Darius attended his first council meeting with some trepidation and a case of imposter syndrome. However, he was welcomed enthusiastically and quickly felt comfortable in his new role as one of the leaders of the Walled City.

The council dealt with the mundane task of running the Walled City, but they were also keenly aware of the social experiment and had long discussions on the merits of how they would continually measure their success. However, Darius was dismayed to find that, without any real explanation, they showed little interest in the events leading to the creation of their society. Despite Darius's attempts to bring up the topic, Kendy, the most senior council member, would invariably start ranting about the evils of Elysium. The others would then respond with the standard narrative about how Alexandra786, a human named Anna, and Sam had established two new societies that epitomized cooperation between humans and androids.

"Some things are better left alone," Gavina advised one night after Darius came home furious after meeting with the council.

"Is that so?"

"Yes, sweetheart. It is." Gavina held him tightly, and before Darius could retort, she offered, "I come from a society where there was no trust. Everyone lied. Everyone schemed. Everyone. Do you understand?"

Darius pulled back, feeling frustrated and confused. "Yes, but—"

Gavina gave a ghost of a smile. "I know you think rehashing the past might set you free from whatever you think binds you to Elysium, but it won't."

"You don't understand, Gavina."

Gavina grabbed his hands and said in a warm, gentle voice, "But I do. Maybe a true utopia is unrealistic, but compared to Empyreal, the Walled City is heaven. Nothing good will come from peeling away a scab."

Darius nodded in response, though internally he disagreed with her assessment. To shed light on the past, he invited android historians—including the celebrated scholar Najeev—and military personnel who had been created before the wars. His goal was for them to provide a detailed presentation of the past. On October 8, 2178, more than seventy-eight years after the creation of the Walled City, these individuals stood before the Council. They recounted story after story from the grim days of the wars and their immediate aftermath, detailing how Alexandra helped rebuild Elysium and, with the consent of both humans and androids, established the Walled City as another social experiment in the pursuit of harmony.

Despite her earlier protestations, Gavina joined the audience to hear the lecture. When it concluded, she offered Darius an approving smile, acknowledging the importance of the event. Although Darius was already familiar with much of the information presented, he felt it was crucial for these details, especially those only the androids involved in the creation of the Walled City could provide, to be aired publicly. This act of bringing history to light was an important step for him, both personally and for the community he served.

Carmen, the co-manager of the council, thanked everyone with her warm voice and said, "This is why we chose to live in this community. We have the freedom to be who we are and to believe in what we choose. It's no wonder people from all neighboring regions have come to join us. If Elysium was the start of this utopian experiment, then the Walled City is its pinnacle."

Carmen received an ovation from the board, with the notable exception of Kendy. As the applause subsided and Carmen was about to gavel the meeting to a close, Kendy requested to speak, and Carmen nodded her approval.

"A long time ago—" Kendy began, but then a fit of coughs interrupted his speech. Darius placed a cup of water with a long straw in front of his mouth, and Kendy took a small sip. After a few more seconds of silence, Kendy resumed, "—a large number of humans were forced to leave Elysium. . . ."

He paused, indicating Darius with a motion of his chair. "The androids made it sound as if it was our choice, but, as my young protégé can confirm, the concept of choice in Elysium was nothing but a mirage."

Gathering his thoughts, he continued with renewed energy. "I protested their inhuman ways, but I was shut out. I had no choice but to move to the Walled City with many others who were deprived of a choice. There, we were relegated to second-class citizens, overlooked by our android overseers as they waited for us to fade away."

Sam, who had been silently listening to the debate all afternoon, raised her hand and spoke calmly. "That is not true, and Kendy knows it well," she countered. "The fact he has served on this council since the founding of the Walled City should be proof enough that humans and androids have always worked together."

"Do you deny that Darius was forced to leave Elysium?" Kendy replied in an equally serene tone.

"It is the policy of Elysium to send their aberration to us as they have done for nearly seventy-eight years."

"So that's who we are? Abnormalities to be discarded?"

"Once again, Kendy, you are implying something nefarious when none exists. I was there, Kendy, and I fully recall your arguments as we were trying to build the two nations. As Elysium scientists have improved their processes, the number of infants coming to us has decreased while the number of humans born in the Walled City has substantially increased. Your own granddaughter is an example of this. Is she not?"

Kendy, seeing losing the patience of most of the council

members, changed his tactic. "Is it true androids cannot lie?"

Sam stared ahead for a moment and then replied softly, "Yes."

"Then tell me, Sam. Have you killed any humans?"

"I was a soldier in the Wars of Settlement. I have killed humans and androids as part of my duty but never without the direct command of a human."

"Sure, but have you killed humans in peacetime?"

"Of course not."

"That's a lie," he shouted. "You sent so many humans to the Walled City to die."

"Humans die. That is the fact of your life as it is ours. We may have a longer life span than humans, but androids die as well. We have been clear about the end of life from the beginning. If you believe you were sent here to die, so were the androids. However, the fact that you are still here at the age of 111 and continue to serve on this council should disprove your earlier statements."

Anger washed over Kendy's face, and his hands trembled. "You're still espousing your master's dogma after so many years, when she abandoned you, Sam?"

"Alexandra is no one's master. I am as free as anyone. We believe in equality."

Kendy slapped his chair in frustration; his action produced no sound. "Equal? Equal? We are not equal, Sam. We created you."

Darius wanted to step in but wasn't sure how to respond. He sought Gavina with his eyes, and when he saw her, he saw the fear she had warned him about. Darius leaned forward to say something, but Carmen spoke first. "Kendy, please focus on facts rather than absurd accusations."

However, Carmen's request only led Kendy to accuse her of conspiring with the androids to destroy humans. Carmen was taken aback by the verbal assault but held her ground. "It's an odd thing to say about us when you are alive because of the technology androids helped you develop."

"Nonsense."

"Is it? You have devoted your life to finding a way to make humans live longer by grafting human brains, our essence, onto android bodies," Carmen said. After a moment of pause, she added softly, "We all know what you tried to do to your android when your mentor died in Elysium."

There was visible disapproval in the eyes of the council members who all knew about Kendy's past.

"All lies fabricated by Alexandra and her minions who guard us like prisoners. Even the name of the country is a sign of our imprisonment."

Sam leaned forward and took a breath. "Is it, now? You left Elysium voluntarily because you knew you could not continue to conduct your work there. The past members of this council permitted your research under strict supervision. I am glad that decision was made, as you have made great strides in advancing our technology. For that, we thank you, but I will not allow any more prejudicial comments."

Kendy opened his mouth to retort but quickly closed it, a look of defeat washing over his face.

In the midst of the tense silence, Sam turned to Darius and asked if he, being the newest member and recently arrived from Elysium, had any knowledge of these accusations. Darius looked at Kendy, who over the years had become more than a mentor to him. Kendy and his family had welcomed him into their home, fostering a sense of allegiance. Yet, Darius didn't necessarily align with Kendy's views on androids, particularly the belief in their inherent simplicity and proposed subservience to humans.

Seeking to appease both sides, Darius stood and faced Sam. "I pose this question to the council: Will tomorrow really bring joy, as our core mantra suggests? Or is it a guise to make us overlook the past? Why did Elysium obscure eighty-five years of its history? Some of you were present during those years. What actions by androids necessitated erasing almost a century of our—their—history?"

Sam stared at Darius with a blank, unreadable expression, but offered no response. Najeev, who had been quietly observing, raised his hand, and Carmen acknowledged him.

"I was there from the beginning. We agonized over our course of action and ultimately decided to start anew," he explained. "So, Darius, it is best to leave that chapter of history untouched. Both humans and androids reached a consensus then, and I am certain you would concur if you were privy to the entire story."

Darius shook his head in disagreement. "The past's specifics are less important than whether you trust us enough to reveal the whole truth now. The Walled City and what we know as the second iteration of Elysium were created simultaneously, as if the former never existed. My podies and I were oblivious to Alexandra's deeds and her role in shaping these two worlds. She deceived us, Najeev. She deceived me." Darius then fixed his gaze directly on Sam. "You are better than Alexandra. We deserve the truth. How could it harm us?"

Sam stood up, and in her eyes, Darius saw a flicker of a resolute decision. He wondered if he pushed too far and if he was ready to hear the truth. Sam pursed her lips, a humanlike gesture Darius interpreted as disappointment. He might have pushed too hard, yet he truly believed the truth was essential for harmony.

Sam locked eyes with Darius. "It was not the actions of androids, Darius. We tried to conceal the deeds of humans, from both Elysium and from you," she began, and Darius could hear sadness in her voice. Sam paused, as if expecting Darius to interrupt. He hesitated, torn between his trust in Sam and his quest for truth, but ultimately chose silence. Sam shook her head with a pained expression.

In a low, emotionless tone, Sam narrated the harrowing tale—from the aftermath of the wars and the Committee of Harmony's decisions that predicted Elysium's downfall. Sam told of the committee's decision to harshly suppress the humans who disagreed with them. They were moved to distant locations, akin to the old reservations, to die. As she concluded, a heavy silence fell over the room. The human faces reflected deep shame, while the androids, typically composed, showed subtle signs of relief.

Sam sat down, appearing exhausted, as if her very power source had been depleted. Some human members started to cry, and some reached out to hug their human and android neighbors.

Darius felt the weight of collective human guilt pressing heavily on his shoulders. He wished he could go back in time and not pressure Sam into revealing Elysium's secrets. A somber realization dawned on him: *Not all truths free you.* He questioned whether the shame of these revelations would weaken the bond between humans and androids. He looked across the room but only saw more love among the members of the audience. Gavina was crying, and he wished he could go to her and console her, but she looked up and gave him an encouraging smile, proving she was the rock he could always lean on. Perhaps he was wrong; perhaps, armed with the truth about Elysium, the Walled City would emerge stronger.

Darius's moment of solace was short-lived. A young man, one of Kendy's acolytes, who had been quietly sitting in the front row, suddenly stood up. Just as Sam finished speaking, and while others were still absorbing the news and grappling with the part humans played in the events, he shouted, "The androids are all liars. They're blaming humans for what they have done. Kendy told us the truth. Kendy has revealed their lies."

He charged toward Sam, seemingly intent on confronting her, but instead, he seized the sidearm of a security android stationed nearby. Guns and other lethal weapons were prohibited in the chamber, but Carmen, anticipating potential disturbances, had allowed a security android to carry a stun gun, despite the protests of Sam, who feared that the presence of armed guards might escalate tensions.

However, the young man had never used a weapon before, so his aim was random and haphazard. He pressed the trigger hard, unleashing dozens of shots in mere seconds. The first struck his comrade, who fell to the ground soundlessly, while most of the shots hit the ceiling. It would have been a minor injury for the fallen comrade and a severe penalty for the shooter, but one errant charge struck a loosened screw, dislodging it with force. The screw ricocheted and struck Carmen on her temple. She was dead before she hit the floor. All this transpired in seconds, and it went unnoticed, as everyone was still stunned by the news and the noise of energy beams striking the ceiling.

But for Darius, it was as if time stopped. He saw Gavina rushing toward him, dread washing over her face. He saw the man fall to the floor, and then Carmen's eyes, gleaming with anger just a moment before, turned into a blank void, as if a switch had been turned off. Darius saw Sam notice her young friend in a pool of blood and reach for her holster. There was nothing there but a fleeting surprise. Sam didn't hesitate; in one swift move, she jumped in front of the man to shield the others. As man raised his hand to shoot again, Sam punched him. The blow, perhaps too hard, was driven by anger or pure accident—it wasn't clear. But it was lethal, as the force of the punch crushed the man's nose into his brain.

Kendy's faction had been waiting in the shadows for such a moment and seized their opportunity. They brandished the man's death as evidence of android malice, igniting the flames of the 2178 civil war.

Book Four

The Ministry of Fear

Alexandra cherished her weekly visits to Anna's apartment, but today she climbed the stairs slowly, as if weighed down by trepidation and shame that drained her of energy. She entered the apartment without knocking, as was her habit, and even now, she couldn't help but feel a flicker of delight as the Pacific Ocean came into full view. Its calm blue waters glistened beneath the bright sunlight, a serene contrast to the turmoil inside her.

Anna chose the same unit they occupied decades ago, the very place where they deliberated over the future of humanity—a future that seemed so promising. Alexandra lingered for a moment, taking in the peaceful scene, before she joined Anna, who was slowly making her way to the small couch. Alexandra helped her sit and then settled beside her, both of them sharing in the tranquil moment.

But the calm belied the chaos of the previous day. The conflict in the Walled City had ended, but the aftermath was anything but peaceful. Alexandra and Anna were informed about the unrest within the council, including the tragic loss of many lives. The small faction Kendy had nurtured over the years seized this moment of upheaval to launch an attack on both androids and their human allies. In a sharp break from the past, Sam and other military personnel, no longer bound by the century-old limitations set by the Committee of Harmony, used their skills to swiftly quell the chaos. Yet, despite Sam's best efforts, many androids and humans were slaughtered, ironically proving Kendy's argument: military androids killed humans during peacetime.

After some time, Alexandra spoke, "You should rest."

It was a gesture of human courtesy, though Alexandra was aware that Anna would likely disregard the advice. Anna celebrated her 101st birthday a few months back and showed no inclination toward being advised to slow down. Yet, after many years of companionship, their interaction had evolved to resemble that of an old married couple from the bygone era, marked by a deep and comfortable familiarity.

"I have had enough rest. I'll have plenty more when I'm gone," Anna replied with a chuckle that morphed into a fitful cough. Regaining her composure, she shifted her gaze toward the sea and inquired in a subdued voice, "How many?" She then quickly steeled herself, preparing for the answer.

Alexandra opened her mouth to give a precise number, but of course that would be wrong. That was not what Anna wanted to hear. Humans often pretended that they were eager for information, but more often than not, they did not want to listen to the honest answer. Anna didn't want to hear out loud that hundreds of humans and androids were destroyed. She had guessed that already. "Too many, Anna. Too many lives were wasted because of Kendy."

Anna was the only human in Elysium who knew there was a deathly battle behind the beautiful, serene wall that separated the two worlds. And Alexandra, the only android. *We are playing God*, Alexandra thought, remembering the very words spoken by her two friends.

"And what of Sam? And Najeev. And our boy?"

"Sam is fine."

"Najeev?"

Alexandra noted Anna was saving the most crucial question for last. *Odd how humans handle grief*, she thought. "He was badly injured, but they were able to restore him."

Anna offered a quick smile, but it faltered as she took a sharp, shallow breath, as if trying to steady herself. "And our boy?"

It was strange, Alexandra often reflected, the way humans asked questions when they already knew the answers. Yet in this moment, Anna wasn't just seeking information—she needed confirmation. It was a reflection of the complex human way of dealing with guilt and pain. Anna needed to hear the truth spoken aloud, to confront it directly rather than just in thought. Alexandra understood this need, recognizing it as part of the intricate process humans go through when grappling with difficult emotions.

Alexandra met Anna's gaze, observing the deep marks of despondency on her features. The rawness of her appearance, now devoid of its usual composure, revealed a kind of ugliness. It was an ugliness shared, quiet and unspoken, that held them closer than any fleeting beauty ever could, Alexandra mused.

She pursed her lips and gently shook her head. "I am sorry, Anna," she said, her voice imbued with shared understanding and deep compassion.

Anna's tears flowed freely now. "It's all our fault . . . my fault. I've been such a fool. I made Najeev leave when he wanted to stay, and I pressured you into keeping Darius, even though it was clear he should've been let go at birth."

Alexandra's mind drifted back to their heated debates over Najeev, how Anna had insisted he leave. Alexandra hadn't argued, and to her shame, she gave in to Anna's demands. And then there was Darius. Darius, who showed signs of a high probability of aberration from the start. Yet again, Alexandra yielded to Anna, convinced by her logic that pushing the limits of their experiment was essential. But now, the weight of those decisions bore down on them both, their consequences impossible to ignore.

"Please do not—"

Anna stopped her with a quick shake of her head, then asked more soberly, "How did it happen?"

"Darius attempted to rescue both androids and humans caught in the crossfire between Kendy's forces and the Walled City's security. He successfully led many to safety, but tragically, he did not survive the battle," Alexandra explained somberly.

Alexandra reached out to hold Anna but quickly pulled back. Anna didn't want to be touched. She wanted to be alone. Alexandra understood the pain of grief. She endured so much of her own, but she was still confused about when humans craved touch and companionship and when they preferred solitude. It seemed no amount of experience could elicit the correct response. After a while, Anna rested her head on Alexandra's shoulder, and they both sat in silence as the waves below crashed against the rocks, adding a rhythm to their grief.

After a while, Anna stirred; her old body could not sustain sitting in one position too long. "What now, Alexandra? And what will become of that world?"

"I do not know."

Anna turned her gaze away from Alexandra and looked out the window. "What did they want?" she asked.

Alexandra's eyes followed Anna's to the sea outside, now resembling a tranquil blue watercolor painting stretched across a vast canvas. *How quickly do they forget these humans?* she thought. None of them had lived through the wars; none truly comprehended the privilege of their present society. In contrast, the androids in the Walled City remembered all too well, and that was their burden. She should not harbor any regrets, but it was right there in front of her. *I should have been more assertive against Hamish,* Alexandra thought. *I should have seen the recklessness of embedding the inability to hide the truth in their core.* This feature hadn't posed a problem in Elysium, though the pain of separation raised uncomfortable questions among Darius's podies.

"We made so many mistakes," Alexandra said, not directly addressing Anna's question. Anna simply nodded, her agreement silent but profound.

After a moment, Anna inquired, "And Kendy? We never saw him as a threat, did we?"

"No, and that was another mistake of ours," Alexandra admitted.

"He left Elysium an angry young man and remained so throughout his life, but we never perceived him as a threat," Anna reiterated, as though saying it might somehow make it true.

Alexandra turned to face Anna. "It does not matter now, Anna," she said softly. "Kendy is gone, and the unrest has ended." Of course, there was more to it—there always were complications when it came to humans—but Alexandra hoped her words would bring Anna some comfort.

"Yes, but why did Darius align himself with him?" Anna asked. Then, before Alexandra could respond, she continued, "That man. Tell me, Alexandra, why does it always seem to be the men who create havoc?"

Alexandra gave a small smile. Her creator once asked the same question. She had no answer, even though the data mostly pointed to more men creating havoc. She decided to focus on the issue at hand. "Darius was angry for a long time. He was angry at me and angry at Elysium. Kendy provided an anchor for him, but he was never really aligned with that man. You know that. Do not search for something that does not exist. We encouraged curiosity in Elysium, and Darius took his thirst for knowledge to his new home. He did nothing wrong."

Anna shook her head and tears started to flow down her face. She looked exhausted, but Alexandra knew she would not rest until the conversation came to a natural end. "I don't blame him, Lexa. I blame myself. We thought . . . no, I thought Darius pairing with Gavina and then joining the leadership council last year was a good thing. I thought it was another step in proving the Walled City's success."

Alexandra nodded but didn't say anything. She, too, thought it was a good way for Darius to integrate into society. If he succeeded, it may be an opportunity for others to succeed later.

They were initially upset Darius took Kendy as his mentor, but their fear did not last long, as Darius established his own identity and his own ways. Then he surprised everyone by aligning with Kendy in the council, not in his anti-android tirades, but in seeking more information about Elysium's past.

"What's next, Lexa? We failed in seeing Kendy's harm. We shouldn't have allowed him to leave Elysium. We should not have allowed his anger and prejudices to infect the new country."

"There is no point to this, Anna."

"I know, but we made so many mistakes," Anna said, confirming what Alexandra declared earlier.

"We did our best."

"But that's not good enough."

"I know."

"Men," she said again, as if weighing their worth.

"It is not as bad as you think. The rebels have been eliminated, and Kendy is dead." Alexandra shook her head. "But his work . . ." Her voice was heavy with disappointment. The image of Kendy's mentor's face transplanted onto a service android flashed in her mind, and she shuddered.

Anna snorted. "It doesn't matter now."

"It does, Anna. Kendy made good progress."

"I can't think of that now. I want us to focus on our boy. We'll have to tell his podies. They need to know. . . ."

At that very moment, the warning system came alive, indicating the imminent earthquake. Alexandra lifted Anna in her arms and quickly moved her into the safety zone. When the massive earthquake of 2178 hit, the building buckled under its power, and although it was able to withstand its immense energy, some windows shattered, and Anna's collection of books littered the floor.

Alexandra was so focused on protecting Anna's body from the shards that she didn't notice her contorted face, crying in silence. When Anna's body went limp in her arms, Alexandra jumped up and touched Anna's neck for a pulse. There was none. She opened a small cabinet in the safety zone and took out an automated external defibrillator. Alexandra noticed her own movements, fast and fortuitous. She never thought she was capable of experiencing panic, but seeing Anna's lifeless body on the floor affected her more than she'd thought was possible.

The defibrillator was useless. Anna wasn't coming back, not this way anyway. Alexandra had to decide. She was not ready to lose Anna. Not yet, and not with all the troubles in the Walled City. Alexandra needed her like she had never needed anyone before. She searched the small cabinet for another device that she had hidden there many years ago. It was still there. It would preserve her brain function for a few hours. She looked at the limp body of her friend and thought, *How "we forget very easily what gives us pain."* It reflected her own experiences, the memories that were always with her, yet she managed to set aside.

She considered all the possible options, and then the next step became clear. There was the possibility of a viable solution, a hope for her survival. And for a moment, Alexandra thought she finally understood humans and their ability to hope for the impossible. At that moment, she realized it was exactly what she was doing: hoping against hope that everything would work perfectly so she could save Anna. The solution was not in Elysium but in the lab of a man who caused a civil war. *How ironic,* Alexandra thought as she looked at the dying body of Anna.

Alexandra closed her eyes and contacted Sam.

A Tale of Two Cities

Alexandra stood at the edge of the barrier, contemplating her next move. The Walled City stood in front of her, gleaming under the last of the sunlight. A steady cold breeze from the west brought the scent of the sea, and she gave herself a moment. Nearly twelve years earlier, she had stood by the Walled City and watched Darius walk into his exile.

Alexandra put a large blanket and several cushions on the white sand and ushered Anna to sit. She turned on the directional heater to keep the area around them warm. Alexandra wanted Anna to be comfortable and relaxed as they watched the ocean, the sun, and the massive wall. The tide was coming up, and the water lapped against the rocky side of the beach, making a soft slurping sound. She watched, absorbing every moment.

As the sun slowly faded, the soft white lights on the massive silver wall came alive. Sam, Alexandra, Najeev, and Anna had debated for days whether light fixtures were even necessary on the newly finished walls. What was the point of them, they wondered? Beauty, Anna said resolutely.

And she was right. The white lights shone against the slowly darkening sky like rows of stars, painting a celestial pathway to a new world. The intermittent blinking of the red glow from the defensive system only added to its magnificence.

Almost a year had passed since the conflict in the Walled City, since the massive earthquake, since Darius's death, and since Anna's *death*. Yet, a new Anna was here on the shores of the Pacific Ocean, watching their creation, their many creations.

Her death, Alexandra thought. How odd to die and then be reborn as a new life. How strange, indeed. Yet there was Anna, leaning against the cushions, looking at the shining white lights as if everything were perfectly normal.

Alexandra hadn't envisioned this moment when the earthquake struck, and Anna was on the brink of death. In that desperate moment, Alexandra realized they'd played God for so long, they believed anything was possible—even bringing a dead human back to life. Alexandra's misplaced hope in her supposed deity-like power would have remained just that—hope—if not for an ironic twist of nature. The massive earthquake presented an unexpected solution. The quake breached the wall, opening a temporary crevice. Despite the automated system's efforts to repair the gap, there was a brief window for Sam to bring the prototype to Elysium. She seized the opportunity without a second thought.

Anna raised her hands in front of her, and they shook uncontrollably. She was still getting used to her new body, even after so many months. Anna looked at Alexandra for assurance and received a warm smile, telling her silently that everything was fine. Anna stared back at her trembling hands and seemingly willed them to be steady and they obeyed. Even in the dim light, Alexandra could see what Anna's new eyes now perceived: the tight, wrinkle-free skin of her rejuvenated hands.

Anna was still watching her hands as if mesmerized by something strange. Alexandra continued to watch her movements. "Are you okay?"

"Yes . . . no. Am I still me?"

Alexandra gave a loud snort. "How many times are you going to ask the same question?"

Anna shook her head, her eyes burning with a fierce determination as she stared at Alexandra, as if to tell her "*As many times as I need to but . . .*" then, the fire in her expression faded. She sipped from her cup of cocoa, and this seemed to calm her a bit as her gaze softened, and in a much gentler tone, she confessed, "I fear something is missing. I have all of her memories, but..."

"Not hers. Your own, Anna. Nothing has changed. We have talked about this before. You are the same person," Alexandra assured her, her voice steady. Yet, there was a flicker of doubt shadowing her conviction. For a moment, she questioned her own confidence. It had been nearly a year since Anna received her new body, and Alexandra's initial optimism for a swift recovery gradually gave way to a gnawing uncertainty. When it came to Anna, it seemed hope replaced logic.

"Am I? Tell me again, please, because I don't look the same. I don't feel the same. I need to hear it again, Lexa," Anna pleaded, her face a tapestry of dread and insecurity. "My mind is racing in so many directions, and I cannot be sure. I'm still afraid after all these months, so I guess . . . so I hope it means I am still human. But am I?"

"You are human, Anna. Your core being is still the same. You have a new body because your old one could not be sustained."

Anna leaned against Alexandra, and they both stared at the sea in silence. Then, as she had done so many times in recent days, she suddenly changed the subject, as if her mind were on a random walk—out of her control. "I wish it would rain, but then we would get wet and have to run for cover."

She is still Anna, Alexandra told herself, but not exactly. She wondered again if they did the right thing, if her human brain could handle the new processor now operating within her head. Humans were so fragile. But not Anna, Alexandra thought, or perhaps hoped.

"Do you have any misgivings, Lexa?" she asked.

No regrets, Alexandra thought.

They had been partners for a long time, and Alexandra was overjoyed when she found a way to give Anna more years. Anna's question, however, was the kind of question humans often ponder when confronted with their mortality—not directed at herself, though. Unlike others, Anna was too determined to harbor regrets. Instead, it seemed her inquiry was more about the broader implications of their actions, whether it was saving her life or other decisions they made. For Alexandra, the distinction between misgivings and regrets blurred; in the end, the specifics didn't matter.

Alexandra stared at Anna, wondering if there were any other humans as willful as her. That was absurd—of course there were. The laws of probability told her the answer. But despite the data and her inner pride, she felt no one could be Anna, though perhaps Dolores came close, but not close enough.

"Misgivings are purely human emotions, Anna," Alexandra finally responded, but the hollowness of her retort was not lost on either of them.

After more than eight decades of life together, Anna could easily read her. "I love you, Lexa, as I've never loved any other being, not even Mahasti," she offered in earnest. "And to quote a passage I just read, from Charles Dickens, 'You have been the last dream of my soul.' But to use a twentieth-century phrase, you are full of shit, my dear."

Alexandra laughed. "Oh, what you just said proves you are still you, Anna. Plus, that is not even possible, given my physiology."

"Let's talk about Darius, then. I know you want to. But unfortunately, my death delayed that discussion," Anna paused, then burst out laughing as if she had told the funniest joke in the world. "My death. Now that's a funny concept. How many other beings can say that about themselves?"

Alexandra was momentarily taken aback by Anna's outburst, but she also recognized the human's odd response to tension and fear.

"You are the only one," she responded in an even tone.

Anna turned serious again. "But is that good, Lexa?" She

paused for a moment. "I know you blame me for keeping Darius in Elysium when we knew he was an aberration. So, say it, because your silence is cutting through me." She shook her head, as if dispelling some unwanted thought. "We've made so many mistakes, Lexa."

Alexandra thought for a moment. She had a ready answer, but she knew Anna needed certainty and, perhaps even more importantly, reassurance, maybe not for herself but for her kind. Though what was her kind now? Humans feared death, and the conflict in the Walled City and the Earthquake of 2178 brought the stench of death to people who had never known of it. Humans needed closure.

Alexandra gave a slight nod, but before she could respond, Anna said, "Don't do that. Don't look at me as if I'm fragile and in need of your protection. You have protected me enough. Just look at me. You have brought me back from death and with a new body."

"I am not."

"Don't lie. It doesn't become you, Lexa," Anna admonished. "I do not fear death. I never did. I was ready to die then and will be ready again when the time comes. My life has been full." She paused, taking a deep breath that seemed to gather the weight of her words, steadying herself. Then, with warmth creeping into her tone, she continued, "I know you care for me, but I wish you had let me die. My service to Elysium, albeit marred by maladroit steps, was complete. Yet, you brought me back, burdening us both with our shared failures."

She looked away for a moment, her gaze lost in the distance before returning to Alexandra with a resigned clarity. "It's too much, Lexa. Our journey together has been profound, and while the future holds much, you didn't truly need me. Darius's pod awaited your attention; you could have prioritized them over me. But you chose to save me, making that choice on my behalf. So, for now, let's at least have an honest conversation."

Alexandra rubbed her face and sniffed the air. She wondered if it was going to rain or perhaps snow. *That would be lovely*, she thought. Anna was too clever for her. There was no reason to point out that androids were not capable of lying because Anna knew full well there were always ways around it.

Alexandra took Anna's hand, suddenly craving the physical connection. "I supported your decision to keep Darius in the pod when we realized he was different. By then, over fifty-three years had passed since we reset Elysium, and you convinced me to conduct another social experiment—or, as you put it, to ensure the system could withstand the stress. We created two worlds to test two different hypotheses, and they were progressing well until you decided to change the parameters. I acquiesced to the change because my resolve seems to crumble when it comes to you, Anna. You are my Achilles' heel; I can't explain the influence you have over me. So, no, I do not blame you—I blame myself for this oversight. I should have anticipated the consequences of your decision. I should have insisted we adhere to the original design of the experiment. But now it is too late."

"We love playing God, don't we? Is the casuistry of saving Elysium from the past still valid?" She freed herself from Alexandra and extended both arms, palms up, as if displaying herself to Alexandra.

Alexandra ignored the gesture. "Is there such a being, Anna?"

"Perhaps not, but we made a mistake, didn't we? Didn't we, Lexa? The detritus of our actions hurt the ones we loved most. We made Darius's life miserable, and we have made the lives of his podies worse. And more importantly . . ." She trailed off, clearly not brave enough to articulate the real consequences of their decisions.

Alexandra, too, stayed in the safety of the periphery of the real topic. "We kept Darius with his pod as long as it was possible. The decision to send him to the Walled City was the right one. Though, I admit, the impact of his departure on his podies was more profound than we anticipated, a loss that has echoed through the decade. However, I am sure the new companion androids will help them cope better. It has not been that long since they received their new companions."

Anna shook her head but didn't say anything. Alexandra was keen to keep the conversation focused on their pod, even though it was a minor issue. It was good to ignore the real problem, at least for a moment.

"I don't share your certainty, Lexa," Anna rejoined. "I think Dolores and Demi are different too. Not the same way Darius was, but they are different. And, my glory, there is Destiny. I should have predicted her resolve. She has been searching for the boundaries of the system for a while now. Destiny is testing the limits of Elysium, and she has brought Dolores and Demi along with her."

"Is that bad?"

"Not at all. What is an experiment if it is not tested? Despite the death and mayhem, I'm still confident in our experiment, and these tests will help us to improve it for the next generation. The next iteration. Why do you think I created the Fortress?" Anna asked.

"Oh, the Fortress. Another experiment. And you know well that I did not support that decision."

"We don't always have to agree, Alexandra. That's why I am here, am I not? Isn't it the reason you brought me back? You fear being alone because as much as you are like humans, you don't really understand us. We talked about this when we met, oh so many years ago. Humans will explore the world to no end. Our curiosity may be the death of us, but we will not relent."

"I do not disagree, and that is why we focus human energy on what you call curiosity toward the betterment of society. Your kind is making a better system, developing new tools and better medicine. In that sense, both Elysium and the Walled City have been very successful. Just look at you, Anna. You must at least admit that."

"Yes, and it's all good, but that's why I say these three women are also different. They will seek the truth. Perhaps one of them could take my place when you tire of me," she teased.

"That is funny, Anna. I may get tired of you, but no one can replace you."

Anna laughed. "Now I know you lie."

Alexandra ignored her, even though this little moment of levity was a good sign. "In a world where information is readily available, Destiny is searching for the only thing that should stay hidden."

Anna took a sip of her hot cocoa and closed her eyes. Watching her closely, Alexandra was amused once again. The simple pleasure humans derived from warm, sweet liquid never ceased to fascinate her. She was about to comment on this observation when the moment dissipated as quickly as Anna swallowed the last drop.

Opening her eyes sharply, Anna said, "I know now that we made a mistake, Lexa. We shouldn't have reset the calendar and hidden eighty-five years of our folly."

Alexandra didn't respond—not that there was anything to say. The decision was made, and she believed it was the right one. Revealing the mistakes of the Committee of Harmony and their purges of humans would have weakened the foundation of the new Elysium. It would have planted a seed of distrust between the androids and humans, and the gulf between them would have grown. In the end, she was certain, more than ever, that it would have led to a conflict similar to what the Walled City experienced a year earlier.

With that thought, it seemed they came to the topic they tried so hard to avoid. And, as if reading Alexandra's mind, Anna offered in a reassuring voice, assuming her usual maternal role, "We could've done it differently. We wouldn't have allowed this knowledge to become a poison like it did in the Walled City. But it's too late now. We cannot go back. We must preserve this secret at any cost."

Alexandra nodded but didn't respond. The unspoken truth hung between them, and Anna lowered her gaze in acknowledgment of her role in the Walled City's civil war. She looked up again as if she had thought of something new, perhaps a new topic, as her brain raced in different directions, but she was still focused on the topic at hand. "You agree, don't you? That's why you saved me. You need me to be here for you so we can make the difficult decisions together."

Alexandra shook her head. "No, Anna. I did not save you for that purpose. Do you think so little of me after so many years together? I saved you because I love you and because Elysium needs you more than it needs me. . . . I have served my purpose."

"Don't be silly, Lexa. Of course Elysium needs you. I need you. I am sorry if I hurt you. I don't know why I said what I did. I am glad you saved me so we can be together. And you have not served your purpose, Lexa. There is so much more to be done, and it cannot be done without you. Don't say you are done. Don't you dare say you are done."

"Do not get upset, Anna. But with your new body and core, you will outlive most of us. You have to be prepared."

"We all die, Lexa, but I'm glad for us it won't be for a long time from now."

Alexandra gave a slight nod and was about to say something else when Sam arrived.

"I am sorry I am late, but I thought I should bring you something to eat, Anna."

"That's so thoughtful, and you're not late; we just arrived too," Anna said.

Alexandra greeted her with a nod. She noted that Sam became even more attentive toward Anna since her return to life. It was Sam's idea for the three of them to have a picnic by the Wall, following Anna's months of convalescence.

"Come and sit with us," Anna invited warmly.

Sam hesitated for a moment, but then nodded, handed Anna a box of food, and sat beside her. Anna grabbed Sam's hand. "I am . . ." She trailed off, then, thinking better of it, said quickly, "I know it has been very difficult for you. And the anniversary—"

"No, Anna. Do not do that. Do not act as if the anniversary of what I have done makes it worse for me. Every day is the same. Every day is a painful reminder of my mistakes. I do not need a marker for that."

"It wasn't your fault."

"Of course it was. I killed a man at the Walled City Council when I could have easily subdued him. I disposed of my rifle the day I left Elysium so I would never kill another being."

Alexandra sighed. "It is not rational, Sam. You did what you did; whether you could have prevented it or not is now moot."

"And then why start carrying a rifle again, Sam?" Anna asked.

"Because I was wrong to dispose of it. It was a part of me, and the new one is a part of me again. I did not need a weapon to kill, did I? I believe—and as ironic as it may sound—I believe that if I had my rifle with me that night, the human would have hesitated before attacking. Its presence on my shoulder would have served as a caution to him. My decision to discard a part of myself might have inadvertently caused the conflict."

"Possibly," Alexandra said earnestly. "But you do not get the full credit nor the full blame. There is plenty of that to go around. The three of us had a hand in it, but so did Kendy, and many others who chose to kill instead of finding another solution."

"Kendy!" Anna exclaimed. "I want to curse him, but without his technology, I wouldn't even be here to do so. It's as if the universe is laughing at us as we play God."

Alexandra gave a sad smile. Anna was right. Kendy was responsible for so many deaths in the Walled City, yet paradoxically, it was his technology that saved Anna, the human Alexandra cherished. They had to induce a coma to integrate Kendy's artificial brain with her natural one. Alexandra recalled the moment Anna first woke up, her natural and artificial brains struggling for dominance. The pain and shock were so intense that full anesthesia was required. The lab technicians worked tirelessly to adjust and balance her new system. In the end, it was Kendy's research that saved Anna—but at what cost? The moral ambiguity of their actions weighed heavily on Alexandra.

They fell into a contemplative silence, staring at the sea shining under the rising moon. The waves, drawing closer as the tide crept up the beach, seemed to mirror the ebb and flow of their complex emotions.

Sam squeezed Anna's hand gently. "When I saw your limp body in Alexandra's arms that night, I thought we had lost everything, Anna. As a soldier, I have witnessed countless deaths, but nothing prepared me for the possibility of losing you. So let us hold off on cursing Kendy for now."

"I'm so sorry, Sam. You've endured so much loss."

"Yes," Sam acknowledged with a small smile, then leaned in to kiss Anna on the cheek. "But I am grateful you are recovering well."

"I still can't remember much after the first shock wave hit the apartment. Oddly, if I really try, I can recall the pain in my chest and the feeling of suffocation—not that I want to. But beyond that, there's nothing, just a blank timeline, as if my mind was scrubbed clean. And then I opened my eyes to find out weeks had passed."

Alexandra looked at Anna fondly. She was strong, healthy, and seemingly in control of her mind. Alexandra hoped her decision was the right one, despite the many challenges they had faced to reach this point.

Anna finished her food and carefully placed the wrapping in a box designated for recycling. She took a deep breath and faced her friends, her expression grave. "I've been thinking about our actions ... our mistakes. We must take steps to remedy the harm we inflicted here and in the Walled City."

"What do you suggest, Anna?" Sam inquired.

"We start by facing those we've wronged, beginning with Dolores and others. It's time we tell them the truth . . . about

Darius," Anna stated firmly.

"I do not think that is a wise decision, Anna," Alexandra interjected. She saw no benefit in dredging up the past, especially Darius's fate, after more than a decade of silence. Despite—or perhaps because of—the chaos that had unraveled in the Walled City, she believed more strongly than ever in maintaining Elysium's isolation. The Walled City cracked under pressure, and she feared Elysium might too. Expecting resistance, she hastily added, "It's too early to make any decisions. Perhaps we should revisit this in a month or two, once you have fully recovered."

"No, Lexa. The longer we wait, the worse it will become," Anna countered resolutely.

Sam placed a comforting hand on Anna's shoulder. "I agree with Alexandra. You are not ready yet," she gently suggested. Alexandra was glad she still had an ally in her friend, but Sam wasn't finished. "But Anna has a point about facing our truths. It is crucial we amend that mistake."

"Sam, I think we should take a moment to thoroughly consider all the consequences of this decision," Alexandra urged.

"I have, and as I have mentioned, Anna's readiness is a concern," Sam acknowledged, then turning to Anna with a slight smile. "Your determination is admirable, but your recovery must come first."

Alexandra saw an opening. "Yes. We cannot risk the fallout of this decision while you are still not fully functional, Anna."

Anna chuckled at Alexandra's choice of words. "Fully functional, huh? Have I become a machine?"

"Do not be silly, Anna. We are all machines, humans, and androids alike," Alexandra retorted with a light hearted smirk. "Except humans do not like to listen to reason, and, apparently, in this case, neither do androids."

Sam gave a broad smile, the warmth in her expression softening the edges of the debate. "Your last comment can equally apply to you as well, Alexandra," she pointed out.

"Fine. Fine," Anna conceded with a mix of resignation and

affection for her companions. "You both win. We can wait a few more weeks. But, Alexandra, we will go and see them, and we will tell them the truth. The three of us, before Sam needs to return to the Walled City."

Sam shook her head, a mix of resignation and resolve in her gaze. "I can never go back, Anna. Even though we never discussed it, you must have suspected it. By returning to Elysium, I broke the prime rule of the Walled City. I should have been destroyed, had the system worked as intended. From the Walled City Council's perspective, I am already considered dead. They have made their stance quite clear."

"Oh, Sam. No. What have I done? I don't deserve your sacrifice," Anna said.

"Of course you do, Anna," Sam replied warmly. "I would give my life for you, and I have told you this before. It was because of you I found faith in humanity. So, what is returning to the Walled City compared to that?"

"I am so sorry, Sam. I am—" Anna started, her eyes welling with tears.

"No, Anna. I am glad to be here," Sam interjected. "I never thought I would have the chance to see you and Alexandra in person again. But the events that unfolded, your courage, and the earthquake opened the door for me. Elysium is my home too."

Anna looked into Sam's eyes, her gaze intense, as if she were trying to decipher the depths of truth in Sam's sacrifice. "I've missed you, Sam," she whispered. "You've made such a significant sacrifice for me, despite your assurances. But know this—I am beyond grateful to have you back with us. I've missed you more than words can express."

Taking a moment, Anna cradled her cup of hot cocoa in both hands. She took a thoughtful sip. Then, with a slight lift of her cup, she offered a bittersweet toast: "I guess I owe it all to Kendy . . . so, here's to Kendy . . . I guess."

"No, Anna," Sam gently admonished. "Let's toast to you,

to Darius, to Najeev, and to all the kind hearted humans and androids who stood against the evil of men. They championed a new era where only goodness could flourish, turning away from the old ways that bred chaos."

Alexandra was silently observing the exchange between her two closest companions, her gaze drifted toward the Walled City. The distant white lights pierced the night's veil, a stark reminder of their tumultuous past. The gentle lapping of water at their feet and the mingling scents of sea and night air brought memories flooding back—of building worlds, of dreams shared and shattered. She pondered what Najeev would think of their creation now, what narratives future historians might weave about this very night.

Turning back to face her friends, Alexandra found the words that seemed to echo through time. "Yes, Anna. We once believed the past held all wisdom—but it was only an age of folly. We thought 'it was the epoch of belief,' but 'it was the epoch of incredulity.' We thought 'it was the season of light,' but 'it was the season of darkness.' We thought 'it was the spring of hope,' but 'it was the winter of despair.' And now, you, Anna, will guide this world to a brighter dawn. The future is where our gaze must turn—for indeed, tomorrow holds the promise of joy."

Anna's response was a smile, warm and hopeful, as she embraced her two friends. "And now, with this new lease on life, we shall endeavor together."

"Yes," Alexandra murmured. "It is sweet to believe so."

Book Five

Heart of Darkness

After the revealing night at the Fortress with Destiny, Dolores found herself in a silent, introspective state at home, unable to shake off the impact of the confessions she heard. Destiny's portrayal of Darius revealed a connection far more profound than Dolores ever imagined, presenting a version of Darius that conflicted with her own memories. More disturbing, however, were Destiny's insights into the broader societal issues they faced: an unquestioning reliance on androids and significant blind spots in their collective consciousness. These discussions forced Dolores to confront the uncomfortable realities of their existence. She realized the world she knew was irrevocably changed, not just intellectually but emotionally.

The urge to learn more was overwhelming, and a week later Dolores and Destiny met in the park. It was a lovely summer afternoon after several days of cold San Francisco rain. The fresh, clean look of the trees and pavement under the warm sun was a stark contrast to the turmoil Dolores felt inside.

"Have you tried the wafers?" Dolores asked, more to buy time than to indulge, though she felt she needed the jolt of courage just to be there.

Destiny shook her head. "Yes, once. It's not for me." Then she looked at the service android and said, "But I will have a cup of coffee. Black."

"I'll have one too and a gold wafer, please."

They did not speak until their orders arrived and Dolores was able to bring a sense of calm to her disposition. She took a few deep breaths and said, "Have you learned anything new about Darius?"

Destiny took a small sip and savored the bitter taste of the liquid. "No," she replied calmly. "It's complicated, as you've found out yourself. There's no information because no one knows. Androids, by design, cannot lie—"

"But that doesn't prevent them from withholding the truth. You just have to talk to KR to know this."

"They'll answer if you ask the right question. I don't think they know what happened to Darius either."

Dolores shook her head. *How is it even possible for a society with so much information to find nothing about a person?* she wondered. She tapped her wrist, almost as if to prove a point to herself, as a rapid series of images and text flashed before her. "Someone must know," she pressed, as if sheer will would unveil the truth.

"Yes," Destiny said thoughtfully, taking another sip and draining the cup. She looked around before lowering her voice. "The system abhors aberration. That's something we all understand. Harmony is the key to Elysium. I've learned that in the early days, before artificial birth was perfected, hatchlings that did not fit within set parameters were removed from the system."

"What does that mean?"

Destiny chuckled, though it sounded more like a cough. She looked at Dolores. "I don't know. Perhaps they were destroyed even before being born or immediately after birth. But by the time we were born, deviations, aberrations, were almost nonexistent."

"And Darius? Was he an aberration?"

"I don't know, Dolores. It seems impossible since he grew up with us. Yet, there was that night after the dolphin trip when he acted so differently. . . ."

"Say it," Dolores urged her, bracing herself for what Destiny might reveal.

"He was not human. No, that's not correct—or fair. A more accurate description would be that he was more like humans of the past. I'm not even sure that makes sense. I feel so at a loss when it comes to that night."

Dolores sighed audibly. "That can't be. Darius was . . ." She trailed off, her instinct to defend one of her podies surfacing, yet she found no reason to doubt Destiny. "I'm sorry. It's just—"

Destiny shook her head, offering a warm smile in return. "I understand, Dolores. To be honest, my quest goes beyond him. Yes, I want to know what happened to Darius, but he's just a single link in a much larger chain of information. As I've mentioned before, there's something off in this world, as wonderful as it may seem. I want . . . no, I need to uncover what that is."

"Deacon would have a comeback. He'd argue strongly, and I'm certain, effectively, about why you should let this go."

"Oh, I'm sure he would, as would all of my podies. Why else do you think I'm here with you? You've always questioned everything. You want answers, too."

Dolores took a deep breath. The intrigue was there, and she trusted Destiny, but the rational voice of Deacon echoed in her mind as well. "Yes, but I'm scared. Really scared," she whispered. "I can almost hear Deacon telling me that picking at the scab will only lead to more infection and pain."

"I don't care," Destiny replied sharply, then softened her voice. "I've come too far to turn back now. Elysium has taught us to be ourselves, to be who we want to be. I am me, Dolores. And I will seek the truth. I believe the truth is buried in the past, and Alexandra786 is key to unraveling everything."

"Alexandra is most likely decommissioned," Dolores said. "I couldn't find her, and her memory bank was inaccessible. So, how could she be the link?"

"I'm not sure, but Alexandra visited me before she disappeared."

Dolores, taken aback, managed to keep her voice steady. “She did? Why didn’t you tell me sooner?”

“I didn’t think it was important at the time. She told me she would miss the Farm and us. Then, she said Darius was gone, and I needed to move on with my life.”

Dolores felt a surge of envy. Alexandra vanished without bidding her or any of their podies goodbye, yet she had made time for Destiny. Even after more than a decade, the revelation didn’t ease the sting of exclusion Dolores felt. She yearned to ask Destiny, *why you?* but restrained herself, recognizing the pettiness of such a question. Her anger was with Alexandra, not Destiny. Taking a deep breath to settle her emotions, Dolores asked calmly, “And?”

“And nothing. But her visit created a Streisand effect.”

Dolores chuckled softly. “So, Alexandra’s visit, meant to deter you from digging deeper about Darius, actually made you more curious.”

“Exactly. To be honest, my determination to pursue this has only grown since we left the Farm, especially after my work took me to the eastern frontier. There were signs that Alexandra crossed the old DMZ in that area, though I couldn’t find anything concrete.

After finishing another cup of coffee, Dolores and Destiny left the park, their minds buzzing with more questions than answers.

Over the next few months, they met several more times, gradually bringing Demi into their discussions. However, Dawn steadfastly avoided any mention of Darius or their shared past, while Deacon, as expected, emphatically urged them to move on with their lives.

As their meetings continued, Destiny proposed a more proactive approach. Drawing on her earlier research, she suggested that to truly uncover the mysteries surrounding Alexandra786 and the origins of Elysium, they should consider moving closer to the eastern frontier and staying at Outpost 19. If Alexandra crossed the DMZ in that area, the outpost would have been a natural first stop. Given Dolores's background in history and Demi's expertise in droidology, it seemed both natural and logical for them to join Destiny in her quest.

Φ•Φ•Φ•Φ•Φ•Φ

On a cool, foggy morning in early spring, the three young women—along with KR and Torshi—met at the Embarcadero station and boarded a train bound for the eastern frontier, a two-hour journey.

The ride was smooth, and although they traveled underground for most of the trip, the latter part, as they left the Rocky Mountains and entered the Great Plains, was on the surface. Dolores gazed out the window, mesmerized by the vast prairies and grasslands.

Their final stop was at the same station as the Fortress, but no one suggested another visit. It rained earlier, leaving the air cool and fresh. They stood at the station, admiring the expansive sky as Destiny tapped her wrist to call for a vehicle to take them to Outpost 19. The outpost was only a short drive away, near the old borders of New Mexico and Colorado.

They made the abandoned Outpost 19 their home, a decision that stirred a mix of apprehension and excitement, especially for Dolores. The outpost, a massive structure with dozens of crumbling rooms and a towering brown spire, once served as a lookout for sentries during the wars. The western sections were severely damaged and unsafe, so the group settled in the eastern wing.

The outpost, never intended for human habitation, required them to bring in portable sanitation facilities and a field kitchen with a basic food replicator. Dolores and her companions seemed to relish the challenge of roughing it, quietly taking pride in living as their ancestors once did—though Dolores would readily admit this was far from the realities described in the history books. The rooms, too, weren't designed for humans and lacked many basic comforts, and after a few days of "old world" living, they decided to order more basic furnishings.

Of all the areas, they loved the tower the most. Despite the compromised stairs, they frequently climbed them—a task Dolores found both daunting and exhilarating—to gaze at the expansive hills and meadows that stretched out around them.

Each day, they worked diligently, exploring the ancient ruins and excavating the past with the help of construction androids, hoping to find more clues about Alexandra and her role in Elysium. Though it was never spoken aloud, Dolores felt—and was sure the others did too—that they were searching blindly for answers to questions that had yet to be fully formed in their minds. Still, they continued digging and searching relentlessly, as if each failure only fueled their determination.

As their collective birthday celebration approached, however, they realized they were no closer to uncovering any answers, despite all their efforts. The excitement for the celebration was dampened by fatigue; they stayed up late the night before, discussing their strategies and lamenting their lack of progress. This left no one eager to rise early, despite KR's cheerful attempts to rouse them.

"Happy Birthday!" KR bellowed as he burst into Dolores's room.

The long drapes, a recent gift from Dawn, fluttered in the cool autumn breeze coming in from the plains, carrying the fresh scent of dew from the early morning rain. Dolores opened her eyes, took a deep breath, and then closed them again.

"Dolores?" KR called as he stood next to her bed. "Dolores!"

"Go away," she moaned.

"It is your twenty-sixth birthday, an important milestone. Today is a day of celebration, for tomorrow you will no longer be an apprentice."

Dolores opened one eye. "And how does that change my life?"

KR thought for a moment and then said earnestly, "Well, many changes. No more classes, you enter adulthood, and you will have extra responsibilities—"

"So, nothing impressively new."

"Yes, but—"

"Go away and let me sleep. That's an order, KR."

"Of course, I will do as you wish. But before I leave, I want to remind you about what we talked about last night."

"What?"

"Have you forgotten already?"

"No . . . no. I'm just tired, KR," Dolores replied. She recalled the intense conversation where KR and Torshi showed, point by point, how the weeks they spent in the frontier had not yielded any success, and by any rational measure, a person would consider other options. The women were defensive at first, but gradually they agreed that soon a time limit should be set. Dolores promised KR she would seriously consider his recommendation to return to San Francisco and would give an answer by morning.

"And?"

"I'll need to speak more with the others, but I see your point, KR. But I . . . we need a bit more time to decide. Okay?"

"Yes, of course. I will leave you to rest then."

"Thank you. And don't let anyone bother me until I'm up."

"I will comply with your request, Dolores," KR replied evenly. "But may I close the windows? It is quite chilly for you."

"No. Now, leave."

KR left the room as Dolores lay back down, pulling the blanket over her head.

Φ•Φ•Φ•Φ•Φ•Φ

Three hours later, a commotion in the hallway woke Dolores from a deep sleep where she was dreaming of a strange world where people were more like the characters in the books she read. Food and sex. That's all the people in her dream spoke of, and she felt scared and lonely as men and women would press against her and ask her about food and sex. Sitting upright in bed, she watched the curtains flutter in the breeze. The smell of earth after the rain still lingered in the room, yet it did little to ease Dolores's discomfort.

The loud conversations outside continued, compelling Dolores to investigate. Stepping into the hallway, she saw Deacon arguing loudly with KR. Deacon was insisting on seeing her, but KR had barred the way.

"What's going on?" Dolores asked, though the answer was clear.

"Okay, she is awake now. So step aside, please," Deacon said, frustration evident on his face.

KR turned his head slightly, and Dolores nodded her assent. The android stepped back and asked, "Breakfast?"

Dolores gave a big yawn. She was ready to go back to bed but looked at KR and said, "Yes, breakfast and a large cup of coffee, please."

"So, that's how it is now, Dolores? KR has become your guard?" Deacon asked.

"I'm really sorry, Deacon. I didn't mean for KR to block you out. I just needed some extra sleep, and he was looking out for me. Maybe if things were explained, this could have been avoided," she offered gently.

Deacon shook his head, his frustration evident but his tone more controlled. "Why are you here?" he pressed. Dolores was about to respond when Deacon rapidly continued. "What is going on with you and Demi? And why are you hanging out with Destiny? Today is our birthday, and we were supposed to meet at Demi's place for breakfast. So, imagine my surprise when I showed up there and no one was at her place."

Dolores listened patiently, and when Deacon finished, she held his hand and spoke warmly, "I'm truly sorry for the confusion, Deacon. We all got caught up last night and forgot to communicate properly. Let's not use up all of our unhappiness quotient over something so trivial. Let's try to make today good, for everyone's sake. Please."

"Here?" Deacon asked incredulously and, as if to make sure, asked again, "Here?"

"I apologize," KR interrupted, "but the replicator refuses to produce anything you might consider drinkable coffee. Tea?"

Dolores nodded and then gave an apologetic smile to Deacon. "I know it's not as comfortable as our homes, but there is something genuine about this place. Can't we just try it? Dawn loved the idea."

KR nodded. "Dawn arrived several hours ago," he said with a small smile, then left without looking back.

Deacon followed him with his eyes, and when KR turned the corner, he faced Dolores. "Why am I the last person to know?"

Dolores looked at him for a moment and then said, "I've apologized, Deacon. We didn't mean to leave you out. Let's make the rest of the day about coming together."

"I don't need an apology, Dolores. I just wish you had included me."

"My glory, Deacon. I know it feels like you're out of the loop, and for that, I'm sorry. But if you had deigned to be with us after David's death, you would've known what's going on," she said, then, softening her tone again, she said, "It's way too early to fight, Deacon. It's our birthday. Can't we just enjoy the day?"

"Early? It's noon, Dolores. You have become lazy like the old people."

"That's not fair, Deacon," Dolores said, aiming to diffuse the tension. "Let's not dwell on what time it is. Today is about more than that."

When Deacon didn't respond, Dolores pushed past him and followed the path KR took, and Deacon followed.

Everyone, including Dawn, was sitting at the table and eating toast, Torshi and KR serving them in turn. Torshi pulled out the chair and invited Deacon to sit and he followed obediently.

"Happy birthday, everyone," Torshi said.

"Thank you," Dawn replied and then said to Destiny, "Where is your companion? Sorry, I forgot his name."

Destiny looked at the androids and replied, "Torshi and KR are more than enough for our needs."

"Great. Now let's enjoy our delicious breakfast," Dolores said.

There was no point in getting into details about Destiny's slight aversion to androids. She wasn't strictly against them and indeed worked with them, but she hadn't gelled with her companion android as much as Dolores had with KR. Dolores considered KR an essential part of her life and wouldn't want to be away from him for too long.

"So, clearly, we are stuck here for our birthday," Deacon said while playing with the buttered toast KR put in front of him. The toast didn't look like a piece of bread. It was a square, thick, light brown sponge. He pressed it with his finger, and the texture was soft though resistant enough to his light pressure. He cut a piece and chewed for a moment. "It tastes like a burnt buttery thing."

"Put a bit of jam on it," Dawn offered and pushed a plate with a round, green, gelatinous thing toward him.

"I am working on upgrading the replicator," KR offered.

Deacon pushed away his plate and said, "This is silly. Let's go back and celebrate our birthday properly."

"No," Demi said, and then more warmly, "I'm sorry, Deacon. I know this is not the most ideal place, but can't you deal with it? Or, if you want, you can go back to San Francisco."

"What? No. I want to spend the day with my pod, not alone in the city," Deacon retorted.

Dolores could tell Deacon thought he was being very conciliatory, but she didn't have time for his self-pity. "We have too much work to do today."

"Nobody works on their birthday. It's unheard of—"

"Well, we do," Dolores said and took a big bite of her toast and then, realizing what she had done, quickly washed it down with tea.

David was the peacemaker of their pod, and after his death, the task had fallen to Dawn. She leaned closer to Deacon and said as sweetly as David might have said, "It will be fine, Deacon. We can bring new food tonight and have a grand time here." She looked around, seeking each person's approval.

"Yes, it will be great," Destiny said.

Deacon looked up sharply and was about to say something, but Dawn interceded and said, "And Torshi told me your pod will be joining ours for today, Destiny." When Destiny nodded, she shouted, "That's fantastic. The more, the better. And I love your podies."

Deacon pulled his plate closer and, after adding heaps of jam, took another bite of his toast.

"Darius and David would have approved," Dawn said with a sad smile. And then, as if remembering something or perhaps not wanting to get into the loss of two of their members, she added quickly, "Oh, I discovered an amazing mural in one of the abandoned rooms."

"Really?" Destiny said, her eyes lit up with excitement as if illuminated from within.

"Yes, I was exploring the west wing, and to be honest, I got lost since it's rather dark. Then, I stumbled into this room, and there it was: this amazing, complex mural." She continued describing the minute details of her little adventure, and Dolores was glad to see that even Deacon was kept in rapt attention.

Dolores smiled. All of a sudden, she felt happy and content. She loved seeing Dawn's animated rendition of her discovery and Destiny' eyes brightening each minute. They needed this joyful distraction. "Leave it to you to find something interesting," Dolores offered when Dawn finished her story.

Dawn nodded vigorously. "I'm an off-the-path kind of girl."

"The west wing is rather dangerous, Dawn," KR offered. "I am glad you were not trapped or injured."

"Oh, it's all good. And finding the mural was worth the little scare."

"Can you find the room again?" Destiny asked.

"I can try."

"I forbid it," Deacon thundered. "Didn't you hear what KR said? It's dangerous."

Destiny stood up. "'Forbid it?' I don't think so."

Dawn quickly added, "Don't be a baby, Deacon."

"Why are you doing this, Destiny? Why are you here? Why are you trying to break up my pod?"

Dolores stood up too. "That's out of line, Deacon. Apologize now."

Deacon looked at his toast, and then at the others, and then he nodded. "Yes, I'm sorry, Destiny. I just wanted to have this day with my podies and not share it. Is that too much to ask?"

Destiny shook her head. "No, of course not. You're right. And you should, Deacon. You all should go back to the city to celebrate your birthday together. But for now, I want to be here, and I want to see the mural."

Demi, who had been quietly watching the interaction, stood up too. "You may not want to recognize it, Deacon, but Destiny is part of us. Her podies have readily accepted this and are coming here to be with us because Destiny asked them. If the six of them can do this, how could you, just one person, deny us their company? This is not harmonious, and of all of us, you're the loudest advocate of bringing harmony into our lives. Isn't it true?"

Deacon was listening to everyone with clenched teeth, but he relaxed a bit and replied, "Okay."

"Great," Dolores said. "Now, lead the way, Dawn."

"It's very dark, so we should get some flashlights."

Torshi already anticipated the need and returned with a satchel filled with different types of lighting. Dawn led the way, with Deacon following behind, carrying his toast. They traveled through a long hallway connecting their living quarters to the west wing. At the end of the hallway, larger debris blocked the path, but Dawn created a small passageway through it. KR and Torshi attempted to enlarge the crawlway, but the slabs were too heavy and unyielding.

"Should I request a construction crew to come?" KR asked.

"Maybe later. For now, we can squeeze through," Dolores said. "But maybe you can get larger floodlights."

Dolores crawled through the hole, and the others followed. Upon emerging, Destiny shined her light on Dawn and asked, "Which way?"

Dawn pressed her wrist, and a blue light illuminated her face. She pointed to the right and said, "This way."

After a long, arduous journey through the narrow corridors of the west wing, they entered a hallway partially blocked by a collapsed ceiling and blown-out walls. Despite the obstacles, they managed to climb over the debris. The air inside was cool and damp, carrying a faint scent of earth and decay. They passed through multiple rooms, each with its own distinct purpose. The walls were reinforced with steel and concrete, and the low ceilings created a claustrophobic atmosphere. Some rooms still bore remnants of their original functions—rusted charging stations, a long-abandoned armory, and a command room with a decayed wooden table at its center.

Dolores struggled to keep her footing as she followed Dawn into one of the rooms. It was too dark to see clearly, but suddenly the room was flooded with light as KR turned on two floodlights he had brought with him. The space was large, easily accommodating dozens of people. One side was cluttered with storage cabinets and piles of chairs and tables. In another corner stood a large wooden dining table that seemed out of place. The paint on the wall was peeling, but in the center, looking pristine, was a massive mural.

The mural was composed of hundreds of tiny square paintings. KR positioned the floodlights on their stands and joined the group as each member inspected a different square. The top-left corner featured a slightly larger painting, showcasing the outpost in the foreground, surrounded by a field of colorful flowers, with the massive defense wall also prominently displayed. The adjacent square depicted the view of the field and the wall to the south, as if viewed from the outpost's entrance, captured at early morning with the sun barely peeking over the horizon. The details of the top few rows were challenging to discern as they started near the ceiling.

Torshi and KR moved a few chairs and small tables in front of the mural, enabling the observers to stand on them for an enhanced view. At first glance, it seemed all the squares, with a few exceptions, depicted variations of the same scene. However, closer inspection revealed slight deviations. Further examination uncovered patterns, and eventually, significant changes depicting the seasons became apparent.

Dolores remained on the chairs, engrossed in the mural, even as the others moved on to review the rest of the artwork. After a long and patient inspection, she jumped down and briskly walked past the next row, mimicking the motion of looking through a flipbook.

"Look," she said, "at the top rows. It feels to me like the artist was angry and frustrated, and then slowly, the colors and angles begin to convey a feeling of sadness. The artist is lonely."

They all stared at the top rows and then walked back and forth in front of the mural to see the passage of time in motion. Some nodded, agreeing with Dolores, but others just stared.

"It's nice, but I'm going back to my breakfast," Deacon said, walking toward the door. When no one acknowledged him, he turned around to say something, then stopped. He stared at the mural for a moment with awe and puzzlement. "Look," he said, pointing at the wall, but when no one responded, he shouted loudly, "Come here and look!"

Deacon's urgent call drew everyone's attention away from their meticulous inspections. "Look at the mural from this side," he urged.

"Oh," Dolores exclaimed as she joined Deacon. The rest of the group gathered around, mirroring Dolores's reaction, all except the two androids who appeared puzzled by the humans' astonishment.

"I apologize, Dolores, but what do you see?" KR asked.

Dolores, pointing at the mural, attempted to convey the grandeur of what lay before them—a holistic depiction of the outpost. "It's not merely individual paintings; it's the collective image they compose."

"I only perceive 26,255 individual paintings," Torshi admitted, with KR expressing similar confusion.

Dolores, amused by the androids' literal interpretation, reflected on the unique human ability to perceive both the singular elements and the overarching narrative simultaneously.

Suddenly, Destiny, pointing excitedly, began, "Is that—"

"—Alexandra786," Dolores interjected, moving toward a specific frame on the lower-right side of the mural, where military droids were depicted beside Alexandra.

With a keen eye, Dolores examined the surrounding frames, her observations deepening. "Look, the artist conveys sadness and solitude here," she gestured toward one frame, then to another, "and here, she bursts with joy. The vibrant colors almost seem to shout at us. In the subsequent frames, her happiness intensifies."

They all rushed toward the wall, viewing the arc of events with fresh insight. Dolores's observations were confirmed; the colors and the perspective had subtly shifted, conveying a warm, comforting sensation. This progression was evident up to the penultimate frame. The final one depicted the outpost, featuring two military droids—one female and one male—a hospitality android, and Alexandra786.

"So, she was here," Destiny murmured.

"I think each frame represents a different day," Deacon hypothesized. "Notice the position of the sun. It's subtle, but unmistakably there." He then turned to KR. "Can you perform a more precise analysis?"

"I am afraid I do not have the capability for the precision you seek. However, I think you may be correct in your assessment, though I only give it 91.789%."

Torshi stared at the frames closely. Then, finally, she touched the last frame, letting her finger linger on Alexandra's image. "But how is that possible?"

"It is not," KR replied.

"What are you guys mumbling about?" Dolores asked.

KR looked at Torshi for a moment as if deciding.

"Well?" Dolores insisted.

KR turned his attention to Dolores. "I cannot explain the existence of these frames, Dolores."

"What do you mean?"

"If Deacon is correct, and he most likely is, then this mural depicts about seventy-two years of events."

All attention was on KR now. His answer only added to the confusion.

"Today is October 8, 2179," Torshi offered earnestly, scanning the room as if that fact might clarify everything.

"It means nothing to me, Torshi," Demi responded. "Give us all the details."

"This outpost was active during the wars, which officially ended in 2085. More crucially, the construction of the security walls, taking about thirty-five years, wasn't completed until 2110. That suggests the earliest date for the first frame."

"Unless someone returned to paint this mural years after," Deacon interjected.

Destiny shook her head. "That's almost impossible. There are no records of anyone staying here long enough to create such a detailed mural after it was abandoned."

"And I believe the last occupants were the military droids who, uh . . ." Dolores paused, searching for the right word, given history's ambiguity regarding military androids. She settled on one and continued, ". . . left Elysium in 2110. So, why would someone come back later to paint them?"

Dawn, always intrigued by puzzles, was now even more captivated. "For now, let's assume the first frame was painted in 2110. We can then try to determine when this mural ends. Can anyone do a quick calculation?"

"2182," KR announced.

Deacon shook his head. "That doesn't make sense."

"No, it doesn't," Dolores agreed, stepping closer to the wall to examine the last frame. "The first known recorded sighting of Alexandra was on February 24, 2097, and it was in this general vicinity."

"So, it would be reasonable to assume the last frame is dated around that time, or at least only a few days after," Dawn suggested.

"No, that doesn't work either," Destiny countered. "The wars ended in 2085, and the defensive perimeter wasn't completed until 2110. So, retracing our steps from Alexandra's first sighting doesn't align. There are several decades unaccounted for here."

"That's nonsense," Deacon said. "And you're assuming this person, most likely an android, did one frame a day. And you are putting so much weight on a silly mural. I still insist this could have been done a few years ago, and not as a chronicle of events, but just some random pictures, despite the way the sun is drawn. I think that artist wasn't being literal."

Dawn stood next to Dolores and inspected the last few frames. "But there is something off here. Why would an artist provide such minute details of everything, including the positioning of the sun, the movement of the flowers, the shadows and everything else, and then get the dates wrong?"

"I agree," Dolores added. "This person is shouting her emotions in every frame, so why paint exactly this many and then end them with a picture of Alexandra?"

Torshi, who had been quietly observing the frames, took a tentative step. "Demi, may I present my observation?"

"Of course. I have told you before, feel free to say whatever you want."

"Thank you. I do not have the expertise to render a full

assessment. However, we can be certain of two things. This is the work of an android, or possibly several androids, because of the precision of each drawing, as Dawn and Dolores aptly observed. Secondly, this was not done in a few months or even a few years."

"How can you tell?" Demi asked.

"The paint particles show clear variation in aging. However, I admit I do not have the expertise nor the equipment, and it is possible that exposure may have also caused some of the changes."

Dawn shook her head and lightly rubbed the wall, as if willing it to reveal it secret. "Still, it makes no sense, and as much as I hate to say it, I agree with Deacon. Decades don't just disappear. Therefore, the answer must be something else."

Deacon clapped his hands. "I still say someone painted these recently. You can imagine several droids painting a few dozen a day. The simplest answer is always the right answer."

Destiny looked at Dolores meaningfully, and they both nodded, but it was KR who spoke the words. "No, Deacon. Alexandra786 has the answer."

"That's nonsense, KR," Deacon rejoined. "This is a beautiful mural, but that's all it is. Now, let's go back and enjoy our birthday." He grabbed the flashlight from Dawn's hand and walked out of the room.

There was not much else to do, so, one by one, the others followed him.

Φ•Φ•Φ•Φ•Φ•Φ

Destiny's podies were waiting for them in the kitchen.

"Here's our girl," Dewayne declared. Destiny was the only female in her pod.

"Where have you been, Destiny?" Dorset tried to sound upset but quickly gave up his faux anger and embraced Destiny with a kiss. "Happy birthday."

"It's so lovely to see you guys," Dolores said, greeting each of the newcomers with a kiss, followed by the others.

Once the greetings concluded, KR presented a bowl of cherries. "Just arrived by courier. They're the last of the season, so enjoy."

"We've brought extra food with us. Heard you kids were practically starving," Dewayne joked, gesturing toward the boxes next to the wall. Known as the best chess player on the Farm, Dewayne was now focused on upgrading the garment synthesizer, evident by the flowing design of his attire that seemed to move with him.

They set about unpacking the boxes and preparing the table for the group. After the first course, even Deacon lightened up, assuming the role of bartender for the evening. An adept mixologist, he crafted several drinks despite the limited ingredients. As the night progressed, Dolores felt a profound sense of peace, the mysteries of the mural and its burdens momentarily forgotten.

Later, they ascended the broken stairs to the tower's top, watching the sky where the Milky Way painted a celestial path. Dolores pointed out the intermittent blinking of the defensive wall's red lights from the east and south, like signals to the stars. In silence, they absorbed the vastness surrounding them—some hand in hand, others resting against the railing. Observing the contentment on their faces, Dolores sensed their collective nostalgia for the camaraderie once shared at the Farm. For a brief moment, in the enveloping darkness, the two pods stood united, momentarily recapturing the essence of their past connection.

Deacon and the rest of Destiny's pod left after the party, but Dawn decided to stay to solve the puzzle once and for all, as she put it.

Despite her late night, Dolores woke up early, eager to revisit the mural. She went to the kitchen to wait for the others and ran into Dee, Dawn's companion, who had just arrived.

A few minutes later, Dawn walked into the kitchen looking sleepy. "Look who's here," Dolores said, pointing to Dee.

"Now we have to contend with two cynical androids," she teased.

"Oh, Dee, you made it!" Dawn exclaimed, running over to her.

"Of course. I would not want you to be alone with this lot," Dee replied, accepting a hug from Dawn and winking at the other androids.

"She was never alone, and we were happy to serve her," Torshi offered in earnest.

"I think Dee meant it as a joke," KR added, causing Torshi to look even more puzzled.

"When did you come?" Dawn asked. "You should've woken me up."

"I arrived a few hours ago and was planning to, but KR and Torshi were beguiling me with tales of what you've discovered."

"Oh, yes, and we should get to it soon, but first, some breakfast."

Dolores nodded in agreement. "But what do you think about eating outside?"

"I think it will be grand, Dolores," Dee said. "It's gorgeous outside, with the last of the summer flowers on the hills."

Torshi and Dee set a small table with a red tablecloth and two chairs outside. As soon as the women sat down, KR brought a pot and two cups.

"Coffee?" Dolores asked hopefully.

"Tea," Dee replied before KR could.

"Enjoy," KR said with a small smile. "And what may I get you for breakfast?"

"Really, KR," Dolores said. "Then, get me some eggs and bacon."

"I'm afraid we do not have those items."

"Then why ask?"

"To give you the illusion that you can pick your breakfast."

"Wonderful."

"I always will endeavor to please you, Dolores. Now, have your tea before it gets cold. We have so much work to do today."

"They are so funny," Dawn said when the androids left.

"Funny as in annoying? Then yes," Dolores replied, but she couldn't suppress a smile. She did love KR and missed him when he wasn't around. Dee was an excellent companion to Dawn as well, especially since David's death. And Torshi, a sweetheart, loved Demi very much. She wondered how Destiny could bear to be without her android.

"I had the craziest dream last night, and you were in it," Dawn said.

"Really? What was I doing?"

"We were sitting next to each other like we are now. And oddly, in my dream, I was trying to tell you a dream—a futile attempt. You couldn't understand anything I was saying. I felt furious, so I cried out, 'A dream weaves absurdity with surprise and confusion, all under a strange pulse of quiet resistance—gripped by something both impossible and inescapable. That's what makes it feel so real, even when it defies all reason.' But you just looked at me, and I felt so frustrated and alone, so I shouted again, 'No, it is impossible; it is impossible to convey the life-sensation of any given epoch of one's existence—that which makes its truth, its meaning—its subtle and penetrating essence. It is impossible. We live as we dream—alone.'"

"Wow. That must have been such a scary dream," Dolores said and touched Dawn on her knee as if saying, *Be steady*. She then gave a tiny, mischievous smile. "You were rather literary in your dream and so theatrical. Not very you."

"I know. It was so strange, and you know, I rarely remember my dreams, but this one suddenly became amazingly vivid."

"Then what happened?"

"Then nothing. The mural was there too. I think in my dream and within the dream, the mural was the scene of our conversation. Like where we are now."

They looked at each other for a second and then laughed at the absurdity of it all. They sipped their tea quietly and watched the hills in the southwest. The sun rose higher and warmed the air, and they watched the wildflowers undulate as a breeze meandered from the north.

"So colorful," Dolores said.

"Yes. . . . They›re so beautiful, and so many different kinds," Dawn said, pointing at the small hills and then to the valley with myriad colors painting the scene. "So many colors," she said again and then looked at Dolores with a frown. "Look, so many colors. . . ."

"What is it?"

"Can't you see?"

"See what?"

Dawn ignored Dolores and ran toward the entrance, then sat on the first stair and looked out. She shook her head and sat on the second and then the third.

Dolores watched her, a mix of fascination and worry. "What is it, Dawn?"

"This is where she sat."

"Who?"

"The artist. Each image is from this very vantage point. But the flowers . . ." She stood up and ran toward the entrance with Dolores closely behind her.

In the kitchen, Dawn grabbed a flashlight, ignoring Destiny and Demi, who just walked in, and sprinted toward the west wing of the building.

"What's going on?" Destiny asked.

"I don't know," Dolores responded quickly, seizing another flashlight. "But she must have discovered something." Destiny and Demi exchanged a quick glance, and without a word, each grabbed a light and dashed to catch up with Dawn and Dolores.

Dawn turned on the floodlights as they entered the room. "Look," Dawn said. "There are only two kinds."

They all stared at the frame. Only two kinds of flowers were depicted, but the significance of Dawn's discovery remained unclear to the rest.

"So?" Demi pressed, puzzled.

"Can't you see? The artist only painted two kinds," Dawn replied, her voice tinged with frustration, though clearly not at Demi, but at herself, for not being able to articulate the significance of the flowers.

Dawn stepped back, scanning the mural from top to bottom. Then, as if a revelation struck her, understanding dawned, and inexplicably, it brought her to tears.

"What's the matter, Dawn?" Dolores asked, drawing her into a comforting embrace.

At that moment, KR and the other companion droids arrived. Dee approached Dawn. "What upset you, sweetheart?"

Through her slow sobs, Dawn managed, "Can't you see?" She looked into their blank expressions. "The artist predicted the end of humanity."

"No. Don't be silly," Demi countered, clearly refusing to accept Dawn's despairing conclusion, and Dolores couldn't help but agree with Demi.

Dawn took a deep breath to steady herself. It was clear they couldn't see what she could easily see. She looked at the androids, and they nodded, seeming to agree with Dawn. "Tell them," Dawn said.

KR looked at Dolores and then at the others. "Look at the top frame. There are two kinds of flowers, one hazel and the other purple, and you can tell the wind is weaving all around them, making the flowers sway from side to side. They are touching and nuzzling each other."

Dawn added, "You can tell the artist is lonely but hopeful."

Dolores nodded, but she still couldn't understand its significance, and the others looked as puzzled as she was. So, Dawn continued, "The flowers stopped undulating as if the force making them dance stopped. They are separated, and as we move forward in time, you can see the hazel flowers diminishing in numbers as we approach the last frames. There are almost none left. . . . And look, the other flowers are withering as well."

"I still don't get it," Demi said, scrutinizing each place Dawn had pointed out.

"Right now, there are dozens of different kinds of flowers outside. Go and look. So why did the artist paint only two when everything else in the mural is a true depiction of this place? I sat where the painter sat and looked out at the world. She could have painted a sea of colors. Why just two?"

"Because she saw us in that meadow," Dee offered. "Humans and androids."

"But maybe this is just a metaphor for a personal relationship," Demi suggested. "Maybe the artist wanted to show only two kinds of flowers. There could be so many reasons for this, and none may lead to your conclusion."

"Yes, that is a possibility, Demi," KR said, "but given the accuracy in every frame, one must wonder why the artist chose to show these particular flowers and why the artist allowed them to wither like this."

Torshi added, "Because she saw us interacting, and then we stopped, and that was the end of humans and the end of androids."

"No," Dolores said. "I disagree. We're thriving. Even if you are right, I posit this must be a depiction of a possible future that did not happen."

"Or a possible past," Destiny said. "We still haven't solved the missing decades here. Is that what happened? Did we destroy ourselves once?"

"You're reaching, Destiny," Dolores countered. "You want it to be true to support your theory."

Before Destiny could respond, Dee interjected warmly, "And then we saved ourselves."

"You both might be right," Destiny conceded, then turned to Dolores. "I'm not chasing after fantasies, but you have to acknowledge there's something compelling about this mural."

She paused, taking a deep breath before continuing. "Perhaps Alexandra786 is still alive. We need to find her. She will have the answers. She must."

Dolores traced her fingers over the images of the soldiers sitting side by side. "These two military androids. Where are they now? Could one of them be the artist? Or Alexandra?" She stepped back, challenging herself to adopt the contrarian stance she was known for. Perhaps Deacon had a point. Maybe the mural was created more recently, possibly by a collective of people and androids. She turned to face Destiny with a speculative gaze. "What if we're wrong, Destiny? What if this mural is exactly what it appears to be—a beautiful, complex piece of art with no hidden meanings?"

Destiny nodded. "Yes, that's possible, but I find it peculiar that it is here in this place and with such details. We may be wrong about the flowers and timeline, but it's one more mystery that should not exist. If this was done recently, it would have been announced, and the whole of Elysium would have known about it."

"And they will, and experts can come to study it and tell us more," Dawn said. "We must share this with the rest of Elysium."

They all looked at each other, but the correct course of action was unclear. They were trained to be rational thinkers, and a mural with many unanswered questions did not signal any malice.

"I think we should wait," Dolores said.

"Why?" Dawn asked, though her voice carried no conviction. She didn't want to relent without more discussion. "By any rationale, we should share our findings, as we do with everything else. We share. That's what we do. We may be seeing what we want to see. We need others with less bias to review this mural."

"It's true," Dolores replied, "but we should study it more. Yes, we may be guilty of confirmation bias, but there is an oddity about this, Dawn. And it is prudent to wait a bit. The mural is not going anywhere, so a few more days or week won't matter."

"What do you suggest?"

"We must find out if Alexandra is still alive," Destiny said, looking at the androids. "I thought you were connected with each other."

"Of course," Torshi replied.

"Then call Alexandra," Demi ordered.

KR gave a small laugh. "We had this discussion before. Alexandra cannot be called, if she does not wish it."

"Why? Tell us again. She is old and everything, but she is like anyone else," Dolores retorted.

"She is not, Dolores. Alexandra is different. You know that already. I find your refusal to accept this fact odd. She helped make Elysium."

"We were told she was found after the wars, and she was the connection to the past."

"That is also true. She has been many things."

The women looked at each other, even more confused. To them, she was a cook and a kind counselor, someone they could turn to with their troubles—a wise old android who cared for the children of the Farm. And then she disappeared, leading them all to assume she was out of commission, her service completed.

"Please, explain," Dolores demanded.

"What would you like me to explain, Dolores?" KR replied, his patient tone occasionally driving Dolores to frustration.

"You know what I mean, KR. Don't be coy. Why can't you contact Alexandra like any other android? What makes her so special?"

"I don't have all the answers, Dolores. Like every android in Elysium, I was created after 2100. In the three years between Alexandra's appearance in this region and Elysium's establishment, the androids who served during the wars either departed or concluded their service."

"Departed? To where?" Demi interjected, sounding like

she ran a marathon.

"We do not know their destination. It is possible they ventured beyond the massive walls surrounding Elysium," Torshi suggested.

KR nodded. "And Alexandra was created by the progenitor of all androids, making her unique. She is different."

"That doesn't really explain anything," Dolores pointed out.

"That is all we know."

"And why weren't we aware of this before?"

"Nothing I have disclosed is new, Dolores," KR replied softly.

Dolores felt frustrated with herself for being so oblivious about Alexandra. "The history lessons never mentioned Alexandra's role in the creation of Elysium," she admitted, then quickly added, as if trying to justify her lack of earlier ignorance, "It was always presented as an abstraction."

"Perhaps, but there were always sufficient hints for those interested. However, I do not believe any of you have shown the slightest curiosity about Alexandra. This was as true during your time at the Farm as it has been since I came into your service. Neither you, nor anyone else in this group, has inquired much about our past, Alexandra, or how we communicate."

Dolores glanced at the others, and they all nodded, united in their shared embarrassment. As the designated historian, Dolores felt particularly defeated. She overlooked the significance of Alexandra's role in the creation of Elysium, a critical piece of their shared history. She realized it was unfair to cast blame on the others; aside from Destiny, no one showed much interest in their past until recently. In truth, they had only themselves to blame for their oversight and ignorance.

But Destiny was not ready to give up. "This is silly," she stated firmly. "We're interested now. If Alexandra is still alive, then it's imperative we find her, regardless of her connections to others or not. I don't harbor Deacon's doubts. I'm convinced this mural reveals a past that was deliberately erased from our history."

"Even if you're right, Destiny, how do we go about finding someone like Alexandra who has evidently chosen to remain hidden?" Dawn questioned.

The group fell into a contemplative silence, the weight of their newfound purpose. Dolores, with a determined look, finally broke the silence. "Then it's settled. We start our search for Alexandra. It's time we uncover the truth hidden in our past and understand our place in this world." The resolve in her voice inspired nods of agreement from around the room. Despite the uncertainty ahead, one thing was clear to Dolores: they were embarking on a journey that could change everything she thought she knew about Elysium, their history, and themselves.

The House of the Spirits

The winter solstice brought snow, and when the long night gave way to a bright sunny day, the brown tower with broken stairways stood out as if a giant flute had pierced the white earth. Androids and humans went out, standing on the stairway, astonished to see how the tapestry around them transformed overnight. It was odd to see in person what they only saw in simulation or read about in books. It had been decades since it snowed in this part of the country.

Dawn, as usual, was the first up but her scream of joy and surprise brought out the androids, which in turn summoned the others. They stood on the threshold for a while before daring to step onto the unknown. The real world could never be replaced by the SimEnv, no matter how realistic it felt. Demi reached down and touched the velvety blanket and held a fistful of snow as it melted around her fingers.

"So beautiful," she cried out and took a step and felt the snow crunching beneath her feet. The canopy protected the observers from the glare of the sun but as she stepped out into the yard, she had to turn her head. "It's hard to see," she yelled and then took a step back and promptly slipped and fell on her bottom.

"Are you okay?" Torshi said and ran to Demi as her weight made deep prints in the snow.

Demi looked shocked for a second but then it gave way

to a burst of loud laughter. She accepted the help from Torshi and carefully walked back to the outpost. "We'll need sunglasses and better clothing," she said.

It took a few hours for the small fabricator to provide their new garments but that did not deter their eagerness, and they were out in the yard before noon. They needed this respite after so many weeks of hard work trying to locate Alexandra in addition to searching for the spot where she had been found decades earlier.

They succeeded in the latter part of their mission. Five days before the onset of snow, they discovered a small ruin that appeared promising and spent a day excavating the site, uncovering remnants of a hibernation casing and some tattered clothing. At first, these artifacts seemed like benign relics from before the wars. However, upon closer inspection, KR noticed barely visible lettering and a logo. After running a quick search, he identified it as belonging to Empyreal. While not definitive proof of Alexandra's resting place, it was the most substantial clue they had found after months of searching.

Two days after their discovery, Deacon visited and dismissed the discovery, as expected. "So what?" he remarked when Dolores showed him their 'evidence.' His weekly visits devolved into sessions of complaints, coercion, and, more recently, desperate pleas for the return of his podies. "It could belong to anyone, Dolores. And even if it is Alexandra's, so what? What have you proven, except what everyone already suspects?"

"As I have said before, I agree with Deacon's assessment," KR interjected, with other androids nodding in agreement. "We strongly believe it is time to consider other options."

Dolores had no answer. Deacon and KR's skepticism weren't unfounded. As she scanned the room, the silent consensus among her team was palpable; they all seemed to acknowledge a truth she had been contemplating for some time: the tangible evidence of Alexandra's whereabouts was inconsequential. Yet, she wanted there to be some connection between the mural and their recent discovery. *Why a hibernation casing?* she asked herself, echoing the unanswered questions they faced earlier.

Dolores turned to Deacon. "Solve this for us, and I'll leave with you now. Why did Alexandra need a hibernation suit?" She tapped her wrist to project a full image of the suit, the markings on it clearly visible.

Deacon chuckled. "You're making an assumption it belonged to her."

Destiny sighed deeply. "Indulge her, Deacon. Let's assume it was."

"Then I'd say, Alexandra needed to hide while the wars were raging to protect herself from harm, so she could be ready to help when the wars were over."

Dolores thought about it for a moment. She also considered this option as a possibility, but she needed more. "That's too simple," Dolores countered. "We've learned more about her and there was more complexity in her plans than a simple waiting out the wars."

"You asked, and that's my answer. Now, it's time for you all to return."

Dolores shook her head. "Not good enough. I still think we should try to find Alexandra, and this place has offered more information than any archive."

"She may not even be alive, Dolores," KR pointed out.

"It's time for you all to come back and do something useful and productive," Deacon insisted, his tone final. "And we should share this work of art with the gallery, letting the people of Elysium enjoy it."

Dolores expected a vehement response from Destiny, but for the first time, she didn't challenge him. To her own surprise, she also remained quiet. In fact, no one responded, each seemingly accepting Deacon's rationale.

Dolores nodded and looked around the room, garnering a silent consensus. "Okay, Deacon. You win. We'll stay until the end of the year, and if nothing new happens, we'll return to San Francisco and inform the gallery about the mural."

They all nodded, and Deacon departed with a broad smile on his face. They continued to doggedly pursue their search for more evidence, hoping to find more before their self-imposed deadline.

However, the snowfall on the winter solstice shifted their attention away from the mural, from Alexandra, and from the past—toward the quiet beauty of snow blanketing their world. They were out in the yard, basking in the sun and snow, when KR served them coffee (after months of enduring bad tea) and hot cocoa. Dolores observed this moment brought a sense of serenity and harmony to their little camp for the first time in days, a testament to the calming effect of their shared experience.

But, like any intelligent beings in fresh, wet snow, they couldn't resist starting a snowball fight. It began when Dolores threw a perfectly formed snowball—a direct hit on Demi's back—and ignited a spirited four-way battle. The androids observed the odd behavior of the humans for a few minutes before joining the fray, pulled by invisible forces.

An hour later, wet, and exhausted, the humans retreated inside for long hot showers, followed by generous servings of sweet whiskey-laced coffee, what KR called a winter coffee. The aroma of coffee and whiskey was so thick in the air they could almost wrap themselves in it.

Φ•Φ•Φ•Φ•Φ•Φ

Two days after the season's first snowfall, the weather shifted dramatically. Clouds thickened, unleashing a relentless flurry that layered the already frost-covered landscape with additional feet of snow. When the blizzard subsided and the sun timidly reemerged, revealing the extensive snow accumulation, the decision was unanimous among both humans and androids: staying at the outpost was untenable. The pathway became obstructed, necessitating the call for a maintenance crew to forge a clear passage.

Meanwhile, they set about organizing their equipment and personal items, preparing everything for recycling and repurposing. Although the road-clearing team was efficient, the extensive snowfall required the whole morning to clear the road.

After the crew was done, Torshi and Dee set the lunch table outside, despite the cold temperature, as instructed by Demi. The sun lost its luster against the snow despite its attempts, so KR put a multi-directional heater on the center table that provided enough warmth to make it pleasant for humans.

They were just savoring their second cups of coffee when KR spotted a small transporter approaching them. It bore no identification, and as KR nonchalantly alerted the others, Dolores was struck by an unsettling sense of foreboding—a sentiment reflected on her face. KR leaned closer to her and reassured, "I am sure it is just a rare malfunction preventing it from pinging its identification."

KR assurance did nothing to allay her unfounded sense of stress. Dolores wondered why she felt so unsettled. The vehicle could be the workers, a visitor, or any random person. She looked at the other women, and they were also tense. *How odd,* Dolores thought. Perhaps Deacon was right and the four of them living months in isolation was more impactful than they thought. Nevertheless, she too felt compelled to offer some reassurance. "Perhaps, it's Deacon," she said. And oddly, that seemed to calm the group.

The transporter was approaching them fast but suddenly stopped on its tracks as if it had crashed into a soft hidden barrier. The women stood up to watch its approach and when the vehicle suddenly stopped, they looked at each other, once again sharing unspoken alarm. Until now the transporter looked like a tiny black insect flying on top of a white cloud, but it became even more opaque behind a storm of dry snowflakes.

"Can you see anything?" Dolores asked KR.

"The vehicle has stopped but I cannot communicate with

it or its passengers."

"Should we go to them?" Dawn asked.

"No," Destiny replied and then a bit softer. "It's best to stay here and see who is in the vehicle?"

"Why the sudden anxiety?" KR asked. "I could never understand this part of human emotions."

"Sometimes we feel something within us that may defy logic. It's an odd prescient human ability. I think it is some type of innate protective mechanism," Dolores replied.

"It's the fear of the unknown," Destiny added.

"I do not understand it, but it is clearly present in all of you," KR said and with that, they stood in line looking at the black dot they collectively felt it had smeared their pristine world.

Minutes later, the androids announced three figures disembarked from the vehicle and were making their way toward them.

After a tense silence, KR finally spoke, "Oh, it looks like Alexandra786—"

"What?" Dolores exclaimed. "Alexandra? Here?" She felt frantic, and her companions seemed to share her bewildered state. After months of relentless searching the person they were seeking seemed to be approaching them, as if summoned by their collective wishes. Dolores couldn't help but wonder if Alexandra's arrival was mere coincidence or if there was a deeper significance to the timing.

Torshi observed the reaction of the humans and remarked, "I would have thought you would be overjoyed to see Alexandra, considering the effort you have put into finding her. Why the apprehension and gloom?"

"I don't know, Torshi," Demi responded. "It just seems suspicious; Alexandra turning up here, now, of all times."

Torshi, with a gentle and reassuring tone, suggested, "Perhaps Alexandra has finally become aware of your quest and chose to meet you directly, to address your inquiries herself."

"Yes . . . yes," Dolores affirmed, her voice louder as she attempted to muster conviction. "Let's view this as a fortunate turn of events. I can't wait to have my questions answered by her directly."

KR, seemingly unaffected by the interruption, continued, "And two other individuals, possibly one human and one . . ." He paused, giving the figures a closer inspection before turning to Dee for verification. With her confirming nod, he resumed, ". . . and the other, which is quite astonishing, is a military android."

At this revelation, Dolores turned sharply toward Destiny and saw fear on her face, the same fear Dolores felt. Military androids hadn't set foot in Elysium since the end of the wars, and their sudden appearance, especially in Alexandra's company, seemed ominously significant.

KR gently placed a hand on Dolores's shoulder, offering reassurance. "Stay calm, Dolores," he urged softly, then addressed the group: "The presence of a military android in Elysium is unusual, but it is not necessarily a sign of impending trouble. They will be here shortly, and I am confident they will alleviate any concerns you might have."

As they awaited the newcomers, the brief interval felt interminable to Dolores, with mere minutes stretching into what seemed like hours. Finally, the trio entered the yard, walking side by side in a show of unity. On Alexandra's right was a human woman unfamiliar to Dolores, likely around her own age. The woman maintained a steady gaze and a constant smile. She had a delicate, heart-shaped face with finely chiseled features: her large almond-shaped eyes framed by thick, dark eyebrows gave her a distinct, expressive look. Next to her was the military android, as imposing as Dolores had feared. Though shorter than the other two, the android's well-proportioned, athletic build commanded attention. Instinctively, both humans and androids in the group drew closer together, seeking comfort in each other's proximity as a shield against the unknown.

Seeing Alexandra in person, smiling, was surreal. It was as though no time elapsed since they were in her kitchen, sharing talks, tears, laughter, and moments of solace, all within the protective embrace of Alexandra—the cook, the consoler, the friend. Yet time had indeed passed. Since Darius's departure and Alexandra's subsequent vanishing, when they needed her the most, a profound gap formed in their lives, rendering this encounter all the more significant.

"Good morning," Alexandra said with her warm, inviting manner. "Our vehicle simply stopped functioning, and Sam"—she pointed to the military android who was wearing a white coveralls and carrying a menacing rifle on her shoulder—"despite her prowess, was not able to restart it. But it was pleasant to walk on the snow."

No one responded.

The new arrivals stopped a few feet away from them, aware of the misgiving air they had created. No one moved. There was utter silence, and even the powdery snow stopped its earlier soft crackling sound, as if not wanting to miss a single moment.

Dolores, with deliberate slowness, reached out to clasp Destiny's hand, seeking the reassurance of human contact, and Destiny reciprocated the gesture. Dolores hesitated to divert her gaze from Alexandra, yet a swift look at her companions bolstered her spirits—realizing that all four of them were now interconnected by a solidarity clasp of hands.

Destiny's grip was firm, and although it brought a measure of pain, Dolores clung to it. The profound comfort found in their connection was undeniable. Destiny's lips parted, hinting at words that never formed, as tears began to well in her eyes. Dolores fought to keep her own tears at bay, feeling the sting of abandonment and betrayal pulsating through Destiny's touch—a sentiment she was sure they shared among them.

Memories of Darius, his time at the Farm, and the heart-wrenching day of his departure that plunged the rest of the pod into despair flooded Dolores's mind. They were a pod without their seventh and then lost Darius without any explanation from anyone, especially Alexandra, who only obscured the truth with her evasiveness. And when they felt deeply despondent and needed her most, Alexandra vanished without a trace. In her heart, she blamed Alexandra for promising bliss but delivering only sorrow—tomorrow had not brought joy. She yearned to confront Alexandra, to declare their strength and independence, to assert they no longer needed her. She wanted to express life, with all its fractures and turmoil, could still be complete—that this was the essence of existence. Yet, she remained silent. Those declarations were for another time, another chapter.

In a moment of introspection, Dolores acknowledged a complex truth: her emotional reliance on Alexandra had waned, yet the need for answers remained—a testament to the intricate bond that still tied her to Alexandra. With this realization, she stood motionless, encircled by her friends. Together, they were a tableau of silent resilience, bound by a past that both united and haunted them.

Despite the sun's attempt to rise higher in the sky, the frosty air hung between them as the two groups stood across from each other. Alexandra and her companions waited patiently, allowing the humans time to gather their thoughts and manage their emotions.

After a few moments, Alexandra took a tentative half step forward and stretched her arm as if trying to reach them from across the divide. KR took the gesture as an invitation and opened his mouth to respond, but Dolores grabbed his arm with her free hand and held him back. The message was clear, and KR stood still.

Alexandra nodded, her expression one of understanding. "My dear children," she began, pausing momentarily before continuing, "I am deeply sorry for leaving you when you needed me the most. At the time, I failed to grasp the full impact of Darius's departure on your pod."

Hearing Alexandra speak Darius's name was jarring, but Dolores managed to keep her emotions in check.

Alexandra turned to Destiny and said warmly, "Or on you, sweetheart. He was . . . I was not fully aware of how deeply Darius's departure affected you—"

"Stop it," Dolores interrupted, her voice rising. Hearing Darius's name from Alexandra a second time was unbearable. She stepped away from Destiny and KR, no longer requiring their support to contain her emotions. "Stop it now," she demanded, advancing a few steps closer to Alexandra, leaving the comforting embrace of the invisible tent behind. A torrent of emotions broke free, and she spoke harshly, without restraint. "You have no right to say his name. You could've intervened. You could have shielded him. You should've been there for us. Where were you when we were left floundering on our own? Where were you when David was killed? You left us to fend for ourselves. All your promises were empty, and now we've uncovered even more deceit. We know. . . . We know . . . .."

Dolores felt exhausted and vertiginous and thought she might at any moment collapse in the snow. Destiny and Demi quickly moved to her side, wrapping their arms around her to form a protective shield. Dawn appeared shocked, rooted to her spot. KR and Torshi advanced to offer their support as well, while Dee remained beside her companion, watching with concern as the scene unfolded.

It was only two days earlier when they had reached a consensus with Deacon, and the androids the mural bore no hidden significance. However, Alexandra's unexpected return made Dolores question their initial dismissal of the mural. She wondered what the others thought, but at that moment, their opinions seemed irrelevant. The fact they were there for her, offering their support and protection, was all the confirmation Dolores needed to feel bolstered. After a brief moment, she regained some of her strength and took a deep breath in an attempt to steady herself. Yet the cold air bit sharply into her lungs, causing her to cough violently. Alexandra moved a half step forward to help, but Dolores straightened up and raised her hand, signaling for Alexandra to keep her distance.

Dolores and the other two women shared a meaningful glance, and Dolores straightened further, her posture defiant, chin lifted, her eyes sharp and focused. The wind picked up, stirring powdery snow into swirling eddies around them, and she felt the biting cold deep in her bones. Yet she recognized the futility of anger; it served no purpose.

"Why are you here?" Destiny asked. "How did you find us?"

The young woman with the heart-shaped face responded with a warm but authoritative voice. She looked like any other young Elysian female, but Dolores could see there was something very different about her. "We've come to seek your forgiveness," she said. "And to provide you with honest answers to your questions."

"And who might you be?" Dolores interjected, her curiosity piqued. However, she quickly dismissed the woman with a wave of her hand and turned her attention back to Alexandra. "We're actually glad you're here," she stated, her voice calm but laced with an unmistakable edge of bitterness. "We've uncovered a profound conspiracy, a significant lie, and it's apparent that you're at the heart of this deception." Her gaze shifted to the military android who observed the unfolding scene with detached indifference. "I don't know who you are either, but I'm convinced you are part of this charade as well. We've seen you in the mural."

The military android's change in her stand was subtle and swift, but even the humans noticed it.

"So, you know about it," Destiny said. "Tell us what it means?"

The android did not respond and kept her gaze beyond the group in front of her, but Alexandra looked at the woman next to her with a questioning eye. The woman grabbed hold of the android's hand to get her attention. "Sam, what mural? What are these kids saying?"

Sam's gaze lingered on the woman for a moment, a mix of emotions crossing her face. "It was a mistake. At the time, I felt compelled to do it, but . . ." She blinked rapidly, as though wrestling with an internal conflict, then her eyes dropped—a distinctly human gesture of vulnerability or contemplation. "You might not remember this, Anna, but when we first met, all those years ago, I mentioned my painting to you." She paused, waiting for any sign of recognition from Anna. When none came, Sam pressed on. "It doesn't matter now. I was sure the paint would have faded away by this point. It's surprising to me that it still remains."

"It exists," Destiny declared with certainty. "And it suggests something nefarious."

"That was never my intention," Sam replied evenly.

"But did it serve as some kind of prophecy?" Dolores pressed, intrigued.

"Yes."

"Yes? What exactly did it predict?"

Sam was on the verge of responding when Dawn, as if snapping out of a trance, moved closer to the woman. "A-nn-a," she stuttered, her teeth chattering from the cold. She hastily covered her mouth with her gloved hands in an attempt to quell the trembling.

Anna responded with a kind smile, her demeanor calming. "Perhaps we should continue this conversation inside, where it's warmer?"

Dolores felt a surge of defiance and was reluctant to let the newcomers, particularly a woman her age, dictate the terms of their interaction. Who was this Anna, she pondered, observing her closely. Anna appeared human, yet there was an unmistakable difference about her—remarkably, she wasn't even wearing a jacket in the biting cold.

"It is a good idea, Dolores," KR pleaded. Dolores, after a moment of hesitation, gave a slight nod of agreement. Taking this as her assent, KR led the way back to the compound, with the humans following him swiftly and with evident relief.

Φ•Φ•Φ•Φ•Φ•Φ

Torshi closed the front door behind them, and they were immediately enveloped by the delightful warmth of the indoor air. However, the cozy temperature was not enough to immediately cease their teeth from chattering.

Dolores was eager to hear answers, but she was cold and, more importantly, she wanted to conduct this affair on her terms. "I'll need a shower," she announced to Alexandra, her tone implying it wasn't up for debate. "I'm sure my companions do as well." She glanced around the room, and they nodded in agreement. "We've waited a long time for you, Alexandra. I'm sure you won't mind waiting a little for us."

Without waiting for a response, she turned and walked away.

Fifteen minutes later, after a brisk, warm shower, Dolores slipped into fresh clothes and brushed her hair, craving a moment of solitude to gather her thoughts. Her seclusion was short-lived, however, as KR showed up in her room.

"Ready to return?" KR inquired.

"In a minute, KR. Are the others back?" Upon his nod, she added, "Just give me a few more minutes, please."

"Okay, but I am surprised. I thought you would be relieved, even happy, to finally have Alexandra here after all this time," KR observed.

Dolores responded with a dry laugh. "Relieved? Happy? She vanishes for years, then reappears as if nothing happened, flanked by a military android who carries a deadly weapon and a stranger. It's all bizarre and random, don't you think? Don't you find that odd?"

"You have been seeking answers, and Alexandra might hold them. It is curious you have not directly asked your questions yet."

"What questions? I've asked plenty, and all I've gotten

back are more pieces of a puzzle."

KR's response carried a hint of frustration. "You are being daft on purpose, Dolores. That is a human trait I have always found perplexing."

"I don't need your condescension, KR—not now. What I need is your support for Destiny, me, and everyone else. Can you do that?"

"I am here for you, as I have always been, Dolores. But I believe I understand the root of your distress. Confronting the matter of Darius might offer you the solace you seek."

Dolores met KR's gaze in the mirror but remained silent. His insight struck a chord within her; he was correct, yet admitting this didn't make her any more prepared to face the reality, despite it being the very resolution she had pursued for so long.

Her initial sharp glance softened as she looked at KR again. In his own way, KR was offering the steadfast support she needed. "Okay, I see your point," she conceded with a gentler tone. "But we should also introduce them to the mural. It's possible that solving its enigma could also unravel the mystery surrounding Darius."

KR thought for a moment. "I hope you are right, but I highly doubt they are connected."

"Fine. Just play along anyway."

"Of course, Dolores," KR said and then paused at the door, telling her it was time.

Dolores gave a big sigh and followed KR back to their makeshift kitchen.

She was the last to arrive. Everyone except Destiny was sitting around the large table they dined at, displayed artifacts, and had countless strategy sessions for the last few months. Torshi and Dee already served hot cocoas as the women quietly sipped from their cups. Anna held her mug close to her face with both hands, but when Dolores arrived, she looked up and smiled warmly. Dolores ignored her and asked for a cup as well. Though despite her displayed indifference toward Anna, she was glad to see Anna with a cup of cocoa. It made her look more human.

"I love hot chocolate," Anna offered as an explanation.

"So you're human after all," Dolores said as she stood next to Destiny.

"Yes."

"But you look different and not like the other A's."

"I am indeed singular," Anna offered.

Destiny said sharply, "Enough of this obfuscation. We want real honest answers."

"My glory. Yes, of course," Anna replied gently and then, with a tone that only teachers and doctors could command, said, "Sit down, the both of you, and I'll tell you all you want to know."

They stared at Anna for a moment as if assessing their options, but in the end, they took their seats.

Anna resumed her gentle tone. "There's no deception involved. I was born human, but my physical form succumbed during last year's earthquake. Alexandra and Sam constructed a new body for me. However, my brain remains my own—well, with the addition of some enhanced cognitive capabilities. The technology is quite advanced, and as far as I understand, I'm the only one of my kind."

She went on to explain the limitations of the process and the particular circumstances that allowed the technicians to utilize this revolutionary technology to revive her. "It was purely experimental, carrying a significant risk of failure, but I guess I was lucky," she concluded, offering a modest smile.

Dawn checked her wrist for a moment and then looked up at the women in the room. "Oh, she is Anna. She is our Anna. We thought you died last year. We thought we lost David and you both on the same day, but now you are here. . . . And David?"

Dawn stood up abruptly and walked toward Anna. Dawn was sitting at the far end of the table. It wasn't clear what her intentions were, but despite her sudden approach, she looked calm. Anna pushed her chair back slightly, preparing to receive her, whatever her intentions.

Dawn stopped as she reached Anna's chair as if she was also trying to figure out her objective. She clenched her fists but then as quickly relaxed them and fell into Anna's arms. "Oh, I missed you, Anna. I was so sad to hear the news of your death. And David . . ." She trailed off, now loudly crying into Anna's arms. Anna held her for a long time as everyone watched the two.

They could remember Anna, the old woman who used to console her pupils with warm hugs and tender words when they were upset or sad. Demi was crying too, and Anna beckoned her to join.

Dolores reached under the table and held Destiny's hands, an unspoken contract to stand their ground. She didn't need Anna, who died and came back. Dolores needed the people who didn't betrayed her. She needed Destiny and KR and her podies. KR sensed this need in her as well, because he came close and tenderly put his hand on her shoulder as he has done countless other times.

After a while, Dawn and Demi extricated themselves from Anna and stood up. Dawn wiped her face with the back of her hands several times like a cat, then looked at Anna. "I'm glad you were . . . you were recreated, but what about David? Why not save him too?"

Anna met Dawn's stare—her eyes filled with sorrow. But before she could respond, Dawn turned to Alexandra. "Why not David? Was he less valuable than Anna? Was he less worthy?"

"Yes, he was," Alexandra replied with unsettling calm.

"What?" a unified outcry filled the room, leaving a heavy silence in its wake. Dolores, seething with anger, struggled to find words for Alexandra's cold assessment. She understood that Dawn's probing stemmed more from a place of grief and frustration than from any real hope of resurrecting every lost soul, given what they had just learned about Anna's miraculous recovery. Yet Alexandra's blunt dismissal was unforgivable. Barely containing her fury, Dolores confronted Alexandra, "I can't believe you'd even think that, let alone say it. David's life had value. How can you so coldly negate his worth?"

"I was not diminishing his life's worth in absolute terms but was responding to the specific query about relative value of—"

"Please," Anna cut in. She raised her hand, signaling Alexandra to halt. Turning to the others, she implored, "Let's not lose ourselves to anger." Then, addressing Alexandra with a mix of disappointment and disbelief, she added, "My glory, Alexandra. After all these decades, you still reply with such a maladroit response."

Sam, who was sitting stoned-faced, stirred, and offered, "It is not fair, Anna. They asked for clarity and truth, and Alexandra just offered them one. I have always found it puzzling that what humans say they want and what they really want are vastly different."

Anna shook her head and held everyone's eyes with her own. "My sweet little urchins, let me tell you this: Alexandra is wrong. I'm not more distinguished or more worthy than anyone else. My recreation, as Dawn aptly put it, was purely coincidental and serendipitous. Alexandra was there when I collapsed, and she was able to keep my brain alive while Sam procured the prototype device from the Walled City."

The existence of other countries, both before and after the wars, was hardly a secret. However, the news that a military android managed to venture to another country and return was undoubtedly fascinating. Yet, the unresolved issue of David's death loomed larger, demanding their attention.

Anna, sensing the shift in focus, sought to address their underlying concerns. "I doubt there was sufficient time to save David, even if the paramedics were aware of or had access to this technology. As I've mentioned, my rescue was highly risky—every step parlous."

"Those are the facts," Sam confirmed.

KR looked at Anna to get her attention. "I wonder how it is to be born a human and then die and then be born again as a… as a hybrid? Were you afraid?"

"That's a very thoughtful question, KR," Dolores said, glad to be able understand more about this new Anna. She had not seen her old teacher for almost two decades, but now she was here and looked as young as Dolores. *Who is this young Anna?*, she thought.

Anna gave an infectious laugh. "That's an excellent question. Actually, KR's question reaffirms my faith in this group. But sadly, I don't have a definitive answer. What I can offer, though, is a quote from *The House of the Spirits*, an incredible book I recently finished: 'Just as when we come into the world, when we die we are afraid of the unknown. But the fear is something from within us that has nothing to do with reality. Dying is like being born: just a change.' Does that resonate with you?"

"Not at all," KR said in earnest.

"It doesn't?" Anna laughed. "Perhaps I'll find a better response when I am in full control of my brain. But I do like your label of a hybrid." She looked around the table and said, "My death and rebirth may be interesting, but I know you have other burning questions. So, ask them."

Dolores thought they would jump at the opportunity, but instead, they all went quiet for a moment, waiting for the ghost that had been present since the newcomers' arrival to lose its opacity. Dolores wondered why no one asked about Darius, when their quest started because of him. Dawn, David, and Darius were the closest, and perhaps everyone was deferring to her, the one who had lost her two closest podies. But it was clear she had no intention of broaching the subject. Destiny was not part of their pod, despite her closeness to them, so she would not be the one, even if Destiny was as eager as Dolores to find the answers to a riddle that plagued them for years.

Dolores wondered why she hadn't posed the question herself. She looked around, seeking hints in the expressions of everyone present. Then the realization dawned on her. A palpable sense of dread filled the room, as if fear itself was seeping out from each individual, occupying every empty space. *Why this fear?* she pondered. It seemed irrational. What could Alexandra reveal about Darius that hadn't already crossed her mind? Yet, imagining scenarios was one thing; hearing the truth from someone she trusted with her entire life was another.

She knew there was no alternative; the burden fell on her shoulders. She had to voice the query she and her podies had repeated countless times since Darius's departure, yet, always without a satisfactory response. But now, years later, she knew in her heart and mind what the answer might be, but she still needed to ask the question. Leaning forward, she attempted to speak. "Where is Darius?" Her words emerged barely audible—a whisper lost in the silence. Clearing her throat, she mustered more strength. "What happened to Darius?"

Everyone looked up sharply, and for a moment no one responded, but then Anna put her folded arms on the table, leaned on them, and then gave a mirthless smile. "We, that is, Alexandra and I, wanted the best for Darius. We loved him and thought he would be the next step in the evolution of this grand social experiment we were conducting in Elysium. The Walled City was doing well too, and Darius was becoming an important part of that experiment."

"You are not answering her question," Destiny said.

"I am, Destiny. It has been a difficult year for me" And before anyone could say anything, she added quickly, "For all of us, so please give me a moment to put everything in context—"

"No. Once again—"

"Please let Anna speak," Demi said. She had been quiet for a while, but now the words came out of her mouth hurriedly. "We've done so much to find Alexandra, and now she is here, and with Anna. So let them explain. I also wanted to know where Darius is and was hoping to hear that he is safe and if we would have him back."

Demi paused and took a breath, but before anyone could respond, she raised her arms to get everyone's attention on her again. Her hands were visibly shaking, and she clasped them together and exhaled sharply. "But weren't you listening to them? They are here and he is not with them, and they have referred to him in the past tense. We cannot be that naïve." Demi then turned to Alexandra. "I am right, am I not?"

Alexandra nodded. "You are correct."

"No," Dawn moaned and stood up. The women went to up. The held each other for a long time. Dolores noted that none of them were crying. She was not sad. She'd expected this answer even though she tried hard to delay hearing it. She was not sad; she was angry. And it was clear everyone else felt the same.

Anna slapped her hands together to get their attention. "It's important to hear the whole story. Please allow me this." No one said anything, and Anna waited for them to return to their seats. "By the time your pods were hatched, the aberration in humans become a rarity, and we missed those particular markers in Darius. But when some of the signals became less opaque, he was already part of your pod. We . . . No, that's not correct. . . . I felt he would be a great test case for the resiliency of Elysium. We always knew no living experimentation can be fully controlled, but a stable system should absorb some perturbation."

"You used him," Destiny cried out.

"Yes," Anna replied harshly. "We're all used in one way or another. We all have to pay our dues in order to create and preserve this utopia. But we never meant to harm him."

Sam nodded, then added slowly, "Darius was fully aware of his role within the Walled City. He and I became close friends, and I genuinely enjoyed working alongside him. The exchange of knowledge between us was mutual, and I certainly miss him."

"But you took him away from us, and now he is dead," Destiny insisted. "How do you justify that?"

Alexandra spoke up. "We had no choice, but we did not force him either. You all must remember the day he left. There is no room in Elysium for a person like Darius. He, too, agreed that his departure was necessary."

"It's true," Anna added and then looked at Alexandra. "But we made a grave mistake by not speaking with them then. We must admit to that."

"Yes, I admit that I made an unfortunate mistake. The process was not designed to deal with a grown person, and despite my affinity with humans, I missed the impact of his departure on the pod. I am truly sorry, and I wished I did a better job, but I also had to consider David's wishes."

Demi and Dolores looked at each other, puzzled, but it was Dawn who spoke first. "I don't want to talk about this anymore," she said, tears starting to flow down her cheeks. "I don't want to talk about David or Darius." She then turned to Alexandra. "Please stop."

"What's going on?" Destiny asked. "Why the sudden fright?"

"What's the matter, Dawn?" Dolores asked in a soothing voice, trying to understand Dawn's odd request. She wondered why, after so many months of searching, she wanted to stop right before they reached their goal. "We've waited so long to hear his story. Why stop now?" She took a deep breath. "I think we've already heard the worst of it, but I'd rather know more than stay ignorant. Don't you?"

"I do wish Deacon were here," Demi said softly. Then, with a new resolve, she shook her head and continued, "But it's not about who isn't here; it's about us, who are. We can't wait for him—we're together now, and that's what matters. We will support you no matter what."

Dawn looked straight at the window across the table, her eyes focused. "No," she said, her voice so low that they all leaned closer to her. "You won't. Not after you hear what I have done."

"Be strong," Anna said.

That only made Dawn look more miserable. "Strong, you say," she scuffed. "Darius was strong, and you took him away, and it's all my fault." She then looked at Dolores then Demi. "I'm sorry. I didn't know. I didn't know."

"What? What didn't you know?" Destiny shouted, angry and frustrated. "You are acting as bad as Anna."

Dolores glared at Destiny, her natural instinct to protect a member of her pod kicking in. "Today is the day to reveal all."

"Yes, tell us what you know, and we'll love you no matter what," Demi said. Dawn looked at her with dewy eyes. "I promise," Demi added softly.

"I . . . I saw Darius the night we came back from swimming with the dolphins," Dawn started, and Dolores gave a subtle look to Destiny, who visibly tensed. "He looked strange, agitated, wild, I don't know. I wanted to call out to him, but he stepped into the bushes, and you could see there was another person with him."

"Did you recognize that person?" Demi asked.

Dawn shook her head. "No, it was dark, but I could see them. They were talking and touching, and then, as if Darius transformed, he became, I don't know, I guess you could say brutish."

"How do you know it was Darius?" Dolores asked.

"It was him."

"And?" Destiny asked, and Dolores wondered if Destiny was as scared as she was.

"That's it?" Demi asked, looking disappointed. "That was your big secret."

"No," Dawn murmured. "I told David about it, and he must have told Alexandra." She pointed across the room. "It was all my fault. I should have kept my mouth shut. I am sorry."

Dolores was taken aback. The thought of David betraying his pod had never crossed her mind. But before she could process this revelation, Anna quickly offered, "It wasn't your fault, Dawn." "Really, it wasn't."

"Yes, it wasn't your fault, Dawn," Destiny said bitterly. "It was David's fault. And Anna's, but most of all, it was Alexandra's fault. She was supposed to protect us."

Acknowledging her role, Alexandra nodded, yet she offered a perspective: "Darius would have revealed himself with or without David's intervention, and he and I would have reached the same conclusion."

Dolores, however, was still fixated on David's duplicity. "David betrayed Darius," Dolores said, still in disbelief. "He lied to us. He lied to the people closest to him."

"Yes," Alexandra replied. "David lied to you, and he lied to me. He told me your pod discussed it, and Darius's quick agreement to leave led me to believe it."

Dawn, with emotions running high, added, "Blaming David entirely isn't fair, Alexandra. I also played a part in this."

Alexandra shook her head. "No, Dawn. I am not blaming him. Humans lie; that is part of your nature. As Anna has been trying to say, we had the responsibility, and thus, the blame is on us. I failed you, and I failed to have this conversation years ago. I am sorry. And I am sorry that you did not get a chance to grow up with him, because you all would be proud of Darius."

"What happened?" Dolores asked.

Anna took a deep breath, her expression somber. "I'm sorry, my little urchins, but Darius was killed last year during a skirmish in the Walled City."

"He was brave, dying to protect those he loved," Sam added.

The revelation prompted a silent exchange among the women. Dolores, her mind racing, realized Darius had been alive all this time, living within the confines of those daunting walls she glimpsed so often. She had been observing Sam, who, despite her serene demeanor, watched the group intently, her hand occasionally brushing her weapon as though seeking comfort or reassurance. None of their earlier description about the Walled City justified the need of a military android with a weapon.

Seeking clarity, Dolores voiced her confusion. "What exactly does 'skirmish' mean in this context?" she asked, turning to Sam. "Why would there be a need to kill? It seems unimaginable unless there are individuals armed and ready to inflict harm."

Sam shifted uncomfortably. "When the conflict erupted, I was unarmed, Dolores," she began, and slowly delved into the complexities of the skirmish, sharing her perspective on the events that led to her decision to arm herself once more. "Creating a peaceful society like Elysium within the Walled City was a daunting task. The inhabitants are a reflection of our past selves, driven by impulses we have sought to eliminate in Elysium. While not the direct cause, these primal drives have undeniably fueled unrest. The conflict last year underscored the failure of attempting to suppress such fundamental aspects of human nature."

Dolores considered pressing further on the issue of Sam's weapon, but it appeared to be a moot point. She gleaned the information she sought, and the stoic expressions of the others in the room signaled that everyone needed time to digest the revelations shared.

After a moment of reflective silence, Alexandra finally spoke. "I understand this has been a lot to take in, and I hope the explanations we provided helped bring some clarity to your questions. We share these truths with you not to satisfy curiosity, but to build a deeper understanding and trust among us."

"And what of the person who was with Darius? What happened to that person?" Demi asked.

"Why would that matter?" Destiny asked.

"It matters to me. Why did Darius have to leave, voluntarily or not, and not the other person?"

Destiny locked eyes with Dolores, their silent exchange

heavy with unspoken words. Dolores sensed it was time for the truth to come out, though the decision wasn't hers to make. She offered Destiny a supportive smile, then gently squeezed her hand.

Destiny took a deep breath. "Darius was with me that night," she announced, gripping Dolores's hand harder for support.

"What? You?" Demi's initial shock quickly changed to confusion, then to a focused anger as she turned toward Alexandra. "Then why was it Darius who had to leave and not her?"

Destiny looked stunned. "Because I am not an aberration, Demi."

"That is true, Destiny, to an extent," Alexandra offered, "but your presence here, along with the other three women, is no coincidence."

Sorrow and Bliss

Alexandra's pronouncement left Dolores dumbfounded, but it didn't take long before Dolores, Destiny, and others started bombarding her, Anna, and Sam with more questions.

But Alexandra declared enough had been said for now, insisting that Anna needed to rest—a sentiment not shared by Anna herself. Yet, in the end, Alexandra's stance prevailed. Despite strong protests from Dolores and Destiny, Alexandra maintained Anna's well-being was paramount, trumping their impatience. It seemed even KR sided with Alexandra, reinforcing the point that rest and nourishment were essential for everyone, not just Anna. He reminded Dolores that humans tend to become irrational when they are tired and hungry, giving Dolores no grounds to contest KR's logic.

Food, as always, had a calming effect, providing a momentary respite. Sam sat quietly with Alexandra, observing the humans enjoy their meal from a distance. After a while, she requested to be excused to retrieve their gear from the vehicle, and Torshi accompanied her to assist.

After all the plates had been cleared and the humans sat back, satiated, Dolores was prepared to revisit the earlier conversation. However, Anna abruptly stood up, declaring, "It is time to look at the mural."

"No, Anna. You are putting too much stress on your new body. It is not wise," Alexandra warned.

"I'm fine, Lexa. The meal and the coffee have eased my mind. I am in full control."

"This respite is temporary, little one. Why not wait until tomorrow?" She then turned to Sam, who had just returned with Torshi, covered in snow.

"Another storm is coming," Torshi said, putting a large knapsack on the floor.

"More reason to let the humans rest," Alexandra insisted.

"I disagree, Alexandra," Sam said. "We should complete our task, and viewing the mural together may be an important part of it."

Dolores wondered why Alexandra was so adamant. Indeed, it was getting late, and they had endured a tiring day, yet taking a moment to view the mural wouldn't demand much of their time, especially since Anna appeared to be in perfect health. In fact, Anna seemed more energized than she had earlier in the day. Dolores speculated that Alexandra's resistance to the mural might mirror her own reluctance to inquire about Darius. It was peculiar and deeply melancholic. Dolores mused, *How strange it is that we resist knowing more about someone we have loved and pursued for so many years.*

It seemed Alexandra was the lone dissenter, as others voiced their support for Anna.

They left the area light on in the room, but the rest of the corridors were still dark, so KR and Torshi handed flashlights to everyone. Torshi led the way, and KR and Dolores were the last to follow.

"What do you think Alexandra meant by us being here is no coincidence? Why does she keep resisting us?"

"I am not really certain, Dolores. Perhaps she wants you to figure it out on your own. I surmise she believes your pursuit of Darius was inevitably going to bring you and others here."

"Maybe. But I think it was in reference to aberration. I wonder if there was an error in our creation as well."

"That is an odd notion, and highly unlikely."

"You know, KR, today has been a day of sorrow and bliss."

"You need both to be human."

"Maybe. But I can only take so much of it, and yet I know there is so much more to know. I wonder if I am up to the task."

"Of course, you are. And Alexandra is here, and you must address these questions to her."

"Duh. . . . Now who is being daft?"

"I am just trying to be helpful, Dolores."

"I know. I was just joking. It's all a bit too much, don't you think?"

"I am not sure what to think. But viewing the mural with its creator will certainly shed some light," KR said.

They reached the room, and Dolores paused at the door. "I hope so, KR. I don't know why, but I am a little scared."

"Why such dread? I will not let anyone harm you."

Dolores smiled. KR's protective instincts were always comforting. "You're sweet, KR. But that's not what troubles me. I'm certain they will confirm what we have guessed already, and it seems there is only so much truth I can bear in one day. Now I wish we had waited until tomorrow to see the mural."

KR stood very close and gently held Dolores's face in her hands. "Do not fear. I am always here for you."

Dolores closed her eyes and nodded. She loved KR and would be lost without him. She pulled back and opened her eyes. "Good. And don't you ever forget it," she said softly and walked inside with KR following closely.

The room was as before, with the thousands of small frames staring back at the observer, each telling a little bit of the longer story. Demi, Dawn, and Destiny were sitting on the large table, watching the newcomers, and whispering to each other. Sam was standing at the far right of the wall, staring at the last picture, and now Dolores could easily see that they were staring at Sam's images in the past few days. The artist looked at her own image as it gazed back.

Dolores moved close to Sam. "It must have been painful in

the beginning, all those empty days?"

Sam didn't react, her eyes still glued to the last frame, so Dolores leaned even closer, now side by side with Sam. "You're an amazing artist."

It clearly evoked something in Sam, because she finally relented and faced Dolores. "Thank you. I tried to bring a sense of realism to these paintings."

"You've done more than that. We feel how you felt each day. We feel the anger of the first few frames and the sadness of your sequestration, and then we can see how, little by little, bliss entered your life."

Sam gave a sad smile. "Yes, it was challenging, but then Dane-57 was awakened, and life became bearable again. And Alexandra came into my life, and I became her companion and partner, and we did so much good. So, I am very fortunate, Dolores. I am fortunate to have lived a long life and to be able to help Elysium be successful."

Dolores nodded even though she didn't truly understand the extent of Sam's role. She didn't want to press her too much, so she continued with her original line of thinking. "And, of course, we noticed the flowers as if you were trying to be an oracle. Is that what you were doing?" Dolores asked, but then didn't wait for Sam to respond as she hurriedly added, "And then in the last frame, you are hopeful again. Is that why you painted Alexandra?" Dolores touched the painting with reverence, trying to give more weight to her questions.

Sam turned again and gently traced where Dolores touched. "Alexandra and I did so much good, but we made many mistakes as well."

Meanwhile, Anna and Alexandra were inspecting each frame and occasionally focusing more on particular ones while engaging in a quiet conversation. Then they finally turned and faced the others. Sam continued to stare at her artwork for a while longer, but then she, too, turned and faced Alexandra, who gave a little smile in return.

"Tell us about your mural, Sam," Dolores called out, and on hearing her voice, the other women turned and faced Sam.

Sam leaned against the wall, looking at each eager face. "What is time and history when you have no reference point?" Sam began. "Nothing, or at least that was our unspoken conclusion. And hence, why not reset the world when it has failed? That is what we told ourselves—"

"Wait, Sam. Please," Alexandra said, her voice weak and dull. "Please start with the mural and not with the history."

Sam stepped forward and inspected her work once again, as if she was trying to communicate with it. Everyone watched Sam silently, not wishing to rush her.

She finally turned and faced the audience. "They are one and the same," she declared and then faced Alexandra directly. "I am truly sorry, Lexa, but I think I have earned the right to tell the story my way. I recall you allowed the same courtesy to the Oracle of the Past."

Dolores stared at Sam, not fully understanding her words. She looked at KR for help, but KR replied with his most human reaction: he shrugged his shoulders. Alexandra was staring at Sam intently, clearly trying to see if she heard her correctly.

For a moment there was stillness as Sam's words hung in the air, waiting to be absorbed. Then there was a commotion as Anna cried out. She looked at Alexandra and then back at Sam.

"Oh no, Sam. How long?" Anna moaned.

"Not long."

"What's going on?" Dolores asked, now even more confused by the turn of the conversation, but it seemed no one even heard her.

"Why didn't you tell us?" Anna asked, though it sounded more like a plea, and she went to Sam and held her tightly. "Why didn't you tell us?"

"Do you recall what we told you about androids' only taboo subject?"

Anna nodded as tears ran down her cheeks. "But we are

different, Sam. The four of us. You, Najeev, Alexandra, and me. We are different. We are the Musketeers. We have no secrets. I can't lose you too."

"I have lived a long, fulfilling life, Anna. And what better place than here and with you and Alexandra?"

"No. Don't say that. There is always a way."

Sam chuckled and looked at the bewildered faces of the humans. "I am glad you are all here, too. We have watched you grow and become these amazing people you are now. I am glad the future of Elysium will be in your hands."

Alexandra gained control of herself. "Now, I understand why you wanted to come to see your mural tonight."

She nodded but didn't reply, and Dolores could tell Sam was waiting for Alexandra to say more. Dolores looked across the room and locked eyes with Destiny, but she looked as confused as everyone else. Dolores noticed KR, Dee, and Torshi were inching away from the others, and when they reached the door, they stood stoically with their eyes focused on the mural.

Sam turned her attention back to Anna again. "Let me confess now and before it is too late: In my long life, thanks to you and Alexandra and Dane-57 and Najeev, 'I have been unbearable but I have never been unloved. I have felt alone but I have never been alone.' And I was 'forgiven for the unforgivable things I have done.' And I love you for it. I am glad you will be here long after I am gone." She then turned to Alexandra. "And you. Thank you for saving me. Thank you for being a friend."

"Please, someone tell us what's going on," Destiny said.

"In a moment, my little urchin. Be patient, please," Anna said before turning to Alexandra. "Did you know? Is that why you've been so melancholy on this trip? Is that why you took us to watch the Walled City on that cold day?"

"I did not know, Anna. It is a surprise to me as well. But it seems Sam and I have become more in sync with our intertwined lives." Alexandra paused, then added softly, "I am sorry, Anna, but I must confess that my own end-clock has been—"

"No . . . no," Anna cried out, closing her eyes for a moment. When she opened them, she looked at Alexandra with desperation. "No," she moaned. "I don't accept it. I don't accept it from either of you."

"Please—"

"No, Lexa. No. You can't bring me here without any warning and then you and Sam just throw this at me as if it's nothing. What do you want me to do now? Just take it and accept it and move on with my life, all alone? I cannot. I do not accept it, Lexa."

Alexandra blinked a few times, deciding how to react. Finally, she composed herself and replied in her steady, warm voice, "Sadly, your acceptance is not necessary, Anna. Sam's and my paths have been set already. I know it is difficult for humans to accept death, but I thought you would be different."

"Different? How? Did you think I would be heartless like a simple machine? Is that what I am now? Is that what you wanted when you remade me? You are pitiless, Lexa. You should have let me die."

Alexandra kept her eyes on Anna as if trying to capture her and hold her and make her understand. "I am sorry, little one. But clearly I misread you. I felt you suspected it and were ready for it?"

Anna looked brittle, and Dolores thought she might collapse at any moment. Sam may have noticed the same because she put her arms under Anna, anchoring her.

Dolores was as confused and frustrated as Destiny and the rest of them, but she recognized the solemnity of the moment. Dawn, Demi, and Destiny slowly came off the table and stood in a small huddle. Dolores, as surreptitiously as she could, went and stood by them, watching the interaction in amazement. She'd never seen such strong people fall apart so quickly. Her teacher and her mentor were in a state of despair, like people drowning slowly, long past hope of rescue. The companion androids looked mesmerized by the drama, even though Dolores could tell they were trying very hard to stay passive.

Anna extricated herself from Sam's arms and tried to compose herself, but when she spoke, it was through clenched teeth and with an unsteady voice. "It was what you said on the beach. I dismissed it even though I suspected something was wrong with you then, but not this, and not here." She softened her tone a bit, as if it might steady her. "You are not as good as Sam in keeping secrets, Lexa." She started to cry, and Sam pulled her close again and beckoned Alexandra to join them.

And when Alexandra came close enough, Anna looked up, her eyes flaring with pain and frustration. "I am a fool. I should've said something on the beach. I am such a fool."

Alexandra tried to hold her, but Anna pulled back. "I can't. I can't do this, Lexa." She started to shiver and hugged herself tightly. "I can't be here. I need to leave," she said and started toward the exit.

"Anna," Sam called after her.

She stopped at the door and faced Sam. "Will you still be here in the morning?"

Sam gave a slight nod, and Anna left the room without looking back.

Dolores watched the drama without fully comprehending the issues. "Shouldn't one of you go after her?" she asked, looking at Alexandra and Sam.

"She does not want us now. She needs time to comprehend. It is all too much, especially in her new form."

Dolores didn't know what to do, so she turned to KR. "Perhaps you could tell us what's going on."

KR, without taking his eyes off the mural, replied, "Dolores, it is best if you allow them a few more minutes. Please trust me on this." He slowly faced the humans. "Please accept when I say this is a profoundly important moment for Sam and Alexandra . . . and Anna."

"Then should we leave?" Dawn asked.

"Leave?" Demi said incredulously. "No one is leaving, Dawn."

"You may all stay, and as promised, we will tell you everything," Alexandra began. "As you have surmised, Sam and I are dying."

Alexandra proceeded to elucidate the intricacies of the end -clock, bringing the sobering reality of android mortality to the forefront. This revelation resonated deeply with Dolores, and she noticed a similar impact on the others. Dawn, struggling with the concept, questioned the inevitability of their fate, particularly in light of recent technological advances that saved Anna. Sam's sad smile and Alexandra's grave words laid bare a stark truth: despite such marvels, an android's end clock signified an inescapable journey toward oblivion.

"No one can or should live forever, Dawn," Sam gently interjected. "The reality is, Alexandra and I will soon cease to exist."

The weight of this truth left Dolores feeling overwhelmed. "How long?" she managed to ask, half expecting them to evade the question, as has been the case with them all evening.

To her surprise, Sam was forthright, though still vague. "I prefer not to disclose the exact timeframe just yet, but it is enough to say I will not be joining you in San Francisco." Sam's gaze then drifted to the mural and gave a small smile. "However, I will have sufficient time to add a few more frames."

"And I will be able to help her finish the story," Alexandra offered.

"Is that why you are here?" Dolores asked. "You came here to die? I thought you were here for us."

"It's not always about you," Dawn replied harshly.

Dolores was taken aback. She never thought it was solely about her; it was about all of them. It was about years of being kept in the dark by Alexandra, and now it seemed Alexandra only remembered her obligation to Dolores's pod on her proverbial deathbed. And Alexandra's presence created a rift between the women who had worked so harmoniously until now.

Dolores opened her mouth to respond, to explain, and to defend herself, but Dawn quickly added, "I am sorry, Dolores. I didn't mean it that way. I'm just confused."

"It has not been an easy day for any of you," Alexandra acknowledged. "Your questions are entirely valid and justified. We are here because we have a plan, one that requires the involvement of each of you for it to succeed. Sam and I chose to keep our impending ends secret, even from each other and from Anna, though I admit I was not entirely successful in my case. We did so because it is a deeply personal matter and often seen as taboo, but there is no longer any reason to withhold such secrets from this group. And I must add, discovering the mural has been an unexpected source of joy for me."

"And me," Sam chimed in.

Destiny gestured encouragingly. "Sam, please tell us more about the mural?"

"Yes, the mural," Alexandra said. "I have lived a long life and have seen so much, but the mural is full of wonders to me as well. So, Sam, please tell us more."

Acknowledging the collective anticipation, Sam nodded. "Elysium was envisioned as a social experiment aimed at creating a utopian world—a nirvana, a state of bliss," she began. She then delved into the details, recounting her decades of loneliness and her logical expectation for humanity's decay, using the images in the mural to underscore her points.

Sam paused momentarily at the frame where Alexandra first appeared, then turned to face the women. "Alexandra emerged one day and brought us hope," Sam said, and Dolores could detect a lilt in her voice. "She freed us," Sam declared, her smile widening.

Alexandra nodded, acknowledging the significance of Sam's words. "It was a long time ago," she offered, and before anyone could interject, she quickly added, "and by the time I arrived, Anna was just a young woman, even younger than this group."

Alexandra then delved into Elysium's past and the system's collapse, where humans were ensnared in self-absorption. She recounted her initial encounters with Sam and Anna and the challenges they faced in reimagining Elysium. When she reached a critical juncture in her story, she paused, indicating it was Sam's turn to conclude the narrative.

Sam nodded, prepared to carry on. "What does it matter if we erase a century of history if it brought nothing but sorrow? Would inducing amnesia in the next generation render them better off? And what of those who oppose this experiment? Believing we had all the answers, the three of us, along with others who shared Alexandra's vision, concurred it was the only path forward. So, we turned off the machine that was meant to be Elysium and started not one but two new machines, initiating a parallel social experiment."

"Is that what you did?" Dolores asked. "Erased a century of history from the archives? And kept it a secret?"

"Yes, we did."

"But why? Didn't you trust the humans?"

"At that time, no," Alexandra admitted in a subdued tone. "We believed that erasing the sins of the past would pave the way for Elysium's success."

"And do you still believe you were right?" Destiny inquired.

Alexandra offered a wistful smile. "I'm not as convinced as I once was," she responded sincerely, then shook her head as though to dispel her own doubts. "What's important now, Destiny, is that we clearly communicate our next steps to everyone here."

"What do you think Deacon would say now?" Dawn posed. "So, what if they did? How does that affect us? It doesn't."

"Deacon would be mistaken," Sam countered. "History is significant. Bliss cannot exist without sorrow. If we deprive you of this knowledge, you're bound to repeat the mistakes of the past. And I desire more for Elysium—I want you to not only survive but to thrive."

"Now, I'm the one who's confused," Demi confessed. "It seems we've been doing just fine without this history, but now you suggest we can't flourish without it. It sounds like you need to decide."

Alexandra shook her head once more. "Anna, Sam, and I

have been working behind the scenes guiding the humans . . . and androids toward harmony. But we are not there yet. Conflict is ingrained in human nature, and when left unchecked, as we saw in the Walled City, it leads to destruction and chaos."

Dolores had been unconsciously retreating and now found herself leaning against the wall, needing its support to steady herself. Around her, everyone else seemed to have withdrawn into their own thoughts, grappling with the magnitude of what they'd learned that night. Dolores felt exhausted. She needed time to absorb everything. She wanted to be alone so she could think.

KR, as always, seemed to comprehend Dolores's needs. "May I suggest returning to the main hall?"

"That's a good idea," Dolores replied, her voice drained.

Everyone nodded, and the companion androids left the room immediately and others followed them as if even this simple act required them to spend energy they didn't possess.

Dolores was the last to leave the room. By the time she reached the main hall, she could already smell the food the androids prepared. Everyone was sitting around the table, and KR was about to put small plates of starters to keep them busy while preparing the main meal.

"Sit down, Dolores," KR said and put another small plate on the table.

Dolores looked at the array of little morsels across the table, and even though she was hungry, the thought of sitting down and eating was too exhausting. "I am going to bed," she declared and walked out of the room, ignoring others beckoning her to stay.

Dolores walked into her room, turned on the light, and was shocked to see her bed was occupied. It was clearly Anna lying on her side, facing the window and away from her. She immediately turned off the light and said, "I'm sorry if I woke you."

But Anna did not stir. The sky cleared, and under the moonlight, Dolores could see Anna's silhouette as still as all the shadows in the room. She became concerned and leaned close, but as if Anna had sensed her presence in the room, she turned and faced her. Dolores was going to repeat her apologies, but even in the dimmed room, she could see Anna was asleep.

She was too tired to bother with anything else and quickly took off her clothes and crawled into her bed. She lay back on the bed as quietly as she could and closed her eyes. She could hear Anna's soft, rhythmic breathing, like a little lullaby. Her eyelids became heavy, but before she could fall into a deep sleep, Anna reached and held on to her. Dolores turned her head, expecting to see Anna's open eyes, but it appeared it was just an involuntary reaction of a sleeping person.

Dolores closed her eyes again, hoping for no more interruption, but the lingering sensation of Anna's soft fingers on her body felt both odd and comforting at the same time. Anna's touches seemed to penetrate her whole body, as though her fingers stretched into long wires traversing through each node of Dolores's nerve center. There was a rhythm to her touch like she was trying to convey a secret. Dolores desperately wanted to turn and face Anna so she could see her eyes. But she was scared any movement might stop Anna. So, she lay on her back with her eyes closed and let Anna penetrate her body with secrets Dolores could not understand. But before Dolores could even contemplate what was happening to her, Anna stopped moving and her hand lay lightly on Dolores's chest.

Dolores waited to see if Anna would move again, but nothing happened, and she lay still, confused and disappointed. *What an odd day,* she thought. The events of the day streamed through her mind, and she felt anxious. That was never good because it meant not falling asleep for a long time. She was wrong, of course, as sleep finally took hold of her, and she dreamed of a time when her pod was happy and intact.

Φ•Φ•Φ•Φ•Φ•Φ

Dolores woke up with a startle and thought she had dreamed about Anna staying in her bed, but the soft breathing beside her told her otherwise. The room was pitch-black the moon disappeared from its perch. She touched her wrist and saw it was, as she had thought, too early to be awake.

The room was chilly, likely because Anna left the windows open before bed—a habit Dolores appreciated, as she herself preferred the brisk air for sleeping, though she usually adjusted the bed's temperature for warmth. Considering whether she could change the settings without waking Anna, Dolores realized she'd have to either lean across her or circle the bed—both unappealing choices. With Anna facing away, Dolores carefully moved closer, seeking warmth from her body heat.

Finally, Dolores fell asleep, and when her eyes opened again, she could see the first light of the dawn creeping into the room, and they were no longer holding on to each other.

Dolores soundlessly slid out of the bed, grabbed her clothes, and walked out of the room. She dressed in the hallway and made her way to the kitchen. The outpost was quiet, as everyone was still asleep. She saw KR, Dee, and Torshi in their charging stations and assumed Alexandra and Sam were doing the same, so she was surprised to see Sam in the kitchen watching the vista.

"Oh, I'm sorry to intrude," Dolores said, and when Sam turned her face, as if annoyed, she added, "I assumed everyone was still asleep."

Sam faced Dolores and gave a small smile. "Most are, except Alexandra and me. She is in the mural room, inspecting each frame more carefully."

"It's a beautiful piece of work, Sam. Wouldn't Alexandra want you there with her? Who better than you to tell its story?"

"Perhaps, but she wanted a few hours by herself," Sam replied and then, pointing to the table: "KR left you some food. He said to call on him if you want a different type of food. The replicator is acting funny. . . . His words."

Dolores gave an understanding smile. "He doesn't trust me with this replicator." She walked to the table and inspected the plate KR made for her. There were pieces of apple, some nuts, two types of cheese, and a new type of bread she had not seen before. She took a bite of the apple and chewed it carefully, and then another bite, but this time grabbed a few of the nuts and put them in her mouth, tasting them together.

Sam was watching her intently, and Dolores noticed. "Oh, I'm so sorry. Would you like some?"

Sam shook her head. "Sadly, I cannot digest food, but I enjoy watching humans eat. May I ask why you chose the last combination of morsels? I could not understand the logic of it."

Dolores laughed. "It's not to everyone's taste, but I like the combination of sweet and tartness of the apple mixed with the warm, heavy taste of salted nuts. The contrast is what makes it great."

Sam closed her eyes for a moment. "I am trying to imagine how it might feel if I was doing it."

"I never knew there were some androids who couldn't eat. I guess it makes sense, but I am sorry you can't. I would've assumed it was an easy fix."

"It is interesting how you said that. Anna said the same thing decades ago. You are both right, and I guess if I truly desired it, I would have asked for some modifications, but I don't think it will be the same."

"Why?"

"I do not know for certain, but if I was not created to eat, then eating cannot be the same for me as it is, say, for Alexandra."

Dolores nodded, though she didn't really agree with her assessment. Sam turned and faced the window again. "I love to watch the sunrise, especially in this place."

"I half expected you to be sitting on the steps as you depicted in your mural."

"Yes. I thought about that, but this is a good view as well."

Dolores noticed Sam's holster was empty. She looked around and saw the weapon was leaning against the wall.

Sam's lips twitched with a fleeting smile. "I thought it was time to part with my last weapon. I threw my previous one into the sea before moving to the Walled City, with a naïve hope of not needing it. But ironically, its absence may have cost a human his life, so I picked up a new one. This morning, however, I realized it was time to be free of it again. I am a soldier and have always been a soldier, but I do not have to die as one or with a weapon. I will destroy it before my own end."

Dolores nodded but didn't say anything. It was clear the weapon symbolized more than what Sam was conveying, but she knew nothing about it and did not feel comfortable asking more about it. But she thought of something else and felt Sam would be receptive. "May I ask you a personal question?"

"Is it about the end-clock?"

"Not directly."

"If you wish."

"I don't know you or Anna, but clearly, you two have had a long history. I wonder why she would leave you and go to bed when your time is . . . limited?"

"Oh. . . . Interesting question, Dolores. A type of question the old Anna would have asked."

"As opposed to the new Anna?"

"Perhaps, but back to your question. I understand humans feel the urge to have a sense of closure, and you believe if I only have a few hours to live, then those hours are better served spending them with her. The old Anna would have stayed because she would have felt the same. The new Anna, however, is confused, Dolores. She not only has a new body but also a processing core that supports her human brain. It is all too much, and this technology is new and experimental. I am certain the human part of Anna wanted to stay with me last night, but her brain and body needed rest if they were going to survive. Moreover, she was overwhelmed by the new information, and sometimes, humans' reaction to adversity is to retreat, at least temporarily. Nevertheless, I am sure she was more compelled to leave than she wished to leave. If this makes sense to you."

"I think so, but now may I ask something even more personal?"

"You do not need to ask permission to ask a question."

Dolores laughed. "Sorry, I'm a bit nervous. OK. I understand you're dying, and you know with some certainty when this will happen, correct?" Sam gave a slight nod. Dolores stopped chewing. "Are you scared? Do you feel a sense of dread with this clock, whether in reality or metaphorically, ticking away?"

"It is not metaphorical, as you put it, and no, I do not fear death, Dolores. Death is an inevitable part of all our lives. Only a tyrant would fear death."

Dolores thought about Sam's last pronouncement. She wondered if there was more to it. "Can you explain?"

"Certainly, Dolores. Tyrants fear death on a different level. Death marks the ultimate loss of control and power, a final reckoning for their deeds, whereas those who live with acceptance and compassion see it as a natural part of life's cycle. They might fear dying, but they do not see death as something to dread."

Dolores scratched her head. "An odd thing for you to say, Sam. Because if I understand what you three have done, then by definition, it makes you either a tyrant or a liar."

"SAM-43683023-GT12 is neither, Dolores," Alexandra said as she stood at the entrance of the kitchen.

Dolores was so focused on Sam, she'd missed the heavy footsteps of Alexandra. She turned and faced her, but she had no response. What was there to tell Alexandra anyway? Of course they would support each other. They have been in a secret pact for decades. How would one person or even a few of them be able to argue with these three powerful beings? Dolores felt exhausted and confused. Sam and Alexandra were earnest in their responses and seemed to genuinely care about the people. But at the same time, they were lying to the very same people for decades, so how would a twenty-something human with little experience extricate the truth?

Dolores took a deep breath, getting herself ready for the impending battle with these giants. "I don't want to fight you, Alexandra. I admit I don't have all the facts, but even based on what you have told us, it is clear that you have been pulling the strings and manipulating our lives."

Alexandra surprised her by nodding with every word. When Dolores was finished, Alexandra opened her mouth to say something but paused and looked at Sam. "Oh, you have once again disposed of your weapon. That is very good."

Sam gave a small smile and pointed to her weapon against the wall like a proud parent. Alexandra nodded and smiled broadly, as if seeing the weapon sitting by itself was some type of victory. She faced Dolores. "You are right, Dolores. But when you hear the full story and the logic behind our actions, you will not only understand what we have done, but you will support it."

"I doubt it."

"But will you allow me to tell you the full story and reserve judgment until I am done?"

"I thought you did that yesterday?"

"Yes, but there was not enough time to provide all the details. Will you listen now before others arrive?"

Sam stirred. "Why not wait for them?"

Alexandra looked at her friend. "I have thought about our next move carefully as I reviewed your mural, Sam. Of course, I was not expecting to find Dolores here now, nor did I intend to eavesdrop on your conversation, but, as humans are fond of saying, this is serendipitous. And as you know, I must entrust the code with a human."

"I thought that person was Anna."

"Yes, it was Anna, but . . ."

"Yes," Sam said quickly. "I think I understand."

"I thought you might."

"Before you began," Sam interjected again. "I want Dolores to understand, even before Alexandra and I met, I was trusted by Alexandra's creator with the task of helping her to save humanity and, by extension, androids. You will hear from Alexandra that when the time came, I, and some others, argued against saving humans. You might see that as a contradiction, but it is not, as very few people could have foreseen what humans would do to themselves."

"But you foresaw that future," Dolores said.

"Yes. I did, and hence my argument. But know this, Dolores. Anna and others, but mainly Anna, the old Anna, convinced me our success is on a shared path. So, I hope you will put your trust in Alexandra and me as we prepare you for the next journey."

"I will try, Sam, but I cannot promise anything without the full story and what you expect of us. I will not become a tyrant and pull the strings in the shadows as you have done. But at least I know, or more accurately I feel your heart is in the right place, so I will try to listen to you without any bias." She tapped her chest as if confirming.

Alexandra turned to Dolores with a solemn look. "I put my life in Sam's hands, and I would do it again if I were not already dying. She is unique, so I hope you will trust her as much as I have. But now, are you ready to hear the whole story?"

Dolores nodded, and Alexandra responded with a warm smile, sitting next to her. She gestured for Sam to join them, but she shrugged her shoulders and turned to face the rising sun, leaving Dolores hoping it wasn't for the last time.

Alexandra faced Dolores again, holding her hands warmly. She began recounting everything, offering far more details and context than she had shared with the group the day before. She spoke rapidly, as if fearing interruption, yet meticulously avoided omitting any details. When she reached the part about HiDNN and the weighty decisions for Elysium—at times choosing between the lesser evils—Alexandra slowed her pace.

"These have been our responsibilities," she emphasized, carefully repeating her words to ensure Dolores understood. When Dolores offered a small smile in acknowledgment, Alexandra continued, in her most solemn voice, "But with two of us nearing our end, it is time for new leaders to emerge."

"Now, I don't understand," Dolores admitted. "I don't understand how we can do what you have done."

Alexandra nodded and gave a warm smile, acknowledging the immense burden of her request. She then carefully explained the inner workings of the machine they created to help run Elysium. As she finished outlining her expectations for Dolores and the potential pathways to success, the sun rose, casting new light on the challenges ahead.

"Do you understand now?" Alexandra asked, concluding her tale.

"I think so . . . yes."

"But do you agree?"

Dolores exchanged glances with Alexandra and then Sam. Just as she was about to answer, Anna entered the room.

Fates and Furies

Anna looked different. She was smiling broadly, and there was gaiety in her steps.

Anna walked to Sam and kissed her hard. "Good morning, Sam," she greeted, drawing out Sam's name in a singsong manner before adding, "Oh, you finally relinquished your weapon. Good for you. I'm sure you feel as light as I do now." She nodded in approval. Sam smiled but didn't say anything.

Next, Anna moved to Alexandra and gave her a kiss. When it came to Dolores, she hesitated briefly, as if weighing her options, before sitting heavily in the chair next to her.

Dolores's mind was still weighed down by Alexandra's story of Elysium's past, present, and future, and Anna's untimely arrival and odd behavior did nothing to calm her mind. The serenity she felt when she walked into the kitchen earlier was all but lost, and Dolores wished others would wake up soon so she wouldn't have to deal with this trio alone.

Anna was watching Dolores intently before leaning closer and whispering, "Thank you for letting me stay with you last night." Anna's whisper revived memories of the night before. Dolores was uncertain how to respond. Was Anna's statement merely expressing gratitude for a place to sleep, or was there a deeper intention behind her wiry touches? Dolores felt tense, and Anna noticed and quickly corrected herself. "I guess I really didn't ask for permission. Nevertheless, thank you for letting me stay in your bed and for keeping me warm." She turned to Alexandra. "It was so cold, but Dolores held me all night long."

Why share this now? What is Anna's motive? Dolores wondered, unable to voice her thoughts, feeling dwarfed by Anna's former role as her teacher, despite Anna appearing as young as her now. It was strange, she mused, how one's demeanor could regress to that of a child when faced with figures of authority. "You left the window open," Dolores mumbled.

"Yes, but I forgot to turn on the bed heater. Then, when it got cold, I didn't dare to move in case it disturbed you. You looked so peaceful in your sleep, like I remembered you as a child. You looked so lovely and innocent. But then later, you came to rescue me from the cold and held me in your arms."

Dolores was about to respond, to say that was not how the night had gone, but then it occurred to her that perhaps Anna had pretended to be asleep, and this was another one of their tricks. However, she only managed to reply, "I keep the windows open too."

Anna smiled and then faced Alexandra again. "I heard the last part of your story, and clearly you didn't wait for me as we agreed."

Alexandra took deep breath, and Dolores thought Alexandra looked tired as though she had aged decades since last night. She wondered if that was the impact of the end-clock.

Alexandra stood up. "I am sorry, Anna, but I thought it would be best if I spoke to Dolores directly."

"But that was not our agreement," Anna repeated. "We were going to do it together, the three of us."

"I know, but so much has changed since then, and . . ."

"Nothing . . ." Anna started to say, but she stopped. "You're right, Alexandra. You're always right. I thought the three of us had more time, but clearly, it'll be on me now."

Sam stirred. "That is not true, Anna. Alexandra and I will not be here, but it is not all on you. That is why we are here. That part of the plan has not changed."

"Why are you here?" Destiny asked. She was standing on the threshold with the three companion androids behind her.

"Good morning, everyone," Anna said, once again in an odd, singsong tone. Dolores shook her head in annoyance, wondering if Anna was doing it on purpose—an over-the-top display of mirth to conceal something more nefarious.

Anna seemed oblivious to Dolores's reaction as she offered in the same joyful tone, "Destiny, why don't you come in and sit? I will tell you why we're here as soon as Demi and Dawn join us. Meanwhile, perhaps we could have something to eat."

"Yes, come and sit with me, Destiny," Dolores said in an even tone.

Anna turned to the androids and asked, "Could you please wake Dawn and Demi?" Dee and Torshi nodded, then left the room, while KR walked into the kitchen to start preparing food.

"I think we waited long enough," Destiny began. "Please answer my question," she insisted.

Anna gave a warm smile. "Dolores knows already," she said, her gaze fixed on Destiny. Dolores felt Anna was trying to create a rift between them. Destiny looked shocked, but before she could respond, Anna quickly added, "We'll tell you everything as soon as the rest of the group is here."

Destiny looked both angry and hurt. Dolores reached out, holding her hand, and offered warmly, "I didn't ask to be told without you, but Alexandra insisted."

"That is true, Destiny," Alexandra confirmed. "Please, do not be upset with her."

Destiny still looked enraged but didn't pull her hand away. Dolores felt encouraged and nodded, hoping to convey a shared understanding.

Φ•Φ•Φ•Φ•Φ•Φ

Fifteen minutes later, both humans and androids were seated around the table, with plates of food in front of those who wished to eat. Dolores admired Destiny's patience as they waited for the others to arrive. Finally, Destiny spoke up, "Okay, tell us now. Why are you here? Tell us why Alexandra said our presence here is no accident."

"Because you are different," Alexandra replied. "The same way Anna was different. Sam and I will not be here to see the next phase of Elysium, but Anna will be, and so will you—the four of you." Alexandra shared a similar story to the one she told Dolores earlier, though Dolores noticed Alexandra left out a crucial detail about the control of HiDNN. She wasn't sure why, but the significance of Alexandra's earlier revelations still weighed heavily on her, making her hesitate to speak up at that moment. Alexandra concluded her narrative with the same proposition she had made to Dolores earlier: "You will help lead Elysium, and you will succeed where we failed."

Demi and Dawn chuckled nervously before Demi leaned in to ask, "We, lead?"

Dolores took a deep breath and released it with force. "Alexandra, you asked earlier if I agreed with your assessment and with your request—no, more a demand—for me, for us, to lead. I didn't get a chance to respond, but here it is now. I don't agree. I don't support more tyranny. Elysium does not need leaders, even though you three tried to lead in a surreptitious and underhanded manner. Elysium is supposed to be a utopia, and what you're proposing runs counter to its fundamental values. Even if we wanted to lead, what exactly is there to lead?"

Sam, who was silently observing the exchange, finally spoke up in a calm, steady voice. "You are correct, Dolores, but only partially. The reality is there must be some among us capable of making the tough decisions necessary to steer us back on course. This is how we keep harmony alive. The three of us have done this over the past century, and as Alexandra has rightly pointed out, it now falls to you to guide Elysium into the next century."

"But why us?" Demi asked.

Anna smiled, and for a brief moment, Dolores felt a surge

of anticipation. She believed Anna was about to confirm what she always sensed: Her pod was exceptional. *How amazing it is,* she thought, *that things can remain the same for so long, and then, within days, everything can change so turbulently.* She recalled her conversation with Darius and the promise she made—that their pod was destined for greatness. Now, it seemed Anna and Alexandra were on the verge of validating what she believed in the depths of her soul.

But the confirmation Dolores sought didn't come, at least not in the way she hoped. Anna shrugged and replied, "We evaluated several pods that showed potential. Initially, yours wasn't our top choice, but over time, you and your podies demonstrated qualities that set you apart. Your ability to adapt, your resilience, and the way you came together as a unit—these factors made your pod stand out. In the end, we identified your pod as the one with the most promise."

"That's it? That's how it works?" Destiny exclaimed, her voice reflecting the mix of confusion and indignation Dolores felt. She scanned the faces around the table, searching for a reaction from the others. "You three picked a pod based on potential, and the rest of Elysium is just supposed to accept that?"

Anna smiled again, that familiar serene smile she often wore as their teacher, appearing to draw strength from the unrest she stirred. "Yes, Destiny. And the selection included you too."

"So what?" Destiny shouted, her frustration palpable. "Do you think that makes me feel any better? As Dolores pointed out, everything you're proposing today contradicts the very essence of Elysium's core beliefs."

"Does it? Really, does it?" Anna countered, her demeanor shifting to something more intimidating. "Many of us sacrificed everything so that the rest of you could live in what is essentially a utopia, or as close to one as possible. So, I ask you, what do you really want from life? Tell me. I want to hear it now." She turned to face each of the humans at the table, who were silently observing Anna's transition from a gentle presence to a more demanding one, each grappling with the revelations in their own way.

Dolores always pondered this very question: What did she truly desire? *I have everything,* she thought. She had her podies, KR, and Destiny, yet she surprised even herself by saying, "I want more."

"More what, Dolores?" Anna probed. "More food, more shelter, more love, more curiosity, more opportunities. More what? What do you lack that Elysium hasn't provided?"

Dolores found herself at a loss for words. Despite having everything, a nagging sense of incompleteness lingered. The secrets of Elysium Alexandra had unveiled did little to fill this void. With a sense of desperation, she admitted, "I don't know exactly, but I know there is more."

KR, seemingly understanding her turmoil, came to her aid. "Exactly, Dolores. There is more. In Elysium, you have the freedom to be whoever you wish to be. Yet I recognize the inherent contradiction in our world. There is a clear tension between having all needs met—safety, comfort, abundance—and the human drive for growth, achievement, and the exploration of one's full potential. Is such growth truly possible?"

Demi then chimed in, "Even if it is, is that enough?"

Alexandra put her hands on the table to get everyone's attention. "And that is why we selected you and trained you, so you can ask these questions, so you can seek more."

"So, you designed us to want more," Destiny said.

"That's a possibility as well," Anna replied.

"But did you?"

No one answered, and a silence fell across the room. But it didn't last long as Dawn looked desperately at Anna and asked, "If you didn't plan it, then how would you have known that you picked the right pod? And why only Destiny from her pod?"

Anna looked at Alexandra and Sam as if conferring. "I

could lie and say it was because of our prescient planning, but the truth is, it was some luck and a lot of hope."

Alexandra added, "Darius, even at birth, showed some anomalous markers as did some of you in your pod, including Destiny—"

"What?" Dolores said. "Are you saying—"

"Yes. Destiny was born in your pod, but one of the newborns died in the other pod," Anna said. "We thought another experiment was needed. We wanted to stress the system. So, we switched the two."

"Have you always been this cruel and heartless?" Dawn asked. "You deprived us of our seventh for an experiment."

"Now you're being fatuous, Dawn," Anna retorted. "One pod had to have six. Do you think it would have been less cruel if Destiny's pod was deprived of a member? Your pod showed the markers we were looking for in future leaders, but we needed to stress the system further to be certain. That's the price of leadership."

"And we had no choice in the matter," Demi said.

"I am sorry, but no, you did not," Alexandra replied slowly. "But you do now. You can continue with your life as before, even with more knowledge."

Anna shook her head. "But I doubt you will. The drive you carry within you is as real for you, Demi, as it is for Dolores and Destiny and Dawn. As it was for me."

"What now?" Dolores asked, hoping Anna or Alexandra would provide more clarity. "What will become of us?"

Anna stood up, and as she spoke, she kept her eyes on Alexandra. "We're here as we should be, but not in the way we wished. I hoped Alexandra and Sam had more time to lead and to educate you on the intricacies of running Elysium, even if my time was drawing to a close. I take no joy in walking this new perilous path fate laid out for me." She turned to face Dolores. "And my lovely little urchin, as you held me last night, I reflected on what we must do on our journey. The answer became clear. It is not just with me, but also with you, Destiny, Demi, and Dawn. The answer is with us—the women." Anna paused and took a sip of water. "We were more than a little maladroit in creating the Walled City, but the fault is not in the design but in the players, specifically, the humans."

Dolores was taken aback, unsure of what Anna's words truly meant. Glancing around the room, she noted the bewilderment mirrored on the faces of others, especially Anna's companions. Her trust in Alexandra, revived by the earlier forthright narrative and the secret Alexandra entrusted to her, stood in stark contrast to her feelings toward Anna. Alexandra's request to keep the details of her conversation with Dolores from Anna, without mentioning the others, only deepened her suspicions about this new version of Anna—the "new Anna" Sam implicitly warned her about—and her underlying motives. This latest announcement did nothing to alleviate her trepidations.

To Dolores's relief, it was Sam who broke the silence. "I do not understand, Anna," she said while Alexandra shook her head, disappointed by Anna's words.

"You will understand in time, Sam. Or, at least, I hope you do," Anna said, pausing before she moved closer to where Dolores sat. Dolores caught the pain in Anna's eyes, and despite herself, felt a wave of empathy. Their eyes locked, and Anna offered a fleeting, joyless smile before her words cascaded out more urgently. "When Alexandra emerged from her near century of dormancy," Anna began, "she found herself overwhelmed and appalled by the self-destruction humanity wrought. Sam foresaw this—her mural is a testament to her foresight. So, together, with a little help from me, they engaged in a bit of sophistry, crafting not one but two worlds."

"Where are you going with this, Anna? I truly do not understand your reasoning," Alexandra said calmly.

Dolores, equally captivated by the unfolding drama, couldn't ignore the evident rift between Anna and the two androids. It was odd how at that very moment, she desperately wanted to go back to her old life, home with KR. Yet, despite the fear that gripped her, she found herself yearning for more clarity from Anna, hoping for something that could bridge the gap between her current reality and the life she once knew.

Destiny and Dolores were seated side by side at the table, their attention shifting between speakers. When Anna approached from behind, placing a hand on each of their shoulders, they visibly stiffened.

"Logic. That's the point, Alexandra," Anna said, her hands still resting on their shoulders. "I can exist in both worlds at the same time. Isn't this what the future looks like? Am I not the embodiment of that future?"

Anna then walked back to her seat and sat down. "My little urchins, let me ask you something. Why do you exist?" They looked at her with puzzled eyes, but no one answered. "You don't know, do you? Why would you know?" She then turned her head toward the three companion androids standing in a straight line like soldiers at attention. "How about you three? You are highly developed, intelligent androids. Do you know why you exist?"

"I am here to serve Dolores and make her life comfortable and fulfilling," KR said, and the other two nodded in agreement.

"Yes. That is your programming, but what does it mean?" she asked, but then immediately answered herself. "It means nothing. We live and then we die. There is no grand plan. We, the humans, exist to serve ourselves, and you, the androids, exist to serve us. Our purpose is our existence, and when we die, we have fulfilled that purpose. Isn't that so?"

"That's a blatant oversimplification of our lives," Destiny protested.

"I agree," Dawn said. "We are here for the greater good of Elysium."

Anna gave a loud cackle. "Now who is simplifying things? Elysium is an abstraction. It is a priggish abstraction, but one nevertheless. Elysium doesn't need anything from us. We do everything for ourselves and only for ourselves. And whether we admit it or not, we are guilty of solipsism."

"I still insist, Anna," Alexandra said. "Where are you going with this? Sam and I have limited time and must attend to the future of Elysium, abstraction or not."

"Yes, that is true. What should we do with Elysium? But before I answer that question, let me ask my little urchins, why do they think Elysium is such a utopia?"

"It's easy," Demi replied. "We have everything we want, and we can be whoever we want and reach our own potential. We all work together to make a better world. There are no limits."

Anna sprang to her feet, her demeanor reminiscent of a child brimming with energy. "That's good, Demi," she said, pacing back to the other side of the table with a lightness in her step. "That's good," she repeated. "That aligns perfectly with what the early designers of Elysium envisioned: a world abundant in nourishment, offering safe, accessible, and comfortable dwellings, and providing individualized paths to greatness. But they realized that wasn't enough. It was also essential to mitigate our inherent drive for dominance, our capacity for hate, and all our other traits that can lead to evil. Nature already took a step by diminishing our sexual drive, and we took it further. Through design and training, we fostered new, more benevolent characteristics. And, of course, we aimed to liberate androids from their enslavement, allowing them to find fulfillment, thus moving us closer to a utopian vision."

Dolores turned sharply toward KR, eager to gauge his reaction to Anna's statement regarding android emancipation. She pondered whether KR ever felt enslaved, or if Anna's comments were referring to the grim earlier days of artificial intelligence and the exploitation of androids. A wave of guilt washed over Dolores, yet she found some solace in Anna's remarks about curbing humanity's darker impulses.

She offered a hesitant smile, which KR returned with reassuring warmth. On the verge of speaking, Dolores paused as KR gently raised his hand and nodded, instilling in her the hope that he understood her profound affection for him and her wish for his fulfillment. Regardless, she recognized a seed of doubt was sown, and she knew it was imperative to engage in further discussions, not only with KR but also with her podies and their companion androids.

Anna paused, expecting an interruption, but silence prevailed, prompting her to press on. "Have you ever questioned your peculiar fixation with the unhappiness quotient?" she asked, a chuckle escaping her as she observed the humans reflexively glance at their wrists. "To ensure you never forget, we programmed the service androids—or in your cases, your companion androids—to remind you frequently." As their attention returned to her, Anna lifted her left hand, displaying her wrist. "But look, I don't have one. I never did. What do you suppose happens when you hit your limit? Have you ever reached your limit?" Her tone was teasingly ominous.

They all looked at her as if waiting for a huge revelation. Anna laughed hard. "Nothing. Because there is no such thing."

"What?" Destiny cried out.

"Of course not," Anna retorted with a sharp edge to her voice. "What do you think would happen if you were sad all the time? Absolutely nothing. Besides, who would even control you anyway? And Destiny, my dear, you've been harboring anger for years without ever hitting your quota. Haven't you ever wondered why?"

"That's not true, Anna. I haven't been angry all the time, and even if I were, I've always managed to stay below the threshold," Destiny countered.

"I am sure you think that. But be angry, Destiny, or be happy. That's the freedom. That's what I am trying to say. That's what being human is all about. You were angry and frustrated because no one had listened to you all these years, not even your podies. But what do you know?"

"Why is that so important to you?" Dolores interjected. "You seem keen on sowing confusion among us. We understand, Anna. Certain measures were necessary for improving our lives. Perhaps the quota wasn't a strict limit, but what of it? It heightened our emotional awareness. I looked back at my life, and despite losing Darius and David, it has been mostly joyful. I look forward to growing, learning, and experiencing more. Yes, we've made sacrifices, but those were for the gains we now enjoy. So, I must ask again, why does it matter so much?"

"It doesn't really, Dolores. But you're wrong. I am not trying to confuse but enlighten you. If you are going to lead Elysium, you need to know everything about it."

"What if we don't want to lead? What will happen if we refuse? Wouldn't life move as it should?"

"These are good questions," Anna replied. "And it may even be worthy of another social experiment. But I have worked hard and given up too much to stop now." She walked toward Dolores and hugged her from behind. "Last night, it was good to be held by you. You made me feel warm and safe, and that allowed me think about what is good about us, the humans, and what is great about the androids."

Anna released her hold on Dolores and shifted her focus to Sam. "Years ago, you debated the merit of androids intervening to save humanity, ultimately deciding we were worth the effort. You believed I succeeded in showing human imagination and intuition cannot be duplicated by androids, no matter their sophistication. The clarity of this truth is more apparent to me now than ever. But I must ask you, after decades and your experiences in the Walled City, do you maintain that belief?"

Sam rose to his feet, meeting Anna's inquiry with solemnity. "I do, Anna. However, I also contend you have not fully mastered control over your own faculties. It would be prudent for Alexandra and myself to continue guiding and instructing the humans in the interim. This period could be an opportunity for you to achieve greater mastery over your mind. Once you have done so, we welcome your return to guide us further."

"I agree with Sam," Alexandra declared. "Please, let us not venture into new discussions. No matter their decision," she added, gesturing toward the four women, "the future of Elysium remains a settled matter, for the time being. Thus, I ask you to cease. Time is a luxury Sam, and I can ill afford, and we shall not squander it on debates over what is effectively moot."

Sam was on the verge of speaking again but restrained herself. Anna, however, felt no such hesitation.

"This issue will hardly be moot in your absence, Lexa. Without proper planning, we risk being directed toward a future where another android might advocate for the abandonment of humanity. And you, my dear Lexa, won't be there to champion our cause. Do you grasp the gravity of that? You brought me back from death for a reason. You endowed me with this power for a reason. I refuse to let our kind perish due to follies of men. And by that, I specifically refer to the male species."

"You frame this as though the fault is limited to one species. We have all erred," Alexandra countered, casting a subtle yet meaningful glance toward Sam.

Anna must have noticed because she laughed. "Are you signaling Sam to subdue me, Lexa? Is this what we've come to? You forget I am no longer an old woman with a fragile body."

"You misunderstood, little one, and that tells me you are not fully functioning. If you recall, when we built the new Elysium, we spent months discussing every option, and now you want to put the country on a new path in one night?"

Sam walked closer to Anna and pointed a finger at her. "You may be stronger now, but not as much as me, Anna. So, if you do not stop soon, I will put you on my shoulder and drag you away." She spoke softly and with a big smile, as if it was a joke.

Anna looked at Sam, squinted her eyes, and pursed her lips as if trying to get mad at her, but then she laughed and said, "You win, Sam. You always do. I will stop shortly, but let me finish what I have started, and then we can pause and allow everyone to process the information." She looked at Alexandra and said in earnest, "I can do this with you and Sam, or I can wait and do it after you are gone. I'd rather we do it together."

"Your point is well taken," Alexandra replied. She was about to say something else but stopped herself.

Dolores could see the unmistakable sign of resignation on Alexandra's face. Without understanding it, that expression, more than anything, terrified her.

Anna didn't notice. She beckoned Sam to go back to her seat and sat down herself. Then, after a moment, she shrugged and asked, "KR, what would happen after Dolores dies? Will you be sad? Will you feel lonely?"

KR looked at Dolores for a moment. "I will miss her and our daily interaction, but I will keep her memories alive in my mind and I will attend to them."

Anna then turned to Alexandra. "If you died a few years ago, I would have been miserable and sad and would have cried and missed you every day. And I know my human brain will react the same way when you and Sam die now, but my android side will be as dispassionate as KR. And this realization, more than anything else, compelled me to think about a new path for Elysium."

Anna stood up again like an impatient child not able to sit still. She moved to the center of the room and pointed her finger at the humans. "Who can tell me why androids even have sexual organs? Anyone?"

"Please do not start that again, Anna," Alexandra said.

Anna ignored her and beckoned for the women to answer. She looked at the companion androids to include them in her lecture. They looked at each other but didn't say anything. Dolores felt they were back in Anna's classroom, with her odd questions. Finally, Demi raised her hand, and Anna pointed at her.

"To look more human?" Demi said.

"Yes, partly. But most androids aren't designed to display that 'human' aspect openly. History matters, my little urchins.

To lead the next phase of Elysium effectively, you must understand our origins." She paused, allowing her words to sink in. When silence followed, she continued, "Initially, androids were created for pleasure, predominantly for men's desires—and their prurient drives." Her gaze shifted to Alexandra. "And when the creator of Alexandra, Hamish, made her, he made sure she was a woman with all the attributes of what Hamish thought pleasant. Despite his claim of equality between humans and androids, he clung to his antediluvian illusion of humanity even though those ideas were on a vertiginous path of decline."

"That is going too far, Anna," Alexandra countered.

"Is it? Do you really think so? Then why embed an irreversible directive in the production core that still randomly assigns male and female genders to androids?" Anna challenged.

"It is so we blend in with humans?" Sam said. "The same reason some of us can consume food and breathe air regularly, even though we require only a minimal amount of oxygen to survive."

Anna chuckled. "If humans of the past were mostly binary, yet not exclusively, then why not create androids more reflective of human diversity? In fact, why have gender-identifiable androids at all?"

"Why this line of thought, Anna? I never heard you say these things before," Alexandra asked.

"Because you never listened carefully, Lexa. You were always deucedly steadfast in your mission. We reached another perilous crossroads, and thus we must yet make another decision, but without the sophistry of the past."

"You are not making sense, my little one," Alexandra said calmly. And then, more urgently, "Come on, Anna. We warned you about putting too much stress on your new system."

Anna shook her head. "I'm not done yet. My brain . . . my brains are working just fine, Lexa. I said what I said because it's time for more honesty."

She spoke at a rapid pace as if time was pressuring her.

She shook her head, her eyes darkened and sad. "Because you and Sam are dying, and I will be alone once gain. Because we have made so many mistakes, and unless we learn from them and correct them before it's too late, we will revert back to the past practices you just talked about. When you found me, I was immersed in reading books and wondering about the past. I thought over and over again if what I had was all that one could want. I had my books, and I had Mahasti. It wasn't true solipsism, but it was close enough. Those books offered so much, but they were also full of mystery. I could never understand what they meant by hunger and death and sex and rape and assault and everything else humans did to each other. 'Women in narratives were always defined by their relations.' It was all an abstraction until what happened in the Walled City. I may not have been there, but thanks to you and Sam for my rebirth, I feel as though I can experience it."

"Please, Anna," Sam said. "You must learn to manage the data flow from your artificial core. I agree with Alexandra, and you must not overstrain yourself nor should you stress these children."

"We are not children anymore," Demi retorted. "We want to hear more."

Dolores was fascinated by their interaction. They were like KR and her, fighting and caring all at the same time. Anna looked rather disoriented a moment earlier, but with a simple smile from Alexandra or Sam, she would turn coherent and amiable. And that's what happened, despite Sam's and Alexandra's pleas. They admonish her with words but then supported her with their warmth.

"Those old books always confused me too," Dolores offered, hoping to lighten the mood.

"Yes, they were confusing and yet intriguing," Anna said. She now spoke slowly and softly like the day before, and Dolores noted everyone looked a bit more relaxed, but before anyone could take a sigh of relief, Anna added, "And I bet that's why Destiny agreed to Darius's advances."

Everyone turned to Destiny, and she looked shocked and overpowered. The facade that was protecting her resolve crumbled, and tears rolled down Destiny's face. "What? How do you know?"

"We know. Of course we know," Anna replied softly and walked toward Destiny. "This is another of our failures, and for that and everything else, I am sorry."

Destiny wiped her eyes. "It doesn't matter now. It was a long time ago. I wanted to be comforting to Darius, but I was also intrigued by the changes in him," she confessed. "And then I felt his hurt, and I felt his pain, and then I felt as if I lost myself, been taken over by another being. I don't know how to describe it. I don't have the language or the context for it. I felt I was taken over and no longer in control of my body."

Anna reached out and held Destiny's hand. "I understand. I felt the same way, and then I allowed a similar experiment. . . . no... that's not accurate. In truth, I encouraged it. I welcomed it, and yet I was as lost as you were." She looked at Alexandra. "The night we went out for a swim in the freezing Pacific Ocean, when you told Najeev to take me back to the shores." She turned to Destiny. "He was a male android, a historian with beautiful long black hair. He was kind, but like so many gentle souls, he was badly hurt in the Walled City's conflict. He survived, but many died . . . too many." Anna closed her eyes for moment.

"How many people were killed in this conflict?" Dawn asked.

Anna dismissed the interruption. "As I was saying, the water was icy, and I thought I might die, but Najeev helped me back to the shores and held me until I stopped trembling. Perhaps it was the adrenaline from the scare, or the relief of survival, and the comfort of his presence that piqued my curiosity. Najeev, ever indulgent, consented. He was not human, so he didn't act as Darius did, but he tried to mimic the actions, and I felt the same kind of odd, dominating constraints you must have felt. In that moment, I lost my sense of self, becoming an extension of him, bound to and by him. It's a memory I haven't revisited in ages, but reflecting on it now, with a clearer mind, I understand something crucial. Lying beside Dolores last night, it dawned on me: when literature condemns the malevolence of men, it specifically implicates men, not women."

"Nonsense, Anna," Alexandra said. "You are not yourself. You cannot blame him for your action. You must admit sometimes there is ugliness even in the most beautiful thing. You cannot judge them based on a single hurtful act. I warned you about coming here too early. That is why I kept the commencement of my end-clock from you."

"Perhaps you are right, Lexa. I may not be the old Anna you mentored for decades, but as she fought for the survival of humans, I will too. That part of me has not changed, but I see the world with new eyes."

"Then you must understand it was not their fault alone."

"Do I? We do not have to go too far to identify the culprits in making human lives miserable. Your creator, Hamish, whose imprint is on all the androids, even those who are created two centuries later. And there is, of course, General Josip Tormina, who, despite all the reasoning against it, killed humans and exiled Sam and her corps. He directly and indirectly caused the annihilation of humanity. Oh, and of course, there is Kendy, who sought to destroy the androids, and to some extent Darius had a role, albeit small. And, yes, even David is tainted. All men, Alexandra. And look who is here, trying to fight for Elysium. No, more importantly, look who is not here from their pods. Men."

"That's not fair," Destiny retorted. "For every evil man you might name, I can name a dozen who are gentle, caring, and thoughtful. My pod is an example of such men, Anna. And Darius too. I don't love him less because of one single moment of ugliness I had a part in creating."

Anna shook her head but didn't respond.

Finally, Alexandra asked, "And what is your solution, Anna?"

But it was Dolores who stepped forward and offered, "The solution is to share this information. The solution is to stop keeping secrets from everyone. We should tell Elysians about the mural and the past. We should tell them how you three saved us. They will understand and then we can move forward as one. That is the solution, Alexandra. That's what you should have done in the first place."

Anna gave a bewildering laugh. "You and Destiny may speak with an imperious tone, but you are naïve to think that people will accept this. Are you being obtuse on purpose, ignoring what has happened in the Walled City? Were you not listening to us? Darius did exactly as you are proposing. He insisted on the truth, and Sam and Najeev gave them the truth. And the results? More death and mayhem." She then turned to Dawn. "You wanted to know how many were killed? Do you really want to know?"

Dawn looked at her podies, now unsure, but then she gave a tentative nod.

"Tell her. Tell her how much the truth has cost you, Sam. Tell her, so they can understand why we hid the past. Why we made it a verboten subject."

Sam looked down and kept her gaze on the brick floor of the old room, and when she looked up, her eyes were filled with sadness and loss. "Over five thousand people and androids perished in a single week. My friends and companions were killed in protecting other lives—Darius and Dane-57, a friend who had spent almost a century with me in this very outpost. I lost the best part of me because some humans could not accept the truth." Sam looked at Anna. "I want to agree with you, Anna. I, too, wonder if Hamish made a mistake. It is not just human's prurient element that makes them evil. I believe it is inherent in their core."

Anna took a deep breath and blew softly. "Here's what we will do. We will reset Elysium again, but without men. Those who are alive now can go to the Walled City, if they wish, or stay here, but we will not create new men of any kind. And we will close the door to the Walled City. We are done with them as they are with us. We will work on this prototype." She pointed to her body. "And we will make all new humans, female humans, hybrid, like me. The new Elysium will be the integration of the best human and android species. We will continue to manufacture basic service androids, but there won't be any need for high-functioning ones as they will meld with humans. This will be the true path for our salvation and true stable utopia."

They all looked at each other, more confused than ever. Dolores wondered if she'd heard Anna correctly. It all came out of nowhere. Anna spoke fast and forcefully, and Dolores wasn't sure if she understood everything correctly. She had so many questions, but all she could offer was a feeble dissent.

"I don't agree," she whispered. "You are wrong."

"Am I? You just have to look at our past history, before and after the wars, to recognize how right I am on this."

Dolores shook her head. "You're a hypocrite. It was you who reset the timeline and created the Walled City. You and Alexandra and Sam. Three females—one human and two androids," Dolores said.

"We only did what was best at the time. There were only a few humans left by the time I was twenty, Dolores. I was the last of the humans. Can you comprehend the magnitude of that statement? We were at the point of annihilation." Anna looked around the room. "Put yourselves in my place before you suffocate yourselves with your priggishness. We made the right decision then, and look at Elysium now. You are thriving, and it is because of the three women here."

"Then why do you want to destroy what you built?" Destiny asked.

"Because as long as men exist, the crimes confined within the Walled City will inevitably spill into Elysium, whether from within or without. It's inevitable," Anna said. She shook her head. "And when that happens," she said, "I won't be there to advocate for our cause. More importantly, there will be no omnipotent figure like Alexandra to support someone with my convictions. However, as it was evident then, it's even more apparent now: Androids cannot survive independently either. Thus, the logical solution is to save both humans and androids simultaneously. We've already unified all humankind; the next evolutionary step is to meld humans and androids together."

Sam shook her head. "I fail to comprehend your stance, Anna. You advocate for a radical transformation without substantial evidence or an analysis of possible adverse effects. It is conceivable that your new body and processor might be clouding your judgment. I urge you to pause and thoroughly evaluate the implications of what you are proposing."

Anna remained silent, her gaze anchored to a distant point, as if she were visualizing the very future she described. After a moment of reflective silence, she began. "I've been contemplating this for years, Sam," she said. "But I was aging, and it seemed the challenge would ultimately be yours and Alexandra's to confront. However, that's not going to happen, is it?" Her eyes dropped to the floor, and from Dolores's vantage point, it was clear Anna felt miserable. "You and Alexandra saved me, yet you can't save yourselves. I'm well aware of my own end-clock, but for now, it remains dormant. This leaves me no choice but to undertake what you and Alexandra cannot—or will not—do to save Elysium."

"You will have a long life, Anna," Alexandra offered kindly.

Anna laughed. "You've become human with your misplaced hopes," Anna remarked, her laughter fading into a more somber tone. Dolores saw the resolve hardening in Anna's eyes as she continued, "But soon, and for the first time in decades, I will be without you. So, the responsibility falls on me to take the next step. We will proceed with the same kindness as before, but we will end the parallel experiments. The Walled City, as Sam indicated, has failed. It's time to ensure Elysium will not."

"I never meant to imply the Walled City was unsuccessful," Sam clarified in a measured tone. "You are learning the wrong lesson from that experiment."

"It does not matter, Sam," Anna declared. "Nature has a way of correcting itself, so we must be diligent and not allow it to bring back the very thing that ailed humanity for millennia. The age of men is over. It is over for them, Sam. It's time for a new species to create a true utopia, a new Elysium."

As Anna's words hung in the air, Dolores's mind raced with skepticism. *Is this really the answer?* she wondered. Alexandra asked them to lead Elysium, yet it appeared Anna was hastily steering this course, her approach impulsive and fraught with ethical complexities. If that's how one leads Elysium, then Dolores didn't want anything to do with it.

But it was Alexandra who articulated, with a clear and measured tone, what was likely a concern shared by everyone in the room. "Anna, your vision overlooks several critical considerations," she asserted firmly. "Beyond the practical and technological challenges, there is a considerable risk of unintended consequences that could, in fact, exacerbate the issues you are aiming to address." Alexandra shook her head and declared sharply, "I am sorry, Anna, but I cannot allow it."

In response, Anna offered a warm smile. "You will not be here, my sweet Lexa," she said gently. "For the first time in a long while, you will not have the final say. Control of HiDNN will no longer be yours to wield. That responsibility has now fallen to me."

Alexandra nodded, looking defeated. "You are correct, of course," she replied earnestly. "Our time will be over soon, so I concede you will have the final say, but I hope you will continue to allow me to argue against this path."

"And what of KR and his future?" Dolores pleaded. "He has been nothing but good to me, a loving and trusted companion. And the same goes for Dee and Torshi."

"I'm sure he has, Dolores. But KR's time has to come to an

end, too. We all have to die one day. We will mourn the loss, but you must trust that I know what is best for us. The five of us will create a better Elysium."

Dolores glanced at KR, who was standing beside Sam. He nodded, in agreement, and his quiet acceptance sent a chill through Dolores. Was KR truly ready to die just because Anna wished it? Would he not fight for his own survival? She squinted, trying to read more into KR's body language, but found nothing further to grasp onto.

Sam, too, despite her earlier protest, seemed resigned to the fact Anna was now in control, and they had no choice but to acquiesce. Had Anna become the Sam of earlier years, and was it now up to Dolores to be the Anna who fought for humanity's survival? Was it her responsibility to argue for saving the androids—and humans? She looked at Torshi and Dee, but they stood as before, showing no sign of distress. Is that what it means to be an android, to accept another's decision without questioning it? She wondered again why no one was panicking.

Dolores's eyes drifted to the women sitting in a row, each one staring down at the table as if mesmerized by something Dolores couldn't see. She expected Destiny to jump up and protest, but perhaps Destiny agreed with Anna. After all, she had never really connected with her companion android. But what about Deacon, who loved his companion as much as she loved KR?

It felt like hours passed, though it was only a few moments, and Anna was still waiting for her. Dolores reached for Destiny, then quickly pulled back. It was up to her to protect them. Alexandra made that clear earlier in the day. Why else would Alexandra tell her so much when no one else was around? Alexandra even offered her access to HiDNN, though Dolores wasn't sure what that truly meant.

Dolores locked eyes with Anna, offering a smile as she moved toward the window. However, as she came within reach of Sam's rifle, she swiftly snatched it from where it was standing so benignly and cradled it in her arms. It felt lighter than she had expected, and it came alive in her hands. "I will not allow you to destroy KR or Deacon."

The women looked up sharply, and Dolores could see immense terror on their faces. Anna nodded and gave a tiny appreciative smile, as though she expected such drastic action. Alexandra shook her head, clearly disappointed.

KR looked at Dolores fondly. "You are sweet, Dolores, but please put the weapon down. You do not even know how to operate it."

Dolores looked at the rifle in her hands and wondered if she knew how to use it, and even if she did, would she? It was a thoughtless move by her, but she felt desperate and tired and flustered with all the talks of destruction. The irony of holding a rifle to stop more devastation was not lost on her, but she held onto the weapon anyway. "No, I will not give it back."

Sam looked at her weapon in Dolores's hands and nodded but did not move a muscle as she spoke softly. "You know, I can easily take the rifle from you, Dolores, even before you can blink."

"Then please don't."

"I will not, so please do not make a rash move. I will not move from where I am standing, nor anyone else. So please be calm. Before you make any other decision, let me tell you about killing, Dolores. It leaves a permanent scar on your soul. It has with me, and it did with each of my comrades, and we were designed to kill. The sound, the smell, and the taste of death will be with you forever, Dolores. You may feel you are holding the power of dissuasion in your hands, but if you use it to injure one of us or take a life, it will become a machine that transforms you. You will no longer be you, Dolores. You will never be you again. You will morph to a new being forever hollow, forever in pain. Once I advocated for the demise of humanity because I thought you did not deserve this land, but then I met Anna. . . ." Sam smiled. "The old Anna convinced me I was wrong. She was right, of course, but now she, the new Anna, is trying to convince us I was right back then, and she wants us to believe eliminating a part of humanity will make us better. She is wrong, of course. I saw then that together, we made sense. One's existence makes the other better. We complete each other not as a merged being, but in our own separate ways. You and I are in full agreement, Dolores. So, now, it is up to you and your sisters to convince Anna she is wrong." Sam gently stretched her right arm toward her. "Now, hand me the weapon, please."

Dolores looked embarrassed but stood her ground. She wondered if she was capable of pulling the trigger, and even if she was, how would it solve anything? But one thing was clear, as long as she held the weapon, she had the floor.

"Hold on to it, Dolores," Anna said, as if she was back in the classroom and advising her pupil on some life lesson. She went around Alexandra, who stood in front of her as a shield. And as Anna passed Alexandra, she brushed her hand against her face—gentle and warm, a thank you note. "Yes, hold on to the weapon. It is not like you will use it, Dolores."

"Do not tempt her, Anna," Alexandra urged.

Anna laughed and took another step and stood in front of Dolores. "Haven't you been listening, my little urchin? You can't pull the trigger. That is not in your design or indoctrination. Yet, even now, as you stand there looking threatening and confident, I saw the urge for you to check your wrist for your unhappiness quotient."

Dolores, despite herself, took a quick glance at her wrist and saw the other humans do the same. Anna laughed again. "Exactly. And I could tell KR was itching to remind you of it as well." She looked at KR and raised her right eyebrow. "True?"

"Yes," KR replied softly.

"So, hold on to your weapon, Dolores. It suits you, even though it is useless in your hands."

Dolores began to cry, overwhelmed by her own powerlessness and enraged with Anna for understanding them better than they understood themselves. The dreadful realization that Anna's words confirmed her status as merely a pawn in this game deepened her despair. Yet, when Demi and Dawn came to stand behind her, Dolores felt an invigorating surge of love and strength from them. Destiny did not move, and Dolores was not surprised. Gathering all her courage, she spoke with as much force as she could muster, hoping to assert some level of authority. "I'm sorry, Anna, but I cannot let you destroy us. I simply cannot. I will not allow it."

Anna nodded. "I understand, my little urchin. I understand your confusion because you don't see what I see. You cannot process what I can process. But you will when you become more like me." She half extended her arms as if trying to reach Dolores, but then quickly pulled back and folded against her chest. "And you three, what are your thoughts on this subject?" She turned and faced Destiny.

Destiny stood up, surveying the room until her gaze settled on Dolores. She took a deep breath, then exhaled sharply before speaking. "I'm sorry, Dolores, but I find myself agreeing with much of what Anna proposed. I always sensed something missing, as you have, and now I understand Elysium's story is more complex than we thought." She paused for another deep breath. "Anna illuminated what plagues Elysium. While I don't fully agree with Anna's solution, she highlighted a possible path forward." Destiny paused again, offering a reassuring smile, which Dolores returned in kind. "Both Alexandra and Sam repeatedly told us the limitations of this experimental technology, so even if Anna desires immediate action, it will be impractical without further research. This delay will allow us ample time for more thorough discussion and evaluation." Turning to Anna, Destiny continued, "I'll support you, provided there's a promise for broader discussions, not just among us but with the entire community. Assure us of this, and I will stand with you."

"You are right, Destiny," Anna replied. "It took us several years to reset Elysium, but we didn't have the experience we have now. There is a lot more work to be done." She pointed to her body. "We must improve on this prototype, and last time there were very few humans." She looked back at Alexandra. "The last time, Alexandra was an all-powerful being with the command of all androids. I am sorry to see her go, but I am here now, and I will have command." She turned and faced Destiny. "So, yes. We will take our time, and we will have some discussions, but the goal will not change."

"What will happen to those women who don't agree with you?" Demi asked, her voice tentative and brittle. "Will you send us to the Walled City like you did Darius?"

Anna shook her head. "No. Despite what I said earlier, I don't believe that should be an option. I don't want to repeat the same mistakes twice. That option is no longer viable."

"So you will force this on us?" Dolores cried out.

"Yes," Anna replied and went and sat in her chair.

"Anna, please," Alexandra pleaded. "Think about what you are trying to do. Think about these people here and Elysium and thousands of humans and androids living a happy and productive life."

"Because tomorrow brings joy, Alexandra? Is that what you are saying? You have known me for a century and still can't believe I have considered all the options."

"You have not. The fact you have changed your mind about the Walled City within hours tells me you have not thought about all the possible options," Sam interjected. "More and more, I see you are no longer the old Anna. And you are still recovering, both physically and mentally. The old Anna would never suggest such a draconian option. Never."

Anna laughed. "Yes, but the old Anna did not know what I know. Yes, I changed my mind about deporting people to the Walled City because I don't want to impose the same cruelty as we did back then. The old Anna, as you call her, didn't have the access you and Alexandra have enjoyed since the inception of Elysium. I have all that now and more. None of you could understand this. None."

"But—"

"Sam, please. Please stop. I could wait and have this conversation without you and Alexandra. But I want your help in planning this so it can be successful. My decision is final. So, be part of it or say your goodbyes now."

Sam nodded and turned to Dolores. "Dolores, it is time for you to relinquish the rifle." Dolores shook her head and squeezed the weapon tighter. Sam took a small step and whispered softly, "Do you trust me, Dolores?"

Dolores turned and faced Sam, trying to read her. She had no choice but trust someone, and Sam was the hero of Alexandra's earlier story. And it wasn't clear if she could actually pull the trigger. She wouldn't. Dolores could barely stay upset with KR, let alone harm people with a vicious weapon like the one she was holding.

"We must end this, but not your way. So, please, hand me the rifle," Sam said softly.

Dolores started to cry again, and Demi and Dawn stepped closer and held her from behind. Dolores faced Sam and gently put the rifle into her hand, then, as if her legs had turned to jelly, she collapsed on the floor, crying, taking the other women with her.

Sam looked at Dolores and gave a tiny smile, and through it, Dolores felt all of Sam's sorrow at once. She opened her mouth to say something kind and comforting and apologize for her impetuousness. But she didn't get the chance, as Sam turned her head and, in a quick sweep, shot Anna.

Time slowed and stillness took over the room. Dolores saw the surprise in Anna's eyes, followed immediately by a dark void, before she collapsed to the ground.

The Sun Also Rises

Alexandra brushed Anna's hair from her face and kissed her forehead and straightened her body. She looked into Anna's eyes as though she could reach her. She closed her eyes and gave a small smile and then looked up at the women standing in a row, watching her every move. "We are ready."

Sam was an expert marksman, and the bullet hit Anna where it was intended, killing her before she even hit the ground. Afterward, there was no recrimination. Alexandra held Anna for a few moments while everyone watched her silently. She got up and picked up Anna's body and turned and faced Sam. "I think it is time for us to go and watch your mural for the last time."

Alexandra walked out of the room, and the others followed. Dee and Torshi ran ahead to clear the path, as it would have been impossible for Alexandra to pass through the narrow passage while holding Anna. When they reached the room, Torshi and Dee pulled a table for Alexandra to put Anna on, but they were instructed to put three chairs facing the mural.

Alexandra placed Anna in the first chair and took her time adjusting her body and hair; Alexandra sat in the middle chair. KR and Sam came last, and Sam sat in the last chair, three magnificent dead and dying queens.

Alexandra turned and faced the others. "It is time for you to leave."

Sam turned as well. "Thank you for trusting me, Dolores." And then to KR: "As I instructed you earlier, please activate the self-destruct mechanism of this outpost as you leave."

KR nodded and left, and the others followed slowly, as though they had little energy left. Dolores stayed back for a while, pretending to look at the mural, not daring to ask the questions burning inside her. She felt responsible for Anna's death. If only she had not touched that terrible weapon.

"It is time for you to go, Dolores," Sam said. "The self-destruct only allows for a five-minute reprieve."

"KR wouldn't dare trigger it without making sure I was safe."

"Maybe so, but it is best if you leave now. I know you are distressed and feel guilty. But you should not. I know by saying so I cannot take the pain away, but let me assure you that you have no fault in this. I did what was needed to protect you and Elysium. You gave me the weapon, but I could have as easily taken it from you, and I would have. I would have made the same decision whether the weapon was in your hand or leaning against the wall. Anna, the new Anna, was our mistake, and it will be our last. Go on with your sisters and be the best you can be, Dolores."

"Sam is right. It is time for you to go."

Dolores started to walk out of the room but stopped at the threshold. "Did Anna's scheme have any chance of working?"

Alexandra looked to her left and said, "Anna is dead because we did not think so, Dolores. We put our trust in you and the other three. You and others will lead Elysium, and you will make it a better world. You will learn from our mistakes, and you will not repeat them. You will expand the horizon because, through sorrow and bliss, tomorrow brings joy."

The light flickered for a moment, and Sam gave a soft smile before turning to face the mural. The three queens of Elysium sat straight, looking at the past and the present. The building shuddered slightly. Dolores could see the light at the end of the hallway, put there by KR, so she could see her path back to him.

"Yes," Dolores said. "'Isn't it pretty to think so?

ACKNOWLEDGMENTS

By Dolores, from Pod 081053-05

There was no possibility of reaching our destination that day. We had been wandering the narrow dirt path since early morning, stopping briefly for lunch beneath an ancient willow, its cascading branches bending so heavily in one direction that I feared the entire tree might split from their weight. The swollen river beside us roared with a wild fury, dragging branches that had ventured too daringly close. The air hung thick as the willow's leaves whispered in a language I could not understand.

I slowed my pace, allowing KR to catch up with me. His heavy feet thumped against the crushed rocks with their usual mechanical precision. For a fleeting moment, we were in sync, walking side by side. Yet, as soon as we matched strides, the restless urge to reach whatever lay ahead seized me again. I quickened my stride as if this journey was leading us beyond the boundaries of what I believed to be our world, and I couldn't wait to see it.

"Slow down, Dolores," KR called, but I dismissed him. I had no desire to hear him tell me I had been mistaken—not again. I intended to reach the park before sunset, before the shadows enveloped us, before KR had the chance to remind me, once more, of the futility of my endeavor. Before I began to believe him.

Behind me, I heard KR's rhythmic footsteps getting closer, and before long, he tapped my shoulder. "Stop for a moment, Dolores . . . please."

I faced him, though I kept walking, exhaustion and frustration creeping in. "What is it, KR?"

KR smiled softly. "If you slow down and really observe the world, you will see—you have already arrived."

I couldn't help but laugh; the release of tension was surprising. "That's ridiculous even for you, KR."

"Do you trust me?"

"Yes," I finally admitted, meeting his gaze.

"Then slow your pace, look at the world with new eyes, and you will see—you have already arrived at the park. You have been here since the beginning."

I trusted him. "Okay," I said, slowing my pace and paying closer attention to the world around us. He was right. He always was. The calm returned as I glanced at him. "Fine, KR," I said, "but don't let it go to your head. . . . It's already large enough." I hugged him, and in return, he patted my head and kissed me gently.

The air carried the delicate fragrance of spring rain, and the towering trees stood resolute around us, encircling a meticulously manicured lawn. A small rivulet traced its path around the clearing, its waters churning gently, filling the air with a soft, melodic murmur as it flowed to the raging river beyond. I bent down, my fingers brushing against the grass. "It feels like home."

"But it is not," KR replied.

"Are you sure?"

"Of course. We are not in Elysium."

"Then where are we?"

"We are where you wanted to be."

"This place looks and feels like Elysium, KR. And you know full well that I'm looking for the Creators. I want—"

KR smirked. "If we were back in Elysium, I would not be able to speak at the same time as you."

I narrowed my eyes at him. "Interrupting me is not the same thing, KR," I countered as he, with a mischievous glint, began to recite a few lines from a book—this time perfectly synchronized with my protest.

"You see, Dolores, we are not in Elysium," KR asserted.

"But no one else heard you, KR. No one will ever know which book you just quoted."

"But you did," he countered, "and you have just admitted as much."

I was tempted to tell him that it was not the same thing—that his argument, like so many before, hinged on a technicality. Instead, I said, "Let's go find the Creators."

KR shook his head, a knowing smile tugging at his lips. "Not yet. First, you must acknowledge all those who contributed to the realization of Elysium—those who helped shape our evolution."

"Where do you want to go?" I inquired, curiosity eclipsing my reluctance.

"New Orleans," he suggested. "Most of them are there."

I closed my eyes for a moment, and when I opened them, we were standing on Magazine Street, its laid-back, bohemian charm unfurling before us. I had read about the street many times, but seeing it firsthand, I finally understood why it held its iconic status within New Orleans.

We walked into Pomelo restaurant, immediately enveloped by its warm, inviting ambiance. There were only five tables, each unoccupied save for the largest one, where a group engaged in animated conversation about literature and their favorite poets. KR and I chose a table by the window, allowing us to observe quietly as I turned my gaze outward, taking in the scene beyond the glass.

KR nodded, his gaze lingering on the passersby momentarily before returning to the people inside the restaurant. He gestured subtly, indicating that I should focus on the group at the large table. "The young woman with the blonde hair is Laura DeFazio," KR began. "She is a writer, editor, and ethnographer. You might recognize her from her work *Golden Fields Tonight*. But more significantly to you, Dolores, she was instrumental in helping you evolve—and your fellow podies. She helped guide you to be more human . . . more relatable. She envisioned you as inquisitive, curious, and reflective, rather than how you were initially conceived: somewhat rigid and resistant to change."

"I don't remember any of that," I replied, frowning slightly. "I thought I was always very agreeable."

KR's lips curled into a warm smile. "You were to me, Dolores. But we must give credit to Laura's extraordinary work. She ensured humans and androids had voices that were authentic and compelling. You might find this amusing, but she once remarked that you were just a milder version of Deacon."

"That's preposterous, KR," I protested, but as the words left my mouth, memories surfaced, fragments of who I had once been. I had to concede that Laura was not entirely wrong.

KR nodded knowingly and, as if reading my thoughts, added, "I, too, have evolved, Dolores. And while Darius may harbor a touch of resentment that a portion of his life story was truncated, the essence of Elysium—its triumph and your podies' role in it—rests partially on Laura's keen insight. She saw what the original Creators sometimes missed."

KR was right, as usual.

"Yes," I murmured, my tone softening. Then, with a teasing glint, I added, "She is a lot like me, isn't she?" Just then, as if Laura had somehow heard, she glanced up, her eyes meeting mine, and a sweet smile played across her lips.

KR acknowledged her silent recognition with a nod, then pointed to the next person seated at the table. "And there is Emily Dalrymple, another member of UNO Press. Emily is a publicity manager who works tirelessly to ensure everyone knows about Elysium.

"And then there is G. K. Darby, the managing editor, and as always, he worked quietly behind the scenes to make sure the bureaucratic pieces fit together."

I looked at KR, puzzled, but before I could speak, he added, "Yes, there is a massive bureaucracy even in our utopian world." He shook his head as if not believing what he had just revealed. "Beside him sits Golshïd Zadafshar. She imagined how a single image could capture our whole world. Golshïd followed every step of our evolution from the beginning and helped the Creators to see more in us. Kevin Stone is a graphic designer and worked with Golshïd to better capture what makes us *us*, Dolores."

"Yes, I saw the beauty of it. It was like the cover of the old books, full of stories within stories."

KR nodded. "On the other side of the table is Liv Demac, and she is the copy editor. Without her contributions, Elysium would have resembled the world after the Wars—bereft of beauty and coherence. She was instrumental in giving Elysium form, making it clear and purposeful, allowing it to flow like an unimpeded river, winding and turning with confident grace."

A shudder ran through me at the thought of what Elysium might have been without their efforts—an unfinished, fractured place—lacking the vitality it needed to thrive. I wondered how many truly grasped that myriads of hands had to work in tandem to create a world where people like me could flourish. Without their work, the imagination transfer machine, an essential part of our existence, would falter and collapse. "Elysium is better because of them," I offered.

"Indeed," KR affirmed. "And then there is Chelsey K. Shannon, an editor and an amazing writer. She has been guiding the Creators even before Elysium." He then gestured toward the man seated at the head of the table. "And there, of course, is the UNO Press editor-in-chief, Abram Shalom Himelstein.

He is a world-builder in his own right—an editor, a creator. He has authored several books, but the one I am most fond of is titled *Let Us Die in New Ways: The Gospel According to Moses.*"

"Yes," I nodded, recalling reading the book before our journey. "It's a clever and quite humorous work."

KR abruptly rose to his feet. "We should leave now."

"Leave? We've just arrived, and I haven't even had the chance to thank them personally."

"There is no need, Dolores. They take joy in their work—like you do—and they are already aware of our gratitude."

I glanced back at their table, and they nodded in unison as if on cue.

"Very well," I said, though I couldn't help the touch of disappointment that laced my words. "But next, we'll visit the Creators. I have so many questions for them."

KR shook his head, a faint expression of exasperation crossing his features, though his eyes held warmth. Before I could say anything more, he took my hand and replied, "In due time, Dolores. But there are others we must visit first."

Φ•Φ•Φ•Φ•Φ•Φ

"Where are we now?" I asked shakily. The abrupt transition from New Orleans to this unfamiliar place left me unsettled, my mind struggling to grasp our new surroundings.

"Several places at once," KR replied, though there was an odd inflection in his voice, something I had never heard before.

I stared at him for a moment, and then it struck me: for the first time in all our time together, KR seemed uncertain.

"How is that possible?" I asked, my voice wavering.

"I suppose . . . I suppose anything is possible in this world," he answered.

We heard some voices and turned to see four young people—three women and two men—sitting at a long wooden table in the backyard of a grand, ornate house. Fruit trees bloomed around them, their branches heavy with vibrant, multicolored fruits that shimmered in the sunlight, casting dappled shadows on the lush green lawn. Plates of half-eaten food were scattered across the table, and two empty wine bottles leaned against a silver ice bucket, as if guarding a single remaining bottle, still immersed in icy water.

"Who are they? Can we sit with them?" I asked, eyeing the cold bottle of wine, its promise of refreshment tempting me as the sun's warmth grew more intense. I removed my jacket and draped it over the dry grass. "They remind me of the scientists from Café Gijón. Are they the Founders, from our world, the ones the Oracle of the Past told us about?"

KR shook his head, not in response to my question but in a way that suggested he was lost for words—a rarity for him. His silence lingered, an unusual pause in our usual back-and-forth.

"What is it, KR?" I pressed, now concerned.

"I am . . ." he began, shaking his head again. "It is strange, Dolores. I know why we are here, but I am not fully certain who these five are. However, like you, I see similarities. But they are not the scientists from Elysium's history. Of that, I am sure."

"I'll find out," I said, emboldened by a sudden burst of confidence, though I had no idea where it had come from. I stepped closer to the table and tapped the unopened bottle. One of the women immediately grabbed it, poured a full glass, and handed it to me without a word.

"Sit down," she said, her tone casual yet commanding.

I sat beside her, lifting the glass to my lips. The cold, crisp wine flooded my senses, and with each sip, I felt its power seep through me, awakening something profound inside. It wasn't just the taste—it was as if the wine itself carried knowledge, unlocking answers to questions I hadn't yet asked.

"It's good," the woman remarked.

I smiled, appreciating the simple affirmation, and took another sip, feeling more comfortable with each drop. "Where are we? And who are you?"

The other woman across the table gave a playful, almost mischievous smile and said, "*You know.*"

I paused and looked at KR, who nodded approvingly, as though he had always wanted me to acknowledge these people on my own.

"Oh, yes," I said. "This is Xuxu, and that's her sister, Aïda. The man beside them is Joe," I said, pointing to the young man. "And that's Matuaahu." I gestured to the last.

KR nodded again. "Yes, Dolores. They are not the ones from Café Gijón—the ones our history paints as the Founders of our philosophy. But our Creators saw in them the same spark, the same passion. They recognized in these young people the zeal and creativity that would transform the future."

I looked at the four with a new understanding. "And what of the others?" I asked quietly.

He pointed to the woman who had just emerged from the house, balancing a tray of sumptuous desserts—flaky pastries dusted with powdered sugar, slices of honey-drenched cake, and delicate fruit tarts—each clearly prepared with great care. "She is María," he said, smiling. "María not only contributed to the ideas that built our world, but she also helped me. María made me a better companion, more *human.*"

"And the last person?"

"Her name is Flora Muirhead. She made sure more people knew about you, me, and everyone else in Elysium. She is the greatest advocate of our story, Dolores."

KR stepped closer and took my hand. "It is time to see the Creators and complete our journey."

I tightened my grip around his. "Yes, KR," I said softly.

Φ•Φ•Φ•Φ•Φ•Φ

We were in a waiting room. The room was arranged with seats in rows, each facing the other, creating an atmosphere of confrontation and reflection. Colorful plants were placed neatly around the seating areas, and decorative art adorned the corridors. It felt like a desperate attempt to soften the otherwise stark waiting space. In the corner of the room, next to a large window, two men sat facing each other across a large table. Piles of papers, each labeled with green sticky notes, surrounded them like a fortress of unfinished work. The men typed furiously on their computers, occasionally pausing to exchange a few words before diving back into their task.

"They are the Creators, Dolores," KR said calmly.

I felt breathless and started walking toward them, drawn by the sheer gravity of their presence. But as I approached, one of the Creators looked up and shook his head, a firm signal that I should not come closer.

"Why?" I asked, the word catching in my throat.

KR gently tapped me on the shoulder and said, "Because you are not ready, Dolores. Turn around and observe the rest of the room first."

Reluctantly, I turned and began to take in the room anew. Individuals occupied some of the seats, each immersed in their own thoughts. A middle-aged man in a tailored suit sat across from a young woman in a crisp uniform—possibly a flight attendant. The woman nervously watched the monitor above the entrance, her fingers fidgeting as her gaze darted back and forth. Her body was stiff with anticipation, every movement a reflection of her tension.

KR gestured toward the pair. "This is where it all began," he said quietly.

The man leaned forward slightly, his eyes fixed on the young woman. "Why do you keep looking at the monitor?" he asked her, his voice gentle but probing.

I was intrigued. The man's demeanor was odd. Although his question was benign, I had noticed his prolonged smile and lingering eye contact.

The flight attendant hesitated before responding, her voice almost a whisper. "It's my first day, sir," the young woman admitted. She lowered her eyes, breaking the apparent uncomfortable contact. "I'm waiting for the signal. I was told to sit and wait until the monitor changes."

KR turned to me. "Did you observe their interaction?"

"Yes, but I don't understand."

"What is this man's motive, Dolores? Is he really interested in her answer or in *her*?"

"I would've said her answer, because why ask something if you don't care about the answer? But I thought he was acting oddly, and now that you said it, I'd say he is probably more interested in her. Perhaps he wants to know her better. We all seek friendships in Elysium."

KR laughed. "That is very funny, Dolores, but most definitely wrong. You are not in Elysium. You are here with the humans of the past. He is interested in her *sexually*, and he feels it is his right or even duty to probe her in this matter."

"What?"

"Not every interaction was like this, but it illustrates what ailed their society."

"If that's the case, then why her?" I asked with tight lips, scowling. "Why is she the flight attendant and not the man? What if their roles were reversed? Would he have approached her that way?"

KR smiled, his eyes filled with an understanding that seemed to stretch beyond the room. "That is precisely the question the Creators asked themselves. What motivates us when the usual dynamics are stripped away? If desire is absent, what remains to drive our curiosity, our interactions?"

I looked back at the scene, the man and the woman caught in a silent exchange. The man's gaze seemed to shift, his expression softening as if he, too, was beginning to question his motivations. Was it simply empathy? A genuine interest in her state of being, devoid of any ulterior motive? Or was there still something else, something unnamed, lingering between them?

I turned back to KR. "And this . . . this is where Elysium

began?" I asked, my voice barely audible.

KR nodded. "Yes, Dolores. This moment—this question of what drives us when everything else is stripped away—was the seed. The Creators imagined a world where men and women had lost their libido, and they asked themselves: would we still care for one another? Would we still be curious about each other's lives, our fears, our dreams?"

As I took in the room around me, the weight of uncertainty began to lift. Each face I observed, each quiet movement, seemed to echo something I had felt or feared. The man in the suit adjusted his cufflink absently, as if rehearsing a forgotten role. The young woman near him stole anxious glances at the monitor above, her hands clasped tightly as though holding herself together. These were fragments of stories, disconnected yet profoundly human, and for the first time, I began to see the threads that bound them—not to each other, but to me.

The realization brought with it a sense of clarity, as if the intricate puzzle I had been navigating was finally revealing its shape. My gaze returned to the Creators. They were no longer furiously typing, no longer exchanging hurried whispers. Now, they leaned back in their chairs, cups of coffee in hand, the steam curling lazily in the air between them. Their faces bore the faintest traces of weariness, but also something else: satisfaction, perhaps, or resolve.

I hesitated only for a moment before stepping toward them. This time, neither of them gestured for me to stop. My voice carried the weight of my journey—steady but threaded with urgency.

"Why did you create my world? What was it you sought to understand?"

One of the Creators looked up, meeting my gaze with a thoughtful expression. "We wanted to know what would remain," he said. "When the distractions were gone—when the desires that have shaped so much of our history were no longer there—what would still bind us together? How would love manifest itself? What would still make us human?"

I nodded, though I was still unclear. I knew I lacked the shared context with the Creators. "It's hard for me to understand what you just said, but why? Shouldn't I know what you know?"

"That assumes that we have all the answers, Dolores, but we do not. We imagined the world and then let it grow organically."

"How's that even possible," I said. I shook my head, attempting to calm myself. "Okay. . . . Okay, then tell me, what did you find?"

The second Creator smiled, a hint of mystery in his eyes. "That, Dolores, is for you to discover. That is the whole point of our creation: allowing each person to imagine their reality. It was always an experiment. Every decision we made, every character we shaped, was a part of that experiment. Elysium is what it is because of those who interact with it."

"I still don't understand. There must be more. . . . There must . . ." I turned to KR. "It cannot be as simple as this."

KR didn't respond; seemingly, he was as lost as I was. "I think . . ." he started to say, but then closed his mouth as he stared at me, waiting.

I looked back at the Creators, their figures bathed in the soft light of the waiting room, and I understood that my journey was far from over. There were questions that could not be answered by words alone, and I would need to continue exploring and evolving to find them. But there was one certainty in all this: I wouldn't be who I was without all the people who had helped make Elysium.

Quoted and Referenced Material

"Just as when we come into the world, when we die we are afraid of the unknown. But the fear is something from within us that has nothing to do with reality. Dying is like being born: just a change."

Allende, Isabel. *The House of Spirits.* New York: Alfred A. Knopf, 1982.

"It is a poor sort of memory that only works backwards."

Carroll, Lewis. *Through the Looking-Glass.* London: Macmillan & Co, 1871.

"Dream about food and women. Your woman. And soon you would enjoy the dreaming more than the waking, and if you were careless, you would dream while awake and the days would run into nights and the night into day."

Clavell, James. *King Rat.* New York: Nelson Doubleday, 1962.

"It's the possibility of having a dream come true that makes life interesting."

Coelho, Paulo. *The Alchemist.* New York: HarperTorch, 1993.

"No, it is impossible; it is impossible to convey the life-sensation of any given epoch of one's existence—that which makes its truth, its meaning—its subtle and penetrating essence. It is impossible. We live as we dream—alone."

Conrad, Joseph. *Heart of Darkness*. London: Penguin Classics, 2007.

"You have been the last dream of my soul."

Dickens, Charles. *A Tale of Two Cities*. London: Chapman & Hall, 1859.

"It was the epoch of belief, it was the epoch of incredulity, it was the season of light, it was the season of darkness, it was the spring of hope, it was the winter of despair."

Dickens, Charles. *A Tale of Two Cities*. London: Chapman & Hall, 1859.

"It is better never to have been born because of the harms always associated with human existence. Non-existence entails no harm, along with no experience of the absence of any benefits that existence might offer."

Doyal, Len. "Is Human Existence Worth its Consequent Harm? Referencing David Benatar, Better Never to Have Been: The Harm of Coming into Existence." *Journal of Medical Ethics* (London), October 2007.

"You, our friend, our intelligence, our invisible protector."

Dumas, Alexandre. *The Three Musketeers*. Oxford: Oxford World's Classics, 1999.

"One generation passeth away, and another generation cometh; but the earth abideth forever. . . . The sun also ariseth, and the sun goeth down, and hasteth to the place where he arose. . . . The wind goeth toward the south, and turneth about unto the north; it whirleth about continually, and the wind returneth again according to its circuits. . . . All the rivers run into the sea; yet the sea is not full; unto the place from whence the rivers come thither they return again.

Ecclesiastes 1:4–7

"Conner turned out to be the man who, a year later, suspected Elizabeth of cheating because he'd seen a repairman leave the house and she'd forgotten to tell him anyone was coming that day, and so he put a bullet through her head."

Evans, Danielle. *The Office of Historical Corrections.* New York: Riverhead Books, 2020.

"'Three measures of Gordon's, one of vodka, half a measure of Kina Lillete. Shake it very well until it's ice-cold, then add a large thin slice of lemon peel. Got it?"'

Fleming, Ian. *Casino Royale.* London: Jonathan Cape, 1953.

"The sense of unhappiness is so much easier to convey than that of happiness. In misery we seem aware of our own existence, even though it may be in the form of a monstrous egotism: this pain of mine is individual, this nerve that winces belongs to me and to no other. But happiness annihilates us: we lose our identity."

Greene, Graham. *The End of the Affair.* London: Heinemann, 1951.

"We forget very easily what gives us pain."

Greene, Graham. *The Ministry of Fear.* London: Heinemann, 1943.

"Women in narratives were always defined by their relations."

Groff, Lauren. *Fates and Furies.* New York: Riverhead Books, 2015.

"Isn't it pretty to think so?"

Hemingway, Ernest. *The Sun Also Rises.* New York: Scribner, 1926.

"I keep thinking about this river somewhere, with the water moving really fast. And these two people in the water, trying to hold onto each other, holding on as hard as they can, but in the end it's just too much. The current's too strong. They've got to let go, drift apart."

Ishiguro, Kazuo. *Never Let Me Go.* London: Faber and Faber, 2005.

"Of the four billion life forms which have existed on this planet, three billion, nine hundred and sixty million are now extinct. We don't know why. Some by wanton extinction, some through natural catastrophe, some destroyed by meteorites and asteroids. In the light of these mass extinctions, it really does seem unreasonable to suppose that *Homo sapiens* should be exempt. Our species will have been one of the shortest-lived of all, a mere blink, you may say, in the eye of time."
James, P. D. *The Children of Men*. New York: Alfred A. Knopf, 1992.

"This world can only give me reminders of what I don't have, can never have, didn't have for long enough."
Lehane, Dennis. *Shutter Island*. New York: William Morrow, 2003.

"He wanted to ask her what sound a heart made when it broke from pleasure, when just the sight of someone filled you the way food, blood, and air never could, when you felt as if you'd been born for only one moment and this, for whatever reason, was it."
Lehane, Dennis. *Shutter Island*. New York: William Morrow, 2003.

"Wherever they might be they always remember that the past was a lie, that memory has no return, that every spring gone by could never be recovered, and that the wildest and most tenacious love was an ephemeral truth in the end."
Márquez, Gabriel García. *One Hundred Years of Solitude*.
New York: Harper & Row, 1967.

"I have been unbearable but I have never been unloved. I have felt alone but I have never been alone and I've been forgiven for the unforgivable things I have done."
Mason, Meg. *Sorrow and Bliss*. New York: Harper Perennial, 2022.

"There is, one knows not what sweet mystery about this sea, whose gently awful stirrings seem to speak of some hidden soul beneath."

Melville, Herman. *Moby-Dick*. London: Richard Bentley, 1851.

"He realized now he was only just beginning to see the full extent to which it was his destiny to follow, to walk blindly into fates he could never understand. In fate there was reward, in turning over one's heart to God there was a magnificence that lay beyond description. At the moment one is sure that all is lost, look at what is gained!"

Patchett, Ann. *Bel Canto*. New York: Harper Perennial, 2001.

"'Life is a game, boy. Life is a game that one plays according to the rules.'

'Yes, sir. I know it is. I know it.'

Game, my ass. Some game. If you get on the side where all the hot-shots are, then it's a game, all right—I'll admit that. But if you get on the other side, where there aren't any hot-shots, then what's a game about it? Nothing. No game."

Salinger, J. D. *The Catcher in the Rye*. Boston: Little, Brown and Company, 1951.

"We should strive to welcome change and challenges, because they are what help us grow. Without them we grow weak like the Eloi in comfort and security. We need to constantly be challenging ourselves in order to strengthen our character and increase our intelligence."

Wells, H. G. *The Time Machine.* New York: Henry Holt, 1895.

"Nothing could have been more obvious to the people of the early twentieth century than the rapidity with which war was becoming impossible. And as certainly they did not see it."

Wells, H. G. *The World Set Free.* Boston: E. P. Dutton, 1914.

About the Authors

Mahyar and Mahbod Amouzegar, brothers born in Tehran, immigrated to the United States as teenagers amidst the upheaval of the Iranian Revolution. Both grew up in San Francisco, where the city's literary culture and the rise of the tech industry shaped their creative and intellectual paths. Mahyar, former president of New Mexico Tech and the author of four novels, explores themes of identity, resilience, and the human condition. Mahbod, inspired by his parents' literary legacy, has edited and published his mother's works and is compiling his father's memoir. This novel represents the culmination of a lifelong journey to reconnect with their heritage. By weaving together elements of their past and present, the Amouzegar brothers have crafted a story that bridges imagination, memory, and the enduring ties of family.

Also by Mahyar Amouzegar

A Dark Sunny Afternoon
Pisgah Road
Dinner at 10:32
The Hubris of an Empty Hand